For Those in Peril on the Sea

by

Max Blue

PublishAmerica
Baltimore

First printing

ISBN: 1-59286-419-8
PUBLISHED BY PUBLISHAMERICA BOOK PUBLISHERS
www.publishamerica.com
Baltimore

Printed in the United States of America

BOOKS BY MAX BLUE

GOD IS ALIVE AND PLAYING THIRD BASE FOR THE APPLETON PAPERMAKERS

GIESSOW'S COTTAGE FARM

HIGHER ED

The Bismark Pacheco adventures:

MURDER AT THE CAT

CIELITO LINDO

These books are available from all on-line booksellers.

Eternal Father, strong to save,
Whose arm doth bind the restless wave,
Who bids the mighty ocean deep
Its own eternal vigil keep.
Oh hear us as we cry to Thee,
For those in peril on the sea.

...The Navy Hymn

Dedicated to

Oliver LaGrone and Ernest Sommerfeld

And, of course, to the luminous Liddy
who never fails to show up, page after page after page.

Acknowledgments:

The author wishes to acknowledge that parts of this book are derived from *The Republic* by Plato.

Also, the author acknowledges the inspiration derived from African folk tales as documented in *Tales From The Story Hat* by Verna Aardema (Coward-McCann, Inc. New York, 1960.)

PROLOGUE

Silent as death was the room. Only the occasional rattle of the window and moan of the wind broke the monotony. The old man slowly got up from his chair by the window, rearranged the shabby blanket over his shoulders, and moved with short, halting steps to a small table where he bent to turn on a battered radio.

"...clouds thickening late in the afternoon. Blizzard conditions are expected with accumulations up to eight inches. Temperatures will fall to zero degrees or below. Wind chill factor of forty below. You are advised to stay inside if at all possible..."

The old man returned to his chair, where he watched the wind-blown snow rise in great clouds, blocking the sun and causing oddly shaped shadows to be cast on the frozen ground. At intervals the gusts subsided, and the bright sun reflected with dazzling brilliance on the freshly fallen snow. Each flake, it seemed, caught the rays, bounced them around, and discarded them to be seen as sparkling gems to the attentive eye.

"...and now, live from the Chapel of King's College in Cambridge, England, we present a Festival of Nine Lessons and Carols. The program combines the readings of Biblical Christmas lessons with performances of traditional hymns and carols..."

The old man was alone with his memories, but they were rich, and he reviewed them often. These days his needs were few, which matched his resources. He wanted to get through another winter. He looked forward to spring, and to sitting on a bench in Riverfront Park with his friend Sparks. They liked to watch the boats on the river and swap sea stories; both had served many years in the Navy, mostly at sea.

"...with righteousness He shall judge the poor..."

As the snow swirled before his eyes, it was transformed into salt spray...

...He struggled to keep his balance on the wildly gyrating, ice-slick deck of a U.S. Navy World War II Geary class Destroyer. The admirals and politicians liked to call these ships "the greyhounds of the fleet." The men who made them go called them tin cans and rust buckets.

A crew of three men in life jackets huddled close to the bulkhead, port side, just forward of the amidships passageway. He saw the fear in their eyes, and measured it against his own. As Boatswain's Mate First Class, he had been in charge of more fueling details than he could count, but he had never seen one like this. The sea was the enemy, and it was attacking from all sides with battleship force. He could see waves crashing over the bridge, 50 feet above him.

"Okay, you shit-birds, let's get some fuckin' lifelines rigged here, whaddaya think this is, a fuckin' picnic?" he shouted above the roar of the sea.

"What the fuck's goin' on, Boats? The Old Man tryin' get us all killed?" It was Vink, Boatswain's Mate Third Class, arms like 16-inch shells, the strongest man on the ship, and probably in the whole Seventh Fleet.

"Never mind about the Old Man, he wouldn't have us out here if he didn't think we could handle it."

Boats was not as confident as he sounded. He knew the captain was fueling out of desperation. Normally they fueled at sea every six or seven days, but the weather had been so rotten the Old Man had put it off for four extra days hoping for a break; instead, it got worse. Boats also knew that running out of fuel was of less concern than restoring ballast. In a sea like this, with fuel tanks depleted, the captain was worried about capsizing.

Boats trusted the captain; had trusted him since the first day he came aboard in Nagoya. The captain was a redheaded Irishman, rough as a barnacle, and fearless as a hammerhead shark. Boats remembered the first time the skipper took the con leaving Nagoya. They were tied up alongside a dock, and no sooner had the "All lines clear" call gone to the bridge, than he heard a quiet but firm voice of authority say, "All back full." The ship had shot backwards from the dock and into the channel in an instant. The captain knew the crew was watching him, and the cheer from the fantail let him know they liked his style.

Boats also remembered how the Old Man had backed him the last time Vink got in trouble on liberty in Sasebo. He had simply told the captain, "I need Vink." Now the captain needed him, and he didn't have to be reminded.

The ship was maneuvering to come alongside an aircraft carrier they could barely make out, laboring in the heavy seas several thousand yards ahead. *Just our luck,* he thought, *to get mixed up with a bunch of flyboys instead of some real Navy tanker-men who know what they're doing.* This would not be easy, but he knew the captain had the con, and Chief Petzhold had the helm, and this comforted him. It was no time for amateurs.

"...and the Angel of the Lord seduced the Virgin Mary..."

"You got everything under control, Boats?" The high-pitched voice from behind jarred him. It was Ensign Craig, an Engineering Division Officer.

Boats thought, *Why can't this little shit just go away and leave us alone? All he can do is get in the way.* He threw a half-salute at the ensign and shouted, "Yes, sir."

Ensign Craig was a hopeless case. Out of some ROT corps school in Texas. A pharmacist, for Christ's sake, and the Navy wanted to make an engineering officer out of him. The ensign had been aboard for eight months, and still didn't know his ass from the after fan room.

"Look, Mr. Craig..." The words were half out of his mouth when the deck dropped like a falling roller coaster, and a monster wave slammed him against the bulkhead. He managed to stay on his feet, and immediately saw that his men, hooked to the lifeline, were safe.

Ensign Craig was not. The wave caught the young officer off balance and folded his back around a life raft stanchion like a gymnast on a high bar. He crumpled to the deck, and floated quietly off into the wildly tossing sea.

"MAN OVERBOARD!" Boats bellowed.

Seaman Faust on the sound-powered phones relayed the message to the bridge. "Man overboard, port side amidships, this is not a drill."

"...go and search diligently for the young child..."

Boats riveted his eyes to Ensign Craig in the bright orange life jacket growing smaller and smaller in the foaming, swirling sea. The ensign was either paralyzed or unconscious because there was no sign of him struggling.

The ship heeled sharply to port, and rolled at a perilous 45-degree angle as the captain did not hesitate to attempt rescue of the stricken man. The sound from the ship's loudspeakers filled the air, the voice sounding almost nonchalant. "Now hear this. Now hear this. Man overboard, port side. Man overboard, port side. All hands, man your man-overboard stations. This is not a drill. This is not a drill."

They had practiced this procedure until they were sick of it, but always in fair weather. The drill called for putting a whaleboat in the water, but today, Boats thought, *if we try that we might have the whole boat crew in the water.* He knew what he had to do. "Vink," he shouted, "secure this line to the winch, I'm goin' after him." He tied one end of an inch-thick hawser around his waist.

"You're crazy, Boats. You can't swim in that sea."

"When I reach him, I'll signal with the Very Pistol." He patted the holster on his belt, and dived into the water.

Boats was a strong swimmer, but more than strength was needed here. He had gauged the direction and flow of the waves, and as the ship came around, judged the moment to jump that would carry him as close as possible to the man in the water. The surge of the slate gray sea carried him to within 20 yards of the crippled ensign, and he began to swim towards him with all the strength he could muster. Instantly he sensed that he could make headway, and the feeling exhilarated him because he knew that the rescue would be successful. In ten minutes that seemed like hours, he was alongside the helpless officer, who looked at him with grateful eyes. "What took you so long, Boats?" he asked.

Boats secured the line around the ensign's waist and said, "Navy red tape, sir. I had to apply for hazardous duty pay." He fired the Very Pistol.

"...when they saw the star they rejoiced with exceeding great joy..."

Later, in a Yokosuka bar, one of his drinking buddies asked him a question.

"Boats, how come you risk yo black ass to save that pimp ensign's white ass?"

"...he came unto his own and his own received him not..."

Boats didn't know the answer then, and after all these years, he still didn't know the answer. One thing he did know though; whatever the answer was, it had nothing to do with skin color.

"...full of grace and truth ."

>>1<<

BOOKER T.

Booker T. McCan sat beside his pal Snowball Faucett on a sandbag wall stacked above a muddy bank, watching the water slowly recede. Booker T. and Snowball didn't know it but they were carrying on a long and enduring tradition...man's fascination with a great river. For uncounted centuries the Peoria Indians had watched the great Illinois River flood the plain where later a city would arise and take its name from them. Standing on the high bluffs overlooking the plain, late-17th century French explorers were the first white men to see it.

Peoria...Heart of Illinois...June 1939. The sky was clear after the spring rains, and the early summer sun beat on the hard-packed mud, cracking it into artistic patterns that would soon curl and crumble into the dust of August. The dank, musty smell of evaporating mud choked the boys' nostrils.

Booker T. picked up a stone and tried to skip it across the swiftly running water, muttering to himself as it sank like a rock.

"I ain't afraid of Bus Taylor!" he shouted above the rush of the high water.

Snowball smiled, and then laughed out loud in that way of his that sounded like "hunnf." He looked at Booker T., big for his age, and said what he had been saying for what seemed like a month of Sundays. "Booker T., you been sayin' that and sayin' that, and ah been tellin' ya and tellin' ya, if you ain't afraid of Bus Taylor you damn sure ought to be afraid of him because he is not only bigger than you, he is mean and he is tough, and if you don't look out he will flatten yo' ass, and then he will stomp on it. I seen him do it. You better stay away from Bus Taylor."

Booker T. picked up another rock and fired it into the water in a fury of pre-adolescent frustration. "I ain't stayin' away from him, I'm meetin' him next Saturday in back of the school. We'll see if he can handle my new left hook."

Booker T., 12 years old, and only beginning to test his limits, jumped off the sandbag wall, and shadow-boxed on his toes in a wide circle, hooking with his left hand while holding his clenched right fist next to his ear.

Snowball watched disdainfully. He knew Booker T. well; they had been friends since they were five. Booker T. had always been the leader, often an impetuous one, but more than once it was Snowball who saved the day with a restraining voice. "Booker T., what you tryin' to prove?" he asked. "Bus Taylor is in tenth grade and you is only in sixth. You could hit him with left hooks from now 'til Christmas, and he wouldn't even know it."

Booker T. knew Snowball was right, but he hated to admit it. He slammed two more left hooks and a punishing right cross into the phantom Bus Taylor's cast-iron jaw, then sank back down on the sandbag wall.

"Okay, Snowball," he sighed, "what should we do? I can't stand that guy no more…always pushin' little guys around. Thinks he's so damned smart…just 'cause he's bigger than everybody else. We got to do somethin'."

They sat again on the sandbags, watching the swirling brown water, noting an occasional floating log, and once what appeared to be an entire limb from a large oak tree with leaves still attached. Their thoughts swirled like the river around the image of the neighborhood bully, Bus Taylor, and what to do about him. In the menacing neighborhood of south Peoria, bullies were a fact of life they had long learned to live with, mostly by simple avoidance. But the emergence of Bus Taylor was something new. In addition to being mean, he was a liar, a cheat, and a petty thief, but worst of all, he was an extortionist. He collected money from neighborhood kids in exchange for protection, a trick he apparently learned from hearing about the Capone gang and some of their escapades in this part of Illinois. Although Booker T. had doubts about Bus Taylor's toughness, of one thing there was no doubt—this brute had terrorized the neighborhood where they lived on the south side of Peoria for too long.

In June 1939, the great economic depression—the Depression—was a big factor in their lives. While many people were out of work, Booker T. was lucky. His family was not on the dole, and though it was no disgrace to be on relief in these hard times, you could walk a little taller knowing you didn't have to stand in line for a handout. Booker T. had seen men gratefully accept a plate of food from his mother in exchange for performing a few odd jobs around the house; jobs he knew could as easily have been done by his dad or by him. His father worked as a janitor at Manual Training High School, and his mother cleaned for the rich white people who lived in big houses on the bluffs overlooking the river on the north side of the city. His mother caught a bus at five a.m., six days a week, and in the winter she did not get home until after dark. But she was glad to have a job, and never complained. Booker T. helped out where he could. From the time he was 10 years old, he had delivered newspapers. He also ran errands for Mister Kramer, the mortician, and for his friend, Ma Jong, who ran the Shanghai Teahouse on South Washington Street. Booker T. was the baby of the family. He had two married sisters, and a brother, Davey, who had joined the Navy the year before, and was serving on a battleship in the Pacific fleet. He idolized his brother, and rarely did anything without considering what Davey would think about it, or how Davey would do it. Davey had been a star fullback on the high school football team, and a champion boxer in the Golden Gloves.

Booker T. was happy with his life, but now, instead of enjoying the early summer sunshine, and the carefree feeling that went with the absence of homework assignments, his mind was troubled by the nagging threat of this bully. Trouble with Bus Taylor began soon after Davey had gone off to the Navy, and had gotten progressively worse until now he was demanding a cut of Booker T.'s paper route profits. What would Davey do? Booker T. stood and fired another rock into the muddy water. "I'm goin' to see Count," he announced.

Count lived in a shanty hut in the middle of the city dump. He was a man of such antiquity that he had been too old for the Spanish-American War. Booker T. respected him not only for his age, but for his wisdom.

Booker T. found Count in his usual place, sitting in an ancient wicker-backed rocking chair on the shady side of his shack, smoking his pipe, and reading a book. Count looked up from his book and saw Booker T. picking his way through the tangle of worn-out tires, wrecked cars, tired mattresses, smoking piles of cinders, and assorted other discards that made up this part of the Peoria city dump. Count had been a friend to four generations of Booker T.'s family, he was older than Booker T.'s grandfather. When Booker T. was close he asked, "What is it, Booker T.? You look troubled." He felt a particular affection for this young man, who might be the last McCan to come to him for advice.

Before answering, Booker T. looked carefully at Count to be sure he was all right; as young as he was, he felt obliged to look after Count's needs. Booker T. liked to run errands for the old man—three times a week he brought in two gallons of fresh water. "You okay, Count?" he asked. "Can I getcha somethin'?"

This was what Count liked most about Booker T., before talking about his own problems, the boy always asked how Count was. Count knew this concern for others was rare in one so young. "Thank you for asking, Booker T.," he answered. "I'm good, I think...what's troublin' you, son?"

"I got a problem with a bully."

Count closed his book; he had been reading Plato. He took the pipe from his mouth, and knocked the ashes out by tapping the bowl on the side of the chair. "Bus Taylor again?" he asked. "What's he up to now?"

"He knows I'm makin' some money on my paper route, and he says if I don't give him five dollars every Friday, he's gonna beat my brains out."

Booker T. found an empty five-gallon oil can and sat down next to Count. The old man re-lit his pipe, and began to look wise. "Five dollars is a lot of money," he said.

Booker T. agreed. "I make one penny on every daily paper I deliver and two cents for a Sunday...It takes me a long time to make a five-dollar profit."

Count nodded. "And if you give him the five, it won't be long 'til he'll want more."

Booker T. pursed his lips tightly, then slowly nodded his head up and down.

Count knew Booker T. was bright, resourceful, and unafraid. His character was being molded in a harsh environment, but he had been fortunate to grow up with good role models, especially his brother Davey. Count also knew that Booker T. did not require his help to solve this problem, so he sat quietly, waiting for the youth to tell him what he planned to do.

After a long silence, Count provided a verbal nudge. "It's an old puzzle," he said. "How to protect yourself against people who want to take away what you worked for."

"Al Capone would just have him shot."

Count looked closely at Booker T. "You gonna shoot Bus Taylor?" he asked.

"Maybe I should...I think..." Booker T. paused, thinking about it.

Count puffed on his pipe. "Mostly guns cause more problems than they solve," he said.

"If I shot him, they'd probably put me in jail," said Booker T.

Concerned that Booker T. might be serious about shooting Bus Taylor, Count took the opportunity to practice what came quite naturally to him—

discussing a moral dilemma. "So Booker T., are you telling me the only thing that prevents you from shooting Bus Taylor is the threat of going to jail?"

Booker T., only 12 years old, and entirely lacking in guile, answered, "It's not the only thing."

Count asked, "What else?"

"I don't have a gun," Booker T. answered grimly.

Count looked to see if Booker T. was making a joke. Seeing no smile, he asked, "Anything else?"

Booker T. shifted his position on the empty oil can, then said in a soft voice, "The Ten Commandments...Count, do I have to obey the Ten Commandments if Bus Taylor don't?"

Count had been around long enough to know better than to try answering that one straight out. He understood what Socrates had recognized more than 2,000 years ago. Aware that the boy was looking at him, he wondered what Booker T. would say if he answered yes...or no. But Socrates would not let it end there, and neither would he.

"Booker T., tell me what you know about the Ten Commandments."

Booker T. blushed at the question. All he knew was that they came from the Bible and that there were a lot of "thou shalt nots" in there, including "thou shalt not kill" and "thou shalt not steal."Looking away from Count, he said, "They come from the Bible."

"Yes," said Count, "the Old Testament; first in the book of Exodus, then again in Deuteronomy. They were the words of the Lord given to Moses for transmission to the people of Israel, first on Mount Sinai, and later in the Promised Land around Jerusalem. It was also Moses' task to inform the people of Israel that the God who was commanding them was an angry God, and they were threatened with destruction if they did not obey Him."

Booker T. thought about Israel, Mount Sinai, and Jerusalem, wondering if they were real places. He also thought about the God of Moses, and wondered why he was so angry. "Count," he said, "if the words of the Lord were directed to the people of Israel, does that have anything to do with us? Is the God of Moses our God?"

"Maybe, maybe not," Count replied, "but some people think, no matter where it came from, the commandment not to kill people is a pretty good idea. But listen to this...the original language of the Bible was Hebrew, and in some translations of the Ten Commandments, the fifth commandment reads, 'You shall not murder' instead of 'You shall not kill.'"

"Is there a difference?"

"Well," Count said, "it's possible to kill without murdering, but you can't murder without killing."

Booker T. looked up and said, "So it might be okay for me to kill Bus Taylor, but not okay for me to murder him?"

Count puffed on his pipe. "If you set out to kill him," he said, "according to most definitions, you couldn't do it without murdering him. But if you killed him by accident, or even in a fit of anger, it would not be called murder. But that doesn't mean it would be okay. See, there's somethin' for you to learn here, Booker T. It's about how to get along with people in this life, which everybody has to do unless they happen to be a hermit, like me." He laughed a loud and bubbly laugh that Booker T. had heard before. When Count laughed like that, Booker T. knew he was feeling good, and that made him feel good too.

Still smiling, Count continued. "The lesson is this," he said, "...when you see somebody behaving badly and hurting other people, you know that's not the way you want to run your own life. You don't really want to kill him, do you?"

Booker T. shook his head, and looked off into the distance over a pile of cinders and ashes. "I been tryin' to think what Davey might do, Count," he said. "I don't think Davey would kill him, but the problem is I ain't big enough to do what Davey would do, which is to beat the crap out of him. I got to figure some better way...I got some ideas."

Count smiled and waited for Booker T. to tell him of his ideas.

>>2<<

THE GLORY

Two-and-a-half years later on a cold but sunny Sunday morning, Booker T. and Snowball, along with another friend, Zane Tucker, were playing Horse on the school playground basketball court. The Horse rules were simple: if somebody made a shot, the others had one chance to duplicate it exactly or collect another Horse. Five failures…five letters—H-O-R-S-E, meant losing, and nobody took losing lightly.

"Slop shot," said Snowball in disgust as Zane threw up a 20-foot underhanded shot that sailed through the hoop without touching anything but air. The hoop had once supported a net, but countless swishes had long ago shredded it to the few tattered remnants that now remained. It was early December, but the boys did not notice the cold, so intent were they on the game. Horse was a warm-up; when the real game began, they would soon be dripping sweat from the non-stop running up and down the court for up to an hour, sometimes longer, without letup.

"Here comes Elijah," said Snowball. "Hey, he just fell down…He's havin' a fit."

They ran to their friend Elijah Fulton, stretched rigidly on the ground in the throes of a grand mal seizure.

Booker T. took charge. "Snowball, hold his legs. Zane, you hold his arms. I got to get this stick in his mouth before he swallows his tongue."

Booker T. pried the afflicted boy's jaws apart, placed a wooden stick between his teeth, and held his tongue in place with his fingers. They restrained their stricken friend for several minutes, until finally he began to relax, and soon the seizure was over. Elijah lay quietly, though he continued to breathe heavily.

"That was scary," said Snowball. "Booker T., how'd you know what to do?"

"I saw my brother Davey do it," Booker T. shrugged.

They all knew and respected Davey. "Whaddaya hear from Davey?" asked Zane.

"He's a Bo'sun's mate on the battleship *West Virginia*," Booker T. said proudly.

"What's a Bo'sun's mate?" asked Zane.

Booker T. pretended to know more than he actually did. "He takes care of the anchors and things, and he's in charge of the admiral's barge. He's also the heavyweight champion of the ship."

Zane's eyes bulged. "Davey's a heavyweight now? Wow! Is he goin' to fight Joe Louis?"

"Maybe he will," Booker T. said.

Two boys appeared from around the corner. They were running hard and shouting excitedly, "THE JAPS BOMBED PEARL HARBOR! THE COUNTRY'S GOIN' TO WAR!"

When Booker T. thought about it later, he would always remember this moment as if it were a dream: the boys running in slow motion, their arms waving wildly, mouths wide, but with no sound coming out.

When the shouts first reached his ears, Booker T. was thrilled and angry at the same time. Then he thought of Davey. Everyone except Booker T. began jumping around and whooping loudly. Booker T. stood as if rooted, then finally turned away and walked slowly to a bench, where he sat and stared thoughtfully into the distance. At length the boys stopped jumping and crowded around him. "Whatsa matter, Booker T.? Dontcha wanna go fight a war?"

Booker T. said quietly, "Davey's at Pearl Harbor."

"How we gonna find out if Davey's O.K.?" Booker T. looked hopefully at his Ma and Pa. Booker T., along with his mother and father, were gathered around the kitchen table looking at the front page of the Peoria *Evening Journal*. It was Monday, December 8, 1941. The two-inch headlines shouted:

JAPAN WARS ON U.S. AND BRITAIN

The sub-headlines read:

BATTLESHIP OKLAHOMA SET AFIRE BY TORPEDO PLANES

104 SOLDIERS KILLED 300 WOUNDED AT HICKAM FIELD

In the story that followed was the line they dreaded to see:

> *"It was impossible to obtain confirmation or denial that the Oklahoma and West Virginia had been damaged or sunk at Pearl*

> *Harbor, together with 6 or 7 destroyers, and that 350 U.S. airplanes had been caught on the ground."*

Mother McCan spoke. "Booker T.," she said, "we just got to wait. We got to have faith that Davey is all right, and we got to pray to God that Davey stays safe."

"Ma, Pa, I wanna join the Navy. I wanna fight them Japs, and I wanna be with Davey."

"That's a lotta wants, Booker T.," said Mother McCan, "but look, honey, you is only fourteen years old."

"But Ma, I'm big for my age," Booker T. asserted. "I could do it."

"Son," his father said, "you got to finish your schoolin'."

"But Pa, you don't need schoolin' to fight a war," Booker T. pleaded.

Father McCan shook his head. "The war won't last forever, Booker T.," he said. "Fact is, I hear them Japs is just a little bitty country, and we'll whup 'em pretty quick. I hear it'll be like Joe Louis fightin' Willie Pep...a heavyweight against a featherweight. Besides, your brother Davey finished his schoolin', and you know that's what he'd want you to do."

Booker T. knew his Pa was right about that.

"Now, Booker T.," his mother said, "finish your supper, and put on your go to meetin' clothes. We are goin' to a prayer meeting."

The Faith Chapel Church of God and Christ was filled to capacity. The organist was playing "Go Tell It On the Mountain," and the congregation was singing lustily, swaying and clapping hands in time with the music. When the music stopped, Isaiah Quentin Black, who liked to be called Preacher IQ, stepped into the raised pulpit. He was a large, handsome, ebony-colored man wearing a flowing black robe with violet velvet lapels. He spread his arms wide above his head, and in a resonating bass voice said softly, "Praise the Lord."

The congregation repeated in hushed tones, "Praise the Lord. Amen."

"Salvation, glory, and power belong to our God! True and righteous are His judgments."

The congregation responded, "True and righteous are His judgments. Amen."

The preacher shouted, "THE COWARDLY JAPANESE ARE AGENTS OF SATAN AND THEY WILL FEEL THE WRATH OF GOD!" He slammed his fist onto the pulpit.

The congregation sprang to their feet shouting, "AMEN, AMEN, HALLELUJAH, AMEN."

Preacher IQ waited for the congregation to take their seats. They looked up at him expectantly. Once again he began to speak, softly at first, his voice growing louder as he moved through his text.

"The Bible tells us, in the book of Revelations, chapter twelve, verse seven, 'Then war broke out in Heaven. Michael and his angels fought against the dragon, who fought back with his angels; but the dragon was defeated, and he and his angels were thrown out of Heaven'...THEY WERE THROWN OUT OF HEAVEN!"

The congregation shouted in unison, "THROWN OUT OF HEAVEN! AMEN!"

Softly, again with rising voice, Preacher IQ continued, "Now the dragon was that old serpent named the devil. He was thrown down to Earth, and all his angels with him. HOW WONDERFUL FOR THE PEOPLE WHO LIVE IN HEAVEN, GLORY HALLELUJAH!"

"GLORY HALLELUJAH! AMEN!" shouted the congregation.

"How terrible for the Earth and the sea, for the devil has come down to us, and he is filled with rage because he knows he has only a little time left."

Preacher IQ stopped speaking, slowly took a large red handkerchief from his pocket, wiped his brow, and looked at the congregation, many of whom had moved to the edge of their seats.

"Brothers and sisters, the devil is the cowardly Japanese, and their evil allies the craven Nazis, and they have very little time left...**LITTLE** TIME! CAN I HEAR AN AMEN?"

"AMEN!" people stood and shouted again.

Once again, Preacher IQ waited for the congregation to settle down. He knew that on this fateful occasion they were looking to him for inspiration. He reveled in the knowledge, trying with some difficulty to contain his own excitement. He was a young man with a volatile temperament, wondering exactly what his role should be in the coming conflict. He suddenly realized that the congregation was quietly waiting for him to continue.

He cleared his throat. "The Bible tells us...there was an Angel flying high in the air with an eternal message of good news to the peoples of the Earth...to every race, tribe, language, and nation...'FEAR GOD, AND PRAISE HIS GREATNESS! FOR THE TIME HAS COME TO JUDGE MANKIND...WORSHIP HIM WHO MADE HEAVEN, EARTH, SEA, AND THE SPRINGS OF WATER!'

"A second Angel followed the first one saying... 'She has fallen! Great Babylon has fallen! She gave her wine to all peoples, and made them drink it...the strong wine of her immoral lust!'

"A third Angel followed the first two, saying in a loud voice, 'Whosoever worships the beast and its image and receives the mark on his forehead or on his hand will himself drink God's wine, the wine of his anger, which he has poured at full strength into the cup of his wrath!'

"Then a voice from Heaven said...'HAPPY ARE THE DEAD WHO FROM NOW ON DIE IN THE SERVICE OF THE LORD.'"

Preacher IQ paused, allowing tension to mount. He lowered his voice almost to a whisper. The congregation leaned forward in their seats, straining not to miss a word.

"Brothers and sisters, many of your sons, and yes, your daughters too, will die in this holy war, but you must not despair, you must remember the words of the Angel...'Happy are the dead who from now on die in the service of the Lord!' Can I hear an Amen?"

"Amen." This amen was not as enthusiastic, as the congregation pondered the idea of family members dying.

"The Bible says... 'Then I looked, and there was a white cloud, and sitting on the cloud was a being who looked like a man with a gold crown on his head, and a sharp sickle in his hand. Then another Angel went out from the temple and cried out in a loud voice to the one who was sitting on the cloud...use your sickle, and reap the harvest because the right time has come; the Earth is ripe for the harvest.' Then the one who sat on the cloud swung his sickle on the Earth and the Earth's harvest was reaped. Then another Angel, who is in charge of the fire, came from the altar. He shouted in a loud voice to the Angel who had the sharp sickle...'USE YOUR SICKLE AND CUT THE GRAPES FROM THE VINEYARD OF THE EARTH, BECAUSE THE GRAPES ARE RIPE!'

"So the Angel swung his sickle on the Earth, cut the grapes of wrath from the vine, and threw them into the winepress of God's great anger. The grapes were squeezed out in the winepress outside the city, and blood came out of the winepress in a flood two hundred miles long, and about five feet deep."

Preacher IQ pronounced this astonishing statistic in profound awe, to great effect on the congregation, many looking fearful. He nodded to the organist, who began to play a familiar hymn as Preacher IQ and his flock sang first slowly and softly, but with ever-increasing volume and tempo.

"Mine eyes have seen the glory of the coming of the Lord,

He is trampling out the vintage where the grapes of wrath are stored.
He has loosed the blinding lightning of his terrible swift sword.
His truth is marching on.
Glory, glory, hallelujah!
Glory, glory, hallelujah!
GLORY, GLORY, HALLELUJAH!
HIS TRUTH IS MARCHING ON!"

The congregation was on its feet, following Preacher IQ down the aisle, through the lobby, out the door and into the street. They marched north on South Adams Street, picking up followers as they went, singing the refrain over and over. People cheered them from street corners and second-story windows. Nobody asked why they were marching. Everyone knew. The country was at war and, God be praised, it was a Holy war.

The next day, Tuesday, Booker T. and his parents were up early as usual, preparing for work, or school. Booker T. was deep in thought, slowly eating breakfast, and staring at the morning newspaper, the *Peoria Star*. His parents were also silent, but they exchanged worried glances, occasionally looking anxiously at their son.

At length Booker T. sighed. "Ma…Pa, I don't want Davey to die. Not even in the service of the Lord."

"Now, Booker T., don't be blasphemin'," his mother said. "Preacher IQ is right. We must not despair and we must have faith. The Bible says so."

"It ain't fair, Ma. Davey never hurt nobody, 'cept maybe a couple plug-ugly stumblebum prizefighters that don't even count. How come he has to die?"

"Nobody says he has to die. Why do you say he has to die?" his father asked.

"You saw the paper yesterday, Pa…*West Virginia* damaged or sunk…and look at today's paper." He pointed to a column:

> *Japanese newspapers identified the two American battleships declared sunk Sunday at Pearl Harbor, Hawaii, as the 31,800 ton West Virginia and the 29,000 ton Oklahoma.*

"You gonna believe Japanese newspapers?"

"No, Pa, but look at this."

> *The White House announced officially that the attack on the*

island of Oahu, site of Honolulu and the Pearl Harbor naval base, probably has cost about 1,500 lives and resulted in an equal number of wounded persons.

Father McCan shook his head sadly. "I don't want Davey to die either, Booker T.," he said.

They waited for word of his brother, their son. Tuesday…no word. Wednesday…no word. There was brave talk in newspaper editorials:

Japan has asked for it. Now she is going to get it. It was the act of a mad dog, a gangster's parody of every principle of international honor.

Thursday…no word. They were frantic with worry. They feared the worst, and prayed for the best.

Friday…no word.

At last on Saturday morning, a Western Union man knocked on the door, and handed Father McCan a telegram. He signed for it, then stood for a long time staring at the unopened envelope in his hand. Finally, he walked to the kitchen, and laid the envelope on the table. The three family members sat silently, looking from the ominous envelope to each other, and back to the envelope. They sat quietly for many minutes, each aware that what was in that envelope would affect their lives in profound and unimaginable ways. At length, Booker T. said, "Maybe we should burn it. If we don't know, at least we can still hope." But they all knew that the envelope had to be opened.

Mother McCan said, "Before we open it, we should pray."

Joining hands, they bowed their heads. They prayed silently, each in their own way. When at last they raised their heads, Father McCan took out a small pocketknife, and carefully unfolded the gleaming, recently honed blade. He picked up the envelope, neatly slit it open, took out the folded paper, carefully unfolded it, and holding it at arm's length began to read:

"Happy to inform you your son, David A. McCan, Seaman, United States Navy; cited for heroism and valor in the face of hostile enemy action stop For distinguished devotion to duty, extraordinary courage and disregard for his own personal safety during the Japanese attack on Pearl Harbor 7 December 1941 Seaman McCan recommended to receive Navy Cross, United States Navy's highest award for bravery."

His voice trailed off. He lifted his tear-filled eyes, and in a voice cracking with emotion said, "Davey is a hero."

"Wow!" shouted Booker T.

"Praise the Lord," said Mother McCan quietly.

Soon they received a letter from Davey telling what had happened. At the height of the attack, with bombs and torpedoes exploding all around, with machine-gun bullets filling the air like rain, surrounded by fire, smoke, and paralyzing noise, he had taken over an unmanned machine gun on the bridge of the *West Virginia,* and shot down at least two Japanese aircraft. He said he was lucky to survive. He did not know how he had escaped unhurt. He had seen his commanding officer die from a shrapnel wound in the stomach. He had seen many men die. He had seen much pain and suffering. He had seen many courageous acts. He was proud to have been part of it, to have done his duty.

Later in the spring he wrote to tell them about receiving the Navy Cross from Admiral Nimitz on the flight deck of the aircraft carrier *Enterprise*, just before the battle of Midway Island.

Booker T. was excited by these letters, and swelled with pride when he told his friends about what Davey was doing in the war. When Davey told them he had been transferred to the aircraft carrier *Liscomb Bay,* Booker T. stopped worrying about his brother's safety. He thought if Davey could survive the sneak attack on Pearl Harbor, he must be indestructible. Besides, what could be safer than an aircraft carrier?

>> 3 <<

DAVEY IS DEAD; KILLED IN THE WAR

Booker T. read the war news every day. Some days it was good, some days it was bad, but he thought the U.S. was winning. He was glad Davey was not a Marine or an Army infantryman when he read about the fierce fighting on the Pacific islands; the stories about Guadalcanal made him shudder. Then, one day, he was shocked to read that *Liscomb Bay*, Davey's ship, had been torpedoed and sunk while operating in the vicinity of Tarawa Atoll in the Gilbert Islands. An eyewitness account was published in the newspaper. The witness had been aboard the battleship New Mexico three fourths of a mile away.

> *There was a gentle swell and a light southeast breeze, the first light of day was in the sky at 0513 when a torpedo hit Liscomb Bay amidships. There was a terrible explosion. A column of bright orange flame rose a thousand feet in the air. Within a few seconds the aircraft bombs stowed in the hold detonated, and, with a mighty roar, the carrier burst apart as though she were one great bomb, tossing men, planes, deck frames and molten fragments so high that the deck of the New Mexico, 1500 yards to leeward, was showered with fragments of steel, clothing, and human flesh. The entire after third of the escort carrier was demolished. Flames raced through her interior and arose from her flight deck as from a giant torch. Ammunition exploded, sending huge bouquets of fire upward. The flight deck caved in, and, only 23 minutes after being hit, the doomed ship flared up for the last time and sank hissing into a 2300 fathom deep. Fifty three officers and 591 enlisted men were lost; 55 officers and 217 men were rescued, mostly by destroyers Morris and Hughes, many in frightful condition with shattered*

limbs, internal hemorrhages, head concussions and horribly disfiguring burns.

Booker T. was stunned. He refused to believe that Davey was dead. There had been survivors; Davey *must* have been one of them. Once again the family was tortured by an agonizing and interminable wait for official news. In a few days a letter from Davey arrived, and for a moment they were greatly relieved, then confused and disappointed when they realized the letter had been written a month before the sinking. The waiting continued until, again on a Saturday morning, a Western Union messenger arrived with a telegram.

They went through the same ritual as before, staring at the unopened telegram lying on the kitchen table. They once again joined hands in silent prayer, and at last Mother McCan said, "Pa, tell us what it says."

After briefly scanning the message, Father McCan said simply, "Davey is dead."

Booker T.'s heart sank at the awful words.

"Praise the Lord," said Mother McCan softly. Booker T. was speechless.

Booker T. grieved for his brother, but for reasons he didn't understand, he did not cry. For days, he could not get rid of the lump in his throat and the knot in his stomach. At night he lay awake for long hours thinking about his brother, feeling a powerful loneliness. Finally, he went to see his old friend.

"Hello, Booker T.," said Count, "...you look troubled."

"Davey is dead; killed in the war. What does it mean, Count?"

The old man looked closely at his young friend, seeing the sad eyes, sensing the aching anguish. He stood up and turned away, gathering his thoughts. *What does it mean to die?* He walked in a small circle, then returned to his chair, where he sat quietly for a long time. He lighted his pipe and took several puffs. Booker T. sat and watched, waiting patiently. At length Count put his hand on Booker T's shoulder and gave it a squeeze. "You ask a hard question, Booker T. What is the meaning of death?...I lived a long time, seen most everything, but I never died."

"Ma says Davey is in Heaven," said Booker T. "Is it true?"

Count heard the hint of a demand, and looked carefully at Booker T. before replying. "Some say so," he said. "Would you feel better knowing Davey was in Heaven?"

"I think so," answered Booker T. "...But I want him to be right here where I can touch him...rassle with him.... talk to him...you know what I mean, Count?"

Count nodded. "How long has Davey been away?" he asked.

"He joined the Navy six years ago. I was ten years old when he left."

"While he was gone, did it seem like he was dead?"

Booker T. had experienced such thoughts. "In a way it did," he answered. "I couldn't touch him or talk to him. But we got letters. And now..." Booker T's voice trailed off in a choking sob. Count squeezed his shoulder again, and waited while Booker T. cried. "It's okay, Booker T.," he said softly. "Let it all out, son."

When at last Booker T. gained control of his emotions, he sat up and said, "Sorry, Count."

Count squeezed his shoulder again. "Nothin' to be sorry about...it's natural...you got to let go of the grief. Now, Booker T.," he said, "tell me how you remember Davey best."

Booker T. did not hesitate. "The time I saw him wipe out three men with one block that let Boomer Jones score on a fifty-yard touchdown run that beat Central, and gave us the city championship. I was standing on the sideline...the play happened right in front of me. They were running right at me...I could see Davey's eyes...they were fierce! Those three guys never had a chance. Davey dove straight out, and hit the first two guys right at the knees. The third was right behind, and they all went down like tenpins. It was beautiful! You should have heard the crowd. They were chanting 'Boomer, Boomer, Boomer!' But Boomer knew. After he scored, he ran back and handed the ball to Davey. Then the crowd chanted 'Davey. Davey, Davey!' After the game, the Central coach came over and shook Davey's hand." Booker T.'s face flushed with excitement as he recounted the story.

Count smiled and nodded, remembering some things himself—Davey had come to him more than once for advice and counsel. "Booker T.," he said, "your brother Davey was a fine young man, and even though his life was short, things happened to him that never happen to most people who live as long as I have. How many people get to hear a crowd chanting their name in praise? How many people get decorated for bravery by an admiral of the fleet?"

"But think what he could have done if he..." Booker T.'s voice trailed off.

Count nodded. "You're right, Booker T.," he said. "Think what he could have done. That's the tragedy of wars. All those brave young men, dead before their time. Think what they could have done. Maybe one of them could have figured out a way to end wars."

"Who was the bravest man you ever saw?" Booker T. asked.

Count did not have to think long. "Harriet Tubman," he answered.

"A woman?"

"Women can be brave, too, Booker T."

"Who was Harriet Tubman?"

Count pondered the question, he searched the cobwebbed archives of his brain cells—he wanted to get this answer right. "Harriet Tubman," he mused. "...People called her Moses. She led so many slaves to freedom in the North nobody could count 'em all, must have been over three hundred. She'd take ten, fifteen...twenty at a time. Traveled mostly at night, from Maryland to Pennsylvania and New York. I was ten years old when I went with her, I never been so scared. She was tough as a drill sergeant; when she gave an order, nobody asked questions. She carried a pistol, and she wasn't afraid to use it; she knew what would happen if she got caught. They had a bounty on her head, but they never caught her. She was the bravest person I ever saw."

"How old are you, Count?"

Count pondered the question. Sometimes he thought of himself as older than the Earth, but there were times when he thought he was only recently born. He looked at Booker T. wondering if that would make any sense to the boy. "How old am I?" he repeated the question. "I was born sometime around eighteen forty, Booker T.,...that makes me five score and three. One hundred and three years old."

"Did you ever come close to dyin'?"

The old man pulled down his collar and showed the boy a long, ugly scar that angled from his right ear three inches up along his scalp. "I was the same age as your brother Davey when that rifle ball creased my head at Gettysburg," he said. "I was lucky, I only lost the hearing in my right ear. When I woke up I was in a field hospital full of men with missing arms and legs. Right next to me was a rebel from Gadsden, Alabama, who had lost an arm. I got to know him pretty good. I still remember his name...Maynard Large. Maynard didn't want to fight anybody; he didn't know what the war was all about and didn't care. His daddy was a storekeeper, and all he wanted to do was go home and help out. That Alabama boy and me talked about how crazy it all was...how one day everybody tried to kill as many as they could, and the next day they were tryin' to save as many lives as they could; war is strange business."

Count paused to think about the strange business of war. He lighted his pipe. Booker T. sensed that Count had more to say about war, and waited patiently. Presently, Count continued. "We had good doctors at Gettysburg," he said. "I still remember Doctor Jewett from Boston. He made sure all the wounded got plenty to eat. He said the better you ate, the quicker you'd heal. Those that lost arms and legs had to eat a dozen eggs a day. If it hadn't been for all those chicken farmers around Gettysburg, a lot more men would have died."

"We had to memorize Lincoln's Gettysburg address in school," Booker T. said.

Count nodded. "President Lincoln was a great man," he said. "I was there when he gave that address."

"Why was the address so important that we had to memorize it?" Booker T. asked. "Our teacher never told us that, she just told us to memorize it."

"People didn't think it was so important at the time," Count said, "there were way too many fresh graves, and it was hard not to think about 'em. There were a lot of people there, but I don't think many could even hear what he said. I know I couldn't. But time has a way of lettin' us see what's important and what ain't. It seems Lincoln was talkin' about the importance of holdin' together a country that was founded on the principles of 'all men are created equal, and life, liberty, and the pursuit of happiness'. What year is this? Nineteen forty-three? It's been eighty years — four score, since Lincoln spoke those words, and we've managed to hold together, and we' re still pursuin', so maybe the historians are right, maybe it was important. Maybe we need to be reminded once in a while that this country is special, and maybe even worth fightin' for."

Count fell silent. They both sat quietly for a long time.

At length Booker T. spoke. "I want to fight, Count, I wanta go kill some Japs and get even for Davey."

Count stood up and walked a few steps away then turned and came to stand over Booker T., who was still seated. "I wonder if that'll make you feel any better," he said.

"They killed my brother, Count," Booker T. raised his voice, "I want to get even."

Count shook his head. "Revenge is a hollow sport," he said, "But I guess there's some things you got to find out for yourself...My advice is to finish high school before you do anything else; anybody named Booker T. has a name to live up to. And Booker T., while you're still home, be good to your Momma and Papa. They're sufferin' more than you know, and you should try to understand that. Sometimes the best medicine for grief is to help somebody else get over theirs."

Booker T. felt better after talking to Count. He stayed in school another six months, completing his sophomore year. In June, 1944, the day after the school term ended, with troops locked in mortal combat on the Normandy beaches, he put on his "go-to-meetin'" suit, and enlisted in the United States Navy. He was 16 years old. At the recruiting office the day he and his fellow enlistees left, the petty officer in charge put little pins in their lapels that read, "I volunteered for the Navy." Booker T. and 20 other volunteers marched proudly through the streets of Peoria on their way to the train station. People cheered and shouted words of encouragement that made all the marchers feel important. On the station platform, Booker T. said good-bye to his Ma and Pa. His mother cried and said, "Be careful, son. Don't forget to say your prayers."

Booker T. stood tall, looking at the other recruits boarding the train. "Don't worry, Ma," he said. "I'll be all right...G'by, Pa." He gathered his parents together into his arms for a farewell embrace, then moved quickly to board the train. He turned as he mounted the last step, and they saw the smiling, happy face of their surviving son waving confidently as the train began to move.

>>4<<

LOWBALL WHEEL

Booker T. gripped the rail as the big ship rolled leisurely to port; he gazed in fascination at the diminishing distance between him and the gray, forbidding water. For an instant he thought this time the ship would surely capsize, but he did not really care. In fact, he hoped it would, for that would bring an end to his nausea. Instead, as it had done time after endless time, the massive transport vessel found its limit, hung suspended over the trough for a breathless moment, and then began a languid, sickening roll to starboard. Booker T. had been here for hours facing the wind and spray, waiting for relief. That the sea itself would test him, came as a surprise, but as bad as he felt, he knew that he would meet the challenge just as he had met all the other challenges over which he had no control. The sea, like the white establishment, might sicken him, but it could not defeat him.

He continued to seethe with rage when he thought about the reception awaiting them in Norfolk, that eternity of two months ago. They were given little white coats, quartered in Section B (black only), and informed that they would receive training to become mess attendants. What it meant, as they soon discovered, was that they were to be servants for the officers. No words could change it. No protest was persuasive; orders were orders.

But the formal training was now in the past, and the real training had begun. They were westward bound; headed for the war zone—it was September 1944. Not until they were at sea, two days out of San Francisco, were they informed that their destination was Hawaii, a ten-day voyage from Frisco; once there, they would be assigned to permanent duty stations.

Two days out of San Francisco, several thousand men were in the throes of an epidemic—seasickness. From the first retching puke in the forward head, it had spread as swiftly and inexorably as a ten-foot swell. Those present at the inception recoiled in horror, instantly understanding that this affliction was as contagious as polio. Men ran frantically from the scene as though they had seen a roomful of snakes—to no avail. Having seen, and worse, having smelled, they were stricken. And so, like chicken pox, or worse, since there was no immunity, it was disseminated until it seemed that the ship itself suffered the ailment. The great vessel took on an unnatural and ghostly silence; only the movement of the ship's crew, required to stand their watches, attested to the presence of life on board. Food was forgotten; coffee and cigarettes were odious. Men stayed coiled in their sleeping racks (pieces of canvass stretched taut over metal pipe frames), stacked four, five, and six to a tier. They were like bears in hibernation awaiting the signal for a blessed and liberating spring.

Three days the motion continued unabated, then slowly moderated, and finally ended. The fourth day dawned bright and clear, and the sea, its fury spent, was as calm and tranquil as a birdbath. The men stormed the chow lines, making up for lost time. They did calisthenics on the weather decks. They scrubbed down the heads, and held field day in the sleeping compartments. Then, by mid afternoon, their work done, they began the marathon poker games.

For the moment Booker T. was not interested in poker; he was struggling to find his sea legs, even to learn who he was—since boot camp, and it seemed forevermore, Booker T. would be called Mac. He was back at the rail, pondering the vastness of the Pacific Ocean, seeing it for the first time. The warm September sun flowed over him, thawing his sadness, then disposing of it entirely in the spectacular blaze of a horizon cloud sunset. He was stunned by the splendor of the symmetrical rays...scarlet, orange and gold emanating from the blood red semicircle of the horizon sliced sun. Then, with a shock of recognition, he realized that the glorious sunset was an almost exact replica of the enemy battle flag, emblem of the hated Japanese. The thought confused him, yet he was not ignorant of symbolism, his mother had explained the meaning of Holy Communion. But what did this mean? He was not prepared to believe the killer Japs were capable of appreciating, as he did, the pure beauty of this spectacle. Therefore, it must have some other more sinister meaning. But surely a nation, even one as slow-witted as Japan, would not choose the setting sun, a portent of coming darkness, as an emblem. Then he remembered that their symbol was of the rising sun, indistinguishable out of context from the setting sun. He thought about that for a while, then smiled. His job, as it had been for his brother Davey, and for all the others, was to ensure that the symbol which the Japanese perceived as their nation rising to be a world power, was in fact the opposite, the symbol of tyranny sinking into oblivion. He was comforted by the idea, and pleased with himself for thinking of it.

His thoughts returned to the beauty and grandeur of the sunset. He sensed Mother Nature atoning for her vicious assault. But the light glancing off the low clouds, the subtly changing purple hues, was more than atonement—it was seduction. Nature was not a mother she was a temptress, and Mac, never one to avoid temptation, was easy prey.

"Cost ya five to get in the game, Mac. House takes four bits from each pot. Dealer's choice. Pot limit. Whaddaya say?"

Mac hesitated, trying to get his bearings. He had taken a seat when one of the players at the game he was watching had thrown down his cards in disgust and stalked off, swearing loudly.

"Come on, Mac, make up yer mind, we ain't got all day. If ya don't like the set up, git yer ass outa the chair and let somebody else play."

The large, well-muscled houseman, burdened with a five-day growth of very black beard, looked ferocious. He squinted at Mac, oozing hostility from behind a glowing cigar butt jammed in the corner of his mouth. Mac looked at him closely, trying to discern why he looked so ugly. It had something to do with the fact that his dark bushy eyebrows came together in the space above his nose. Mac knew he must do something quickly. He also knew instinctively that the proper stance here was to be bluff and tough, but such demeanor was not in his nature, and he was uneasy; this was not a friendly poker game. He disliked being pressured, yet he wanted to play. For the first time in his life he had money in his pocket—100 dollars. It seemed like a fortune. He could afford to gamble, and besides, he had always been lucky at cards, and considered himself a pretty good poker player.

"How come the house gets a cut of the pot?" Mac asked.

The black-bearded houseman looked at him disdainfully, and unleashed a torrent of abusive words, "Where do ya think the fuckin' cards come from, Mac? The fuckin' moon? If it wasn't fer the fuckin' house, there wouldn't be no fuckin' pot. You gonna fuckin' play?"

Mac looked around the large, low-ceilinged, dimly-lighted compartment. Through clouds of tobacco smoke, everywhere he looked there were poker games in progress; he counted at least 20, but knew there were many more. He heard the rattle of dice, and noted the shouts and groans of several rollicking crap games. Crowds of men surrounded every poker game, waiting for someone to drop out so they could play. For three days the games had been underway, uninterrupted by sleep, food, work, or even calls to muster. The players ignored abandon ship drills though some of the watchers reluctantly deigned to go. Mac looked for a familiar face but found none; for the first time in his life he was among strangers, and felt vaguely threatened. For unexplained and incomprehensible reasons, his friend Snowball had been assigned to the Atlantic fleet while he was sent to the Pacific. Growing up with a highly respected older brother, Booker T., now Mac, had been one of those fortunate few who suffered little from the normal abuses endured by most schoolboys. The lesson for him was that the world is friendly; he had no reason to fear strangers.

"What the hell," said Mac, laying a five-dollar bill on the table, "deal me in."

He was not comfortable with this game; it was not real poker, it was a free-for-all. Dealer's choice meant that every hand was different, making it difficult, if not impossible, to develop a long-range strategy the way he liked to do. He had watched this game long enough to learn that none of the players were very good poker players, reflected by the fact that there were no big winners. Except, of course, the house in the form of the malevolent Blackbeard who continued to rake in 50 cents from each pot. In a serious game, Mac might deliberately lose a hand through a false bluff just to set up a big pot later on, but in this wild game he sensed that such tactics would be wasted. Most of the players seemed distracted, and were barely paying attention; it was as if they were playing for matchsticks.

In spite of his discomfort, Mac felt an unfamiliar and thoroughly exhilarating thrill of adventure. To this point in his life, he had never played poker for more than penny ante, nickels and dimes. This game required a one-dollar ante and bets were limited only by the size of the pot. Headed for the war zone, the men had lost all regard for the value of money…it was, after all, only money. Mac looked around the table at the six other players. They were a mixed lot, to be sure, but in spite of the fact that they were tall, short, light, and dark, they were somehow alike. It started with the uniform—all wore rumpled blue dungarees with white cotton T-shirts showing at the neck under their long sleeved blue shirts, which, without exception found the sleeves rolled up well above the elbow. Dog tags hung from dull metal chains around their necks. They were all in their late teens or early twenties. They all smoked…mostly cigarettes, but some smelly cigars. Surnames were stenciled in black ink above their left side shirt pockets. White sailor hats were perched at various angles on most of the heads.

The current dealer wore a St. Louis Browns baseball cap, and on his shirt, scrawled in crude letters above the neatly stenciled name Muchmore was the word Sugar. He shuffled the cards expertly and announced brightly, "Night baseball. With an umpire. Seven cards. Three down, four up. Threes and nines wild. Three up, you double the pot. Fours, you get a free card. Jack of diamonds is the umpire; get it and you can throw anybody out of the game. Ante up."

The black-bearded houseman stared at the dealer in disbelief. "Is your name really Sugar Muchmore?" he rumbled.

The dealer grinned. "That's what my gal calls me," he said.

Blackbeard sneered. "She around here anywhere? What kinda fruitcake game is this? Night baseball with an umpire? Is this the kinda shit they play in Saint Louie? No wonder them fuckers is in last place."

Sugar Muchmore reached into his back pocket and pulled out a package of chewing tobacco. He looked at the sour houseman through narrowed eyes while placing an enormous wad of tobacco in his mouth. Then he sighed and said, "Them 4- F fuckers ain't in last place, Blackie, they're in first place, and if it wasn't fer this peckerwood war I'd be playin' fer them turds." He thought about that for a moment and then added, "Then they prob'ly would be in last place." Everybody laughed at that, Sugar Muchmore loudest of all.

"Anyway, it's dealer's choice," Sugar said, "and I'm the goddamned dealer, so git yer goddamned money up." He started to deal. Mac wanted no part of night baseball with an umpire. On the first card up he got a three, but rather than double the six-dollar pot, he folded without even looking at his two hole cards.

Sugar Muchmore looked at him in surprise and said, "Hey, Mac, that's a wild card, somethin' wrong with yer head?"

Mac put his hand on top of his head and said, "My head tells me to git the hell outta this game 'cause I always had trouble hittin' a curve ball, and that trey sure looks like a curve ball to me."

Mac watched in disgust as the other players bet with abandon and the pot grew. Blackbeard got a three, doubled the pot to 100 dollars, and eventually won the hand with a royal straight flush. He also won the deal and announced, "Night baseball with an umpire." Groans went up around the table.

"Fuck you, junior birdmen," he said, "I ain't changin' when I'm winnin'. Ante up." He won the pot with five aces, and it was Mac's turn to deal.

Slowly and carefully, Booker T. shuffled the cards, then offered them for

Blackbeard to cut.

"You gonna play baseball, Mac?" Blackbeard asked, cutting the cards with a flourish.

"Five card stud, nothin' wild," Mac said.

Blackbeard rolled up his eyes and said, "You must be from Peoria."

"How'd you know?" Mac asked in genuine surprise.

Blackbeard did not answer, but only looked at him with what could best be described as a shit-eating grin.

Mac won 15 dollars with a pair of nines, edging Blackbeard who had a pair of eights. It was the beginning of a run of luck. In the next two hours, at first playing cautiously, then with increasing recklessness as good cards continued to come his way, Mac's stake grew until it was well over 500 dollars. He hit two inside straights. He began to feel invincible. He fingered the bills in his pockets, wondering how much was there. His head swam with the realization that he was accumulating a large amount of money. His concentration on the game waned as he began to think about what he could do with all that money. He thought about quitting while ahead, but not too seriously. For one thing the losing players would pile abuse on him, but more importantly this money had come so easily he could not resist the opportunity to get even more.

Blackbeard watched Mac scrape in yet another pot, and snarled in his gravely voice, "How come yer so goddamned lucky, Mac?"

"Clean living and the power of prayer," Mac answered; he was feeling good.

Blackbeard looked at him contemptuously. "Bullshit," he snarled. "Gimme them fuckin' cards. Let's see how you do at lowball. Ante up for lowball, you swabs."

Mac looked at the dealer curiously. "How do you play lowball?" he asked, steeling himself for the expected stream of abuse. The other players sat with their eyes averted. Mac sensed that he was not the only one here who had never heard of lowball. Blackbeard exploded with venom. "Oh, for crissake," he spat, "don't you shitballs know nothin? Lowball. Five card draw. Lowest hand wins. Pair up and yer screwed unless you got the lowest pair. Nothin' wild. Ace is low." He started to deal.

Mac waited until all five cards were dealt before picking them up. In five-card draw he liked to patiently squeeze the cards out one at a time, millimeter by fractional millimeter, seeing what tiniest fraction of a card could be revealed before recognition. Now as he did this, he was dismayed to see his run of good cards continue. Three queens, two sixes. Full house. In regular poker a sure winner…in lowball, a garbage hand.

"Bet em' up, Mac."

"Check." Mac was looking at his lovely full house, knowing it was worthless in this game, yet not ready to throw it in; it was too pretty.

The player on Mac's left bet 10 dollars, and all the others called the bet. Mac thought about the vagaries of luck, and the chances that all the players at this table except him had been dealt a bad hand. The thought gave him a warm feeling. It was almost as if he was blessed. Then the stunning realization hit him that Blackbeard had devised a way to turn the world upside down. Good was bad. Bad was good. He was cursed, not blessed. With this sour thought he tossed his cards face down onto the table in disgust and said, "Fold."

"Some big shot you are," taunted Blackbeard, "win all the fuckin' dough, then won't even draw fer a lousy sawbuck."

Stung, and feeling a little guilty, Mac picked up his cards and said, "Okay, okay, I'll call." He put a 10-dollar bill in the pot.

"Cards," rasped Blackbeard, looking at Mac.

Mac looked mournfully at his sensuous full house, and sadly threw away three queens and a six, keeping the other six. "Four," he said.

Blackbeard, laughing maliciously, dealt four cards smartly, looked at the next player, and called impatiently, "Cards?"

Mac automatically, but unenthusiastically, began to squeeze out his new hand. Ace of clubs. *Probably get four aces*, he thought. But he was wrong, as one by anxious one, a two of diamonds, a three of hearts, and a four of clubs oozed out of his sweaty hands. He looked at the forlorn assortment, and after momentary confusion, slowly recognized that this normally useless collection was a powerful hand in lowball. Reflecting on it, while trying hard to maintain a poker face, it occurred to him that indeed he had an unbeatable hand. His mind wandered as he thought of the possibilities. A nudge brought him out of his reverie.

"Wake up, Mac. Bet yer goddamned hand." Blackbeard was incapable of speaking without an edge of hostility.

How should he bet? He must be careful. If he bet too much he would scare everyone off. On the other hand, a large bet after drawing four cards might be seen as a bluff. Just then a voice from the past spoke to him so clearly he turned his head to see if Ma Jong was really there. *"Always check the first bet if you have a really good hand."*

"Check," he said.

"Bet ten," said the man on Mac's left.

"Out."

"Bump ten." The next player put a 20 dollar bill in the pot, and Mac felt a small thrill as he thought, *that's gonna be my money.*

"Too rich for me." The next player dropped out.

"Me too." Another player threw down his cards.

The bet was up to Blackbeard. He fingered his cards, opened in a tight fan, and while examining them closely, growled in a subdued voice, "How much is in the fuckin' pot?"

One of the players quickly counted the pot. "Hundred bucks," he said.

Blackbeard looked around the table without meeting anyone's eyes and said, "Okay, I'm bettin' the fuckin' pot limit. Here's twenty bucks to call the raise." He pushed a 20-dollar bill forward. "And another one twenty to match the fuckin' pot." He pulled a roll of bills from his shirt pocket, casually peeled off six 20-dollar bills, and pitched them into the middle of the table on top of the other randomly scattered greenbacks.

Mac's heart leaped, and blood began to pound in his ears.

Blackbeard looked at Mac triumphantly and growled, "Yer bet, Mac. You got plenty a fuckin' dough. Cost ya one twenty to call."

Mac carefully checked his hand one more time just to be sure. He was conscious of men standing behind him, and held the cards with both hands close to his chin.

"Don't eat the goddamn cards, Mac. Jist shit er get off the pot." Blackbeard chuckled at his own wit.

Mac pulled a wealth of crumpled bills from his shirt pocket, counted 120 dollars, and gently laid the money atop the flourishing pot. Then, trying hard to mask his excitement, he said, "Call." He paused briefly for effect before adding, "and raise." Then, aghast at his own temerity, he placed 200 additional dollars even more gently on the pile, gave it a soft tap, and said, "Cost ya three hundred big ones to play." He looked quickly at the other two players still in the game, and then, trying not very successfully to hide his glee, fixed his gaze on Blackbeard.

Blackbeard sat up straight and stared at Mac, who read only surprise in Blackbeard's face. The crowd around the table increased as word was quickly passed. On the table, in a jumble of crumpled green paper, was 600 dollars.

"Too rich for me."

"I'm out. Go to it, boys."

Once again it was up to Blackbeard. He sensed the drama, and seemed to relish being on-stage and in the spotlight. With practiced malice, he turned to Mac, and summoning untapped resources from his mines of ridicule, snarled, "So that's how they play in Peoria? Check and raise? Okay, shine boy, guess I'll just have to teach you a little lesson."

Blackbeard scanned the crowd to be sure they were appreciating his performance. He nodded to one of the watchers, then whispered in his ear. The man hurried away. Next he took a long black cigar from his pocket and slowly began to unwrap it.

Mac was thinking hard...beads of sweat formed on his forehead. This was not what he had expected. Rapidly he reviewed the situation. *What was Blackbeard up to? What did he mean "teach you a lesson"? How can I lose with a perfect hand?* Still, doubt was in him. But he, too, was on-stage, embarrassed by the unaccustomed attention. Then, searching for unrehearsed lines to achieve the right pitch of bravado, and speaking a bit more loudly than he had intended, he said, "You gonna talk or play poker? Two C's to cover the bet. Put up or shut up."

Blackbeard looked at him with derisive amusement, but was in no hurry. He lighted his cigar, inhaled deeply, and blew a megaphone of smoke, and a baggage of hate in Mac's direction. "What's the fuckin' rush, Mac? You in a fuckin' hurry to lose yer fuckin' dough? I'm coverin' the fuckin' bet and as soon as...ah, here he is." Blackbeard's errand boy returned, and handed him a bundle of $50 bills. Carefully, and with great flourish, Blackbeard began to peel one by one off the stack, and flip them into the middle of the table. Then he announced, "I'm raisin' half a grand."

Squinting from the smoke of the smoldering cigar cocked at a jaunty angle from the corner of his mouth, Blackbeard leaned forward, and from the stack of bills held in his right hand he counted aloud as he flipped them forward. "Five, six, seven, eight, nine, fuckin' ten, eleven, twelve, thirteen, fourteen, fifteen, six-fuckin'-teen. " He laughed riotously and said, "In case you didn't get it, shine boy, that's three hundred to cover your shitty bet, and a five-fuckin'-hundred dollar raise. You still in the fuckin' game?" Again he laughed riotously.

Mac experienced a rush of panic. Something was wrong. Suddenly he knew he would lose. But how could it be? The crowd was now clustered four rows deep, all looking at him. What should he do? He could admit defeat, fold, lose 300 dollars, and remain in the game. That thought repelled him because he remembered he had a perfect hand for lowball, to say nothing of the scalding humiliation. There was no way he could lose. He didn't think he had 500 dollars left, but he could call with what he had. If he did that and lost, he would be broke. But how could he lose with a perfect hand? The worst he could do was tie. With a flash of relief he thought, *That must be it! The bastard has the same hand as me!*

Mac took all the money from his pocket...he counted 347 dollars. He pushed it forward and said shakily, "I'll cover that much of it."

Blackbeard again laughed loudly. "Keep the seven, nigger," he growled, "you might need it for shoe polish." He spread his cards face up on the table and proclaimed, "I got a wheel." The crowd erupted.

Mac looked in astonishment at the ace, two, three, four, and five. A five-high straight. How could that be a low hand? Three of a kind would be lower than that.

Mac was indignant. "What kind of shit you tryin' to pull, Blacky?" he sneered. "How you figger a straight is a low hand?" He spread his ace, two, three, four, and six face up on the table.

Blackbeard laughed sardonically and said, "Not bad, shine boy, but yer wheel is missin' a spoke." He stood, still squinting through his cigar smoke, and reached for the pot with both hands.

Mac stood to his full height. He was three inches taller than Blackbeard, but significantly outweighed. Anger seared his brain. He felt the blood rushing behind his eyes. He seized Blackbeard's right wrist in a steely grip. "Not so fast, asshole. Nobody cheats me outta what's mine."

Blackbeard shook his arm trying to dislodge Mac's grip. "Git yer fuckin' hands off me, nigger," he snarled, and with his free hand reached into his pocket for a switchblade knife. His hand never made it. The knuckles of Mac's left fist caught him on the bridge of the nose just under his left eye, and sent him spinning backwards in a rolling sprawl from which he did not get up. It was a one-punch knockout.

Mac stood with clenched fists over the fallen Blackbeard, his fury only partly abated, waiting for his adversary to get up, ready to deliver another blow. Suddenly he felt a strong hand gripping his shoulder. Looking up, he saw a massive chief petty officer who was clearly taking charge. The chief looked at the crumpled Blackbeard. "The bastard had it coming," he said. "But he's right about the poker, Mac. A wheel beats anything in lowball. If ya don't know the rules ya shouldn't be playin' the game."

Mac found himself back at the rail, wind blowing in his face. He had quickly discarded the notion of suicide, and was trying to clear his head in the cool night air. He had no memory of what happened after the chief took charge; how he got here to the rail was a mystery. He was startled by the brilliance of the moon. He could see clearly the outline of many ships in their convoy. *I'll bet the ship captains would like to pull a shade over that moon.* He shuddered as the word bet crossed his mind. Then he wondered if the moon had been shining like this when his brother Davey's ship was torpedoed. He strained his eyes looking for torpedo wakes. Momentarily he was aware of a form beside him.

"Hello, Mac." The voice was familiar; the face was masked in shadow.

Startled, Mac said, "Who is it?"

"It's Buck Fulton."

"Buck Fulton! I didn't know you were on this ship." Buck Fulton was from Detroit, Booker T. had met him on the first day of boot camp at the Great Lakes Naval Training Station when they found themselves in the same segregated company. Buck Fulton very soon had taken charge of leisure time at boot camp, such as it was, by organizing poker games played with matchsticks. Mac was about to learn that Buck had long since graduated from matchsticks.

Buck said, "I didn't know you were either until I saw what happened at the poker game."

Mac hung his head and said, "I was a damn fool."

"Yer not the first, and ya won't be the last."

Mac looked curiously at Buck Fulton. "Guess not," he said. "Ya know, it ain't so much the money…it's…" Mac was searching for words to express his embarrassment and humiliation. To make a mistake was one thing, but to be revealed as an ignorant cornball in front of such a crowd was a new and shattering experience. Just about every man in that room would rather face a Japanese bayonet than look like a fool in front of his peers.

Buck Fulton cut into Mac's thoughts. "You'll get over it, Mac…most of those guys yer never gonna see again anyway. Look at it this way…anybody who was there learned a pretty good lesson. Hell, there probably wasn't one guy in a hundred there who ever heard of a lowball wheel, but I can guarantee they ain't gonna ferget it now."

Mac thought about that, and actually managed a tight-lipped smile. He said, "I was sittin' there like a dumbass thinkin' about what I was gonna do with all that money. I thought I couldn't lose. I think I learned somethin' too."

Buck Fulton said, "I learned somethin' watchin' you smack that greasy Blackbeard...nobody could say he didn't have it comin'. Now I'm gonna tell you somethin'."

"What?"

Buck looked out at the sea and the bright moonlight, and speaking so quietly Mac strained to hear, said, "I run those games."

Mac wasn't sure he heard right. "What?" he repeated

"I'm the house."

"What?"

Buck turned to look at Mac and said, "Hey, Mac, you sound like a broken record fulla whats. Now listen carefully...I get a cut from every pot...I'm the house."

Mac was incredulous. He said, "Right. Yer the house, and I'm the starboard anchor."

"How much did you lose in that game?" Buck asked.

Mac answered, "Well, I had a hundred bucks when I started, and it was up over five hundred before I crashed. Right now I got seven bucks and change. But like I said, it ain't the money; I ain't goin' nowhere. But what the hell you talkin' about, Buck? How can you be the house?"

"Will you believe me if I give you back the dough you lost?" He handed Mac a 100-dollar bill, the first one Mac had ever seen.

Mac was thunderstruck. "Why you tellin' me?" he asked.

"I can use yer help," answered Buck. "I heard the way that blackbearded son-of-a-bitch talked to you. I don't need white slime like that workin' for me."

Mac was shaking his head in wonder as he looked at Buck Fulton, remembering the matchstick games in the barracks at Great Lakes when Buck had said, "I got plans."

Mac said, "You must have a seabag full of dough if yer inta all those games. How the hell do ya do it?"

"Maybe someday I'll tell ya," answered Buck. "But I will tell ya one thing fer sure. Before I'm done, they're gonna be callin' me Bucks Fulton."

Mac laughed, "They'll prob'ly call you a wheeler-dealer too."

Buck Fulton slapped Mac on the back and said, "You catch on pretty quick." He paused, "Fer a nigger."

They both laughed.

Two days later they docked in Pearl Harbor. Mac and 2,000 other fresh faces lined the rails to gawk in fascination at the place where it had all started. He tried to imagine what it must have been like when the Jap planes came screaming in with no warning that infamous day, almost three years before. He was disappointed at the modesty of the geography; he had expected a grander scale. He thought it should be at least as inspiring as San Francisco harbor, but there was no Golden Gate Bridge here. To be sure, the island of Oahu was impressive enough, emerald green in the bright September sun, and crowned by a towering tree-covered mountain range rising above the morning mist. But Pearl Harbor looked more like an oyster than a pearl. A narrow channel, like the neck of a brandy bottle, seemed to have been dredged out of the sandy beach. The channel was lined on both sides with soaring and majestic royal palm trees, behind which could be seen a series of low white buildings that appeared to be family residences. The mass of the bottle, the deep water harbor itself, was surrounded by flat sandy land, and was choked with ships and boats ranging from the ant-sized captain's gigs of the destroyers and mine sweepers, to the five-city-block-long aircraft carriers and battle wagons. Men lining the rail were called to attention and saluted while the ship's colors were dipped passing the hulk of the battleship *Arizona*, tomb for 2,000 sailors, only its superstructure visible above the oily water. Mac thought of his brother Davey, and the anger flared again.

>> 5 <<

FLAPPER

Near a speck in the Pacific called Peleliu, 4,000 miles west of Pearl Harbor, at precisely the moment when Mac and the transport passed the sunken *Arizona,* Homer Jackson, Lieutenant Junior Grade, USNR, who preferred to be called Flapper, rolled over in his rack and covered his head with a pillow, vainly trying to shut out the clanging insistence of the general quarters alarm.

Flapper Jackson had been through this before...at Tarawa, and at Saipan. He was a shore fire control party officer; it was his job to go ashore with the assault forces, and see to it that his ship delivered naval gunfire support where it was most needed. His ship was the heavy cruiser *Indianapolis,* proud flagship of Admiral Raymond A. Spruance, hero of Midway, and now commander of the Fifth Fleet. Flapper was in no hurry; it would be two hours before the LCVP from the attack transport, loaded with Marines, would stop by the "Indy" to pick up Flapper and his crew before their dash to the beach. Always meticulous in dress and appearance, Flapper got up at last and made his usual preparations. He showered, brushed and flossed his teeth, trimmed his thin mustache, carefully shaved, then laid out freshly creased khakis as though they were white tie and tails and he was going to a formal ball. All personnel in the assault forces had been ordered to wear clean uniforms to minimize the chance of infection should they be wounded, but this was like telling Flapper he had to breathe.

Flapper no longer thought about death. After surviving two bloody landings during which he had seen men literally blown apart, he was convinced that his fate was to die in an old age home, or at worst, from cancer of the prostate. In civilian life he had been a high school math teacher and now, as he felt the thump of the ship's eight-inch guns signaling the start of the pre-assault barrage, he gave his combat boots a quick shine as if he were headed for a class.

The talk in the wardroom had been optimistic as usual. "This will be easy," said his friend Nipper Stewart, main battery control officer, repeating what he had heard from one of the admiral's staff officers. "The main island in this group is called Babel Thwap, or something like that, but we're goin' in on Pelaylu, which can't be more than five miles long. Hell, they probably won't even defend it."

Flapper had heard this kind of talk before, and paid no attention to it. He knew it would not be easy. He had seen the Japanese fight. It would not be easy.

Seabags slung over their shoulders, Mac and the others piled down the gangway, lined up on the dock, noting gratefully that it did not pitch or roll, and were marched to holding barracks a mile away; the barracks would be their temporary home until receiving permanent assignments. Most were hoping for ships in the combat zone; they would not be disappointed. But first they would have to wait. In the Navy, you always had to wait. Each barracks building, accommodating about 100 men, functioned as if it were a small ship. Petty officers were in charge of daily routines; duty sections were on a port and starboard basis.

"Come on, Mac, we got the liberty, let's get goin'. I gotta get to a bank," Bucks Fulton urged.

"How we gonna get to town?" Mac asked. The Pearl Harbor Naval Base and adjoining Hickam Field Air Base were about 10 miles from downtown Honolulu. Bucks Fulton was in a hurry. "I'm gonna get a taxi, I got no time to waste. Come on, let's go."

As they emerged at a quick step from the barracks and headed for the gate, Mac asked, "How much dough you got, Bucks?"

"About 20,000 bucks," he answered, a serious and determined look on his face. "It's a start," he added.

Mac stopped walking, and stared in astonishment at the back of the quick-stepping Bucks Fulton, who slowed and looked back impatiently.

"Come on, Bucks, don't shit me. Yer just kiddin', ain't ya?" Mac was incredulous.

"Yeah, Mac, I'm just kiddin'," said Bucks. "There ain't that much money in the world. You comin' or ain't ya?" Bucks, a man in a hurry, started walking again at a fast pace.

Mac ran to catch up. "I'm comin'," he said breathlessly.

As they waited for a taxi outside the main entrance to the base, Bucks

Fulton looked up at the distant hills and exclaimed, "Holy Christ! Would ya look at that?"

Mac looked to where Bucks was pointing, and gasped. He blinked his eyes, and shook his head in amazement. The rays of the afternoon sun, caught by millions of watery prisms rising from the humid valleys, were diffracted into a riot of rainbows. He counted twelve, one stacked on top of another, one starting where another ended. He was captivated by the vibrant hues, brighter than any colors he had ever seen. "Jesus," he said, "back in Peoria we're lucky if we see one...They say if you can find the end of it you'll find a pot of gold."

"The end of them rainbows must be right where we're standing then," said Bucks Fulton as he patted the money belt concealed under his dress-white jumper.

"Flapper, Flapper...this is Rejoice, can you hear me? Over."

The radio crackled through the howl of battle. Flapper Jackson was 25 yards from the water's edge, stretched flat in a depression on the sand, desperately trying to reduce himself to a single dimension to escape the furious fusillade of hot steel slugs that poured over him in an endless stream. If he wanted to die all he had to do was stand up. But Flapper had some living to do. He twisted his neck without lifting his head, trying to locate his radioman. Just then he felt a hand seize his right ankle in a powerful grip. It was Freddy, the radioman, a tall slender boy from Arkansas, who was experiencing his first opposed amphibious landing. He was weeping uncontrollably. "Make em' stop, Mister Jackson. Make em' stop," he gasped between sobs.

"Stay down, Freddy, we're gonna make it." Flapper was not as confident as he sounded. Their position was exposed and vulnerable; they had nowhere to go but down. He could not determine the source of the fire; it seemed to be coming from everywhere at once, and now a walking mortar barrage was beginning. He saw the explosions near the water's edge, and watched them creep in neat but deadly increments up the sandy beach toward the tree line 75 yards away. On that beach were spread 1,500 men of the third battalion, first Marine division, burrowed into the sand, squirming relentlessly forward like a swarm of inchworms. Flapper's mathematical mind was racing—even if they suffered 75 percent casualties, there would still be almost 400 men to storm the pillboxes and blockhouses that seemed invulnerable to the massive naval and air bombardment they had sustained; it was not a comforting thought.

The radio crackled again, "Flapper, Flapper, this is Rejoice, this is Rejoice, can you hear me? Over." Somehow the voice coming from the big cruiser, lying in the calm waters a mile offshore, sounded much too cool for the desperate situation facing the men on the beach. Flapper took the radio transmitter from the fear-paralyzed Freddy, and responded in a similar vein. He made it sound as if he were speaking on the telephone from a cozy den in front of a crackling fireplace.

"Rejoice, this is Flapper. I hear you loud and clear. Over."

"Flapper, this is Rejoice. Do you have any targets for me? Over."

"Rejoice, this is Flapper. Negative. We're pinned down on beach white one. I can't get my head up high enough to see the tree line, let alone find a target. We're up against concealed pillboxes and blockhouses; they must have ten-foot thick concrete walls. Looks to me like the only way to knock em' out is with satchel charges. You got any of those you can deliver real quick? Over."

Flapper did not expect an answer to this request. At this moment he knew that both he and the firing ship were totally irrelevant. He closed his eyes and waited for the firing to subside, but in fact it intensified.

After a long pause, indicative of a hurried consultation on the cruiser, the radio crackled again, "Flapper, this is Rejoice. Nipper says we're fresh out of satchel charges. Sorry. Write if you get work. Out."

Out is how Flapper felt at the moment. Out of gas. Out of sight. Out of options. Out of luck. Adding to his misery was the heat of the day. Seven degrees north of the equator, just past noon, the smoldering tropical sun seemed close enough to touch.

Flapper opened his eyes to a sight that made his heart leap...flashes of gunfire from a small island, just offshore, about a mile and a half away. The island was strategically located such that guns placed there could enfilade the entire beach, and that was exactly what they were doing...maybe he could do something about it. He unfolded a colorfully gridded map and keyed the radio.

"Rejoice, this is Flapper. I have work. Over."

The response was quick and eager. "Flapper, this is Rejoice. How can I help you? Over."

"This is Flapper. Can you see a small island just south of beach orange three in zone K? Over."

After a short pause he heard, "Rejoice here. Negative, Flapper. Over."

"This is Flapper. Roger, I will direct fire. Standby for firing coordinates.

Over."

"This is Rejoice. Main battery standing by. Over."

"This is Flapper. Zone K...square seven fiver...number one, zero, two, two, fiver, one, seven. Repeat please. I will adjust fire. Over."

"This is Rejoice. Roger, Flapper, I repeat, Zone K...square seven fiver...number one, zero, two, two, fiver, one, seven. Firing ship ready. Over."

"This is Flapper. Commence firing. Over."

"Wilco, Flapper."

Flapper waited expectantly. The ship was beyond his view just as the island was out of the ship's sight. Suddenly he saw two enormous geysers erupt in the water just beyond the island.

"This is Flapper. Down two zero zero. Right two zero zero. Over."

"Roger, Flapper. Down two zero zero. Right two zero zero."

Two salvos exploded on the island.

"This is Flapper. No change in elevation. Left fiver zero. Over."

"Roger, Flapper. No change. Left fiver zero."

Again two eight-inch shells exploded on the island.

"Up fiver zero. No change. Rapid fire. Three salvos. Over."

"Roger, Flapper. Up fiver zero. No change. Three salvos."

Multiple explosions engulfed the gun emplacements on the island.

"This is Flapper. No change. No change. Fire for effect. Over."

"Roger, Flapper. No change. Fire for effect."

Flapper became aware that the hostile fire in his area had almost stopped as shell after eight-inch shell detonated on the enemy position, Marines on the beach were on their feet racing to the tree line.

"Rejoice this is Flapper. Cease firing. Cease firing. Target neutralized. Good shooting, Rejoice. Over."

"Roger, Flapper. Cease firing...Anything else we can do for you? Over."

"This is Flapper. How about a couple of cool gin and tonics?"

"Bring us two gin and tonics, Happy, and if you get em' up here in ten minutes, this is yours." Bucks Fulton waved a 20-dollar bill at the bellboy. Bucks and Mac had just checked into a suite at the Royal Hawaiian Hotel on Waikiki Beach in downtown Honolulu. Mac was dazed at the luxury; he looked around slowly, trying to unscramble his thoughts. Never had he seen such splendor...thick carpets, elegant furniture, crystal light fixtures, original oil paintings of seascapes and landscapes...a large balcony with deck chairs, a mesmerizing view of swaying coconut palms, and the magnificent surf of

Waikiki. What was he doing here? How did he get here? How was he supposed to act? What was he supposed to do? He walked around gingerly touching things to be sure they were real, and that he wasn't just dreaming. He turned to look at Bucks Fulton, who stood by the door grinning at him. "Not bad, eh Mac?" he said. "But you ain't seen nothin' yet."

Mac shook his head in wonder. "You been here before, Bucks?" he asked.

Bucks shook his head. "Nope," he said. "But I dreamed a lot about it. You got to act like you belong."

There was a gentle knock on the door. Bucks opened it to see the broadly smiling oriental bellboy, Happy Sing, holding a tray at shoulder level on which were perched two tall glasses, dripping with condensed moisture, and topped with tiny paper umbrellas stuck into large red cherries.

"At your service, chief, what else can I do for you?" Happy spoke in a cheerful expectant manner in perfect unaccented English. Bucks stuck the 20-dollar bill in Happy's upper pocket and said, "Come in here, Happy, I want to talk to you."

Mac looked suspiciously at the small, elegantly uniformed bellboy. "You ain't a Jap, are ya?" he asked.

Happy looked hurt. "Hey, man," he said, "I was born on this island. My mom and pop are Chinese." In truth, his parents were Japanese, but since the Pearl Harbor attack he had been able to conceal it, and had prospered from the reckless spending of men heading for the war zone.

Bucks placed a stack of 100-dollar bills on the table. Happy looked at them with shining eyes. Mac looked at them with amazement. Bucks noted the reactions with great relish. "Okay, Happy," he said, "here's what you can do for us."

Happy Sing had been through this before, but not in the Princess Kaialani Suite, and not with enlisted men—he was accustomed to dealing with officers—and certainly not with this much money on the table. Happy knew well the tastes of American servicemen...cheap whiskey and cheap women. He kept a supply of brightly colored Hawaiian shirts and plastic leis in his locker.

"When I get back to Pearl I'm gonna get me a case of rotgut whiskey, and spend a week at the Pineapple Playhouse." Flapper's radioman Freddy was speaking.

They were lying in a shallow depression, legacy of a saturation bombardment, 50 yards past the grotesquely twisted and shattered trees marking the end of the beach. One hundred yards ahead, to their surprise and consternation, contrary to intelligence reports, the ground rose sharply. Flapper knew what that rising ground meant—concrete blockhouses, interconnecting caves, and cleverly concealed gun ports…death. Naval gunfire was virtually useless in this situation. Flapper wondered why he didn't just take the rest of the day off. Their battalion was holding the left flank of the line, and it would soon be dark. Night in a foxhole on the front lines was no picnic either. Flapper was all too familiar with the Japanese talent for infiltration and there was the genuine possibility of a night counterattack.

A squad of black Marines was toting cans of fresh water and cases of ammunition up from the beach when yet another mortar barrage began. A muscular sergeant squeezed into the hole with Flapper and Freddy. "Mind if I share your billet?" he asked cheerfully.

"Come on in neighbor," said Flapper. "Sorry I can't offer you a drink."

The sergeant laughed and said, "No problem, neighbor…brought my own. Have a snort." He unhooked a canteen from his belt and handed it to Flapper. Flapper helped himself to a double gulp of brandy, and handed the flask to Freddy. He savored the warm delicious feeling as the potent liquid slid down his throat. "Thanks, Sarge," he said, "that's pretty good stuff."

"Best I could do on short notice," said the sergeant. "These mortars are gettin' pretty hot."

Mortar shells were exploding noisily all around them, and shrapnel was whirring over their heads as they lay pressed against the earth, part sand, part coral.

"Usual twilight barrage," said Flapper casually, "they'll knock it off as soon as it gets dark."

"Yer pretty cool, neighbor. You been through this before," the black Marine said admiringly. It was not a question.

Flapper's mind briefly wandered to the other times he had been through it, but he quickly shook it off and said, "This makes the third time. It ain't what it's cracked up to be."

"First time fer me," said the sergeant. "What's next?"

Flapper did not have to think very hard to answer that question. "They'll try to infiltrate," he said, "probably mount a night counterattack."

Freddy and the sergeant winced at that news, but took some comfort in Flapper's cavalier demeanor.

The sergeant said, "You don't seem worried."

Flapper's voice swelled slightly as he remembered previous encounters.

"We got Marine riflemen on the line. The Japs are no match for them, especially when they are experienced, fresh, and well supplied. Besides, with you here, Sarge, we got a three section watch; that means we can get some sleep."

The sergeant was incredulous. "You mean to tell me yer actually plannin' to sleep out here?" He shook his head in disbelief. "And who said I was gonna stay here anyway? When this barrage lifts, I'm gettin' my men and headin' back to the beach."

Flapper said, "That's not such a good idea, Sarge. Night comes fast in the tropics...when this barrage lifts, it's gonna be black as the inside of a coal mine. I don't think you'll want to be wandering around out here in the dark; those Marine riflemen have hair triggers. You better get word to your men to stay where they are tonight if you want 'em to stay healthy. You probably don't even know the password."

The sergeant scratched his head. "Nobody gave us no password," he said. "We sure as hell never expected to be out here all night, but I get yer point...What's the password?"

"It's always the same," Flapper replied. "The challenge is the name of an American automobile, and the reply is the name of a different American car. Any car will do, as long as it's American."

Freddy piped up, "The Japs don't make cars do they? What if somebody answered Rolls Royce?"

Flapper said, "That's a British car, but they'd probably get by if they pronounced the L. The Japanese language does not include the L."

Freddy turned to the sergeant and asked, "What's your favorite car, Sarge?"

"Studebaker," answered the sergeant with no hesitation.

"Mine too," said Freddy enthusiastically.

Freddy and the black sergeant began a spirited conversation about cars as darkness settled in quickly. Also, as Flapper had predicted, the mortar barrage stopped. The crashing din was followed by a ghostly, pregnant silence.

Suddenly they were startled by the sound of the radio. "Flapper, Flapper, this is Rejoice. Over."

Freddy answered, "Rejoice, this is Flapper. Over."

"Flapper, this is Rejoice. Rejoice is retiring from the area for the night. Your firing ship will be Hound Dog. Please make contact with Hound Dog on frequency shackle, love easy able, unshackle. Over."

Flapper Jackson sighed, took the radio from the puzzled Freddy and said, "Rejoice, this is Flapper. At this moment I am lying in a hole in the ground up to my ass in hot shrapnel. It's so dark I can't see the end of my nose and if I strike a light, the Marine in the hole next to me will shoot me between the eyes if the Japs don't beat him to it…just how in the name of Joseph, Jesus, and Mary do you think I'm going to read a shackle code?" Flapper was usually unflappable, but this time he lost it. He was not finished with his tirade: "And another thing, why is the goddamned frequency such a goddamned secret anyway? Over."

The radio crackled. "Flapper this is Hound Dog on sixer three niner. Disregard last transmission from Rejoice. Anything I can do for you? Over."

Flapper adjusted the frequency on the luminous dial of his transmitter. "Hound Dog, this is Flapper," he said. "Can you throw a little light on the situation? Over."

"Roger, Flapper, our orders are to illuminate throughout the night. Twenty shells per hour. First shell on the way. Out."

A star shell popped like a Roman Candle, high in the sky, casting a dim, eerie, glow over a wide area.

Flapper quickly and expertly assessed the effect, keyed the radio and said, "Hound Dog, this is Flapper. Down two zero zero. Over."

"Wilco, Flapper. Down two zero zero."

In a few moments another shell burst, and the men could see each other if a bit unfocused. The black sergeant looked at Flapper in the gloom and said, "You look green."

Flapper considered briefly and offered, "I feel more like yellow."

"Me too," said Freddy.

The sergeant laughed and said, "I guess this is one time where being black comes in handy."

They lay quietly for a while, their faces close to the ground, looking out at no-man's land, each alone with his own thoughts. At the moment they did not feel threatened, but vaguely snug in the warm, humid, tropical air. Then, close by, a few yards in front, they heard scratching on the coral studded ground.

"What's that?" asked Freddy, his voice edged in fear. "Listen to that, can you hear that, Mr. Jackson?"

Flapper was cool. "Don't panic, Freddy," he said. "I hear it. I think it's a land crab. They're harmless."

Freddy was not convinced. "If I don't see that land crab in about ten seconds I'm blowin' whatever it is outta the water." Freddy was waving a .45 caliber pistol in the air.

Flapper put a firm hand on Freddy's arm and said, "Don't fire that weapon, Freddy. The flash will be like somebody putting a spotlight on us, and then we'll really catch hell. Stay calm, man."

The scratching stopped, and again it was deathly silent on the line. Across a 200-yard stage, upon which hundreds of land crabs now performed their crawly ballet, thousands of edgy men waited, fingering their murderous weapons. None would survive the night unmarked.

At length Flapper spoke. "Okay, I'm gonna catch some sleep. Sarge, you take the first two-hour watch. Freddy, you take the next. Wake me in four hours." Flapper curled himself into a tight ball, and was asleep almost instantly.

Freddy listened to Flapper's steady deep breathing, and shook his head in wonder. "Would you look at that, Sarge? How can he sleep like that out here? You'd think he was on a couch in his momma's parlor; I feel like I won't ever sleep again."

The sergeant was intent on looking for movement in the gray gloom beyond their haven. He held with fierce tenacity a .30 caliber carbine that looked very small in his massive hands. With the setting of the sun had come a chill ocean breeze that caused some of the moisture rising from the tortured ground to condense into small droplets of water forming an increasingly dense fog and reducing visibility to only a few yards. The popping star shells now illuminated a white blanket enveloping the battlefield. On the ground the men on one side cursed, while those on the other side smiled.

After a lengthy silence, during which he imagined all manner of moving shadows, Freddy whispered, "Where you from, Sarge?"

Without taking his eyes from the soupy mess in front of him the sergeant replied, "Little Rock."

Freddy was stunned, and repressing the urge to shout, said in a stage whisper, "The hell you say! I'm from Sweet Home." Sweet Home, Arkansas, was a suburb of Little Rock.

The sergeant now looked at Freddy in astonishment, and not even attempting a whisper, said, "You ain't!"

Freddy, now excited, said enthusiastically, "I am so."

For 45 minutes Freddy and the black sergeant plunged into animated conversation about who played who, what, and where, in recent Arkansas high school football. They became totally oblivious to where they were or what they were doing, escaping into the blessed refuge of happier circumstances and more innocent times.

Ahead of them, in the murk and gloom, little more than the length of a football field away, sly movements went unnoticed until, with the shock and suddenness of a thunderclap, 40 battle tanks, concealed in shallow excavations and covered with sand, coughed to life. The tanks rumbled forward accompanied by the frenzied shrieks of 800 Japanese infantrymen. The thunderous roar resulting from 1,000 Marine riflemen responding with semi-automatic carbines, machine guns, and hand grenades answered. As the sound quickly crescendoed, Freddy could hear distinctly above the din, the unmistakable and terrifying cries of "Banzai, banzai!"

Freddy shook Flapper violently and yelled, "Mister Jackson, Mister Jackson! HERE THEY COME!"

"Here they come," said Bucks Fulton, responding to a quiet knock on the massive oak door. He opened the door, and with a sweeping bow ushered into the room two beautiful Hawaiian girls dressed in long, expensive evening gowns. Around each of their slender necks hung a dazzling orchid lei; a matching orchid was secured in the hair behind their right ears. They were followed by a wildly grinning Happy Sing pushing a cart loaded with a mountainous tray of colorful hors d'oeuvres and a large ice bucket containing a magnum of Dom Perignon champagne.

Bucks and Mac were resplendent in dark trousers with velvet stripes down each leg, sparkling white dinner jackets with red carnations in the lapels, ivory studded shirts and matching cuff links, black bow ties over wing-tipped collars, gleaming patent leather black shoes. Mac felt as good as he looked, and he looked like a prince.

"Well done, Happy," said Bucks, handing him a $100 bill. "Serve the lobster and filet mignon on the balcony in one hour."

The happy man tucked the money into his vest pocket, and said in his most enthusiastic and excited manner, "Yes, sir! Whatever you say, chief."

Later, as they listened to the soft surf and the soothing sounds of "Sweet Leilani" drifting up from the hotel patio ten floors below, Mac looked up at a luminous full moon and said, "Bucks, do you suppose this is what we're fighting for?"

Bucks Fulton, stretched out on a chaise longue, needed no time to think about his reply. "I ain't fightin for nothin', man. I'm a lover, not a fighter, right, honey?"

The beautiful Hawaiian girl kneeling near him leaned closer, and began nibbling his ear.

Blood spurted from the black Marine sergeant's head as part of his left ear ripped off in the savagely clenched teeth of a small, wiry man wearing a brown steel helmet. The sergeant seemed not to notice, and only tightened his crushing bear hug on the bantam warrior, whose dying words were, "Ten deaths for the Emperor!"

From the ground the radio crackled, "Flapper, Flapper, this is Hound Dog. Can you hear me? Over." But Flapper could not hear. He lay unconscious from a vicious blow on the back of the head administered by the same Samurai sword that had forever ended the well-founded fears of Freddy the radioman.

>>6<<

SPRUANCE OF MIDWAY

"Okay, Mac, this is your big chance, don't screw it up. Take this tray of toast and coffee to Admiral Spruance on the bridge. Think you can find it?"

Mac picked up the sparkling silver tray with two hands, and carefully stepped over the hatch combing marking the entrance to the officers' mess galley on the *USS Indianapolis* at sea somewhere in the South Pacific Ocean. "If I ain't back in two hours, send out a search party," he said.

Mac had been aboard the ship only a week, and both he and the chief steward's mate were only half joking. He had been to the bridge twice before, following a third class petty officer through a bewildering maze of narrow passageways, up seven flights of even narrower stairways (he knew he should think of them as ladders, but the transition from Peoria to seaman was still too new), through a final watertight door (hatch) into the wheel house where command decisions were made by the Brass and implemented by the Swabs.

But now he was on his own, and he proceeded cautiously, balancing the admiral's breakfast tray with his right hand, keeping the left hand free to grasp for support should the ship take a sudden pitch or roll. The ship was massive, but so was the sea; if he hadn't learned that on the troop transport during the 10-day journey from San Francisco to Pearl Harbor, he had ample opportunity to digest the lesson aboard the fleet oiler *Lackawanna* on the two week voyage from Pearl to a rendezvous with the *Indianapolis* somewhere near the Palau Islands in the Southwest Pacific. While the fat tanker fueled the sleek cruiser in a gently rolling sea, Mac and a few others were transferred from one ship to the other by that most ancient and honored form of transportation—the Boatswain's Chair. He smiled, remembering the feeling of elation as he swung high above the churning ocean, suspended between the two ships; he had felt reborn, embarking on a new and glorious adventure. So what if he was only a lowly mess attendant? He would make the most of it. He would make his mark. Just as he was savoring the exhilaration of new found power, the deck hands on his new ship had playfully slacked the line, plummeting him towards the swirling sea, then expertly tightened the line so that only his feet got wet...it was an initiation ceremony. When his dripping feet hit the deck of his first ship, he felt like he belonged. But it also reminded him that his destiny remained in the hands of others.

"Watch where yer goin', Mac." A peevish voice brought him out of his reverie as he brushed against another sailor headed in the opposite direction.

"Sorry," said Mac, mounting the steps of the final ladder before the bridge. Stepping onto the bridge from an inside passageway, he was electrified by the panoramic view from a great height of a fast carrier task force turning into the wind, preparatory to launching planes.

"Rudder is right full, sir. New course zero six fiver. Passing three fiver zero." The helmsman, the junior officer of the deck looking over his shoulder, shouted to the officer of the deck, standing outside the wheelhouse on the starboard wing of the bridge.

"Very well," shouted the OOD above the wail of the wind.

"Engine room answers, all ahead flank, turns for twenty-eight knots, sir," shouted the engine order telegraph man. The junior officer of the deck relayed the message to the OOD on the wing. Mac was spellbound watching the curving wakes of four aircraft carriers, three heavy cruisers, two battleships, and 18 destroyers etch parallel patterns of artistic brush strokes on the blue water of the Philippine Sea. Fighting men going into action! His blood rushed at the sight; he could hear trumpets and kettledrums. Sky, water, and ships-of-the-line filled his horizons.

"Hey, Mac, you better move yo' black ass. The admiral don't like cold coffee, an' he don't like late," a friendly voice startled him out of his trance. Quickly he looked around the spacious wheelhouse. The quartermaster, manning the chart board, nodded towards the forward part of the bridge where Mac could see a man in a khaki shirt and blue baseball cap, sitting in an elevated, padded swivel chair behind a glass windbreak, intently watching the maneuvering ships.

Mac approached cautiously. "Good morning, Admiral," he said hesitantly, "here's your toast and coffee."

Admiral Spruance did not turn his head. "Put it down there on the table," he said. The admiral, too, was excited by the spectacle. "Good show, eh? Look at those Cans trying to keep up! They'll do it, too."

Mac set the tray down and poured coffee into a large porcelain mug adorned with crossed anchors and four stars. He handed it to the admiral who took it without looking at him. "Take a lesson in naval seamanship," he said, "look at those Tincans! Right on station. Yes, sir." Mac watched the admiral, wondering if the great man was talking to him or to himself; the admiral had yet to look in his direction. Spruance continued, "Those carrier planes are winning the war, all right, but they couldn't do it without the destroyers. Greyhounds of the fleet. You want to be a sailor? That's the place to do it."

The admiral tasted the coffee and screwed up his face in a grimace. "This coffee tastes like cold bilge water. I like my bilge water hot." He turned to look at Mac. "You're new here," he said. "What's your name, sailor?"

Mac looked into the sky blue eyes and leathery face of a 58-year-old man. Gray streaked his hair, and four gold stars graced the collar of his shirt and the peak of his blue baseball cap. His face was stern, but not unkind.

Mac flushed at the sudden confrontation. "Booker T. McCan, sir," he answered, "...people call me Mac."

The admiral shook his head. "Too many Macs around here," he said. "What does your mother call you?"

Mac was embarrassed. "My momma calls me Booker T., sir."

Spruance nodded. "Good," he said. "Where you from, Booker T.?"

"Peoria, sir."

The admiral smiled broadly. "Peoria," he said. "You don't say...Peoria," he repeated. "Good Midwestern stock. I'm from Indiana. Seems like the farther from the ocean, the better the sailor...I've been at sea almost forty years." He said it proudly. "How long have you been at sea, Booker T.?"

Mac laughed nervously. "I think maybe forty days, sir," he answered, then added quickly, "Do you think I'll get to see some action, sir? I want to kill some Japs." Then before he knew it, he rushed on with thoughts that were never far from his consciousness. "The Japs killed my brother, he was on the *Liscomb Bay*."

Mac didn't know it, but he had the wrong admiral. A different fleet admiral, long time friend and colleague of Spruance, Admiral William "Bull" Halsey was famous throughout the fleet for his slogan "Kill Japs, kill Japs, kill more Japs." Not Spruance. The admiral's face darkened slightly. He looked carefully at Mac, trying to tell if the young man was serious. He squinted hard, knitted his brows, put his hand to his mouth pensively then slowly moved it down to his clean-shaven chin. He sighed deeply, and his eyes seemed to glaze over as he became lost in thought. Clearly, Mac's unexpected question had caught him off guard. He turned away without answering, not out of rudeness, courtliness was his hallmark, but because the question had touched a place in his brain where duty and humanity had been at war for some time. Silently he stared at the fleet in action, but it would be some time before even that spectacle could command his complete attention once more.

"When you gonna let me out of here, Ethel?"

The pretty nurse, whose name was not Ethel, walked to the side of the hospital bed and removed a blood pressure cuff from a pocket of her uniform. "How come you're so anxious to get out of here, Homer? Most guys would be happy to have a soft bed and a good looking nurse to take care of him. That crack on the head must have scrambled your brains."

"Who said I had any brains? And when are you gonna start calling me Flapper? Besides, you been tellin' me what a great club they got over at Mogmog; I wanta try it out. How about a date, Ethel? I used to do a mean jitterbug." Flapper paused briefly then fired off another question. "What did you say the name of this tub was?" Before the nurse could answer he had yet another question. "How did I get here?"

The nurse grimaced and said, "Whoa, whoa, slow down, Homer. Now you see why you're not ready to leave? I've answered those same questions fifty times, and you never remember." It was true, but there was a difference. Where before her patient had asked the questions in a dazed and almost delirious way, now, after two weeks, he was clearly alert, and well on the way to a full recovery. He was one of the lucky, and she was gratified to see it; too often this was not the case. It took a special personality to tend the needs of battle mutilated men, and Lieutenant Susan Land, U.S. Navy Nurse corps, often wondered at her aptitude for it; successful recoveries like Flapper Jackson sustained her. She looked at Flapper's handsome face and eager eyes, and smiled again, then spoke slowly and distinctly, clearly enunciating each word. "Okay, Homer, let's go over it one more time," she said. "This is the hospital ship *Mercy*. We are anchored inside Ulithi Atoll. You are here because a corpsman picked you out of a hole in the ground on Peleliu. You are alive only because you were wearing this steel helmet when the Samurai sword slammed into it." She took a battered steel helmet off a shelf, and showed it to him again. The back of the helmet was split down the middle by a jagged and ugly crease. She continued. "Before you ask again, your radioman, Freddy, is dead, and nobody knows anything about a Negro sergeant. And that's about all I can tell you."

Flapper listened carefully, wincing when she spoke of Freddy. "The last thing I remember," he said, "is going to sleep in that hole. Did we win the fight?"

Susan's eyes flashed with anger, and she spoke a bit louder than she had intended. "Depends on what you call winning," she said, "two thousand killed, eight thousand wounded, and it's still not finished…now they're saying Halsey wanted to bypass the whole thing, that we didn't even need it." Susan's voice cracked and she was on the verge of tears when she thought about the lives wasted for no purpose. She threw a pillow down fiercely. "But we won all right!"

Flapper sat up slowly and tentatively swung his legs to the side of the bed. "When is this thing gonna end, Ethel? And by the way, how many times have I asked you what month and year it is?"

"It's November, 1944, Homer, and if I knew when it was going to…" her voice choked and she paused trying to compose herself "…end…" She could not finish the thought.

Admiral Spruance, lost in thought on the flag bridge of the *Indianapolis*, also did not know when it would end, but he had more information than Flapper and Susan. He had been at the San Francisco conference on October 1 where it was decided that Luzon, rather than Formosa, would be the next major objective, followed by occupation of Iwo Jima in the Bonin Islands, and then Okinawa in the Ryukus. He thought these objectives would be attained by the middle of next summer; after that he could only guess. His thoughts drifted back two and half years to the battle of Midway. By all rights the Japanese should have won. They brought a vastly superior force, but a handful of U.S. carrier-based dive-bombers had made the difference. The result was that instead of occupying Midway Atoll, aimed like a dagger at the heart of the Hawaiian Islands only 1,200 miles away, the humbled Japanese fleet, minus four tactically priceless aircraft carriers, one cruiser, 258 aircraft, and 2,500 men, found itself in full, if not desperate, retreat to their home ports 6,000 miles away. He had been awarded the Distinguished Service Medal, and was proclaimed by a prominent naval historian as one of the greatest admirals in American naval history. He smiled when he thought of this, because he knew that his major contribution to the victory was no more heroic than waiting to be sure the enemy was in range of his planes before giving the order to attack. Furthermore, there were those who criticized him for not pursuing the defeated Japanese, but he knew his decision was correct, and more importantly his superior, Admiral Nimitz, knew he was right. Sometimes being a great admiral meant not attacking; in this case, by pursuing, he would have put the two remaining U.S. carriers, *Enterprise* and *Hornet*, in jeopardy because they would have been in range of Japanese land-based bombers stationed on Wake Island.

Spruance thought about the number of lives spared by his decision to withdraw. Then, the recurring nightmare: how many deaths had he been responsible for? It was his duty to destroy the enemy and therefore expected, condoned, and even cheered, but this was little comfort to him. The young mess attendant wanted to kill some Japs. Did anyone ever derive satisfaction from killing? He grieved over the brave young Americans who had died. He also grieved over the brave young Japanese, though he did not speak of it. In 1907, the year he graduated from the U.S. Naval Academy, he had sailed with President Roosevelt's "Great White Fleet"—16 battleships painted white—on a 14- month, around-the-world goodwill cruise that included a stop in Japan, where he came to know, respect, and even admire the Japanese people. Why did the Japanese high command continue the senseless fight? Japan was like a punch-drunk fighter staggering on the ropes. They could still hand out some punishment, as they were doing now on Leyte, but they could not win this fight, and they knew it. If there were a referee, the U.S. would be declared a winner by technical knockout; to continue was to risk permanent physical and mental damage, but the Japanese high command did not seem to care. He wondered how much they were willing to let the civilian population suffer.

Something else Booker T. said had triggered more painful memories—he was convinced *Liscomb Bay* would have been spared if the Army had not been so slow in taking Makin Island, requiring him to keep the ship on station longer than he wanted to. The episode had caused Army-Marine-Navy frictions that would remain unresolved years after all the arms had been stacked.

Spruance of Midway was jerked back to reality with a start when Booker T. McCan handed him a fresh cup of coffee and said, "Here's your hot bilge water, Admiral."

>>7<<

THE MULES OF MOGMOG

"What I need is 'nother Mogmog Mule. Innkeeper! More ale. How 'bout you, Ethel?"

Susan had reluctantly agreed to accompany Flapper to the USO club on the small island of Mogmog, part of Ulithi Atoll in the Eastern Caroline Islands, a balmy 10 degrees north of the equator. It was not her practice to fraternize with her patients, but she was attracted to Flapper in an odd way she was trying to understand. A veteran of two years in the war zone, Susan had nursed far too many young, vigorous, handsome men, not a few of which she developed a strong affection for. But in Flapper, she saw something different that she would be hard-pressed to explain, and for the moment she did not try. She was well aware of the psychic hazards of wartime romance. She had often contemplated the difference between being one of many young women among few men in USO clubs at home, and one of only a few women among an army of men abroad. Susan recognized that nearly everyone needed somebody to look after them and so, in spite of her better judgment, at this particular time in her life, even for a brief interval, she chose to look after Flapper Jackson. Instinctively she knew it was to her advantage to continue calling him Homer, especially since either because his brain was still muddled, or for reasons of his own, he continued to call her Ethel though she had told him again and again that her name was Susan.

They sat at a table on a wide patio with a stunning view of fighting ships at anchor, significant elements of the Third and Fifth Fleets, ships designed to do violence for the purpose of achieving tranquillity. The sun was setting behind low horizon clouds, and the violets, oranges, and reds of another spectacular earthly light show were beginning to develop. A warm tropical breeze flowed over them. The air was filled with the smell of salt water and wet sand, and the cries of gulls, terns, and pelicans.

Susan sighed. "Another Mogmog Mule and you're going to need a new head, Homer," she said. "That stuff is not ale, it's pure rum. And listen, Homer," she added, "let me remind you, your brains are not entirely unscrambled...you better just take it easy...Get it?"

Flapper looked hurt. "Aw come on, Ethel," he whined, "it's Christmas and we gotta celebrate."

Susan shook her head in despair. "You're confused, Homer," she said. "First of all you don't celebrate Christmas by getting drunk, and second it's not Christmas, it's New Year."

Flapper clapped his hands in hazy joy and loudly exclaimed, "That's what I like about you, Ethel, you always know what year it is..." Suddenly he stopped short, and for a moment seemed almost sober. "Hey!" he shouted joyfully, "I think I know that guy that just walked in. Hey, Nipper! Is that you, Nipper? By god I think it's Nipper. It is Nipper! Nipper Stewart, you old eight inch fart! Where you been?"

The man, Nipper, looked at Flapper in wide-eyed incredulity. "Flapper Jackson?" he cried. "...Flapper! I can't believe it! They told me you were dead."

Nipper Stewart grasped Flapper by the shoulders, and looked him up and down. Both men were grinning foolishly. Nipper pursed his lips, nodded his head up and down, and pronounced Flapper fit. "You look as good as ever, man. Better than ever," he said. "Man, am I ever glad to see you. I was afraid I'd have to break in a new shore fire control officer before our next operation. How did you get here? Let's have a drink...tell me what happened."

Flapper felt good. Two Mogmog Mules provided enough alcohol to bring him to a happy-go-lucky state, and the sudden appearance of an old drinking buddy lifted his spirits another notch. Susan had seen this happen before, and began to drift away, preferring to forego hearing about drinking escapades not nearly as funny as the participants remembered them. But before she could make her discreet escape, Flapper put his arm around her shoulder and said, "All I can tell you is I went to sleep in a foxhole, and woke up looking into Ethel's beautiful face. I thought I was in heaven. I *was* in heaven. No, make that, I *am* in heaven. Nipper, this is Ethel, she's an angel."

Quickly adapting to Flapper's festive mood, Nipper took off his garrison cap, executed a low sweeping bow, and said, "A great pleasure, your holiness, I never met a real angel before."

Susan smiled sweetly, curtsied daintily, and said, "Hello, Nipper. Sorry to disappoint you but I'm no angel, I'm a nurse."

Nipper waved his hand dismissively. "Same difference," he said. "How'd you get mixed up with my old drinking buddy, Flapper?" Before she could answer, he added, "I guess I don't have to warn you about his fast hands."

Susan nodded affirmatively, but before she could reply Flapper protested loudly, "Hey, Nipper, don't give away all my secrets, and stop talking so you can get started on these Mogmog Mules. You're gonna love these babies. Ethel, you should have seen Nipper in action at Trader Vic's in Honolulu." Flapper giggled at the recollection and Nipper grinned broadly. Catching his breath, and speaking through the hilarity, Flapper continued, "He drank three Tarantulas in less than an hour. Nobody else could get through two. 'Course we had to carry him out." Flapper laughed uproariously.

Susan said, "I thought a tarantula was a spider."

"No, no. It's a drink. It's a lot like a Mogmog Mule." Flapper held up a bowl-sized glass with both hands, and with a silly grin on his face, looked through it at Susan.

"Mogmog? You been standin' too many mid watches, Gabe. What you talkin' about? Goin' to Mogmog on liberty."

"No, listen, Mac, didn't you ever look at the chart up in the quartermaster's shack? Mogmog is one of the islands in Ulithi Atoll, where we're anchored. I heard one of the officers call it a fleet recreation center. He said we could go over there and play softball, get drunk, watch a USO show, get drunk, do whatever we want; go on liberty. I ain't been on liberty since the cow had puppies, and the dog had kittens; in fact I ain't even been off this ship fer almost a year. What about you, Mac? When's the last time you pulled a liberty?"

Mac smiled remembering. "September, in Honolulu," he said, "with a buddy of mine from boot camp; just before I got shipped out here." Mac felt a warm glow as he thought about that liberty in the Princess Kailani suite. Not only was it the last, but indeed it was the only liberty he had ever pulled.

"What did you do?"

Mac was not inclined to boast, and he also knew that no one was likely to believe that Bucks Fulton and his style was anything but a delusion. He would be cool. "Went into town," he said. "Messed around a little...the beach was nice but it was too crowded. Not really much to do in that town."

Mac's friend Gabe was a Steward's Mate, Third Class, who had been in the Navy for more than five years. Gabe knew where to go for a good time in Honolulu. He looked at Mac in disbelief, and then smiled in happy remembrance. "You just don't know where to go, man," he said. "Next time you're on liberty in Honolulu, ask somebody where the Pineapple Palace is. I guaran-damn-tee you'll find somethin' to do there. Whoo-ee. Oh man, oh man, oh man." Gabe was a happy man as he thought about good times at the Pineapple Palace. Then he asked, "What happened to your buddy?"

Mac thought about Bucks Fulton, and wondered how much money he was making these days. But he didn't envy him. In fact, he felt a genuine sympathy for Bucks, a sympathy that Bucks would have found ludicrous. To Gabe he said, "He had to stay in Pearl. Got assigned to some admiral's staff. Poor bastard. I'm glad I got into the real Navy. I'm gonna kill some Japs before I'm through."

Once again, Gabe looked at Mac in disbelief. "You must be nuts, man," he said. "How do you think you're gonna kill Japs servin' coffee to the admiral?"

Mac said, "I'm tryin' to get assigned to a gun mount for a battle station."

Gabe shook his head in disgust. "You *are* crazy, man," he said. "First of all, you never seen this ship when she was under air attack. Second, mess attendants never get to do anything but fetch and carry, even during battle. The best you could hope for would be hot shell man on a five-inch gun, and that ain't no picnic either. 'Course it do beat any below decks battle station; if this bucket ever goes down you damn sure don't wanna be caught below decks."

Mac looked surprised. "How could somethin' this big sink?" he asked. "She must be longer than two football fields. I feel pretty safe on this ship."

This time Gabe gave Mac a you-poor-dumb-fool look and said, "Mac, my man, did you ever look at her from the side? She looks like she might break in half all by herself. They call her 'Swayback Maru,' and you can see why. Maru is the Jap word for ship. Whoever designed her must have had his head up his ass, putting the hangar deck in the middle between the two stacks, instead of on the fantail like the new cruisers."

Gabe warmed to the description of the *USS Indianapolis* as a floating disaster waiting to happen. "And another thing," he said, "I heard the Exec telling somebody she's a tender ship because she wasn't built for all the new radar and communications equipment they piled on top of her when the war started. Makes you wonder why Admiral Spruance keeps her as his flagship."

Mac said, "Maybe it's because he's from Indiana."

Gabe snorted, "And one more thing, Mac, don't ever forget that no matter how big, or how stable, if a Jap torpedo hits her in the right spot, she'll damn sure sink. I saw what happened to the *Juneau* at Guadalcanal. So don't get the idea she's so damned safe."

Mac was indignant. "You tryin' to scare me?" he asked. "I ain't afraid. I come out here to kill Japs, and that's what I'm gonna do. I'll find a way."

Gabe looked at him dubiously. "How come you so hot to kill Japs? Most guys out here just tryin' to get home alive and in one piece."

Mac stood a little straighter as he answered this question. "The Japs killed my brother. I vowed to even the score."

Gabe nodded in sympathy, and a small light of understanding shone in his eyes, but he was not entirely convinced. "I'm sorry about yer brother, Mac," he said, "but you ain't the only one to lose a brother in this war you know."

Mac said, "I guess I ain't like other people."

"Flapper, you are some rare bird, you know that?" Nipper Stewart was speaking. "I was only kidding about training a new shore fire control officer. Now you're telling me you really do want to go in again. That's insanity. What are you trying to prove? You don't have to do it you know."

Flapper swayed slightly in his chair. "I'll tell you why, Nipper," he said. "There's more than one reason." Flapper seemed to become sober and serious as he addressed the question. Susan looked at him carefully, and was surprised at his quick mood change. "First, I know I'm not going to die on some crummy Pacific beach. I'm probably the only shore fire control officer who knows that, and it's why I'm the best. The others get overly cautious, and don't always do as well as they could...Ah, here's the Mules. Drink up, Ethel. Drink up, Nipper...To life!" Flapper held up the bowl-shaped glass in both hands. Nipper and Flapper each took a large gulp while Susan looked at them warily, and managed a small sip.

Nipper nodded approvingly. "Right again, Flapper," he said, "good drink." Then he looked at Susan and said, "He's right about something else, too, Ethel. As much as I hate to admit it, he is by far the best fire control officer in the fleet." Then he turned to Flapper and said, "Now, you humble bastard, can you please tell me how you can be so sure you're not going to die on the beach? Is God telling you something the rest of us aren't hearing?"

Flapper put down his drink, and again became serious. He did not look at Susan or Nipper as he spoke, but gazed into the distance beyond the ships and even beyond the sunset. He began to speak quietly about things he thought he could never share with anyone...violence so appalling that words had not been invented to describe it. "After a while you get a feeling," he said. "...The first time I went in at Tarawa, I was terrified. Who wouldn't be? Nobody can tell you what it was like. A man right in front of me had half his face turned into hamburger; he looked at me with the other half for about ten seconds while he died. He didn't cry out, but his half face went through a catalogue of emotions: puzzlement, astonishment, understanding...anger."

Flapper paused, and Susan saw tears forming in his eyes. She started to speak, "Flapper, you don't..." but he cut her off and continued. "I saw a man step on a land mine, and get blown a hundred feet into the air. As he reached the apex of his ascent he rotated slowly, his back to the earth, his arms and legs spread-eagled like he was being supported by a giant fountain of water; then he folded into a dive and crashed head first; he never knew what hit him." Again he paused. Slowly he turned away from the horizon to look at Susan and Nipper who met his gaze with sympathetic eyes.

Now he spoke to them directly. "After you survive something like Tarawa," he said, "not very much scares you...Saipan and Peleliu were bad, of course they were bad, but Tarawa was the worst...The landing craft got hung up on reefs, and the men had to wade ashore in chest deep water under heavy machine gun and mortar fire...it was hideous. Somehow I never felt threatened after Tarawa, and I don't say that to be bragging. But don't get me wrong, I don't intend to stand up under fire and offer myself as a target, I do plan to keep my head down. But hey, look what happened on Peleliu; I get whacked on the back of the head with a Samurai sword, and come out of it with nothing but a big headache. Those Japs are not going to kill me. I know it. So why should I worry about another landing? Maybe I can make a difference."

It was Susan's turn to question. "Are you telling us you want to go in again because you think your presence on the beach will save some lives?" she asked.

Flapper nodded affirmatively. "American lives, yes," he answered.

"That's pretty noble, Homer," Susan said.

"Maybe it looks noble, but that's not really what it's about. It's about being in a spot where your presence has meaning, where things can be better because of what you do. You should know about that, Ethel, a nurse must have that feeling."

Susan agreed up to a point, but still spoke with a wrinkled brow. "Yes, I know the feeling you're talking about, but I'm having some trouble with the idea that saving lives on a hospital ship is the same as saving lives on a bloody beachhead. I guess the difference is that when you save American lives, you do it by costing Japanese lives."

Flapper said, "It's the nature of war. If I direct fire to knock out a Jap pillbox, I might cost the lives of forty Japanese, and save the lives of four hundred Americans."

As Flapper and Susan continued their ever more serious discussion, to the point where each had the vague feeling they were about to unearth a profound truth, Nipper had settled into some serious drinking. He held up his glass, trying to restore the merry mood he was more comfortable with. "Flapper. Ethel," he said. "Hold it. Hold it. This conversation reminds me of the queen ant."

Flapper and Susan looked at Nipper curiously. Nipper grinned and began to tell the story. "There was this queen ant," he said. "She was sitting on top of her hill watching a crew of worker ants struggling to get an enormous dung ball up the hill." Nipper giggled thinking of the queen, swallowed some rum, then continued. "These workers had heaved and pushed, and rolled the shitball almost to the top. The queen was delighted, and was thinking how she could reward the whole crew when suddenly one of the worker ants slipped, the ball got out of control and started to roll back down the hill. Thinking quickly, the queen jumped to her feet, began waggling her antennae at other workers further down the hill, and shouting as loud as her queenly voice would allow: 'Stop the shit! Stop the shit!'"

As he gave the punch line, Nipper shaped his first two fingers into V's, placed them next to his forehead, and began waggling them in comic imitation of a queen ant, complete with bulging eyes.

Giggling, Susan and Flapper picked up their drinks and lifted them towards Nipper. "Okay, okay, your queenship," said Flapper, "let's go watch the USO show."

"Come on, Mac. The USO show on Mogmog starts in twenty minutes, we don't want to miss the next liberty boat."

"I'm comin', Gabe. Just gotta get my shoe tied. Who's in the show? Anybody I know?"

"Somebody told me there were some Hollywood comedians. Maybe Abbott and Costello. I also heard some colored Seabees had got up a pretty good combo."

As they emerged from an inside compartment onto the quarterdeck where the liberty party was assembling for inspection, they saw a vast quantity of warships swaying gently at anchor on the mirror-still waters of the spacious lagoon within Ulithi Atoll. It was not the first time Mac had seen the ominous dark silhouettes etched against a glowing sunset, but as before, he was confused at the juxtaposition between the instruments of destruction fashioned by men, and the artful and pacific backdrop provided by nature.

Gabe took in the spectacle and exclaimed, “Holy shit, Mac, look at all them ships! There must be a thousand. We must be gettin’ ready for one helluva operation. Maybe we’re gonna invade Japan.” Gabe paused and looked worried. “Man, this would make some target, I’ll bet them Japs would love to send a few torpedo planes in here.”

The size and numbers of ships impressed Mac, too, but he wasn’t worried. Unlike Gabe, he knew nothing of the ruin of battle, and so could only think of the enemy as worthless and depraved. “Hell, Gabe,” he said, “there must not be a Jap within a thousand miles of this place. You don’t think we’d bring all these ships here if it wasn’t safe, do you?”

Gabe thought about that for a moment, then his face brightened. “Maybe they all came for the USO show,” he said.

“Good grief, Ethel, honey, you din’t tell me ever man in the Fifth Fleet waszh gonna be here.” Flapper’s speech was beginning to slur as they emerged from the Officers’ Club and headed for the outdoors natural amphitheater where the show was beginning. Men were spread out all around, most sitting on the ground but some on jeeps and trucks, and a few perched happily in trees. A large wooden stage had been constructed, and in six foot high letters across the backdrop was the message:

WE LOVE YOU GUYS — USO

Flapper, Susan, and Nipper were pushing with something less than enthusiasm through a milling mass of men scrambling for seats as a fanfare from the stage heralded the beginning of the festivities.

Flapper was ready to give up. He put his arm around Susan’s shoulder and said, “Come on, Ethel, letsh get out of here. Why don’t you and me jush, s-s-shlip off to some quiet beach and talk about phil-philoshophie? Ole Nipper won’t mind, willya Nipper? Hey! Watch who yer bumpin’ into, shailor.”

“Sorry, sir, I…” Mac’s eyes widened in amazement as he recognized Homer Jackson, his high school mathematics teacher. “Mister Jackson!” he shouted. “It’s me. Booker T. McCan…from Peoria.”

>> 8 <<

IWO JIMA

On Booker T. McCan's 17th birthday, 10 February, 1945, Fast Carrier Task Force 58, Admiral Raymond Spruance in command, sortied Ulithi, determined to engage the enemy. Within the next nine days, TF 58 would deliver the first carrier strike against the Japanese home islands, and would follow that act by supporting Marine landings on Iwo Jima, a small island less than 600 miles southeast of Tokyo. The fire power brought to the assignment was galactic in scope: 11 fleet aircraft carriers, five light aircraft carriers, eight battleships, six heavy cruisers, nine light cruisers, 77 destroyers, 1,200 aircraft, and close to 100,000 men.

Spruance, in his usual spot behind a windbreak on the Flag Bridge of the heavy cruiser *USS Indianapolis*, looked at the vast armada spread beyond his view in all directions. He marveled at the contrast with Midway, an eternity of three years earlier, when people in Peoria and Indianapolis slept peacefully, not knowing that the future of the nation was being decided near Midway, a lovely Pacific atoll thousands of miles away, by the heroic men who manned a mere three aircraft carriers, and a handful of dive bombers.

As usual, Spruance was introspective; he thought of the coming agony. Air Force Major General Curtis LeMay had assured him that Iwo Jima was needed as a refueling and emergency landing field for his B-29s in the planned strategic bombing of the Japanese home islands, but still he was restless. He must have known that with the technology available in 1945, the concept of strategic bombing was something of a joke, and was more likely to result in indiscriminate firebombing of entire cities. He had no way of knowing that the war would be over within six months, and in that time more than a quarter of a million people—10 times as many Japanese as American—would suffer violent death in the narrowly focused bull's-eye of the Japanese home islands.

Five days out of Ulithi, as the massive formation steamed north toward

Japan, Mac and Flapper Jackson stood on the hangar deck amidships of the *Indianapolis* watching destroyers go alongside fleet aircraft carriers for fueling-at-sea operations. Booker T. continued to be astounded at the hardly believable coincidence that of the thousands of possible ships he might have been assigned to he had ended up on the same one as his former teacher. "Mister Jackson," he said, "I still can't believe we ended up on the same ship. Look at all those ships I could have been sent to. It's pretty amazing."

Flapper agreed. "It's pretty amazing all right, Booker T."

Booker T. shuffled his feet and cast a sideways glance at Flapper. "Mr. Jackson, " he said, not looking at him, "there's something..." his voice trailed off.

Flapper looked at his friend, thinking how young he looked, even though Booker T. was as tall as he was, maybe a little taller. "What is it, Booker T.?" he asked.

Booker T. turned to look straight at Flapper. "Well, it's just that...Mr. Jackson," he said, "would it be okay if you just called me Mac? It's just that..." he paused to take a deep breath, "...you see, I'm not the same kid who left Peoria last year...I'm...well I guess I'd just feel better if you called me Mac, like everybody else does."

Flapper nodded agreement. "Okay, Mac," he said, "Sure. I understand perfectly. The Homer Jackson you knew in Peoria is not the same person as the Flapper Jackson you see before you."

Mac reminisced. "You taught me eighth grade algebra." he said, "That was...lemme think..."

Flapper broke in. "September, 1941. I was in the Naval Reserve, and couldn't wait to get in after Pearl Harbor. They called me up in January 1942. I've been away from Peoria for three years." He looked at his former student and said, "But, hey, Mister Mac, how come you're out here at all? You're way too young. You ought to be back in Peoria, chasin' footballs and girls."

The old pain clouded Mac's face. His buoyant mood faded when he thought of how to answer the question...why was he here? "Mister Jackson," he began, "did you know my brother Davey?"

Flapper nodded. "I didn't have him as a student," he said, "but of course everybody at Manual knew about Davey McCan. A super athlete, and I was told, a very good student."

Mac almost smiled thinking of his brother the super athlete. "The Japs killed him," he said. "Davey was on the *Liscomb Bay* when she was torpedoed."

Flapper shook his head sadly. "I'm sorry, Mac," he said. "That's a real shame...I saw that ship go down...It was over in a hurry. We were hanging around those islands way too long."

Mac was surprised. "You were there? That's amazing! I met a guy on the train to Norfolk who survived that sinking; his name was Kevin O'Keefe. He told me that one minute he was asleep in his rack, and the next he was in the water watching the ship go down."

Suddenly Mac had a thought that brought him up short. Was it possible that Davey had also survived? Excitedly he voiced his thought. "Mister Jackson! Do you think it's possible that Davey survived that attack? We got a telegram telling us he died in action, but maybe it was wrong. Do you think it's possible?" Mac quickly convinced himself that Davey was alive. He thought of Davey swimming to a nearby island.

But Flapper quickly put an end to his dream. "I'm sorry, Mac," he said, "but I don't think that's much of a possibility. It's been more than a year, and if you haven't heard any more...all the survivors were picked up by destroyers...sorry, Mac." Flapper quickly changed the subject. "Listen, Mac, tell me what's happening back at good old Manual. What have I been missing?"

Mac tried to remember; he was still thinking of Davey. "It's been almost a year since I was there, Mister Jackson." He hesitated, thought a moment, then said brightly, "Last year we won the city championship in football, basketball, and track."

Flapper smiled broadly. "Good show," he exclaimed. "Did you play?"

Mac was modest and unassuming, a legacy from his brother, he could not speak of his own accomplishments without embarrassment. He said only, "Yes, sir, I played."

Flapper smiled, recalling some of the memorable performances of Mac's brother Davey who played every game with a fierce determination and fluid grace that never failed to excite the audience, and not incidentally, to lift his teammates to higher levels of achievement. He could see that Mac too had the carriage and movements of an athlete. He nodded and said, "I'll bet you did. .So which one is your favorite sport?"

Mac thought a moment. "I don't think I like any one better than the other. They come with the seasons. Football and basketball are team sports...in track you're pretty much on your own. Nothing compares to baseball. I like to win. When you lose it's like...you just feel..." Mac searched for the right words.

Flapper interrupted. "Grantland Rice wrote 'When the one great scorer comes to mark against your name, He writes not that you won or lost, but how you played the game'."

Mac shook his head. "No. You have to win," he said.

Flapper questioned, "Winning trumps everything?"

Mac shook his head vigorously. "Oh yeah," he said, "nothing beats winning."

Flapper had some Socrates in him too. "How do you feel about cheating to win?" he asked.

"What's cheating?" Mac asked rhetorically. "If somebody punches me in the nose, and I punch back harder, is that cheating?" Mac thought a moment then said, "War is like a game, isn't it?"

Flapper nodded. "A murderous game, Booker T.," he said. It would take time for him to remember that this was Mac, not Booker T.

"Is cheating allowed in war?"

Flapper shrugged. "It's hard to talk about cheating when there aren't any rules," he said.

"Do you remember Rex Piper?" Mac asked.

"Sure," Flapper answered. "He was an all-state tackle. Big and quick."

Mac nodded. "That's right," he said. "Rex joined the Marines after he graduated in nineteen forty-two. Last year he came back without his right arm, and with his right leg in a brace. He got hit at Tarawa. Is it cheating to cripple a kid who's not even twenty years old?"

Flapper looked pained. "I was at Tarawa," he said. "Rex was lucky to survive. One of every five Marines in the assault force was killed. It was hideous. A murderous game, Mac."

"Mister Jackson, does the Navy send people ashore during invasions?"

Flapper nodded. "A few. I'm the shore fire control officer for this ship. I go in with the Marines and Army units to direct fire from our main and secondary batteries against targets that might be holding up the troops."

Mac asked eagerly, "Can I go in with you the next time?"

Flapper looked at him in amazement. "Are you crazy? This is not fourth and short, Mac. This is blood on the sand, this is about death and dying."

Mac was still eager. "I want to go. Please. Take me along."

Flapper stared at him in disbelief. "You're really serious," he said. "But you can't go. Forget it. Don't even think about it. For one thing, today is Thursday, and Monday we're landing on Iwo Jima. How do you think I can teach you in four days what you need to know to be of any use, let alone to keep from getting your head blown off?"

Mac persisted. "Mister Jackson," he said, "I joined the Navy for only one reason: to avenge my brother Davey by killing some Japs. This may be my only chance. You always told me I was a quick learner. Remember that eighth grade algebra class?"

Flapper shook his head. "This is not algebra," he said, "and you are still Booker T. McCan. Forget it."

Flapper started to walk away, but Mac followed quickly. "Please, Mister Jackson," he implored, "take me with you. I won't get in the way. I promise."

Flapper continued to walk towards the fantail, talking as he went. Mac, two inches taller, was alongside, matching him stride for stride.

"Booker T.... Mac," Flapper said, "you know the Navy doesn't work that way. Even if I wanted to, I couldn't. You have a duty assignment on this ship, and it doesn't include going ashore with a landing party. Besides that, if something happened to you, how could I explain it to your mom and dad?"

Mac persisted. "Mister Jackson," he said, "I think we both know that my duties on this ship are not gonna change which way this war is goin'...Unless you figure Admiral Spruance might lose some sleep if somebody else brings him his coffee, and from what they tell me the admiral doesn't lose much sleep over anything."

Flapper continued to walk, shaking his head. Mac persisted. Trying to get Flapper to look at him, he said, "Mister Jackson, nothin's gonna happen to me. The Japs can't hurt me. I know it. I have this feeling. They can't hurt me. It's a feeling I have."

Flapper was startled. He stopped walking, and looked at Mac as if seeing him for the first time. The two stood looking at each other, Mac with pleading eyes and a flash of hope, Flapper with puzzled eyes and a touch of confusion.

Flapper said, "Tell me about that feeling."

Mac felt a thrill—he could go, maybe he could go. "It's hard to explain, Mister Jackson," he said. "It's kinda like...you sorta know what' s gonna happen. The first time I saw the Pacific Ocean I knew she was gonna be good for me. 'Course she kicked me around in a storm soon after we left San Francisco, but after it was over, she showed me a splendiferous sunset, and I knew it was gonna be all right. Nothin' bad will happen to me in the Pacific. I know it."

Flapper turned to the rail and stared out at the destroyers hustling back and forth between their stations in the anti-submarine screen and the fuelsupplying carriers steaming on a steady course at a leisurely twelve knots. A warm tropical breeze touched their faces in the bright morning sunshine; salt water spray stung their eyes.

It *was* a game. But what a game! Mac's revelation triggered an understanding in Flapper that surprised him. This ghastly global game was a source of inspiration to his generation—it gave them purpose, a noble cause. This was a game worthy of...of what? Flapper turned his head slightly to look at Mac's boyish, smooth-skinned face now intent on the scurrying ships. "Tell me, Mac," he said, "do you believe in God?"

Mac pulled his head back, widened his eyes in surprise and said, "Sure I do. That's a funny question. Do you think God has something to do with the feeling I have?"

Flapper continued to look out at the vast armada; he spoke dreamily. "I don't know, Mac. I don't know. It's...I have that same feeling...the Japs can't hurt me. I don't brag about it, but I did tell my friend Nipper Stewart, and he made a joke about it...he asked me if God was speaking to me."

"What did you tell him?" Mac asked.

"I told him it's not like that...I'm not hearing voices...but I have this profound sense of security. It's pretty damned irrational when you consider the circumstances. Everybody else is scared shitless, and I feel safe as a baby. Now you tell me you have the same feeling. I don't know what to say."

Mac sensed that Flapper was giving in. He spoke eagerly. "Say you'll let me go in with you next Monday. Maybe that's the way God wants it."

Flapper was giving in, but he was not ready to admit it. He said, "Let me sleep on it, Mac. Maybe you're right. Maybe it's fate. But, for God's sake, don't say anything about it to anybody."

For a long time they watched the fueling operations in silence, both lost in their own thoughts. Then Mac had a thought he wanted to share. "Mister Jackson?"

"Yeah?"

"Mister Jackson, do you think the Japs have the same God we do?"

Hunched down in a corner of the bobbing LCVP, trying to get his sea legs, Mac felt queasy. *This is no time to get seasick*, he thought. The landing craft had made a quick stop at the *Indianapolis* about 0730 to pick up Flapper and his new radioman, Winthrop Isaac. Mac, a full combat pack strapped to his back, tagged along. Nobody asked any questions. It was like carpooling to work on Monday morning.

The boat circled at 4,000 yards—about two miles from the beach, just seaward of the line of departure, waiting for the signal to go in. The LCVP was like a floating box, 25 feet long and 10 feet wide. The sides of the boat, for this was most assuredly a boat and not a ship, and these were certainly sides and not bulkheads, were about eight feet high, which meant that standing on the bottom of the box you could not see anything except other men standing in the bottom of the box. Mac counted 45 Marines in and on the craft. Some were standing in the well of the boat, others were sitting on the gunwales, hoping for a better view of the action. There was much to see, and Mac scrambled to a not very comfortable seat on the edge so that he would not miss anything. He counted seven battleships, seven cruisers, and 10 destroyers, all blazing away with their main batteries, respectively, 16, eight, and five-inch guns. Mac had once stood next to an eight-inch shell on the *Indianapolis*, and pondering the immensity of a 16-inch shell, he wondered how anything could remain alive on the island after a saturation bombardment. He also wondered if he would ever again be able to hear soft music. The noise from the great guns was shattering, but no worse than the head-jarring concussion, which teetered on the edge of bearable pain. But these men had elevated pain thresholds; earplugs were for sissies. The human body is a wondrous contraption.

The water around the firing ships was covered, shroud-like, with landing craft, indeed there seemed to be no water at all, only ships and milling small craft. But with each salvo a moat took shape as the multi-ton steel masses recoiled in accordance with the laws of physics, causing harassed firing officers to frantically recalculate range. The smell of diesel exhaust and smokeless powder filled the air, and pools of rainbow-colored oil slicks floated on the water. Overhead the sky was blue, and fleecy white clouds drifted peacefully in the gentle breeze. Then, with breath-taking suddenness, the firing stopped, and for a brief moment, they could hear water slapping against the side of the boat.

In the brief interval before carrier planes, spewing bombs, rockets, and bullets swarmed over the 4 1/2 x 2 1/2 mile island, Mac got a clear view of Iwo Jima in all its ugliness. From 8,000 yards (the approximate length of the island), it had looked like a joke—a large baseball cap with an extended bill, something a clown might wear—so small that the entire island could be captured in three 35 millimeter camera frames. But now, from 4,000 yards (roughly the width of the island at its widest part), it reminded him of the evil queen's castle in the movie *Snow White and the Seven Dwarfs*. On the left, rising menacingly, 550 feet above the dust and smoke, not looking like a baseball cap, and certainly not like a joke, was the dead volcano, Mount Suribachi. Straight ahead were the narrow landing beaches, backed by a series of black sand terraces. On the right the ground rose 300 feet in a succession of increasingly higher rocky ridges and valleys. Mac could see no trees, only gray-black volcanic sand and rocky outcroppings. There were no signs of life, nor any indication that life had ever existed on this barren, loathsome thing. But out of sight, safe for the moment, in caves and elaborately constructed tunnels and chambers, were 20,000 frightened men determined to defend this land for the glory of the Emperor. For 20 minutes the carrier-based aircraft plastered the sand and rocks, then gave way again to the bombardment ships who picked up the tempo, and for another 20 minutes blasted the island with a withering barrage that caused men in the boats to cower and cover their ears with their hands. Mac shouted in the ear of a tough-looking Marine sergeant perched next to him. "Think there'll be any Japs left when we get there?"

The Marine looked at Mac like he was from another planet, shrugged, and turned his attention back to the beach. He did not shout, but began to speak in a normal tone of voice that caused Mac to lean closer, straining to hear. Other than himself, the Marine was not talking to anyone in particular; he was not trying to instruct. "Won't make no difference," he said. "Them Japs is underground in caves and tunnels. Prob'ly playin' checkers or somethin'. We got to root 'em out jist like we always do...Them swabbies might's well save their damn ammo. B'sides blowin' up a few land mines, 'bout all they're doin' is givin' me a headache." He unleashed a stream of brown liquid from between a gap in his teeth. Mac looked carefully at the Marine sergeant and knew instinctively that this man was a leader; where he went, men would follow. What he said resonated with truth, and men desperate for surcease of terror would look to him for example.

Once again the firing rate accelerated until the incessant thundering crash engulfed them. Then it stopped. They saw planes strafing the beaches, and at last the blue pennant on their control boat dropped, pointing toward the beach like a lance in a medieval joust. The landing craft, with its cargo of veteran and neophyte warriors, wheeled and chugged towards its assigned landing area, beach blue two on the right flank of the attack.

Flapper looked at Mac and bellowed, "We'll hit the beach in about 30 minutes. You feelin' all right? You don't look so hot."

Mac answered, "I'm a little seasick but it's not too bad. Now that we're movin' in I'll be okay."

The tough-looking Marine sergeant sitting next to Mac on the gunwale of the churning LCVP never took his eyes off the distant land, but now spoke. "This yer first landing, ain't it?"

Mac nodded. "How could you tell?" he asked.

The Marine smiled a gap-toothed smile. "You forgot your piece," he said.

Mac was not sure he had heard correctly. "My what?"

"Your piece... Your weapon... Your rifle. You gonna throw rocks at them Japs?"

Mac looked relieved and said proudly, "I'm with the shore fire control party. Anyway I've got a .45." He patted the heavy pistol in the holster on his belt.

The Marine was burdened with more than 50 pounds of survival gear...the steel helmet covering his head weighed three pounds. Mac counted ten hand grenades clipped to his jacket and belt. Slung over his shoulder was a .30 caliber semi-automatic carbine. A cartridge belt around his waist held ten 30-round clips. A 12-inch knife was holstered on his right hip, a .45 caliber pistol on his left. A six-inch holstered dagger was clipped to his right combat boot just above the ankle. A length of quarter inch steel cable, to serve as a garrote, was looped over his belt. He was dressed to kill. He snorted. "That pop gun ain't gonna be much help unless they get awful damn close. But then ya never can tell. Listen, Mac," he said, "my name is Joe, why don't you sorta keep an eye on me and, you know...do what ah do."

Mac was surprised. "How'd you know my name was Mac?"

G.I. Joe, continuing to look ahead, said, "That yer name?"

A young officer with the insignia of the medical corps asked, "How many landings have you made, Joe?"

The sergeant took a moment to answer. "Ah think five, Doc," he said, "but ah sort of lose count. The last one was Pelaylu." He shook his head slowly from side to side with a far-away look in his eyes as he remembered. It was not something he needed to be reminded of just now, but it really did not matter, when the fighting started he knew his veteran's instincts would take over.

The young doctor needed to get some things off his chest. He spoke in short sentences as his thoughts paraded to the podium of his mouth. "I've only been in the service two months. Just graduated from medical school last year. Medical College of San Francisco. Sure didn't expect to be out here so soon. They didn't give me much training for this. Got married last Christmas.

Just before they shipped me out. Never expected to be out here so soon."

The sergeant was sympathetic. "That's pretty rough, Doc," he said without irony. He patted the young doctor on the shoulder. The gesture suggested genuine sympathy rather than the sarcasm the remark might have carried.

The doctor agreed. "Yes, it is. I'm not even sure what I'm supposed to do. I thought I'd be more use back on one of the hospital ships."

"What are ya good at, Doc?" asked Joe.

The doctor brightened. "Surgery," he said. "I'm a surgeon."

"You'll be needed on the beach." Joe said it softly, with conviction.

The doctor asked, "What will it be like on the beach, Joe? Will I be able to set up an aid station? How can you do something like that under fire?"

Joe was silent for a few moments. "Not all landings are the same," he said. "Nobody can tell for sure what it's gonna be like on the beach, but ah can make a pretty good guess. The Navy put a lotta hot steel onto this rock. What it means is that for the first fifteen or twenty minutes on the beach, things will be fairly quiet. That's because it will take the Japs a while to come up outta their holes to man their pillboxes and blockhouses. If ah was you, Doc, ah'd work like hell diggin' in and gettin' things set up in that time 'cause once they get back in position they are gonna make you one helluva busy doctor. How many corpsman and litter bearers do you have?"

The young doctor shook his head. "I don't know," he said.

Each Marine combat battalion of some 1,000 men was assigned about 50 Navy hospital corpsmen and 16 Marine litter bearers. The litter bearers' job required them to walk upright over the battlefield...they had the shortest life expectancy of anyone in the headquarters company.

Joe continued. "Once the firing starts," he said, "if yer lucky, we'll have moved far enough in so they'll be shootin' at us instead of you. But then there's that goddamned hill over there which commands the beach." He pointed to Mount Suribachi. "They'll probably be hittin' the supply craft on the beach with seventy fives from there, so you'll wanna get as far away from the water line as you can. Ah don't think it's gonna be easy, Doc."

Mac, Flapper, and others had been listening to the sergeant's analysis, and now Flapper spoke. "That sounds like a pretty good analysis to me, Sarge. Whatta ya do in civilian life?"

The Marine tilted the steel helmet back on his héad, then deliberately took a package of chewing tobacco out of his back pocket while he pondered the question. Before he answered, he put a large wad into his mouth, chewed it briefly, settled it in place in his left cheek, then fired a brown stream of juice though the gap in his teeth. Slowly he turned to face Flapper and the others, and said proudly, "Ah'm a soldier."

Thunk! The LCVP hit the beach.

"All ashore that's goin' ashore," called the coxswain, cheerfully. "Don't take any wooden nickels, men, they tell me the natives are hostile."

Mac jumped into ankle deep water, and began the run to the beach following Flapper and Isaac. As his feet touched Japanese soil for the first time, they sank over his shoe tops in soft, black volcanic ash, and his run was reduced to a churning, struggling, anxious, foot-by-slogging-foot advance. In places, the ash was above their ankles. But the sergeant was right; for the moment at least, they were unopposed. The naval bombardment continued to pound suspected targets along the spine of the island, but at a more leisurely pace than the frantic pre-landing barrage. They moved as quickly as they could toward the first terrace, 50 yards ahead. When they reached it unharmed, they sat gasping for breath with their backs to the 15- foot terrace, and Flapper tried to make contact with his firing ship, the *Indianapolis*. "Rejoice, Rejoice, this is Flapper. Can you hear me? Over."

The answer came with surprising quickness. "Flapper, this is Rejoice. I hear you loud and clear. Over." The din of battle continued, and Flapper had to hold the two-way radio close to his ear.

"Rejoice, this is Flapper. You may have to speak a little louder or reduce your firing rate. You're making an awful racket. Over."

"Roger, Flapper. We're still working on our assigned quota. If you have targets they will have priority. Do you have any targets? Over."

"Negative, Rejoice. We just got here, and so far no fuss; but don't go too far away. Over."

"Roger, Flapper. Standing by. Out."

>> 9 <<

PRISONER-OF-WAR

Mac was in a state of high excitement as he watched the frenzied activity on the beach. Marines were pouring out of landing craft and dashing for the cover of the black sand terraces. As far as he could see, to his left and right, men were sprawled, rifles in hand against the base of the terrace. Soon all space against the terrace was occupied as a new wave of boats arrived every five minutes. The new arrivals sprawled between the outstretched legs of men from earlier waves.

Mac looked at Flapper. "What now, Mister Jackson?" he asked.

Flapper said, "Listen, Mac, and you too, Isaac. From now on you call me Flapper. This is no time for formalities. Anybody know where Sergeant Joe is?"

Mac pointed. "He's over there Mr. Flapper, looks like they're gettin' ready to move up the terrace."

Flapper said, "Okay. When he moves, we follow."

They sat watching the next assault wave land. Mac noticed that some of the men were falling and not getting up. Flapper saw it also. "The Nips are opening up with rifle fire," he said.

Isaac asked, "How do you know it's rifle fire?"

"Because I can't hear it," answered Flapper. "If it was machine guns we'd hear it, and more men would be falling. Joe was right again. Stand by for machine gun and mortar fire any second now. This is where we can help. When they start to unmask their batteries we call in fire to neutralize them. Keep your eyes open and let me know if you see anything that looks like enemy fire. It may only be a slit in a rock."

Mortar shells began to burst all along the beach. Mac viewed with horror the sight of a charging Marine taking a direct hit from an exploding mortar shell. The man disintegrated before his eyes. A shoulder with attached arm still clutching a rifle soared 40 feet into the air.

"My God." Mac and Isaac repeated again and again as variations on the grisly theme were repeated over and over before their shocked eyes.

Flapper shouted, "Come on guys, this ain't a spectator sport, let's move up where we can see something. We got to help these guys."

Night. Calm after storm. Even though the thunder of naval ordnance continued, it was at a reduced pace. Star shells burst in a supernatural Fourth-of-July burlesque that seemed to illuminate the rock-barren scene for the benefit of ghostly spectators. Mac was alive, so were Flapper and Isaac; they were huddled in a shallow depression scratched out of rock and volcanic ash in a narrow ravine between rocky ridges, several hundred yards from the beach. It had been a day of shattering violence. Just as he had wondered before landing how any living thing could survive the ferocious naval bombardment, now Mac wondered how any of the invaders had been able to weather the savage response of the Japanese defenders. Images of horror filled the vault of his memory: a 10 foot length of human intestine shimmering on the sand; a disembodied, but still beating heart; a flying bladder spraying urine.

Within Mac's head raged another war: it was a struggle to subordinate the ghastly reflections to the reality of ever present and all encompassing danger. Flapper had continually urged them to keep their eyes open, to stay alert, to be on their toes. It was a deadly game of cops and robbers. Somehow it seemed fitting that the most momentous day of his life should be accompanied by background music; throughout the entire grotesque day a familiar refrain resonated through his head: "*mine eyes have seen the glory of the coming of the Lord, he is trampling out the vintage where the grapes of wrath are stored.*" Interspersed between the refrain, the words of Preacher IQ Black echoed louder and louder as the day progressed: "*Happy are the dead who from now on die in the service of the Lord.*"

The Japanese defense was as predicted by Sergeant Joe, but no one could have predicted the problems caused by the complexities of the terrain. Splaying out and down some 300 feet toward the beaches from the plateau in the middle of the island were countless gullies, canyons, and arroyos, crossed and interlaced with ravines, defiles, and gulches. Among these winding, meandering convolutions, skillfully disguised and strategically placed pillboxes and blockhouses covered every avenue with cross-lanes of fire. More than once, Marines had overrun or bypassed positions only to find a firing slit opening at their rear. Moreover, it was not uncommon for firing to break out from a position previously thought destroyed. The enemy was unseen, determined, well supplied, and waiting. A nightmare for attacking troops.

Mac reflected briefly on his own performance. He had not been afraid. Two times he had been the first to spot the source of machine gun fire holding up the advance, and call them to Flapper's attention. Flapper had then proceeded in a calm, professional manner to direct eight-inch shellfire from the *Indianapolis* to silence the instruments of death.

Darkness brought intermission. The firing slacked, stopped, then resumed intermittently. The evening was cool, and the fighters shivered in their holes, ate cold K rations and dreaded the long night.

Isaac whispered, "What's next, Flapper?"

Flapper winced and rolled on his side to be nearer Mac and Isaac. The three were side by side in the small foxhole. Their large combat packs made movement difficult. Even in this cramped space they faded in and out of view as a new star shell burst every five minutes. "I wish you hadn't asked me that, Isaac," said Flapper. "For two reasons. One, the last time somebody asked me that I ended up getting whacked with a Samurai sword, and two, I haven't got the faintest idea what's next. This is my fourth landing, and I thought I'd seen everything, but I don't think anybody has seen anything like this. I mean, who could have guessed that we'd be here not only with Japs all around us but even underneath us? One thing's for sure… nobody's getting much sleep tonight."

They heard movement to their left. "Studebaker," said Flapper in a low voice.

"Buick," came the quick reply. A shadowy figure slid into their hole; they could not see his face.

Flapper said, "I don't know who you are, mister, but, slidin' around out here at night is a good way to get your butt shot off. What the hell's goin' on?"

They heard a familiar voice say, "I'm passin' the word…get ready to move out for a night attack."

"Is that you, Joe?" Flapper asked.

"It's me all right. Is that you, Flapper? How you doin?"

Flapper sighed. "It ain't exactly the Royal Hawaiian, is it?" he grumbled, "but I guess we'll make it all right. How about you, Joe? You makin' it?"

Joe said, "I'm numb, Flapper, it's been a bitch all day…the terrain is the worst I ever seen. But listen, in case I don't get another chance, I wanna tell you somethin'. You and your boys did a helluva job today. Saved my ass a couple of times. Thanks, buddy."

Flapper shrugged. "Don't mention it, Joe," he said, "that's our job. You guys didn't do so bad yourself. But what's this crap about a night attack? I'd think the men could use some rest."

"You got that right, Flapper; but this is one time I think the general is right too. If we can knock out a few pillboxes in the dark it might save some lives once the sun comes up. Also we keep the Japs from restin'. I think our battalion will go into reserve in the morning, then we can get some rest. We're so damned pumped up now we probly couldn't sleep anyway so we might as well keep movin'. Trouble is we don't know where to attack. Them Japs is all round us including underneath us. I could smell some rice and rotten fish cookin' back over there. Anyway, Flapper, ain't much use you comin' on the attack, don't reckon you can call in much fire at night."

"I wanta come with you, Joe," Mac said quietly.

Joe was not surprised; he had seen men volunteer before. He had also seen men run away. He accepted the difference as simply the way things were. This G.I. Joe was a realist, he did not look for reasons, and he did not make judgments. "That okay with you, Flapper? We can use all the help we can get."

Flapper was appalled at the thought of Booker T. going out on a night attack. "No," he said. "Absolutely not. He's not trained for this kind of fighting, Joe. He might do more harm than good."

Mac spoke eagerly. "I'll follow Joe," he said. "I'll do what he does. I'll help him. Please let me go, Flapper."

Flapper shrugged. "You have a real talent for talking me into things, Mac," he said. He sighed again. "I guess since you've come this far you're probably in no more danger if you go than if you stay here."

Joe did not hesitate. "Follow me, Mac," he said, "and remember the password." He was up and running in a low squat.

Mac jumped to his feet. "See ya later, Flapper," he said. "Thanks for everything and don't worry, I'll be okay."

Flapper said, "Be careful, Booker T. Good luck." As Booker T. moved off into the darkness Flapper pondered the absurdity of advising caution in a situation where more than 40,000 men with guns were primed to shoot at anything that moved.

"You know where we're at, Joe? It's awful quiet."

"I'm tryin' to get my bearings, Mac. I think the company's over that way, but I ain't sure. Maybe we ought to sit tight for a bit, and see what happens. I know we're pretty far out on the right flank but I ain't sure which direction we oughta be headin'. That's a fine kettle of fish ain't it? Fight a whole goddamn war and end up gettin' lost like a skunk huntin' it's mamma."

Mac said, "Maybe if we crawled up that hill over there we could get a better idea of which way to go."

"Okay, let's go," said Joe.

They crouched low, and started up a steep incline, Joe leading, Mac following five feet behind. Twenty yards up the hill, without warning Mac heard a groan and saw Joe fall. He froze, raised his pistol, and desperately searched the shadows, trying to figure out what had happened and what to do. Hearing a sound behind him, he whirled in terror. It was a rookie mistake. He should have dropped to a prone position and rolled. He felt a tightness in his throat, and suddenly he was jerked violently off his feet as a garrote tightened around his neck. He thudded to earth, raging with anger and struggling furiously but futilely to free himself. The struggle was brief as he quickly lost consciousness.

---------------*************************------------&&&&&##########-

He was falling into a black hole. He tried to stop his fall by grabbing at hangman's nooses that swayed just beyond his reach. He tumbled and turned in a free fall until entering a maelstrom that whirled him in tighter and tighter circles toward a point of light that grew brighter and brighter as the circles became smaller and smaller until he was blinded by the brilliance. He tried to block out the light by putting his hands over his eyes, only to find his arms tethered to his sides. He struggled to free himself and to escape the blinding light.

"Okay, he's coming around, let's go tell the Baron."

Mac heard the voice but did not understand the words. He stopped struggling when the light was removed, and lay still, trying to organize his thoughts. Was he alive or dead? He opened his eyes, but the darkness was total, he could see nothing; neither could he hear anything. He was in a void. He could not move his arms or his legs. He did not feel any pain, other than tightness in his throat, but his fingers were numb. Was he alive or dead?

I am Booker T. McCan. I am thirsty. I am cold. I am afraid.

THE HELL YOU ARE.

The hell I'm not. I am also uncomfortable.

YOU SURE AS HELL ARE.

I need to piss. I must be alive.

YOU ARE.

Why am I talking to myself?

THERE'S NO ELSE TO TALK TO.

How do you know?

WHY DON'T YOU TRY A HELLO?

"Hello?" He could only speak in a whisper.

Silence.

Where is Sergeant Joe? Where am I? I must be tied up. Am I a prisoner?

YOU DON'T THINK THE SERGEANT TIED YOU UP DO YOU?

Why didn't they kill me? I would have killed them.

ARE YOU SURE?

That's why I came out here isn't it?

THAT'S WHAT YOU KEEP TELLING YOURSELF.

Maybe I should pray.

WHAT ARE YOU WAITING FOR?

Should I pray for a miracle?

YOU GOT A BETTER IDEA?

What's that noise? Uh oh, somebody's coming...

Two Japanese soldiers, one holding a flashlight, descended a flight of concrete steps to where Mac, trussed up like a rolled roast, was lying. The soldiers were from Colonel Takeichi Nishi's 309th Independent Infantry Battalion, and as usual, they were complaining about the colonel who, behind his back, they called "the Baron" because of his regal ways.

"What does the Baron want from this American pig?"

"I think he wants information."

"About what? What can he tell us that we don't already know? The pale-skinned cowards have us trapped on this godforsaken island; they have enough ships and planes to completely cover the ocean and sky; they have enough shells to fill up the volcano; they have enough flame-throwers to forever feed the fires of hell; they have enough men so that even their cowardice does not matter; what can this miserable lump of dog dung tell the Baron that would change any of that?"

The soldier gave Mac a vicious kick in the back.

"Maybe the Baron knows something we don't."

"Nagasato, are you a sane person? Do you really think there is even the remotest chance that you or any of us will leave this island alive?"

Mac lay at the feet of the two soldiers who were engaged in animated conversation that sounded so different from anything he had ever heard; he wondered if even they understood what they were saying. Instinctively he did not move, hoping to avoid another kick.

"Nagasato, let me tell you what I really think about the Baron. I think deep down he really likes the Americans. You know he lived in America for many years. He thinks like an American. I believe he wishes he were still there. Did you see this afternoon when he tried to keep Captain Osuda from shooting that crazy Marine who was running towards our pillbox?"

"Susumu, maybe we shouldn't say bad things about our officers."

"What difference does it make? We will die very soon, and that will be the end of it."

"For you maybe. I plan to go to heaven."

"Heaven? Where is heaven?"

"For me it is a clear mountain stream close to my village on Kyushu. My spirit will take the form of a fish, and I will spend eternity worshipping the Gods and striving for truthfulness and purification."

"Nagasato, I must say I have great envy for your Mountain Sect Shinto. If only my beliefs were as simple. I have even begun to doubt the Deity of the Emperor and the existence of the Goddess of the Rising Sun. I have seen too much pain and suffering. My prayers have been ridiculed. I find it no longer possible to be reverent. I am burdened with hopelessness, and so I reprove the Baron who I believe to be weak and vacillating. He is more like an American than a Japanese."

"Susumu, I think you go too far. Colonel Nishi is descended from the Samurai warriors. You and I have both seen him in action. How many colonels do you know who have killed Americans with their hands?"

"It is true, but nevertheless I think he wastes time by interrogating American prisoners who know nothing. I think he likes to see the surprise on their pathetic faces when he speaks to them in their own language. How I wish I could understand what he says to them. Sometimes I think he just likes to hear them talk. One time I swear he was telling jokes, he even had the prisoner laughing."

"Well this one should be different anyway. We've never brought him one with black skin. Maybe this time the Baron will be surprised."

>>10<<

COLONEL NISHI AND THE Bbrowns

Mac, blindfolded, his arms still arrested tightly at his sides, was led stumbling in the darkness through a narrow winding passageway, up two flights of wooden steps, and finally into a small room carved out of the earth and lighted only by a bare electric bulb hanging from a slim cord. When his blindfold was removed Mac saw that the room was sparely furnished—a table, a chair, a low stool. From somewhere he could hear the melancholy sounds of Duke Ellington's band playing "Mood Indigo." A large, detailed map of the island was secured to one wall. On the table were a field telephone, a bottle of brandy, and two glasses. Sitting behind the table facing away from Mac was a Japanese officer. Other than movies, it was the first Japanese Mac had ever seen. It was the Baron...Colonel Nishi.

The colonel sat quietly for a few moments, smoking a cigarette, listening to the music, allowing Mac to take in the whole alien scene. At last he stood up theatrically, and turned to face the wide-eyed young American. He smiled in satisfaction at the look of astonishment on Mac's face. Mac, with his Hollywood inspired knowledge of what all Japanese looked like, was totally unprepared for Colonel Nishi. First, the colonel did not look at all like a monkey; in fact, Mac was struck by how much he looked like Count, his old mentor in Peoria. Secondly, although Mac had grown to an imposing six feet two inches, the Baron was an inch taller. Third, the colonel did not wear thick glasses, and finally, to Mac's utter confusion, the Baron was wearing a St. Louis Browns baseball cap.

Colonel Nishi stood directly in front of Mac, grasped the chain of his dog tags for a close look, and said, in a basso profundo voice that also caught Mac by surprise, "So you are Booker T. McCan? Welcome to Iwo Jima."

Mac was stunned. Here, standing before him was a man who must be his enemy, who surely intended to kill him, and yet was speaking to him in unaccented English, and appeared to be friendly. It made no sense. It must be a dream.

"Why did you kill my brother?" Mac blurted.

Colonel Nishi blinked, shook his head slightly, stepped back, shook his head again, then turned and poured himself a glass of brandy. He took a large draught, swallowed it slowly, then lighted a cigarette with a small pocket lighter, all the while never taking his eyes off Mac who stood defiantly before him.

"Why did I kill your brother..." The question was repeated as a statement. The colonel stared at Mac in surprise—what was this all about? The colonel circled behind Mac regarding him with some interest...was it possible that he had at long last come across a thoughtful American? One capable of an abstract question? Very well, he would give him an answer.

"It goes back a long way, Mr. McCan," said the Baron. "Before you were born...It goes back forty years." The colonel circled behind Mac once again, his mind rewinding to recall long suppressed memories. He stopped, and spoke to the back of Mac's head. "My family came to America because we were told it was the land of opportunity. My father and mother settled in California, and sent my sister and me to school. We learned. It was a happy time. I became a teacher. A teacher of mathematics."

Colonel Nishi walked in circles around Mac as he spoke. He no longer looked at Mac, but seemed to be gazing into the distance beyond the confining walls of the dismal cell that contained them. "Mood Indigo" continued to play. Mac thought of Flapper Jackson, also a teacher of mathematics.

Colonel Nishi continued. "Your name is Booker T.... I wonder if you know anything about the man you are named for?"

Mac was startled. He had never thought much about his name.

"In nineteen fifteen, the year Booker T. Washington died, I came to Tuskegee Institute in Alabama to teach mathematics. Booker T. Washington founded that school. He knew that education was important, and he built a fine institution at Tuskegee. I was proud to be part of it."

Mac listened in gathering amazement...why was this man telling him this story?

The colonel continued. "I was educated in California, but when I came to Alabama I received a different kind of education. I saw a different side of America. I saw meanness. I saw ignorance. I saw hate. I saw hypocrisy. I saw uneducated white people trying to prove their own worthiness by degrading intelligent and sensitive black professors. I experienced the same degrading practices because, even though I wasn't black, I was different. I was yellow, and I had slanty eyes."

The colonel stopped pacing, and stood facing Mac, looking into his eyes. Mac, his upper body still roped, returned the gaze, never blinking. "Do you know what I'm talking about...NIGGER?" The last word was a shout. Mac blinked. He was confused. This man was the enemy he had sworn to kill. He thought about Kevin O'Keefe. He thought about Bucks Fulton. He thought about his billet as a mess attendant. He thought about his brother Davey as a mess attendant. Colonel Nishi, looking deep into Mac's eyes, found a flicker of understanding.

"Listen carefully, young man," he said, and resumed pacing. He spoke as he paced. "I thought it would be different in the north, so I moved to St. Louis, and began teaching at Soldan High School. In the summer I played baseball." The colonel stopped in front of Mac to see his reaction to this news. Mac was puzzled.

"Yes, baseball," said the colonel. "Does that surprise you? Did you know that baseball is the national game of Japan? You see our countries are not as different as you might think."

This piece of news hit Mac hard. It did not seem right. His anger at the Japanese flared again—another treacherous act; baseball was America's game.

"I was a very good baseball player," the colonel mused, again seeing beyond the walls, talking aloud to himself. "I was a pitcher." He smiled as he recalled desperate lunges at his deliveries.

But now his smile disappeared, and he turned back to Mac. "Our team was called 'the All Nations'," he said. "Listen carefully, McCan, this is important. On that team were three white men...a Catholic, a Protestant, and a Jew...there were also five Negroes, two Cubans, a Hawaiian, an American Indian, and me, a Japanese. If baseball is a metaphor for life, and it is, this team proved to all who could see that people of different races can get along with each other and work together for the benefit of all."

Mac knew little of metaphor. He had once played basketball in Metamora, a hamlet near Peoria, but he, too, had teamed with players of mixed and wildly diverse backgrounds, origins, and beliefs. He was unmoved by the colonel's words. What was there to prove? He remained defiant.

"That team was good enough to compete with the best teams in the country, and we proved it on the field many times. We beat teams with Ty Cobb and Babe Ruth on them." The colonel said it with pride in his voice, and paused to savor the thought. Like all former ball players, when he jogged his memory he could recall singular pitches and plays years after the event. He remembered the sound, and his disgust, when Ruth's bat crashed against what he thought was one of his better pitches.

"Two of the white men on 'the All Nations,' went on to play in the Major Leagues, but the rest of us were not allowed, and believe me it wasn't because we weren't good enough."

The colonel stopped for a moment, as a different thought crossed his mind. He turned again to Mac and said, "Some people blamed your namesake, Booker T. Washington. He once made an important speech in which he said that Negroes and whites should be separated. The powerful white community loved that, and it became the law." He paused. "...In nineteen twenty the Negro National Baseball League was formed, and I got a job playing for the St. Louis Giants. Those were exciting times." Colonel Nishi's eyes shone as he thought of those times. "Think of it, Booker T.," he said, "I was paid to play baseball! Not a pittance either, five dollars a game, and sometimes a bonus for a good performance. Oh, yes. Exciting times. What did we care if the white leagues wouldn't let us in? We had our own league, and we felt good about it. The league had a motto: 'We are the ship, all else the sea.'" The colonel smiled sadly. "Brave words. Defiant words, and yet sorrowful...A ship is always at the mercy of the sea."

As he talked, the colonel paced back and forth, smoking one cigarette after another. He walked to the corner of the room and changed the record that had been turning for some time with no music coming out. He carefully lifted the needle and placed the arm in its cradle. He looked through a stack of black 78 rpm records until he found the one he wanted. He placed it on the rotating turntable and set the needle. The haunting sounds of Billie Holiday singing "Melancholy Baby" filled the room. Momentarily the colonel stood quietly, thinking about the ship, the sea, and the melancholy. Then he resumed pacing.

"The nineteen twenties were good years for me. In the winter I taught mathematics at Soldan High School, and in the summer I played baseball for the St. Louis Stars who replaced the Giants in nineteen twenty-two. That was the year the St. Louis Browns almost won the white American League pennant. George Sisler hit four twenty, but they still lost to the Yankees...by just one game. That loss took on great meaning for me as the years passed. I began to see the Yankees as white America and the Browns as brown America. Another metaphor, Booker T."

Another metaphor. Mac's mind was racing. He was listening carefully, as instructed. White America, brown america. Metaphor. He thought of the glorious sunset on the broad Pacific that night on the troop transport out of San Francisco. He thought of Holy Communion. Metaphor. White America, brown america. Yankees, browns.

The colonel continued. "Beginning with that heart-wrenching loss in nineteen twenty-two, I saw the competition deteriorate, and the Browns took some fearsome beatings over the years." The Colonel turned suddenly to look at Mac and asked, "What year were you born?"

"Nineteen twenty-eight," answered Booker T.

The colonel thought for a moment, looked at Mac sadly, and placed his open palm gently on Mac's cheek. "So young," he said.

Mac flushed in embarrassment. His anger was slipping into curiosity. Did this man really care about him? Or was it just another deception?

"Nineteen twenty-eight," said the colonel. "Yes. The Browns finished third with their new first baseman…Lu Blue. The Yankees ruled. They swept the Cardinals in the World Series. Gehrig homered once in game two, twice in game three, and once in game four. Ruth homered three times in game four. It was brutal. In nineteen thirty-nine the Browns hit bottom: one hundred eleven losses. I, too, hit bottom: too old to play baseball…battered by the Depression. The Browns were me. I was the browns."

Colonel Nishi stopped pacing long enough to change the record. This time it was Lena Horne singing "Stormy Weather." He walked back to the desk, took a handful of steel-tipped darts out of a drawer, and began slinging them in an underhand motion at a corkboard attached to a far wall. The circular board was painted into pie-shaped sections lettered with baseball symbols: 3B, FO, KO, SAC, etc. In the center was a small circle with the symbol HR.

"I always went to Sportsmans Park when the Yankees came to town. Hoping. Hoping this would be the day things would change. It was cruel. The Yankees were so powerful…the Browns were so helpless. Few could stand to watch the ridicule. One day I counted fifty-four people in the grandstand and ten in the bleachers. The park could hold thirty six thousand. It was nineteen thirty-nine; hope had yielded to despair. Do you understand despair, Booker T.?"

Mac had seen despair in the eyes of men sitting on the back steps of his Peoria home, eating the food his mother had prepared. But a new thought boiled to the surface of his understanding. With the Japanese attack on Pearl Harbor, despair had given way to exhilaration. The U.S. was alive and full of purpose. Should we thank the Japanese? Mac did not feel despair at this moment, but he sensed that the colonel did.

"The Browns had an unexcelled ability to break their fans' hearts. How can I forget the day they led the Yankees by two runs with nobody on base and two men out in the top of the ninth? Then, with the suddenness of doom the Yankees loaded the bases on an error and two walks, and brought Gehrig to the plate. In nineteen thirty-nine Gehrig was a dying man, but with a bat in his hand he was still dangerous, and God knows, a man who had punished the Browns unmercifully over the years." The colonel paused as he remembered.

"There was an irony here. Gehrig was a fine man, unthreatened by, and unafraid to speak out for the browns. He saw no reason why they should be prevented from playing in the Major Leagues, and he said so. He, like all the others, played against the browns in exhibition games. He saw the absurdity when brown Cubans like Roberto Estalella were not considered Negroes because they could speak Spanish and so were allowed to play. Your country, Booker T., is riddled with paradox...massive and senseless ill treatment of minorities...beacons of outrage like Gehrig." Once again the colonel paused to reflect.

"Your country is riddled with paradox...AND SO IS MINE!" He threw a handful of darts at the board in an outburst of fury and frustration.

The colonel stalked back and forth, wanting his boiling rage to subside. Only slowly did it do so. He would speak again. He wanted to make his point. Like all the best teachers, he became so lost in his logical thought train that he forgot his audience. Mac was but an onlooker. An onlooker taking furious mental notes. With the last outburst, a new parameter had been introduced into the equation. Mac was beginning to see. Captured by the colonel's intensity, no longer being lectured, he waited for the next point in the lesson. He imagined Gehrig, the good-hearted Yankee, husbanding his energy with slow and menacing bat strokes, glaring with murderous, but not evil, intent at the reluctant pitcher. He imagined the besieged Brownie hurler, the brown, grinding the ball into his hip, walking off the mound to pick up the rosin bag, avoiding the confrontation, seeing the dancing base runners, wishing he did not have to deliver the ball...hoping for a miracle.

"I was afraid to look," the colonel continued. "What I heard made me wince. The crack of ball meeting solid wood. When I looked up I saw the runners circling the bases at the top of their speed. But I also saw, to my amazement, the first baseman camping under a ball hit so high it was almost out of sight. Gehrig had hit it up the elevator shaft, home run distance, but straight up. So high that all three runners, almost as if they knew something, had crossed the plate when the ball finally came down as it had to do…even the Yankees were powerless before the laws of physics. But there is no law that an infield pop up will be caught, and as the ball descended I knew with sickening certainty that it was another cruel joke, and of course, the ball was dropped."

Colonel Nishi slammed a dart with overhand fury into the board.

"I stayed in America one more painful year before returning to Japan. What decided me finally to leave the land of opportunity after thirty years was a symbolic act that demonstrated to me with great clarity that it was not only the browns in America who were downtrodden, mistreated, and exploited, but in fact, all the people were victims, all the people were browns, with the notable exceptions of the wealthy few. Victims of an ethic that exalts only gluttonous and insatiable commerce."

Colonel Nishi slammed a dart into the very center of the board, marked HR, placed Franz Liszt's "Le Prelude" on the turntable, and turned up the volume.

"It was the exiling of a popular hero because he had the temerity to demand payment equal to his worth. Joe Medwick traded to the Brooklyn Dodgers for Ernie Koy and a hundred thousand dollars. Like the Japanese army trading General Kuribayashi to the U.S. Marines for Booker T. McCan and a bag of gold."

A symphony of violins and trumpets swelled to majestic crescendo as the sounds of Liszt's great tone poem flowed over the room.

"Medwick was a St. Louis Cardinal. The fans called him 'Ducky Joe' and 'Muscles.' They loved him, and for good reason. The year before he was traded he had seventy extra base hits, twice as many singles, drove in a hundred seventeen runs, and that was an off year for him. The Cardinals refused to pay him the eighteen thousand dollars he thought he was worth. The St. Louis fans were shocked by the trade, nobody in management asked them what they thought. Nobody in management cared. But the fans cared. Young boys cried, and tried to understand. Old men swore, and tried to understand. Ducky Joe was just reaching his prime. He was twenty-eight years old. For me it was the final blow. I returned to Japan looking for something better."

Colonel Nishi hung his head sadly, gently laid his darts on the table, and once more changed the phonograph record. Mac heard the mournful sounds of Billie Holiday singing "St. Louis Blues."

"And so at last, my adolescent antagonist, we come to the point…why did I kill your brother? I killed him because I, like all of us, am a victim. Foolish and helpless before the crushing power of people and events. In the name of duty required to act on the whims of anonymous brokers. I expected something different when I returned to my native land, but it was a childish and naive expectation. And so I killed your brother and many others, and saw my brothers killed in return. And for what? None of us knew why we were killing except that it was our patriotic duty. What price, glory? Indeed."

Colonel Nishi stopped to face Mac. "Go home, Booker T. McCan," he said. "This is not your war. Stop killing. Take what you have learned back to those you love. Try to make them understand."

The last thing Mac remembered was the soaring clarinet of George Gershwin's "Rhapsody in Blue."

>>11<<

MOMENT OF TRUTH

What is that smell? I never smelled that before. It's making me sick. Why am I so dizzy? I feel like I'm going to puke. Stop this train, I need to get off.

STOP THE TRAIN!

Where's the conductor? Tell the engineer to slow down. This roadbed is too rough to go this fast.

STOP THE TRAIN!

I need help.

WE ALL NEED HELP.

Somebody has to do something or we'll all be turned into hamburger.

SOMEBODY DO SOMETHING!

Oh good grief! We're coming to a tunnel. Why am I on top of the train? I have to get back inside the car. Why don't they stop the train? We're going too fast. Too fast.

WE'RE GOING TO CRASH!

We're going to…

))))))))))))))))))))))))))))))O((((((((((((((((((((((((((((((

CRASH! CRASH! CRASH!

The two running Marines dropped the litter, and rolled into a shell hole trying to avoid the crashing mortar shells that were exploding all around them. Mac sat up on the litter, blinking his eyes and looking around in a state of profound confusion. He saw one of the Marines waving his arms wildly. At first he did not understand, and then, in a flash, he did. He dove headfirst into the shallow excavation alongside the two huddled Marines just as a mortar shell shattered the litter.

"Jeez, Mac, you must be living right," said one of the Marines. Mac looked at him dumbly.

How did I get here? What happened to Colonel Nishi? I know I'm not dreaming now...that mortar shell was real. Where's Flapper? I'm not hurt. Why was I on that litter?

"Why was I on that litter? I'm not hurt."

The Marine litter bearers looked at each other and shrugged. One said, "We found you up there, half buried under a pile of rocks and gravel. If you ain't hurt, yer one of the few around here who ain't, and you got more luck than a bald-assed burglar."

Mac spoke excitedly. "I need to get back to my ship," he said. "No. Wait. I need to find Flapper. Where's Flapper?"

"You may not be hurt, Mac but yer sure as hell screwed up. Why don't ya just lay quiet 'til they ease up on those fuckin' mortars? It won't be long, the bastards are just harassing, then we'll get you down to an aid station where a Doc can have a look at ya."

Mac shook his head. "No, no, I'm okay," he said. "I just need to find Flapper."

"Okay, Mac, I give up. What's a Flapper?"

"Not what, who. Flapper is the shore fire control officer from the *Indianapolis*. I'm his spotter."

The litter bearers looked at each other. "Whaddaya think, Art?" said one. "Should we leave this bird, and go look for somebody who really needs us?"

Art nodded. "Yer right, Squid," he said, "this guy can find his own way. Let's get the hell outta here."

"Okay. Listen, Mac," said Squid. "Why don't you just head over that way," he pointed, "and look for the battalion command post, maybe they can help you find Flopper. But for Christ sake keep yer head down...shit, you ain't even got a helmet."

Mac put his hand on top of his head as if to verify that he did not have a helmet. He shrugged and said, "Not Flopper, Flapper."

"Whatever," said Squid.

Mac said, "His name is Flapper," then added, "Thanks for bringin' me back."

"Don't mention it, Mac, it's our job. Come on, Squid, let's get the hell outta here."

Mac didn't know that the Marine litter bearers had the shortest life expectancy of any group in the landing force. Neither did he know the job was alphabetically assigned in boot camp to the newest and least experienced; at this stage of the war the Marines were far from an all-volunteer outfit.

Eighteen-year-old boys were being drafted. The 16 young litter bearers that landed with the headquarters company of the 3rd battalion, 25th Marine regiment, all had surnames beginning with the letter B. In the grotesque and deranged world of 1945 there was survival value in having your surname begin with Z.

Mac said, "Before you go, can you tell me what day it is?"

"It's Wednesday, Mac."

Mac had one more question. It concerned the sweet sickening smell that permeated the air. "One more thing," he said. "What's that smell?"

The two Marines responded almost in unison as they clambered out of the crater, "It's death."

They looked at the hole in the ground, and the shattered fragments of their former litter, then at each other. "We ain't got no litter, Art," said the Marine called Squid.

"Damned if we do, Squid. We gotta go back to the aid station…Let's go." He took a step, then stopped and turned to Mac, "Listen, Mac," he said, "why don't you follow us? It's back towards the beach, but it makes more sense than tryin' to cut across no-man's land lookin' for battalion headquarters. We got enough to do without pickin' you up again."

In 10 minutes they were at the aid station. It was a combination aid and evacuation station, set up close to the first terrace, 75 yards from the water. Doctors and corpsmen were working within a 20-square yard area roughly defined by a waist high stack of quickly thrown together sandbags. Medical supplies had been dumped on litters all around, and apparently there had been no time to sort them out. Mac saw splints, bandages, packages of sulfanilamide, piles of blankets, bottles of blood plasma, boxes of morphine, and sodium pentothal syrettes. Casualties on stretchers were everywhere. They were placed in rows extending almost to the waterline, awaiting evacuation to the hospital ships. Most of them lay quietly under morphine sedation, patiently waiting to be carried back to civilization, wherever that was. For some it was the beginning of the long trip home. Others with lesser hurts might be back in action sooner than they would like. Many would not live to see the ship. Mac saw a few smiling dreamily. A smile easily translated: *I have survived.* Few here would not have willingly sacrificed an arm or a leg for a life.

Mac recognized the young doctor from the landing craft. The doctor worked diligently and purposefully trying to repair damaged youth. Mac listened attentively as the doctor spoke rapidly to a corpsman. "The black ash is ground into these wounds…no point…no time to clean them here on the beach. Just control the bleeding with pressure dressings. Use tourniquets as needed but be careful…sometimes a tourniquet can cause more harm than good if you don't have time to attend it properly. Administer plasma only if it looks like the patient will die without it…there isn't time and there are so many." He looked around in desperation. "We've got to get them back to the ship as soon as possible." He continued to speak as if he were lecturing a class…or reminding himself. No amount of training could have prepared him for this ordeal. "Treat all abdominal wounds for shock. Cover all penetrating chest wounds with pressure dressings and reinforce with firm strips of adhesive tape. Administer one half grain morphine for pain, and two amytal pills for shell shock." He looked up at the corpsman. "Think you can remember all that?"

"Yessir. That's what they taught us in Corpsman School, sir, thanks for the review."

The doctor said, "Okay, get to work," then noticed Mac. "Hey, Mac, what you standin' there for? If you don't need treatment, and you got nothin' better to do, start filling more sand bags."

Mac picked up a shovel and started to fill bags with the black volcanic ash. Artillery shells began to explode all around; he dived for cover. Mac saw body parts and stretcher fragments fly into the air. The young doctor continued to work.

Can this be true? Are they shelling the wounded? Am I dreaming again?

THIS IS WAR, MAC. THE OBJECT IS TO KILL THE ENEMY. WE ARE THE ENEMY OF THOSE GUNNERS ON THE MOUNTAIN AND UNLESS FLAPPER OR SOMEBODY ELSE DOES SOMETHING QUICK, THEY ARE GOING TO ANNIHILATE EVERYTHING THAT'S MOVING ON THIS BEACH.

Please, God, don't let this happen. Stop this carnage.

HAPPY ARE THE DEAD WHO FROM NOW ON DIE IN THE SERVICE OF THE LORD…LOTTA HAPPY GUYS OUT HERE.

God has forsaken us.

WHAT GOD?

God have mercy.

The shelling slowed, then stopped. Mac could see naval gunfire exploding all across the face of Mount Suribachi. Slowly he got to his feet and surveyed the shattered and still smoking aid and evacuation station. A few doctors and corpsmen were moving around, once again trying to help the wounded. Steam rose from shards of hot killer metal pelted with showers of cool rain. Spruance's vision of agony was understated...wrenching pain permeated and ruled.

"Can I help?" Mac addressed an angry doctor. The doctor was desperate. He looked at Mac and asked, "You know anything about battle dressings?"

Mac said, "No, sir, but I can learn."

The doctor shook his head impatiently. "No time to teach you. Look. Some VP's are landing. You can help, put some casualties aboard."

"Aye, aye, sir." Mac saluted and ran toward the boats.

For 20 minutes Mac helped carry shattered bodies to the landing craft. He saw wounds of every imaginable type, but the majority seemed to be of the extremities, particularly of the legs.

"Ouch! Hey, take it easy, Mac. I ain't a sack of flour, ya know."

Mac had slipped as the boat tilted unexpectedly, causing him to lose his grip on one of the stretcher poles. "Sorry, buddy." Mac was truly sorry. He could only imagine the intense pain, but his imagination was racing.

The coxswain said, "Put him right up there in that rack." The boat was fitted on both sides with attachments to hold the stretchers.

"Okay, that's it. Clear the decks, I'm shovin' off," the coxswain shouted. Mac had to jump from the ramp as it began to close. The coxswain gunned the engine, backed away from the beach, and headed for the offshore armada.

The whole frenetic scene mesmerized Mac.

Now what do I do? I'm not used to making decisions for myself.

WELL MCCAN, OLD BOOKER T., OR WHATEVER YOU'RE CALLING YOURSELF THESE DAYS, IT'S ABOUT TIME YOU STARTED.

Okay. I need to find Flapper, that's where my duty station is. I wonder if he's all right.

OF COURSE HE'S ALL RIGHT. HE'S LIVING UNDER A CHARM JUST LIKE YOU. DID YOU FORGET?

How can I find him?

IF HE'S STILL ON THIS ISLAND. HE MUST BE SOMEWHERE CLOSE TO THE FRONT.

The ships are still firing, he must still be here. Let's see now, which battalion did we come in with?

NOBODY TOLD YOU.

It didn't seem to matter.

WHY DON'T YOU HEAD UP TO THE FRONT WITH A CORPSMAN

OR A TEAM OF LITTER BEARERS?

I don't know.

THEY CAN SHOW YOU WHERE TO GO.

Yeah.

WHEN YOU GET THERE, MAYBE SOMEBODY WILL KNOW WHERE FLAPPER IS.

Yeah...I'm hungry.

MAYBE THERE'S SOME EXTRA K-RATIONS OVER BY THE AID STATION.

I wish the guns would stop.

WHAT ARE YOU GOING TO DO ABOUT COLONEL NISHI?

Who says I have to do anything?

YOU KNOW HE'S RIGHT.

So what if he's right? What can I do about it?

YOU CAN STOP KILLING PEOPLE.

I never killed anybody.

WHAT ABOUT THOSE PILLBOXES YOU SPOTTED?

Those guys were tryin' to kill us...This is getting stupid. I gotta find Flapper.

"Hey, buddy. You headin' up to the front? Can I go with you?" Mac was speaking to a corpsman who was stuffing a bag with battle dressings and plasma units.

The corpsman gave Mac a quick look, and continued with his work. "Ain't you got nothin' better to do?" he asked. "You some kind of spectator or somethin'? This ain't no football game, you know."

"I got separated from my outfit," Mac explained, "and I'm tryin' to find 'em. They must be up front somewhere. It's a shore fire control party from the *Indianapolis.* Just show me where to go if you can."

The corpsman continued to fill his bag; he spoke without looking up. "You from Flapper Jackson's outfit?"

Mac became excited. "Yeah. Yeah. That's it. How'd you know about Flapper?"

"I've seen Flapper in action before. At Peleliu and Saipan. He's the best."

"Have you seen him here? Is he still here? Where is he? Can you help me find him?"

"Okay, okay. Slow down. I think I have an idea where he is." The corpsman looked up at Mac and said, "Look, if yer comin' with me you can carry some supplies. You know anything about first aid?"

Mac was eager. "Not much," he said, "but I can learn." The corpsman nodded and said, "Sure you can. What's yer name? Mine's J.D."

"I'm Booker T. McCan from Peoria. People call me Mac."

"Okay, Mac, fill these two bags with some of this stuff. Two plasma units in each bag, battle dressings, triangular bandages. Fill your pockets with some of those morphine syrettes. You got a sharp knife? You may have to help cut clothing away from wounds. Here take this one, I'll get another. You ain't squeamish, are ya?"

Mac shook his head and said, "Not anymore."

"Okay, take some of those disposable scalpels, and you better get a helmet. Sometimes they help."

Mac had no trouble finding a steel helmet, the beach was littered with them, along with all manner of other equipment. There was no time to clean up the mess, even the most fastidious company commander had better things to do. The sounds of combat crashed, echoed, and reverberated all around, particularly to the northeast. Death and destruction ruled.

The weather had turned foul. Iwo Jima was about the same latitude as Miami, and in February it could be, as it now was, cold and rainy. To the attacking 25th Marines, as to the defending Japanese Second Mixed Brigade, it made little difference. Their blood mixed no less efficiently with black volcanic mud than it did with black volcanic ash. Their misery and terror were already spilling over the top of the scale, and what was cold rain compared to a redhot spinning mortar fragment?

J.D. was ready to move. "Okay, Mac, let's go," he yelled.

Mac scrambled after the hospital corpsman, up the steep bank, across 100 yards of level ground leading to the second terrace, and on to the third terrace. Now they turned toward airfield number two where the fighting seemed heaviest. Mac saw ruined pillboxes, their thick concrete walls turned to rubble by the immensity of naval firepower. Steel rods, intended to reinforce the concrete, were twisted and bent at odd and bizarre angles, serving now as prime targets for the combat photographer's camera. The smell of death was in the air.

Soon they were among the fighters, and J.D. went immediately to work, Mac at his elbow, watching and learning. J.D. was a natural teacher, explaining everything as he went along. Cries of "corpsman, corpsman" could be heard up and down the line as the Marines moved ahead, pressing the attack. J.D. worked quickly and efficiently like the professional he was, seemingly unmoved by the ghastly sight of ripped and bleeding human flesh. He put pressure dressings on abdominal wounds and treated them for shock. He wrapped broken ribs with adhesive tape. He splinted broken arms and legs. He eased the pain with intravenous morphine. He placed a breathing tube below a torn windpipe. Seeing an unconscious Marine bleeding profusely from the neck, he quickly stripped away tissue with a scalpel and clamped the jugular vein.

J.D. took advantage of a lull in the action to light a cigarette. He sat with his back against a hillock and inhaled deeply. Then he looked at Mac and said, "Well, whatta ya think, Mac. Can ya do it?"

Mac said, "I'd like to try, J.D. Seems like you'd feel a lot better savin' lives than takin' em'."

J.D. agreed. "Yeah," he said.

Mac asked, "How many lives have you saved, J.D.?"

J.D. shook his head. "Who knows?" he asked rhetorically. "Hundreds…maybe thousands. I don't count. I just do my job."

Mac said, "You must be one of the best. I never saw anything like what you just been doin'. Amazing. Do you think I could ever be as good as you?"

"Sure you could," said the pleased J.D. "I could teach you. Might take a while though. You still lookin' for Flapper?"

In the excitement and fascination of watching J.D. save lives, Mac had forgotten about Flapper. He said, "I almost forgot, watchin' you operate. Yeah, I better find Flapper."

J.D. stroked his chin and said, "Well look, the last time I saw him he was down in that section over there." He pointed. "Maybe if you kinda nosed over that way, and asked some people as you went, you might catch up with him."

Mac got to his feet. "Okay," he said. "Thanks, J.D., that's what I'll do…Are you stationed on a ship? Where can I get in touch with you?"

J.D. shook his head. "No ship," he said. "Just 25th regiment, 4th Marine division…J.D. Poker. And don't tell me, I already know…I'm an ace."

Mac laughed and started to move away. He moved cautiously down the line, behind the attacking Marines, stepping over tumbled and smashed rocks, shattered trees, and the forlorn remains of low bushes. As he made his way down a gully and around a large boulder, he heard a groan. Following the sound he came upon a soldier lying face down on the muddy earth. He could see blood oozing from a jagged hole in the man's back. Quickly and gently he turned the unconscious man on his side to assess further damage. It was a Japanese soldier. For a moment, Mac was stunned at the recognition, then he quickly reached in his pocket and withdrew the sharp knife J.D. Poker had given him.

>>12<<

ALL THE BLOOD WAS RED

Dear Ma and Pa, March 1, 1945

I'm sorry I didn't write more often. I hope you didn't worry too much. I remember how we waited to hear from Davey. I know it's hard not to but please don't worry about me, really I'm fine and I'm sure I'll be coming home soon. Everybody says the war will be over before long. I can't tell you where I am because of war secrets and you probly wouldn't know even if I told you but there's probly something about it in the Journal or the Star.

You wouldn't believe how lucky I've been. You probly don't remember one of my teachers at Manual. His name is Mr. Jackson and he was my Math teacher and I thought he was a good teacher and all the kids liked him a lot. Well anyway, he's an officer on my ship! Isn't that something? I get to see him a lot and he's helped me learn a lot of things. Also we talk a lot about God and things like that. I knew you'd like that Ma. When you see some of the things I've seen you can't help thinking about God. But don't worry, I'm safe now that I'm back on the ship. Remember when preacher Black read from the Bible where it said: "happy are the dead who from now on die in the service of the Lord?" All I can say is there's a lot of happy people around here.

Maybe I can tell you some of the things that have been happening to me. First, I don't think I'm the same as I was when I left home. At home, you know, everybody always called me Booker T. because that was my name and that's what everybody called me. But when I left home and went to boot camp at Great Lakes last summer, I became a different person and people started calling me Mac. In actual fact, I liked being called Mac. It sort of made me feel like I was growing up and that I wasn't a little kid anymore. Well, after what happened to me last week, which I can't tell you about right now, I'm ready to change my name again because I'm not the same person I was before. I don't want to sound like I'm boasting because I remember what you taught me about that, but I think I'm grown up now. Maybe it's not boasting to say you're grown up.

Anyway, my new name is going to be Boats. That may sound like a funny name to you but in the Navy it's not. A lot of people have that name in the Navy because it means that their job has something to do with taking care of the boats on a ship and also the anchors and things like that. So this is a big change in my life because of that too. It means I'm not going to be a mess attendant anymore. But I'll still be on the same ship so you don't have to worry about that. It's a good ship and everybody likes it. You probly wonder what is the difference between a ship and a boat. Well the difference is that a boat is small enough to be carried by a ship but not the other way around.

I hope you're feeling better Ma. The last letter I got from you was about three weeks ago and you said the winter was bad and that you were having a hard time. I'm not allowed to tell you about the weather here but its not like Peoria. I finally got the Christmas cookies you sent. Thank you. They tasted real good and my friend Gabe said tell you thanks and that his favorite way to eat cookies is with a spoon.

How you doin' Pa? I hope you will send me all the news from school. How is the basketball team doing? I bet not as good as last year. That was some team we had last year wasn't it? I wonder what some of those guys are doing now. Probly gettin' shot at somewhere. But you don't have to worry about me, I'm about as safe as I can be. I got a nice warm place to sleep, dry too which is more than a lot of guys out here can say. I'm getting enough to eat too and the food on the ship is pretty good. Not as good as yours though Ma. Sometimes I think about your chicken and dumplings and then I get homesick so I try to think about other things. Most of the time we get plenty of time to think about things out here.

So after all that I want to tell you about some of the things I've been thinking about now and how I think my life will be different from now on because I'm not the same person I used to be. You remember how I always said I wanted to join the Navy so I could kill some Japs for Davey? Well I've changed my mind and I don't want to kill anybody anymore. Maybe if you see Count you could tell him that. I think he might be interested. The way it happened was funny and I'm not sure I can explain it exactly. I think it came in a dream but I'm not exactly sure. Anyway there was this guy who looked like Count but was really a Jap Colonel. He was wearing a Saint Louis Browns baseball cap so it must have been a dream, right? But he started telling me this story about when he lived in America and how bad he was treated because of his color and that all colored people in America were treated bad just because they weren't white. He said some people blamed Booker T. Washington because he said it was okay to keep Negroes and Whites separate in America and that was what the white people wanted to hear because they said that White blood was different from Negro blood and it shouldn't mix. But Ma and Pa I can tell you I've seen a lot of blood out here and all of it is red.

The next thing he told me was that rich people in America and in Japan were to blame for the war and why should little people like us have to do all the dirty work and the killing? So what good would it do me if I killed some Japs who really had nothing to do with killing Davey and were only trying to get through the war so they could go home to their families? Well the next thing that happened, and this was not a dream, was that I ended up saving a Jap soldier's life. Just think, I came all the way out here to kill Japs for Davey and end up saving one's life. It was really very easy. All I had to do was put a pressure battle dressing on his stomach and back and treat him for shock. I learned how to do it from a Navy coreman named J.D. Poker. That's a funny name isn't it?

Well, I got to go on watch now. I'm learning how to be a helmsman. It's really interesting. I'll tell you all about it when I get home. So like I said, don't worry about me, I'm fine.

Love from your son,
Boats McCan

>>13<<

AN IDEA THUNDERS IN THE NIGHT

The great warship, buttoned up tight, cruised like a phantom in the night at a comfortable eighteen knots, creating a wide wake that stretched for miles through the pacific waters of the northern Philippine sea. The night was ink-black. Flapper Jackson and Boats McCan, sitting on a tightly dogged hatch, three feet apart, on the fantail of *Indianapolis*, could not see each other. Mesmerized by the phosphorescent glow emanating from the churning water of the wake, they sat quietly for a long time, alone with their thoughts, trying to make sense of what was happening to them; their thoughts seethed like the wake. In a three week period they had been slammed like a ping pong ball from the cataclysmic savagery of Iwo Jima, to the ephemeral "peace" of a wild and frenzied five day interlude on Ulithi, complete with Navy nurses and a boogie-woogie band, and now to the apprehension of the two days hence assault on Okinawa. Even a veteran like Flapper Jackson was having difficulty. For a 17-year-old still reeling from his first encounter with violent death, it was like being a straw in a tornado.

Boats spoke quietly. "Sometimes I think the whole thing is a dream," he said.

Flapper stirred and responded. "It's not a dream, Booker T., it's a nightmare." To those who had known him in Peoria, he would always be Booker T. no matter what he decided to call himself.

"How did we survive, Flapper? How could anybody survive Iwo?"

Flapper shook his head and shrugged, but did not answer immediately. He pondered the question, sensing that Boats wanted an answer. At length he said simply, "I don't know."

"Were the other landings that bad?"

Flapper always had an answer for that question. "The landing at Tarawa was worse, but the fighting after the landing was worse at Iwo."

Flapper turned philosophical, a survival tactic in its own right. "To survive has to be a miracle." He paused, gathering his thoughts. "It's like being in a rainstorm and not getting wet." Another long pause he said, "Those that survive must have a special destiny."

Boats, with his own sense of destiny, said, "I prayed hard on that beach. I prayed for God to stop the shelling of the wounded. I don't think God heard me. How does it work, Flapper? Is prayer worth anything?"

Once again Flapper took a long time to answer. The questions were getting harder, and he was only a teacher of mathematics. But teachers are compelled to provide answers, and interminable nights at sea inevitably led to examination of fundamental beliefs. Finally he spoke...hesitantly...searching for words he hoped would emerge in a coherent form. "It's about faith, Booker T.," he said. "You know about that...I confess that my faith is being severely tested. I see the slaughter on the islands and say to myself...no God could allow it. Why kid myself? There is no God; or if there is, He is mean and vindictive which is even worse than not having a God at all."

He paused to organize his churning thoughts. Boats moved to the edge of his seat. Flapper continued. "Or...are these Christian martyrs, sacrificed like Jesus to redeem mankind from mortal sin? I'm not a religious scholar, Booker T., but these things have occurred to me. I have seen men spiritually uplifted after kneeling in shell holes for church services punctuated with exploding shells. The preacher has told them that things will be better in Heaven, and why shouldn't they believe him?"

Flapper paused before continuing. Boats waited. "...Look at all those stars, Booker T.," he said at last. "How can anyone see that and not believe in Divine presence? It's awesome."

Boats remembered nights in Peoria looking at the stars, seeing the Big Dipper and Orion's belt. Then it was possible to count the number of stars in the sky. Here, on the wide ocean, with no competition from city lights, it was a different planet. Twinkling points of light so numerous they masked the black void beyond, illuminating the water with beams moving at 186,000 miles every second. Flapper turned pedantic. "Booker T., do you know what a light-year is?"

Boats answered, "I don't think so. Something to do with time?"

"Not time, Booker T., distance. A light-year is a measure of distance; it's how far a beam of light travels in one year. Do you know how fast light travels?"

Boats imagined himself back in Homer Jackson's classroom; it was not an unpleasant thought. He rummaged his memory files, and found the answer under algebra. "A hundred eighty six thousand miles per second," he said proudly.

Flapper nodded. "Good, Booker T.," he said. "So tell me how many miles light travels in one year." Flapper could not resist; his Socratic instincts ran deep.

"I could figure it out."

"I know you could, Booker T.," Flapper said. "But let me ask you another question. Do you know what a quadrillion is?"

Boats cocked his head and furrowed his brow. "I just know it's an awful big number," he said.

Flapper nodded. "It sure is," he said. "Think about this. If you multiply a million by one thousand you get a billion, if you multiply a billion by one thousand you get a trillion, and if you multiply a trillion by one thousand you get a quadrillion. Now listen to this…in one year, light travels almost six quadrillion miles, and that's what a light-year is."

Flapper was pleased with his explanation; it was as if he had cleared something up in his own mind. He smiled in satisfaction, but his lecture was not finished. "Now, one more thing, Booker T.," he said. "Our sun is a star…only about two hundred and fifty thousand miles away from us, but the next nearest star is almost thirty quadrillion miles away. For some reason, astronomers prefer to say the nearest star, after the sun, is five light-years away. Any way you look at it, those stars out there are so far from us it's beyond comprehension. And try to imagine how far away from each other they are…there's an awful lot of empty space out there."

Boats was trying hard to keep up…it was not hard to believe that the galactic distances were galactic.

Flapper seemed to be finished, but then remembered. "…But wait, I almost forgot…I must mention one of my favorite math terms: the concept of infinity. In mathematics, if a sequence or series of numbers increases without limits, in other words continues to grow indefinitely, the mathematician, to bring order to his equations, says that the limit on the sequence is infinity. Does that make any sense to you, Booker T.?"

Boats scratched his head. He had always done well in mathematics. He said, "Yeah, I think so." Then his mind jumped to the stars as he understood what Flapper was getting at. "So the space beyond the stars never ends, is that it, Flapper?"

A rumble of thunder reached them over the beat of the ship's propellers, although the sky was clear.

Flapper mused. “Listen to that thunder, Booker T.,” he said. “The poet, Ernest Sommerfeld, wrote, ‘An idea thunders in the night...God is saying his prayers...how long ‘til dawn?’ Maybe that’s how it is, Booker T....God, somewhere out there in His infinite Universe, created the Earth and everything on it, and now it’s up to us. He wants to see what we’ll do with it. When He sees us killing each other, He prays we stop.”

Boats’ eyes widened. “God is saying His prayers?”

Flapper sat quietly, letting the thunderous thought percolate. Finally he said wistfully, “Why not? It would explain much. I think we have to look to our poets for answers to these questions...if there are any answers.”

Once again they sat quietly, feeling the rhythm of the ship, looking at the constellations, silenced in the presence of the infinite.

At long last, Boats broke the spell. Young minds can take only so much of the infinite; something earthly was on his mind. “Flapper?”

“Yeah?”

“I need to talk to you about Colonel Nishi.”

“What?”

“About what happened to me that night I left you and Isaac in the foxhole, and went with Sergeant Joe on the night attack.”

“You said Colonel Nishi?”

It was a long story, and Booker T. told it without interruption from Flapper. He described what happened to him from the time he left Flapper and Isaac in the foxhole to the time, two days later, when he was thrilled to hear Flapper’s frantic voice shouting: “Booker T.!” Only to be chilled when he heard Flapper scream: “Don’t move! You’re in the middle of a minefield!” Only then had he noticed the series of small yellow flags, carefully placed by Marine combat engineers to mark the buried mankillers.

Finally with his tale complete, Boats McCan turned to Flapper, the man who had just given him insight into the agonies of God, with a simpler question requiring an infinitely more complex answer, “Why, Flapper? Why can’t Negroes play ball for the St. Louis Browns?”

Flapper Jackson, the perpetual pedagogue, loved nothing better than answering a question with a question of his own that might lead the student in the direction of understanding. He thought he had an answer to Booker T.’s question, incomplete though it might be, like the elusive search for proofs of certain mathematical puzzles. His mind raced for a line of thought that would lead to enlightenment, if not understanding.

"Booker T., do you know the word Semite?"

Boats said, "I think I've heard the word in church, but I'm not sure what it means. Something to do with the Bible?"

Flapper said, "Yes, in the Old Testament story of Noah, in the book of Genesis, we learn that the peoples descended from Shem, Noah's oldest son, became known as Semites. Many of the people living today near the Eastern shore of the Mediterranean Sea, some Arabs, some Jews, are Semites. Today the term most often refers to Jews alone. Many of the ancient Jews, the descendants of Shem, moved North from the land of Israel and settled all over Europe where they thrived. But over the centuries a new religion took hold in Europe; it was called Christianity. It was inevitable that there would be conflict even though Christians and Jews claimed to worship one God. More than a thousand years after the birth of Jesus, someone in the church of Rome got the hideous idea that anyone who did not accept the doctrines of the Roman Catholic Church was guilty of heresy and must be punished. And so the church established a tribunal that lasted almost seven hundred years to investigate and punish those who did not follow church doctrine. You can imagine how much pain and suffering that brought about in the name of God, and you can also imagine that the Jews were prime targets for the inquisitions that followed. It was probably about this time that God began saying his prayers.

"In the Middle Ages, the belief arose in Europe that Jews were killing Christian children, and using their blood for religious rituals, so the Jews became known as blood-suckers. From that time on and it continues today, Jews in Europe have been reviled, feared, and persecuted. I know this, Booker T., because my father told me the story of how his father came to America from Germany in eighteen seventy to escape the injustices. When my father returned from France after World War I he wanted to erase Judaism from our family background so he changed the family name to Jackson, and moved us to the anonymity of the city…the city was St. Louis, where we made a fresh start.

"What has this to do with the St. Louis Browns? It is only to make the point that God appears powerless to prevent discrimination, persecution, injustice, and cruelty to families, clans, tribes, and populations solely because of differences in belief, culture, and, God help us, skin color.

"The world is young, Booker T., only four thousand years of recorded history. What is that compared to a light-year? We marvel at the stupidity that caused young women to be burned as witches in our country only three hundred years ago. Imagine what future generations will think of us for preventing Negroes from playing on the St. Louis Browns because they couldn't speak Spanish. Or what they will think of us for sending thousands of light brigades charging into the valley of death as men have done for centuries, often in the name of religion? Progress toward an ethical world society is measured in millimicrometers, Booker T., but let me tell you this: that progress is nudged forward every time someone chooses to spare a life as you did with that Japanese soldier."

Boats sat in stunned silence at this revelation. Saving the Japanese soldier's life had left him with a warm feeling, but to think that simple act was a nudge toward an ethical world society was a bit deep for him. He was not even sure what an ethical world society was. He was also reflecting on Flapper's Jewish background. He remembered his shock one Sunday morning in Peoria when Preacher IQ Black had solemnly told the congregation that the Jews killed Christ. When his thoughts began spiraling into confused dead ends he decided to change the subject.

"Flapper, do you know anything about Okinawa?"

Flapper, too, was ready to steer away from philosophy, though he felt the vague satisfaction, reserved for teachers, of knowing that he had just learned more than the student had. The thought flitted through his mind that maybe he should have been a rabbi.

"Okinawa is one of the Japanese home islands, Booker T. It's a lot bigger than Iwo Jima. Word in the wardroom is that this will be the toughest landing yet, and that's scary because they said Peleliu and Iwo Jima would be easy. The closer we get to Japan the harder they fight. I guess we shouldn't be surprised."

"Flapper, can I go in with you again on the shore fire control party?"

Flapper was surprised at this question. "You still wanta kill Japs?"

Boats said, "No, that's finished. I just want to be with you."

Flapper smiled. "You want to take care of me?" he asked. "I thought it was my job to take care of you. But listen, Booker T., it doesn't matter, because I'm not going in with the landing this time. I think they're saving me for the invasion of Japan."

Another long silence ensued as they watched shooting stars, and thought about Semites, inquisitions, ethical world societies, and the invasion of Japan. Boats broke the silence.

"What will you do when the war's over, Flapper?"

Flapper stood up and walked towards the rail. His eyes had adjusted to the darkness, and he had no trouble reaching the side, marked by a slim restraining cord. It was risky in bright daylight to stand so close to the side; at night, almost foolhardy. He stood no more than ten feet above the rushing ocean sliding by the sleek side of the battle cruiser, looking down at the salty water as if he might find there an answer to Booker T.'s question. The question had been nagging at him since that day on the beach at Tarawa when he knew he would survive the war. He wanted a cigarette, but at night on deck in a battle zone it was out of the question. He shuddered at the thought of falling overboard, imagining what it would be like, alone on the dark sea, seeing your ship disappear over the horizon. He stayed a few moments, then returned to sit next to Boats, picking up the conversation as if he had not been away. "I guess I'll just go back to being Homer Jackson," he said. "I thought about starting a business...try to get rich like everyone else, but I don't think I'd be very good at it. I thought about staying in the Navy...retire after twenty years and take it easy. I don't think that would work out too well either; it would be pretty dull after this. I'll probably just go back to teaching high school math."

Boats said, "Seems like that would be kinda dull too."

Flapper agreed. "Yeah," he said, "that's the problem isn't it...All this excitement, and then only the occasional excitement of seeing a flicker of understanding in a student's eyes...I've been reading where Congress is working on a G.I. bill that would pay veterans to go to college. I might go to graduate school, maybe law school. I don't know...But what about you? Have you thought about what you're gonna do after the war?"

Boats said, "Not too much, I might just stay in the Navy. I've only been a boatswain's mate a couple of weeks, but I can see I'm really gonna like it. Then, too, I thought about seein' the world like all the Navy recruiting posters used to say."

Flapper said, "Did you ever think about getting out and going to college? You could do it. You have the brains for it."

Boats had not finished high school; he certainly had never thought about college. Flapper caught him by surprise with this question. He was certain that nobody in his family had been to college, and he could not even think of anybody he knew who had been to college. Except Flapper. "Flapper," he said, "you are the only person I ever knew who went to college. I don't know anything about college. Why would I want to go to college?"

Flapper knew that true to its name, Manual Training High School in Peoria taught people how to use their hands, it was not in the business of training students for college. In his three years of teaching at Manual he knew of not a single student who had gone on to college. In South Peoria it was considered a lofty achievement to graduate from high school. Flapper was not sure how to answer this question. He knew there ought to be more to it than Booker T. should go to college just because he had the brains for it. Maybe he should say something about it might help get a better job, but when he thought about that he wondered if it was really true. Strapped for an answer and thinking he ought to say something, he offered, "You could study math and become a teacher."

Boats laughed a bit more merrily than Flapper might have liked, but in the end Flapper, never one to avoid a good joke, even at his own expense, laughed too.

Boats said, "Hey look, the wake has moved, I think we just changed course."

Flapper had also noticed and observed, "Probably just zigzagging. The Japs are almost licked, but they haven't quit yet, and they have plenty of submarines in these waters."

>>14<<

OKINAWA

Friday, March 30, 1945. Good Friday on the Christian calendar. The moon was full, the sea calm after two days of rough weather. It was five minutes past midnight, and Boats was leaving the bridge after being relieved of his helmsman duties. The ship was loafing along at a leisurely 10 knots in formation with eight other cruisers, 10 battleships, and a paltry screen of 20 destroyers. Boats marveled at the brightness of the moon, which allowed him to see land to his left, a series of small islands it appeared, and to his right, a large shadowy presence. They were passing through a 10-mile wide channel approaching their firing position for the pre-landing bombardment of Okinawa.

"Better sleep fast, Boats," his relief called out, "we go to GQ at zero five thirty."

"That's about right for me," said Boats. "How come you're so lucky to get the mid watch?"

The relief cocked his white hat jauntily over one eye and said cheerfully, "I was supposed to have the second dog watch, but I lost it in a crap game. Win some. Lose some." He shrugged, "What the hell."

Boats went below, fell into his rack and was asleep instantly. Like all the crew, he slept with his clothes on.

CLANG! CLANG! CLANG! CLANG! CLANG! CLANG! CLANG!

"GENERAL QUARTERS! GENERAL QUARTERS! ALL HANDS MAN YOUR BATTLE STATIONS! ALL HANDS, MAN YOUR BATTLE STATIONS!"

CLANG! CLANG! CLANG! CLANG! CLANG! CLANG! CLANG!

Men rolled from their bunks grumbling and cursing, grabbing for their shoes, and stumbling through the hatches. Improbably, some men remained immobile and had to be pulled to their shaky feet as the GQ klaxon continued its full-volume clamor.

Boats was pointer for a 40 millimeter gun mount on the port side of the ship, just forward of the number one smoke stack. He jumped into the gun tub, grabbed his life jacket and steel helmet, just in time to hear someone shout, "HOLY SHIT! THERE'S ONE HEADIN' RIGHT FOR US!"

And so there was. They started to fire, but got off only a few wildly ineffective rounds before the plane, flying out of the rising sun, smashed with devastating effect into a bulwark just below them, twisted around, and fell into the sea.

Boats thought he was flying. The force of the plane's impact catapulted him into the air where he slowly turned over and over, his arms outstretched like the wings of a bird, or the arms of a cross. He did not remember hitting the water.

.oooooooooooooooooooo..............................ooooooooooooooooooooooooooooooooooooooooo

How long he had floated in the oily, fiery water he could only guess. It was dark and quiet when he realized that, held up by his life jacket, he was floating aimlessly. He had a monumental headache, and he was completely disoriented; he had no notion of where he was, where he was going, or what he ought to do. He was not afraid, he was not angry, nor was he sad or remorseful. He was at peace. He wondered if he was in heaven. He did not remember praying, but he remembered everything else. The ear-splitting bedlam. The calm face of the Japanese pilot. The fire. If that was hell, which it surely was, then he must now be in heaven. He floated effortlessly, letting himself be carried by the whim of the currents. He relaxed and thrilled to the sensation of being utterly free of responsibility. There was nothing he could do or that he was required to do. He closed his eyes and slept.

He awoke to find himself lying face down on a sandy beach, a bright sun beating on his back; he felt warm all over. He opened his eyes cautiously but did not move. His life jacket was gone, and he was above the high tide line. Someone had dragged or carried him out of the water. The only sounds were from the surf and the occasional squawk of a gull. He closed his eyes and waited, contemplating an enormous thirst and enduring a painful headache.

He felt the gentle touch of a small hand upon his shoulder. *I'm dreaming again.* He felt water dripping on his neck. He did not move, but opened one eye. He was looking into the faces of two small children. They smiled when they saw his eyes widen, and offered him a cup of water. It was then he knew. He was in heaven.

He sat up slowly, took the cup, said "Thank you" and drank the water in one large gulp. The children giggled, and spoke to each other in a language he did not understand. He looked in wonder from one to the other. One was a boy, one a girl; he guessed around seven or eight years old. He wanted to ask them questions, but knew they would not understand. He wanted to return their kindness. He spoke to them earnestly, and as gently as he knew how; he did not want to frighten them. "Hello," he said. "Thank you for the water. It was very nice of you. I was very thirsty."

The children smiled, uncomprehending. They were delighted at the sound of his voice and pleased by his kindly manner.

The boy spoke. "*I am Mikio and this is my sister, Hideko. We live near here. Our father is a fisherman. Why is your skin black?*" He bowed politely.

Boats did not understand a word. He was embarrassed by the bow, amused by the seriousness of the boy, and charmed by the shyness of the girl. He saw that they were waiting for an answer, but knew they would not understand anything he said. He began to draw in the sand with his finger. He drew a face with crossed eyes and a tongue sticking out. The children danced around him and laughed joyously.

Boats saw movement in the trees and bushes beyond the shoreline. The land sloped upward from the beach to high cliffs. He could see the mouth of the Bishi River off to his left. He heard a voice call out from the trees: *"Hey kids, get your little butts off that beach, we're trying to fight a war here."*

The children looked up at once and called back, "*No, no. We are having fun. Leave us alone.*"

Boats looked toward the sea, and saw battleships and cruisers maneuvering to form a line for shore bombardment. He remembered the ritual from Iwo Jima. He never expected to see it from this angle. So much for heaven.

Something needed to be done, but he was not sure what. While searching for a solution to their dilemma he continued to draw in the sand. He drew two vertical lines, crossed them with two horizontal lines, and put an X in the middle square. He motioned to the children, and showed them how to put an O in one of the other spaces. Next, he filled a space with another X, and so proceeded to teach them how to play tic-tac-toe. They learned quickly, and were enchanted with the game just as Boats was enchanted with them. They laughed with unrestrained joy when they completed a row of three O's and Boats feigned tears.

Boats could see landing craft circling near the warships. He heard shouted commands from the tree line. Heaven and hell were about to collide. He saw the turrets of the great warships swing around, and the long barreled guns begin to elevate and depress as if engaged in some elaborate stretching exercises. He began to dig a trench in the sand with his hands. He encouraged the children to do the same, and they did so enthusiastically, thinking it was another game.

He saw flame belch from the big guns, and within an instant the first shell burst; close to the water line and advancing towards them in a walking barrage. Terrified, the children began to run screaming towards the trees with their hands over their ears. Boats knew they could not make it, and jumped up to run after them, determined to get them back to the relative safety of the crude foxhole they had dug in the sand. His long strides quickly closed the short gap between them. He dived and tripped the little girl who was three steps behind her brother. As she fell he saw a piece of shrapnel tear through her right calf muscle, and stared in horror and disbelief at the headless body of the boy as it took three more steps before falling. Mercifully, the girl did not witness her brother's fate. She was screaming in pain as Boats crawled toward her. Before he reached her he felt a searing pain in his head, and a sensation of being sucked into a giant whirlpool.

---------***********----------------&&&&&&&&&&&&&&############

"What happened to the little girl? Where is she? Where am I? How did I get in this bed?" Boats sat straight up in the starched hospital bed, felt a sharp pain in his head, and quietly lay back down. The quick movement left him dizzy, and he lay motionless trying to get his bearings. It was quiet in the room, which amplified the ringing in his ears, a high pitched, unending signal that would be with him as long as he lived..

A wire-thin chief hospital corpsman approached the bed speaking cheerfully with a slight Irish brogue, "Well now, did you decide to wake up then? And how's the head feelin'?"

With his head tight to the pillow and his eyes half shut, Boats muttered, "Where am I?"

"Why darlin', yer back on the Indy-maru. In sick bay."

"Am I sick?"

"Well, now, you got a couple of bumps on the head. Doc thinks it's nothin' serious. Probably have a nice headache for a few days. How's yer memory?"

Boats remembered the children. He said, "They killed the boy, but I don't know about the little girl. What happened to the little girl? How did I get here?"

The chief said, "One of the VP's comin' back from the beach dropped you off." He paused, scratched his head, and said, "All I know about little girls is, thank the Lord, they grow up to be big girls." He scratched his head again, and looked at Boats in a funny way. "Maybe there's more to that bump than the Doc thinks."

Boats' head hurt, but he was not suffering from amnesia and he knew it; the images were too clear, the details too crisp. He knew he had been caught on the beach between the give-no-quarter forces of overwhelming firepower on one side, and fanatical determination on the other. He knew his luck had held, that the difference between him lying here in a clean, dry hospital bed or lying headless on the beach was a matter of millimeters. He knew the little girl had been hit in the leg with shrapnel. Beyond that he was ignorant of her fate.

Boats sat up slowly. "What day is it?" he asked.

"Sure and it's Easter Sunday." The chief made the sign of the cross on his chest, then added, "We just landed a load of troops on Okinawa."

Boats muttered, "I'll bet God loves that."

The chief nodded and said, "It's also April Fool's day." He paused, then added, "I wonder then who the joke is on?"

Boats asked for a drink of water. The chief said, "I guess it's okay." He brought Boats a cup of water. "Now then, darlin', how do you feel?"

"Strange," said Boats. "My head hurts…I'm a little dizzy. But my memory's okay."

The chief leaned close to look into his patient's eyes, which he found still dilated more than normal. He murmured, "Hmm. A concussion, no doubt, and a bit of shock to boot. Your brains are a tot scrambled, I'd say, but all in all, you're a lucky lad you should know. You were grazed by a piece of shrapnel. Another fraction of an inch and you'd be another telegram."

Boats said, "I lead a charmed life."

At that moment Flapper arrived. "You can say that again, Booker…I mean, Boats," he said. "I thought I was lucky, but you got me beat a mile. Two days ago I saw you flying through the air in the shape of a cross, and now you're resurrected on Easter Sunday. Maybe you're the second Messiah. What's it like to be dead and come back to life?"

"Flapper, I was in heaven."

Flapper shot a quick glance at the chief who was busy crossing himself. "Oh," he said, "did you see any angels?"

"Two. A boy and a girl."

Flapper and the chief exchanged a raised eyebrow, rolled eyes look.

Flapper questioned, "Wings? Harps? Sitting on clouds?"

Boats ignored the questions. "The boy had his head blown off by an eight-inch shell burst," he said, "the girl got hit in the leg. Does anybody know what happened to her?"

The chief looked at Flapper and said, "He's been asking about this girl since he woke up."

Flapper said, "Wait a minute, Boats. What are you talking about?"

"On the beach. I got washed up on the beach…there were two children; a boy and a girl. We were on the beach when the shelling started. They got hit. The last thing I remember was trying to help the girl. I saw a shell fragment hit her in the leg. I saw the boy running without a head. It was awful." Boats put his head in his hands, and tried to suppress the sobbing grief he suddenly felt as he recounted the grisly scene on the beach.

Flapper and the chief stood in stunned silence.

At length Boats composed himself, and asked without looking up, "How did I get back here?"

Flapper answered. "A hospital corpsman picked you up on the beach when the Army landed. He put you on a VP. Nobody said anything about children. You sure this isn't another dream?"

Boats shook his head. "Not this time, Flapper," he said. "This was real. There were two children. They spoke to me in a language I couldn't understand, probably Japanese. They were happy. We laughed together."

Flapper was perplexed. "I don't know what to think, Boats. Every time you get out of my sight, you have an amazing experience. First, Colonel Nishi, and now you're playing ring-around-the-rosy in no-man's land. I don't know which is more improbable, this, or listening to a philosophy lecture from a Jap colonel who's in the middle of a battle for his life."

Boats said, "Flapper, these kids were real all right, and they didn't have to speak English for me to understand them. They didn't see me as an enemy, a nigger, or anything except somebody they could have fun with. And now they're probably both dead just because they found me on the beach. Did I tell you they gave me water to drink when I woke up on the beach? It ain't right, Flapper. Kids shouldn't have to die like that."

Flapper nodded wearily, "We all agree on that, Boats," he said. "...You know, Boats, that makes two lives you tried to save. Maybe it's time you got a lifesaving medal. They might call it..." He thought a moment, "...The Congressional Medal of Human Kindness."

"I guess I'd settle for a Good Conduct medal," Boats said.

Flapper laughed. "Not bad, Boats. I think even the Japs would agree that trying to save a child's life is good conduct. But seriously, you should get a Purple Heart for this. What do you think, chief?"

The chief, who had been listening to the conversation in some bemusement, looked up and said, "Not a bit of doubt. I've seen the medal awarded for a lot less than a rap on the head from a shell fragment."

Boats thought about Davey's Navy Cross and Kevin O'Keefe's Congressional Medal of Honor. He questioned, "Does anybody set out to win a medal?"

The chief answered. "We all get some medals, just for being here. But some medals are special. Not everybody gets the Purple Heart, and thank the Lord for that."

Boats looked at Flapper and asked, "So now what happens, Flapper? How much damage did that plane do?"

Flapper frowned. "A lot. Nine men killed and twenty wounded."

"I thought the plane fell in the water," said Boats.

Flapper nodded. "It did," he said, "...after it hit the ship, but a two hundred fifty pound bomb went through three decks and exploded in an oil bunker. Number four shaft was bent thirty degrees, and some geniuses from one of the tenders deep-sixed it before anyone knew what was happening."

Boats asked, "Can we operate with only three shafts?"

"They're sending us to Mare Island for major repairs," Flapper answered.

"Where's Mare Island?"

"Just north of San Francisco."

"San Francisco?"

"Admiral Spruance has shifted his flag to the *New Mexico,* we're headed home, Boats."

>>15<<

COUNT

"I heard you was comin' back, Booker T. I hoped you'd stop to see me."

Boats had found his tortured way back to the Peoria city dump to see Count, his friend and mentor. It was late May, 1945. Count stood up a bit shakily, and extended his hand, smiling warmly; Booker T. had always been special to him. Count looked older than Booker T. remembered, and Booker T., despite the trim uniform and neat row of colorful ribbons, looked younger than Count remembered. But when their eyes met, the bond of understanding, forged in solemn and earnest discussion over the years, was intact and secure.

Boats grasped Count's hand, and was surprised by the strength of his grip, then on a sudden impulse he gathered the old man in a warm bear hug, and was surprised by the broadness of Count's back. "I had to talk to you, Count," he said, "that's the main reason I came home. A lot of things happened to me since the last time I talked to you, I was hopin' you might help me understand some of the things I saw and heard. But first, tell me how you been; you're lookin' fine."

Count laughed and slowly took a seat on a rickety lawn chair, motioning Booker T. to sit also. He spoke carefully and deliberately, but with a firm voice. "Well, thank you for asking, Booker T.," he said. "When you get as old as I am, the first thing you do after you wake up in the morning, is check to see if yer hurtin' anywhere." He paused to consider. Boats waited.

" 'Course yer hurtin' somewhere, but lately my hurts been stayin' pretty much the same, and I learned to live with em'. My rule is: if I don't have any new hurts I'm feelin' pretty good." He chuckled merrily.

Boats laughed along with Count. "I guess that's a good rule for just about everybody," he said.

Count smiled while tapping his pipe to empty the bowl of ashes. He looked carefully at his young friend, envious of his youth and strength. "That's enough about me," he said, "you didn't come here to talk about me. What about you, Booker T.? How you feelin'?...You look a little thin...Your Pa showed me the last letter they got from you in which you said you was grown up. Growing up can be hard."

Boats nodded. "I almost got strangled on Iwo Jima, and I was shaved with a shell fragment on Okinawa. Look at this." He turned and showed Count a long, ugly scar that angled from just above his right ear three inches up along his scalp.

Count looked at the scar. "Hmm," he said, "Close. Close to death, Booker T. Close." He cupped his hand over the back of Booker T.'s head. "Somethin' like that has a way of makin' you grow up fast. Look at this, Booker T." Count turned his head to reveal a scar closely resembling Booker T.'s scar. "I was about the same age as you when I got my sign."

"Sign?" Boats looked questioningly at Count.

Count nodded. "I thought it was a sign from God," he said. "God spared my life. I was marked for a special purpose."

Boats waited expectantly, but Count was silent, pondering the 80 years since ghastly Gettysburg. The old veteran and the young veteran sat in front of Count's shanty, looking at a soft, lovely sunset, triumphant over the rising smoke and jumble of the Peoria city dump. Clouds gathered in the west and they heard the rumble of distant thunder.

Count stirred. "You hear that thunder, Booker T.?" he asked. "You know what that means?"

"God is saying His prayers?"

Count looked hard at Boats for a long time. Boats' eyes met his even gaze. At length Count said, "I believe you is grown up. Tell me what you learned."

Boats was not sure where to begin. In less than a year he had seen so much. His mind was like the dump, smoldering and jumbled. Images danced, one towered—the black sands of Iwo Jima. "If you could have seen the slaughter..."

Count said, "Booker T....I was at Gettysburg."

"I'm sorry, Count. I remember. You were there. My friend Flapper Jackson says that if you share a combat experience you have a bond only those who were there can understand. You and I must have that bond even though we were in different wars."

"We do, Booker T. It's a bond forged in horror. After more than eighty years I can see the carnage in my mind as clear as the day it happened. I hear the screams. Feel the terror."

Again they sat quietly, replaying their nightmares. Count broke the silence. "What counts now is what you do about it," he said. "In your letter you said I might be interested that you stopped wantin' to kill somebody. I am interested. Tell me about it."

Boats said, "You remember I left here with a ragin' hate for the rotten Japs who killed my brother. I swore vengeance on his soul. I wanted only one thing: to kill Japs."

"I remember," said Count.

Boats continued. "On Iwo Jima, I got my chance," he said. "That Jap was layin' at my feet, helpless as a baby, but instead of killin' him I saved his life. I coulda killed him easy as sittin' here. He was the enemy, I was a soldier, it was my duty to kill him…I didn't even think about it, I just bandaged his wounds."

Boats paused, remembering the unexpected feeling of relief and elation. He never doubted it was the right thing to do, and he felt no regrets. He was, however, slightly troubled that the act may have been influenced by the words of Colonel Nishi.

Count began humming a quiet tune as he heard Booker T.'s last words. Boats looked at him and questioned, "Did you ever kill anybody, Count?"

"I had a chance to kill a rebel," Count said. "He was layin' at my feet, helpless as a baby, just like you say." Count paused a moment, then said, "I saved his life."

Their eyes met and held for a few moments as they pondered their shared experience. In the gathering twilight, the thunder rumbled closer.

Boats as always, looked to Count for explanation. "What does it mean, Count?" he asked.

"What it means," said Count, "is that some things don't change. For over two thousand years on this Earth…maybe more…takin' and savin' lives been goin' on, and all the time God been sayin' His prayers."

"Why don't God stop the killin'?" Boats asked. "He must have the power."

Count shook his head. "Who can say? Some philosophers think it's a cosmic duel between God and the Devil…between Good and Evil. But it really don't matter what anybody thinks. Man got to solve his own problems."

The 17-year-old Boats' head was swimming. Faith in God and God's goodwill had served him well growing up in Peoria. It was a comfort to know one could call on the mystical power of God in stressful moments, even though it was understood that not all prayers would be answered. Until the shattering death of his brother he had never questioned his faith. Now his spiritual anchor was dragging.

Boats looked at Count. *This man has lived more than a hundred years, he must have answers.*

HE JUST GAVE YOU AN ANSWER, BOATS. PAY ATTENTION. MAN GOT TO SOLVE HIS OWN PROBLEMS.

"Where do we start, Count?" Boats was ready to save the world. Count would tell him how.

Count was more than 100 years old, but he was not without hope. At 17, he, too, had been ready to save the world, and after almost 90 years, in spite of everything, he had not given up. He was always eager to begin new ventures. In 1920, at the age of 80, he had mapped a 50-year project.

Count looked at Boats and smiled. He reached over, took Boats' hand, squeezed it gently, and said softly, "Oh my, oh my. Where *do* we start? Where do *we* start? Thank you for the we, Booker T., but I believe you have some unfinished business in the Pacific, and I probably won't be here when you return."

Boats began to protest, but Count stopped him with a wave of his hand. "You make me feel young, Booker T.," he said, "and I thank you for that, but my time is almost up, and I won't try to deny it. When do you go back?"

"I'm catchin' a bus next week. My ship is in San Francisco for repairs. I don't know when the ship will leave."

Boats thought about the ship, and tried to imagine what lay ahead. More bombardments, more landings, more violence, more death. "After Okinawa," he said, "it's the home islands; it will be awful."

Boats thought about the fiendishly devised system of blockhouses, pillboxes, and firing pits on Iwo Jima. He thought about the fanatical defenders. "A lot of people will die, Count," he said. "But not me. I'll be safe. My friend, Flapper Jackson, has the same feeling. Does that sound crazy?"

Count smiled and patted Booker T.'s hand. "You will live forever, my young friend," he said, "youth is imperishable."

They sat quietly, watching the night gather, wondering what to do with their immortality. They could see Venus shining brightly and unblinking through a gap in the clouds. A chorus of cicadas began a shrill concert. Thunder rolled across the sky.

"Life moves fast, Booker T.," said Count, "try not to get so caught up that you miss the enjoyment of it."

Boats said, "I did have some good times out there. In Hawaii, and on liberty at Ulithi." He told Count about Bucks Fulton and the Princess Kaialani Suite at the Royal Hawaiian Hotel. Count was a very appreciative audience. He seemed particularly interested in learning more about Bucks Fulton.

"So Bucks Fulton stayed in Hawaii?" Count asked. "Have you stayed in touch with him?"

Boats shook his head and said, "No."

"Too bad," said Count. "Sounds like a good guy to know."

Thoughts of Bucks Fulton caused Boats to connect to Colonel Nishi. "Bucks Fulton had a raging hatred for people with white skin," he said.

Count looked sharply at his young friend. Racial prejudice was something he had never discussed with Booker T. It seemed that was about to change. "It's a mistake to condemn an entire group of people because of a single physical characteristic," Count said. "In the history of this country," he continued, "white skinned people have treated black skinned people badly, nobody could argue otherwise, but it doesn't mean that everybody who has white skin is a bad person."

Boats said, "Bucks thinks that God is white and that He has a powerful hate for people with black skin."

Count nodded. "I thought the same thing when I was a slave," he said.

"What do you think now?" Boats asked.

"I don't think that anymore," Count replied, "remember that thunder, Booker T. Man got to solve his own problems."

Boats then described his encounter with Colonel Nishi in the Iwo Jima cave. When he had related the whole improbable tale he had a question for Count. "Is Colonel Nishi right, Count? Is everybody a victim except for the people who are rich?"

Count lighted his pipe before answering. "What would you say if I told you that I was rich?" Count answered with a question.

Boats could not see Count's eyes in the gathering darkness. The acrid fumes of the surrounding dump assaulted his nostrils. He stared at Count without replying. Count had been known to have his little joke every so often, but if he was joking now Boats did not sense it. On the other hand, how could it not be a joke? "I would ask you why you are living in the city dump."

Count would answer that question in due time, but first he had something else on his mind…something that he had been saving. "Booker T.," he began, then paused. "…Booker T., I've had time to do a lot of thinking, and what you have told me tonight makes me even more sure I'm right…I have come to believe that you have a special destiny…that you're marked for a special purpose, just like me."

Boats looked at Count curiously. Dusk had given way to darkness, and Count was only visible in dim outline, but his deeply wrinkled face was briefly illuminated when he held a lighted match to his pipe. Boats waited. Count took a long draw on his pipe, shifted in his chair, and continued, "Let me tell you a story." He paused again, gathering his thoughts.

"…When the war ended," he began, "I headed West. Worked my way across the country on a wagon train. Arrived in California in eighteen sixty-six; I was twenty-five yearsold. It was wild country…full of people searchin' for gold. I teamed up with an old prospector named Hardly. Rufus Hardly. We got an Indian guide; his name was Blue Cloud. Blue Cloud took us back into the mountains, not too far from San Francisco, and we found more gold than fifty men could carry. Shoot, more than that…it was a mountain of gold. In those days all you had to do was stake a claim, and the land, and everything on it was yours. Old Rufus Hardly was a good man; he was very generous with Blue Cloud and me. So there I was, not even thirty years old…rich, and about to get richer."

Count took a contented puff on his pipe as he recalled those prodigal days of discovery. Boats felt a tingle of excitement trying to imagine his friend Count as a rich young man in the bursting world of 1866 San Francisco. He was eager to learn more. "What did you do?" he asked.

Count continued. "Things wasn't so easy then like they is now," he said. "But Rufus was smart, he showed us what to do. We staked our claim, and built up a real mining operation. Hired people to do the work, hired guards for protection, hauled the gold out, and put it in bank vaults. We was rich, and nobody could take it away from us."

Once again Count paused to puff on his pipe, thinking about the wagons full of gold dust bumping over the dusty trails into San Francisco. "Then I remembered Gettysburg and the special sign," he said. "I thought…God gave me this gold, now what does He want me to do with it?"

"Did he tell you?" Boats asked.

Count shook his head. "Man got to solve his own problems, Booker T.," he said. "I waited for a message. I waited a long time. Then I knew. Man got to solve his own problems. My problem was a whole lot different from most people who was caught up in tryin' to find ways to stay alive, to feed themselves and their families, to stay warm, to avoid pain. One thing was plain to me...that gold...it was worth maybe ten million dollars...was not for my delectation. I should use it to do some good in the world. I was marked to be a do-gooder."

Count stopped to allow himself a satisfied chuckle, and another long draw on his pipe. A waxen moon darted in and out of fast moving clouds. The wind was rising, the thunder more insistent; a storm was imminent. Count stood and folded his chair. "Come inside, Booker T.," he said.

Boats had never been inside Count's shanty. He ducked through the low entrance, and entered the dark room. Count struck a match, and lighted a coal oil lamp placed on a small table. Booker T. looked around in amazement; every available space was filled with books. Homemade shelves extended from earth floor to plank ceiling, packed with books...large books, small books, thin books, fat books. Pamphlets, magazines, and newspapers were everywhere.

Count motioned to a chair. "Sit down, Booker T.," he said. "You look surprised."

Boats swept his arm around the room. "All these books," he said.

Count shrugged. "I need to know," he said. "Want some tea?"

Boats picked up a newspaper from the table. *The Wall Street Journal.* "Tea? Oh. Sure, okay. Thanks." His mind was racing.

Count began heating water over a small alcohol burner.

Boats asked, "Did you do good, Count?"

Count laughed. "Well, I tried," he said. "I've had a long time to figure things out, and I'm still learning. You don't ever stop learning. But just think, Booker T....America in eighteen seventy. Imagine what it was like...no electricity...no radios...no airplanes...no automobiles...an awful lot of horse shit." He laughed again. "...But think of the opportunities; all those things were just ahead. Now they're calling it the industrial revolution. People were figuring out how to do things with machines instead of with their hands. Like pulling the seeds out of a ball of cotton, like sewing a seam. It was a time of momentous change. I was in the middle of it with ten million dollars, and not the wit to know what to do with it. So I did the only thing I knew anything about. I bought land. In California, in Texas, in Illinois, in Pennsylvania, in New York. I even bought some land in Florida. And guess what? By the turn of the century that ten million dollars had increased ten-fold; but that was only the beginning."

Boats was listening carefully, if a bit skeptically. He never had a reason to doubt anything Count had told him before, but here he was, living in the city dump, and talking about millions of dollars as if it were pocket change.

Count saw the wrinkled brow, and answered what he thought was on Boats' mind. "Why was the land worth a hundred million dollars? Depends on where it is. If it's in New York City it's because somebody wants to build a skyscraper on it. If it's in Illinois it's because of what's underneath it. Think about a piece of land here in Illinois, just as one example. First, we have fifteen or so feet of topsoil. You have a growing season of maybe six months, and that soil is so rich you can grow just about anything you want on it, and lots of it, so we get food to feed people and animals. Now if you start to dig down below that topsoil you find layers and layers of coal, and if you keep on going deep enough you find an underground lake of black oil, and a whole universe of natural gas. I guess I don't have to tell you—no oil and coal…no revolution. We got some pretty smart chemists in this country too, Booker T. It didn't take them very long to figure out that by refining that crude oil they could get kerosene for lamps, gasoline for cars and trucks, hundreds of chemicals that could be used for all kinds of things."

Count paused. Boats thought of cars and trucks and chemists bending over test tubes and distillation racks.

"So you see, Booker T., the man who owns the land where all those treasures are buried soon has the power to do just about anything he wants to do. In America it's a free society…if you pay your taxes and don't break the law, well, like they always say…it's a free country."

After waiting a moment and checking Boats' expression to see if he was following the tale, Count plunged ahead. "So what do you do with all the money that's now rolling in by the truckload? You put it in banks where it will be safe, and where it will draw interest."

Boats looked up and said, "I never did understand how banks make any money. You give them money to keep in a safe place and they pay you? That don't make much sense to me. How do they stay in business, Count?"

Count smiled. "It's pretty simple," he said. "They do it by loaning out the money they take in at a higher interest rate. If I put a hundred thousand dollars in a bank, at the end of a year they pay me two thousand dollars in interest. They take my hundred thousand and loan it to somebody who wants to build a house, or start a business, or something, and after a year that somebody has paid five thousand dollars interest to the bank. The bank makes a three thousand dollar profit. Interest rates change, it could be more. The bank is in business to loan money."

Boats nodded understanding, but the more he thought about it the more he wondered if Count was telling him a fairy tale. He had known Count since he was 10 years old, and had never seen any evidence that Count was anything but a very old man living a lonely life in a place that most people tried to stay away from. At the same time Boats was confounded by the presence of all these books.

Count proceeded with his story. "Before long I had more money than the bank," he said. "It was about that time I decided to start my own bank."

Boats was startled by this news. He looked at Count in surprise and increasing suspicion. In Boats' small world, bankers were at the top of the money scale. "You own a bank?" he inquired.

Count looked at Boats' questioning face, and realized how improbable what he was telling must sound like; still, he had to finish the story. "That was almost fifty years ago," he said. "Right now I'd say I own about fifty banks. But hang on, Booker T., let me finish what I want to say…I know it sounds crazy, but believe me, I ain't making it up."

Boats blurted, "Fifty banks! I'm sorry, Count, how can I believe you own fifty banks when you live here in the dump?"

Count explained. "I do not live here in poverty, Booker T.," he said. "I live here because I choose to live here. But where I live don't really matter does it? You'll see the proof in due time. What's important now is that you listen carefully to what I say."

Boats looked for madness in Count's eyes; what he saw was strength, purpose, and determination. In Boats' eyes Count saw doubt giving way to resignation, and as he projected his resolve to the troubled youth, acceptance, and finally, trust.

"I have a vision, Booker T. I see the new century, the new millennium, fifty-five years in the future. I see the new president of the United States taking the oath of office on the Capitol steps in Washington, D.C. I see a bright sunny day. I see adoring crowds of people looking on. I see hope in their eyes. The new president, leading the nation into the twenty-first century is…" He paused for dramatic effect, and said quietly but firmly, "…Booker T. McCan of Illinois."

The 17-year-old Booker T. McCan could only laugh, which he did with great gusto, until he saw that his friend Count was not even smiling, but was looking at him in deadly earnestness. Boats stopped laughing, but still shaking his head, questioned, "Me? President?"

"It's your destiny, Booker T.," said Count.

Boats tried to imagine it as Count had described it, but his screen to the future was blurred. "I'm sorry, Count," he said. "The only thing I can see in the future is that long bus ride to San Francisco next week."

Count nodded. "Yes, of course," he said, "you have unfinished business. You are so young; so much to learn. But if you will acknowledge your destiny, and follow my plan we can do it together."

Boats again looked dubiously at the old man. *This man is over a hundred years old and he is making plans fifty years into the future. Is this another dream? Who is crazy, him or me*? WHY DON'T YOU JUST HUMOR HIM?

"Okay, sure Count, tell me what to do," Boats said.

Count had a plan and would not be distracted by indulgence, in fact indulgence was what he sought. He opened a desk drawer, withdrew a 50-page document clipped into a blue folder, and handed it to Boats. "We can begin with this," he said.

Boats read the label: **SCHOOL FOR PRESIDENTS**. He looked questioningly at Count.

Count said, "The post-war world will be so complex and difficult we can no longer afford to entrust the leadership of the country, and of the world, to people not trained for the job. I believe it is time to begin a formal training program for future presidents, and I intend to do something about it. The document you are holding is the result of a study I commissioned two years ago to make recommendations for a program of higher education aimed at the goal of preparing young men and women for public service leading to the highest levels of government. I have set aside one billion dollars to establish an institution dedicated to this goal."

Boats shook his head in amazement. "It's incredible," he said. "But Count, don't you think we've had some good presidents? I saw men cry on our ship when they announced that President Roosevelt had died. I heard one say, 'What will happen to us now that our leader is dead?'"

Count nodded. "President Roosevelt did a lot of good for our country," he said. "Roosevelt was a great man. He brought us up from despair. He showed us how government should be used to help the people. We'll miss him, no doubt about that. I cried, too, when I heard of his death. Roosevelt and Lincoln. They were the best," he paused, "but Teddy and Wilson were pretty good too."

"Why did you cry for Roosevelt?" Boats asked.

Count considered the question carefully. "It ain't easy to explain your feelings, Booker T.," he said. "Maybe it was because I knew he wouldn't get to finish the war, and so close to the end. Maybe I thought we'd need him after the war. Maybe I felt like I'd lost a friend...Maybe I'm just old and sentimental."

But Count was not presently in a sentimental mood. He was energized by the thought of his School For Presidents, and his vision of Booker T.'s destiny. Now and then he found himself wondering how long he would live, but long ago, while waiting for a fish to bite, he realized that these melancholy moments came when he had unscheduled time on his hands. Returning from that fishing trip he chucked his fishing gear into a convenient Dempsey Dumpster. He seemed to be in good health with no major complaints. When doctors told him he was sound as a dollar he hoped nobody would try to spend him. He had read reports and seen pictures of toothless ancients around the world, some reported to be 120 to 130 years old. He was not interested in setting any records for antiquity, but he would like to be around when Booker T. was inaugurated president. He had given up prayer when he began to notice his prayers were invariably attended by thunder, but he didn't think it was too much to expect to live another 50 years or so. Maybe by that time scientists would understand the aging process, and he could live long enough to accumulate all the money in the world. He almost laughed out loud at that thought. In fact, he did not completely suppress a chuckle. *Then I could be Emperor*, he thought, and laughed again.

Boats was still thinking about the dead president, and was startled to hear what almost sounded like a giggle coming from Count. *Is he okay?* At 17, Boats was convulsed by the sight gag humor of the Ritz Brothers and the Three Stooges, he had trouble with Robert Benchley. He wondered what Count found funny in the death of Roosevelt.

Count composed himself. "Listen, Booker T.," he said. "Here's what I want you to do. Go back and get this war over with as soon as you can. When you have time, study this document; it contains a well balanced, carefully considered account of what a future president of the United States needs to know. And Booker T., as you read and think about what's written here, you will have some ideas of your own, and I want to know about those ideas, so write things down as they occur to you. Also, I want you to begin paying close attention to the actions of Mr. Truman, our new president, and to the actions of future presidents. By the time your turn comes you may see as many as ten different presidents. Learn from them. Consider their successes and their failures; think about how you could do it better. Look for new things, ways you think could improve people's lives. That's what this is all about, Booker T....I warned you I was a do-gooder."

Boats wondered at the excitement he saw rising as Count expanded his vision. He was reminded of Coach Schmidt, his high school football coach, and Lieutenant Allgood, who gave the fevered oration in boot camp, telling them "don't give up the ship." Count was giving him a pep talk. Boats didn't mind; he liked pep talks. But he had questions. "You make it sound like a sure thing, Count. How do you know I'm smart enough to do this? How do you know people will vote for me? And somethin' else…are you setting up a billion-dollar school for just one student? You did say a billion dollars?"

"Whoa, Booker T., let's take one question at a time. The first question is easy—It ain't enough to just be smart, lots of people are smart; to be a leader requires something special that's hard to pin down. I have seen the spark of intelligence and sensibility in you, Booker T. I want to nourish that spark, and fan it into a raging flame focused to wipe out ignorance, cruelty, pain, and suffering. We can do it, Booker T. You can do it."

Something in Boats began to stir.

Count continued. "About votes," he said. "Absolutely right to think of that, Booker T. We live in a democratic society and the people have the final say through their votes. It is our job to make you known to the people as a man they can trust to make their lives better. We have fifty years to accomplish that task. You don't realize it, but you have already made a good start…popular high school athlete…war hero…Purple Heart…a very good start, Booker T."

Count was on his feet relishing the thought of Booker T. the candidate—a great American hero. He moved ahead to the details. "Now about the school," he said. "I did say a billion dollars. Here's the way it works, Booker T. Nine hundred million goes into an endowment fund. It means that money is put into an account that generates income. At ten percent return the account will produce about ninety million a year which will be used to operate the school. The endowment means the school is established to run in perpetuity. Perpetuity…one of my favorite words; it means forever. The remainder of the original one billion will be used for building construction and start-up costs. This school will have the finest teachers in the world, and no, it is not for just one student. I have traveled the world, seen the need. This school will have students from everywhere; it will be most grand."

Boats questioned and Count explained until the dawn's early light.

>>16<<

ONE A.A.

Saturday, July 14, 1945

"All back full."

"Aye aye, sir. All back full." The duty seaman pulled the handles on the engine order telegraph to their full down position. In a heartbeat, the bells chingggged with a melodious and satisfying response.

"Engine room answers all engines back full, sir."

In a flat sea, the dark unrippled water, portentous, as though hiding something below a low morning fog, the *USS Indianapolis* answered the engineer's command, and with startling quickness for a 20-ton vessel, began to move backwards at a steadily increasing speed. The ship was undergoing a number of operational tests 50 miles off the northern California coast during a short shakedown cruise following the Mare Island overhaul.

"All stop." Flapper Jackson, recently promoted to full lieutenant, was the officer of the deck; the ship's captain, four-striper Charles McVay III, was at his side. McVay was third generation U.S. Navy, son of one time Commander-in-Chief, U.S. Asiatic Fleet, Admiral Charles McVay, Jr., now retired.

"Aye aye, sir. All stop."

Chinng, chinng. "Engine room answers, all stop, sir."

An explosion of steam shot into the air and engulfed the bridge as the superheated liquid driving the ship's four propellers looked for a place to go, and found the steam relief valves abaft the bridge. The ship glided several hundred yards through the smooth water as it coasted to a stop.

"Starboard engines ahead full, port engines back full."

The engine order telegraph man executed the order, and suddenly the ship began to rotate to the left in a spinning motion, making 1,000-foot circles in the water.

Flapper smiled, looked at the captain, and said, "She looks pretty good, sir."

McVay agreed, "She sure does, Flapper. Those yard birds have done a good job. I believe she's as good as new; maybe better. And I think you better stop this spin drill before I get dizzy."

"Yes, sir. All stop!" he shouted.

"All stop. Aye aye, sir."

The captain spoke. "Okay, Flapper," he said, "that completes the shakedown tests. Set a course for the Golden Gate at about twelve knots. We ought to be tied up at Mare Island tomorrow morning in time for church."

"Aye aye, sir." Flapper turned to the engine order telegraph man and said, "All engines ahead standard, make turns for twelve knots." He then turned to his junior officer of the deck and said, "Jonesy, get me a course for the Gate."

"Engine room answers, all ahead standard, one hundred fifty revolutions for twelve knots, sir."

"Very well…Helmsman, what's your heading?"

"Steering course two seven zero, sir."

"Very well. Right standard rudder. Jonesy, what's the course?"

The helmsman called, "Right standard rudder, sir. Passing two eight five."

"Zero six five looks pretty good for a start, Flapper. As soon as the navigator gets a new fix we can fine tune it to the sea buoy."

"Very well. Helmsman, steady on course zero six five."

"Aye aye, sir. Steady on course zero six five. Passing zero zero five."

Flapper instinctively walked out of the wheelhouse to the starboard wing of the bridge; it was a reflex action. He knew there were no other ships in the area, and yet when he gave the order for the ship to come right he must see for himself that nothing blocked the way. He was met by a familiar draft of cool salt spray that stung his face in a not unpleasant way. The gold braid and eagle on his cap were edged with green verdigris, evidence of countless reflex actions. The sun was burning its way through the morning fog, and patches of light showed blue water laced with gray and black across the wide empty sea ahead of them. Flapper breathed deeply and savored the quiver of excitement he always felt when he knew this splendid ship, this heavy cruiser, was responding to his command.

"Steady on course zero six five, sir," the helmsman called.

"Very well," Flapper answered. He walked forward to where Captain McVay was standing behind a windbreak watching the great ship's cutwater peel away the pliant brine.

"When will we be shipping out, Captain?" Flapper asked.

Captain McVay, startled from his reverie, hesitated before answering. "Still don't know for sure, Flapper," he said. "I thought we were going to get a chance to run through some training drills, but things have speeded up so much in the past week I don't know what's going on. All of a sudden they seem to be in a hell of a hurry to get us out. God knows we need some training. Since we came to the yard, we've taken on thirty new junior officers and two hundred fifty men, not to mention the new radar and fire control gear. We need time to teach people how to use that stuff, but it doesn't look like we're going to get it."

Captain McVay was an old Navy man, a veteran of many campaigns, and not given to complaining, but he was worried about the level of combat readiness of his ship and crew. With him, as with all good commanders, it was axiomatic that practice makes perfect.

"In any case," he continued, "we should know soon. I report to Admiral Purnell at Naval Headquarters for orders tomorrow morning after we tie up."

McVay pointed to a disturbance in the glassy rolling sea ahead and to the right of the oncoming vessel. "Look at that, Flapper. A school of humpback whales...Makes me feel like an intruder."

Sunday, July 15, 1945

San Francisco, California...Naval Headquarters.

"...And so, Captain McVay, this afternoon you will bring your ship from Mare Island shipyard to Hunter's Point Navy Yard in San Francisco. Sometime tonight you will receive a small but vital top-secret cargo accompanied by two Army officers. Tomorrow at first light, you will sail at all possible speed for Pearl Harbor, where you will drop your passengers, refuel and continue at high speed to Tinian Island where your top-secret cargo will be unloaded. This cargo must be guarded at all costs. Every day you save will cut the length of the war by that much. Do you have any questions?"

Captain McVay's brain was awash with questions, but the most immediate was one he apparently was not allowed to ask: *What the hell is it*? McVay tried without success to keep the curiosity out of his face.

Admiral Purnell, seeing McVay's puzzled expression, said, "Sorry, Captain, you're not allowed to know." He then lowered his voice, and said a bit sheepishly. "The truth is, I don't even know what it is. But the orders are clear...get it there as quick as you can. It's vital."

Captain McVay asked, "Does the cargo require any special handling?"

"Yes. It should be kept as far from the crew as possible, preferably in officers' country. I believe you have some Flag quarters presently unoccupied. I suggest you have a ship fitter weld some padeyes to the deck in one of those compartments, and secure the cargo with steel straps. The two Army officers will stay in the same compartment as long as the cargo is aboard; you will post a Marine guard outside their quarters."

McVay said, "These seem to be most extraordinary precautions, sir." He could not refrain from asking, "Does it have anything to do with bacterial warfare?"

The admiral was not pleased. "Dammit, McVay," he spat, "I don't have any idea what that cargo is, and your job is to deliver it, not ask fool questions."

McVay flushed at the rebuke, but was emboldened to continue. "My officers and crew will be curious, sir. What can I tell them?"

"Tell them only that every day you save will shorten the war by that much."

"Aye aye, sir." McVay saluted and left.

Monday, July 16, 1945...Day one of the Atomic Age
San Francisco...0300 Pacific War Time. Aboard the Indianapolis at Hunter's Point.

WHEE-EEE, WHEE-EEE-OOOO. The boatswain's pipe shrilled over the *Indianapolis'* loud speaker system, unexpectedly snatching men all over the ship from sound sleep. "NOW HEAR THIS, NOW HEAR THIS...HEADS OF DEPARTMENTS MAKE ALL PREPARATIONS FOR GETTING UNDERWAY. SEA AND ANCHOR DETAILS REPORT TO YOUR STATIONS. FIRST DIVISION WORK DETAIL LAY UP TO THE HANGAR DECK...ON THE DOUBLE...NOW HEAR THIS..."

The orders were repeated two times for the benefit of the deep sleepers, and for those who vainly tried to ignore the hated intrusion into their dreams.

"What's goin' on, Boats? Nobody said nothin' about gettin' underway today. My god! It's only zero three hundred. What's so damned important we have to get up in the middle of the fuckin' night? Christ, I didn't get off watch 'til midnight. They tryin' to kill me? Fuck the Navy, I'm goin' back to sleep. Wake me when the war's over."

"Come on, Striker, get yer butt out of that rack...the chief's comin' through.

We're in the work detail, we gotta get up to the hangar deck. Come on."

0400... Boats, Striker, and the rest of the first division work detail lounged on the hangar deck, waiting for something to happen, taking the opportunity to vent their weariness, frustration and exasperation. The yard was deserted and quiet, the pier next to the ship empty.

"Just like the fuckin' Navy, Boats. Haul yer ass outta the rack in the middle of the goddam night then make ya wait around and freeze yer ass off fer no goddam reason. I'm gettin' sick of...holy shit! What's that?"

Boats looked up and said, "It looks like a giant crane walking down the pier. Here comes a couple of Army trucks."

Striker moved closer to Boats, and said in a lowered voice, "Did you notice those guys over there in the shadows on the pier? Looks like they're in civilian clothes. Whadda ya suppose that means?"

"I don't know, Striker, they look like some kinda gangsters."

The Army trucks stopped next to the ship, and the chief boatswain's mate went to get instructions. He was not gone long. Returning quickly he began to issue orders. "Okay, men, listen up," he said. "We got some top-secret cargo to bring aboard. Striker...go down to the First Division paint locker and get a crowbar, a big one. The rest of you swabs go down to that forward truck, and rig that big crate for the gantry. Let's go. On the double."

Striker was incapable of taking an order without a question or complaint. "A crowbar? Did you say a crowbar, chief? How we supposed to tote cargo with a crowbar?"

"Never mind the damn questions, Striker," said the chief, "just get the damn crowbar. McCan, you come with me."

Boats McCan and the chief walked down the gangway to the pier where the rear truck was parked. They walked up a ramp, and into the back of the large truck where the chief showed Boats a small metal cylinder, about the size of two bowling balls, resting in what appeared to be a lead bucket. Boats looked in fascination at the innocent looking object, half expecting it to tell him its secret. "What's top secret about a little old metal cylinder, chief?" he asked.

"Stow the questions, McCan," said the chief, "just carry that damned thing up to the flag lieutenant's quarters, okay? The first lieutenant says this thing will shorten the war, so it must be some kind of secret weapon. Right? You wanna take a guess what it is?"

"Do you know what it is, chief?"

"Listen, McCan, when you been in the Navy as long as me there ain't nothin' you ain't seen," said the chief, who had no idea what the metal cylinder contained or represented. "Hell, yes, I know what it is," he lied. "I'm gonna start a pool in the First Division. For a buck you get to put your guess into the pot. Closest guess wins the pot. You got any ideas you wanna put in? You can be first in."

Boats,McCan, always ready to take a chance, said, "Sure, count me in, but I need to think about it a little first. Let me see if I can lift it. It ain't very big, but it looks heavy."

Boats grasped the handle of the bucket with both hands, and managed to lift it only a fraction of an inch before letting it drop back to the floor of the truck. "Oof," he wheezed, "I can't move it, chief...They gonna try to sink the home islands with this thing?"

Striker appeared with the crowbar. The chief began to give instructions. "Okay. Come on, Striker, get that thing up here. Slip it under the handle to this bucket. That's right. Now you need to get the bar up on your shoulders. Here, both of you get down on your knees, get the bar in place, then just stand up. That way the weight is on your legs and not on your backs. That's right. Good."

Boats and Striker, slowly and with wobbly legs, managed at last to stand, the bar resting uncomfortably on their shoulders, the 200-pound cylinder suspended between like an enormous can of worms.

0430 Pacific War Time. A faint glow of dawn tinted the eastern sky. Flapper Jackson and Boats McCan, along with a large group of curious sailors, congregated at the amidships hangar deck looking at the large wooden crate securely lashed to the deck. The heavy cylinder had been delivered to the officer's quarters. "What do you think it is, Flapper?" asked Boats.

"I don't know, Boats, but they're taking bets in the wardroom, just like in the First Division, and everywhere else on the ship. The best guess in the wardroom is that it's some kind of B.W."

"What's B.W.?"

"Bacterial Warfare."

Boats winced. "Ugh. I thought that stuff's been outlawed."

"It has. So has poison gas."

"Do you think it's something like that, Flapper?"

"No. I don't think our government would stoop to anything like that. Why should we? We're winning the war...Jesus! Did you see that, Boats?"

Boats said, "Yeah, a flash through the sky, right over the city…it looked like it was from far away. What was it?"

Thunder rumbled across the sky. Boats and Flapper looked at each other, both wondering if God was saying a prayer.

Alamagordo, New Mexico…0530. Mountain War Time.

A pistol with a muzzle velocity of 3,000 feet per second fires a bullet that triggers a chain reaction splitting a billion quadrillion uranium nuclei into a billion quadrillion nuclei of lead and other heavy metals, some emitting gamma rays, beta particles, and alpha particles. The energy released is like nothing ever seen in the history of the world. Monday July 16, 1945…day one of the Atomic Age. If this test had failed, the *Indianapolis* would not have sailed.

0800 hours aboard the *Indianapolis.* Men stood at attention saluting the colors, first at the fantail, then at the truck, as colors were shifted prior to getting underway. *Indianapolis* backed smartly away from her berth into the main channel as a forlorn group of eight sailors, the remnants of a band, stood on the pier playing "Anchors Aweigh" to the accompaniment of impious and derisive shouts from the ship's company assembled on the weather decks. At 0820, Boats looked up 500 feet through the morning fog to see the underside of the Golden Gate Bridge as the ship moved briskly to the edge of the Far Eastern World. At 0900 the ship passed Farrolon Light abeam to starboard and set course for Hawaii.

"All ahead flank, make turns for thirty knots," called the officer of the deck

"Aye aye, sir. All ahead flank, turns for thirty knots."

*1600 hours…*Boats and Flapper were coming off the afternoon watch on the bridge. It was a warm sunny day. The ship was plowing the calm water at a frenzied pace…like a truck pushing 100 miles an hour on an open highway.

Flapper shook his head. "Absolutely amazing…seven hours at thirty knots, and no sign of a let up…nobody ever heard of such a thing. The word is we maintain this speed all the way to Hawaii…Amazing! The black gang is goin' nuts. I just hope the old lady can hold up."

Boats had something else on his mind. "Flapper," he said, "can we talk? There's somethin' I want you to look at."

"What is it, Booker T.?" Flapper asked. "You look awfully serious. Is something wrong?"

Boats shook his head. "No, no, it's not that," he said. "Flapper, did you know Count back in Peoria?"

Flapper was in an ebullient mood, exhilarated by the pace of the ship and the sense of mission. "No Count? Is this a joke? I knew plenty of no accounts back in Peoria."

"Count is the name of an old man who lives in the city dump," said Boats.

"An old man lives in the city dump? I don't get it."

"It's a long story, Flapper, and you're probably not gonna believe it, but when I was back home on leave last week I went to see Count. He's an old friend, I've known him for a long time, he's helped me with a lot of things. He's over a hundred years old; he fought at Gettysburg."

Flapper furrowed his brow. "Fought at Gettysburg? And living in the Peoria dump? Come on, Booker T."

Boats started to tell Flapper about Count's great wealth, but decided to hold that choice morsel for later. He wasn't quite sure about that himself, he only had Count's word for it. Still, Count's word was...he thought about Count's word...sacred? "Look, Flapper," he said, "can you wait here just a minute while I get something from my seabag? It's a plan Count gave me. I want you to read it so we can talk about it."

Boats quickly retrieved the blue folder Count had given him and brought it to Flapper. Flapper looked at it curiously and read the title. "School for Presidents? What is this?"

Boats said, "Can you read it tonight and maybe we can talk about it after our watch tomorrow morning?"

>>17<<

SCHOOL FOR PRESIDENTS

Tuesday, July 17, 1945...Day two A.A.

As they had done so often, Flapper and Boats sat on the fantail of the *Indianapolis* watching the trail of bubbling water fall away to the horizon. At thirty knots, the power of the spinning screws pulled the heavy fantail down below the level of the foaming wake. It was an odd feeling...like sitting at the base of a waterfall with the water falling up.

Flapper held the blue folder and shook his head. "It's a stupendous concept, Booker T. A ten-year curriculum to train people for public service. Quite incredible, but damned interesting I must say. Have you read it?"

Boats nodded. "Yes, I have," he said. "Count explained a lot of it to me. We talked all night a couple of times; he means to see it done. When I was with him I really believed it could happen, he was so convincing. But when I read it again on the bus from Peoria, I started wondering if it was just an old man's daydream. That's why I wanted to talk to you about it. You're a teacher, Flapper, I thought you'd know about something like this. What do you think?"

Flapper dipped his head slightly. "If I were a skeptic," he said, "I'd say it's a waste of time, but I guess you know me well enough now to appreciate that's not the way I think. I confess I'm captivated by this concept."

Flapper stopped to consider, then continued. "Look, there are two ways this discussion can go...First, even if we don't think there is a chance in hell it could ever be a reality, we could still have some fun talking about it. Second, if we agree this is a good idea, there is the practical question of how to make it happen."

Boats nodded. "I think it all depends on how long Count lives," he said, "that's what's so crazy about it. He's over a hundred years old, and says he intends to be there when I become president of the United States in the year two thousand. As near as I can tell he would be around a hundred and fifty years old." Boats said it so casually that Flapper did a quick double take.

Flapper restrained his impulse to laugh. Instead he turned this little bombshell over in his mind a few times before responding. He decided to play it straight. "What happens if Count dies?" he asked.

Boats was surprised by this response. He had expected Flapper to scoff at the idea of President Booker T. McCan. "Flapper, do you think I could be president?" he asked.

"Why not?"

Boats did not have to think very hard for a reason why not. "Well for one thing, I'm a Negro," he said.

Flapper shrugged. "I don't think that will matter too much fifty years from now," he said.

Boats shook his head in wonder. "That's the same thing Count said."

"So what happens if Count dies?" Flapper repeated the question.

Boats shook his head. "I don't know," he said. "Seems like he's thought of everything. Acts like he's gonna live forever."

Flapper thought a moment. "So Count intends to set up a School for Presidents," he said, "and Booker T. McCan is the chosen one? How do you feel about it?"

Boats felt the blood rush to his cheeks. He looked sharply at Flapper to see if he was being mocked. Count made it sound so easy, but when he talked to Flapper about it Boats suddenly realized how foolish it sounded. Flapper was asking him how he felt about it. He had decided that he wanted to give it a try, and he was looking for some encouragement from Flapper, but he was put off by Flapper's remark about the chosen one. He liked and respected Flapper, but he was not sure enough of his own position to defend it, and so tried to think of a way to end the discussion. He stood up and said, "Why don't we forget it? It was a dumb idea."

Flapper jumped to his feet. "No, wait a minute, Booker T.," he urged. "I don't think it's a dumb idea at all. I just wondered how you felt about it...what you thought about it."

Boats shrugged his shoulders. "Look, Flapper," he said, "I'm only seventeen years old. It's kind of hard for me to imagine something more than fifty years in the future. In the year two thousand I'll be seventy-two years old, most people that age are dead. I don't know how I feel about that...I guess it makes me sad. But look at this...here's what Count wants me to do...he gave me a schedule."

Booker T. reached in the back pocket of his dungarees and withdrew a sheet of paper folded several times into a small square. He unfolded the sheet, consulted it briefly, and then summarized, with frequent glances at the paper, what Count expected from him for the next fifty-five years. "I stay in the Navy five more years…get out in nineteen fifty…the middle of the century. I'll be twenty-two years old. Count says I need that five years to mature, and also to have a little fun before I settle down to a fifty-year plan. Sow some wild oats, he said. But I also need to use that time to learn how to read and write better. I have to keep a daily journal, and I have to write two letters a week, one to my parents and one to Count. I have to work to make at least Petty Officer First Class before I get out. Count says he doesn't care what the rating is, Boatswain's Mate is okay, but a rating where I have to learn some mathematics would be better. I'm thinking about trying for Electronics Technician. Count says I need to learn how to think, and how to focus on a goal. He also gave me a list of books to read."

Boats paused to see how Flapper was taking all this. Flapper had said he didn't think it was a dumb idea, and he still didn't…extravagant perhaps, but not dumb.

Boats continued. "In nineteen fifty I begin the ten-year School for Presidents. I study how to become a lawyer. From nineteen sixty to nineteen sixty-five I clerk for state, federal, and Supreme Court justices. In nineteen sixty-six I'm thirty nine years old…I begin my political career. I run for public office at the local level…Peoria County Solicitor. Over the next thirty years I serve the public as Illinois State Senator, Mayor of Peoria, Governor of Illinois, and Senator from Illinois on Capitol Hill in Washington. In the year two thousand I run for president of the United States." He looked at Flapper expectantly, not a shade of doubt in his eyes.

Flapper listened in growing awe as Boats nonchalantly ticked off the stops along the route to the White House. He was speechless for a few moments when Boats finished. At length he spoke, unable to keep the skepticism entirely out of his voice. "Is that all?" he asked. "Do you really think you can do all that, Booker T.?"

Boats was artless. "Count says it's my destiny," he said,

Flapper sat turning the whole wild scheme over in his mind. It was not difficult to grasp the global reach of the plan, but the idea of tailoring it for one person over fifty years would take some time for him to assimilate. He decided to play the devil's advocate. "What if you can't handle the ten-year curriculum?" he asked. "Have you looked at it carefully? You have to qualify for two doctorates, one in philosophy and one in law."

Boats shrugged. "I can do it," he said. "I won't have to worry about money, I can just concentrate on my studies."

Flapper was surprised. "You won't have to worry about money?"

"Count is a millionaire," said Boats, "maybe more. The hard part will be getting elected."

Flapper agreed. "You can say that again," he said.

Flapper and Boats lapsed into a long silence, both thinking about the improbable exegesis Boats had just delivered. Flapper wondered what it was like to be a millionaire.

Thursday, July 19, 1945...Day four A.A

Pearl Harbor, Territory of Hawaii. The *Indianapolis,* riding high in the water for lack of fuel, eased through the narrow channel, and coasted to its berth alongside the fuel docks in the snug, nearly empty harbor. The Navy had cleared the harbor to lessen chances of a mishap to the Indy and its precious cargo.

At precisely 1030 hours, Captain McVay ordered, "All stop."

"All stop, aye aye sir... Engine room answers all stop."

"Very well. Secure the sea and anchor details. Call away the fueling details. Tell the engine room to keep all eight boilers on the line. Unload all passengers. Standby to get underway upon completion of fueling."

Flapper handed the captain a printed message. "Captain," he said, "we just got word from the port control office...We set a speed record from San Francisco to Hawaii. Two thousand miles in seventy-four hours. That averages about twenty-eight knots...not bad for a creaky old lady."

Captain McVay smiled. "Damn good, Flapper," he said, "but we're not even halfway there...we still have three thousand miles to go before we can ease up. I'm going to report to CincPacFleet...maintain the bridge watch, I won't be gone long."

"Aye aye, sir."

Six hours later they were underway for Tinian.

Tuesday, July 24, 1945...Day nine A.A.

Boats and Flapper, helmsman and officer of the deck on the second dog watch came off the bridge after being relieved. Flapper was still excited. "Nobody has seen anything like it, Booker T., steaming at flank speed for eight days in a damned row and no sign of a let up .You have to wonder though....If it was so damned important to get those damned things out here so damned fast, why didn't they just put 'em on a damned airplane and fly 'em out?"

Boats got caught up in the flood of damns. "Do you think we'll ever find out what those damned things are, Flapper?" he asked.

Flapper replied, "Damned if I know, Booker T., but I guess we will someday if it really is that important. Some of the officers claim to know, but I doubt if they do. I figure it's something none of us ever heard of...like some Buck Rodgers ray gun. Maybe we'll find out when we get to Tinian in a couple of days."

"I noticed we're not zigzagging," said Boats, "does that mean we don't have to worry about Jap subs?"

"Traveling this fast, no sub can touch us," Flapper replied. "We'd be doing them a favor by zigzagging."

Flapper and Boats found seats in a 40mm gun tub, and watched the evening stars slowly appear. Flapper pointed to an area in the southern sky. "Look at that constellation, Booker T.," he said. "See those four stars? It's called the Southern Cross. It can only be seen in southern latitudes, you can't see it in Peoria. I think it's one of the most beautiful constellations."

The night was velvet black, and the ship was tightly veiled, traveling in a war zone. Soon the sky was nearly saturated with stars. Boats and Flapper sat quietly, drinking in the majesty, feeling small and insignificant.

At length Flapper spoke. "Tell me about Count, Booker T., how did he get so rich?"

Boats repeated the tale Count had told him about the California gold, the purchase of land, the discovery of oil, and the investment in banks.

Flapper was incredulous. "It all seems so unreal, Booker T.," he said. "If he has all that money, why isn't he living in a mansion on a large estate with lots of servants like any good capitalist would? And why is he living in Peoria? In a dump? I'm surprised the city allows him to live there."

Boats said, "He owns the land. He also owns the Caterpillar Tractor Company, the Hiram Walker distillery, and all the banks in town."

Flapper shook his head. "So Count owns Peoria. And all this time I thought it was Al Capone." He looked at Boats who was not laughing. "It's hard to believe, Boats, pardon me if I'm skeptical, but did he give you any evidence that all this was true?"

Boats squirmed at this question; it was one he had been expecting. "That's a good question, Flapper, and the answer is no," he replied.

Flapper sighed. "Okay," he said, "so it's probably just a fantasy. But that's okay, it's fun to talk about."

Boats said, "Maybe it is just a fantasy, Flapper, but maybe it's not. Count gave me this safe deposit box key before I left." He fingered a key on the neck chain holding his dog tags.

Thursday, July 26, 1945...Day eleven A.A.

Ten days and 5,000 miles out of San Francisco, the *Indianapolis* was welcomed to the small Tinian Island harbor with a sigh of relief from the informed, and with great excitement from many who knew only that she was carrying something important. A number of admirals, as well as Army and Marine Corps generals came aboard simply to watch the unloading. The crew was never told what they were carrying.

Late in the day at Tinian, after the mysterious cargo had been unloaded, and after once more taking on fuel, *Indianapolis* weighed anchor, and got underway for the overnight trip to Guam, site of CincPacFleet Admiral Chester Nimitz's headquarters. Admiral Nimitz, along with his staff, and various Navy, Marine Corps, and Army commanders and their staffs, was busily engaged in planning for the invasion of the Japanese home islands, scheduled for three months hence.

Friday, July 27, 1945...Day 12 A.A.

Apra, Guam...Wardroom of the *USS Indianapolis* swinging at anchor in the harbor. Captain McVay addressed his senior officers. "Gentlemen," he said, "let me have your attention, please." The room became quiet. "First, let me congratulate all of you on a job well done. We still don't know the nature of that top-secret cargo, but whatever it was, we delivered it safely in record time so we can all feel we have done our duty. I hope you will convey this message to the junior officers and to the men. And let us hope it is true that we have played a major role in shortening the war, for if it is, we can all be proud to tell our grandchildren.

"Now let me tell you about our new orders. As many of you know, I had hoped we would be allowed to undertake training exercises here in the Guam area, but I am afraid that is not to be. Instead, we will sortie Guam at zero nine hundred tomorrow, and proceed to Leyte at normal cruising speed, which may take some getting used to after the last two weeks." The captain smiled, and a ripple of polite laughter went around the room.

"We should arrive in the Leyte area sometime Tuesday morning, and immediately begin seventeen days of training. I think you will agree that with all the new officers and men aboard, this training is desperately needed to get the old lady back in fighting trim for the invasion of Japan which I can now tell you is at this very moment being planned right here on Guam , and is scheduled for November." The captain beamed. Smiles, nods, and muttered approval filled the room.

"Are there any questions?"

"Captain, will we have an escort to Leyte?"

"No. We will be traveling alone. No escorts are available at the moment. The question was discussed, but it's the feeling at Pac Fleet Headquarters that presently the risks are minimal, and there is no compelling reason to delay our departure because of no escort. In fact, they feel it is so safe we may zigzag at our discretion. My plans are to zigzag during the day, and at night only if the moon is up."

Saturday, July 28, 1945...Day thirteen A.A.

Apra, Guam...At 0900 the *USS Indianapolis* sorties the harbor, and sets course for the southern Philippine Island of Leyte.

Boats and Flapper sat near the end of a long table in the crew's mess. In front of them lay the blue folder containing the curriculum of the School for Presidents. Flapper turned to the first page and said, "Four hundred and fifty years before Christ was born...more than two thousand years ago...Plato wrote *The Republic.* Did you know Count is a Greek scholar? Look here on page one."

Flapper pointed to the three short paragraphs, neatly spaced near the center of the page. He read aloud:

"As the individual soul has three parts, the rational, the spiritual, and the concupiscent, so the State has three corresponding elements—the rulers, the military guardians, and the mass of the population.

Who then are those whom we shall compel to be guardians of the State? Surely they will be those who are wisest about affairs of State, and to whom the State is best administered, and who at the same time have other honors and another and a better life than that of politics.

Until philosophers are kings or kings philosophers states will never have rest from their evils...THE REPUBLIC by Plato...450 B.C."

Flapper looked at Boats and said, "Count wants to make you a philosopher king. You may be the first."

Boats shook his head. "What does it mean, Flapper?" he asked.

Flapper thought he had an idea what it meant. "Have you ever heard of Socrates?" he asked.

Boats shook his head. "No," he answered.

"Okay, here's what I remember from my college course," Flapper began. "*The Republic* was one of the books we studied in Masterpieces of Literature. Socrates is the wisest of the philosophers of Athens, capital of Greece. He talks a lot about good and evil, justice and truth. When he is called wise he says, 'Only God can be called wise.' He prefers to be called a lover of wisdom. Socrates did not actually say states should have philosopher kings...he said that's what he might have said if it had not seemed so extravagant. In *The Republic* Socrates describes the qualities necessary in a philosopher-ruler, and the precise outline his education should take until he is finally prepared to assume responsible office. In a nutshell, Socrates says the ruler should be a warrior-athlete trained in arithmetic, geometry, and astronomy, and should understand that the highest knowledge is the idea of good."

Boats listened with interest. "It's pretty heavy stuff, Flapper," he said. "I'm not sure I see how it has anything to do with being president."

Flapper said, "I think the idea is that the president should be someone who is carefully trained for the job. One who is informed and knowledgeable in all aspects of government, and is committed to working for the public good. It's a magnificent vision, but probably no more practical now than it was two thousand years ago. Socrates himself said it was an extravagant idea, and I think Count knows it too. It's a lofty goal, but what's wrong with lofty goals?"

Boats nodded. "Can we talk about the curriculum?" he asked.

"Why not?" Flapper agreed. "It looks pretty unorthodox. Look at this...it begins with a course in statistics. If you're a mathematician you have to love that. I think Socrates would approve. The rationale is that if you're president you have to think big, and statistics is the science of big numbers. Remember when we talked about billions, trillions, and quadrillions?"

"I remember. It was about how far away the stars are," said Boats.

"Right. But now we're talking about things closer to home. If you're president, you have to make decisions, and plan programs that affect the lives of a hundred million people in the U.S., and maybe a few billion people around the world."

Flapper tapped a pencil on the table as he considered how to proceed. He had not planned this lecture, and wondered where it was headed. "Let me tell you about distribution curves," he said, then drew a graph on a notepad he carried. "Let's look at the distribution of wealth in the U.S...On this vertical axis, the Y axis, we'll put number of people. On the X axis, we'll put annual income, okay? Now let's just say there are a million people in the U.S. who don't have any annual income at all, and let's say the highest amount anyone makes in one year is a hundred thousand dollars, and there are also one million people in this category. So these are the first two points on our graph. On the Y axis these two numbers are the same—one million—but on the X axis they are very far apart. Now let's say the average annual income of all the people in the U.S. is ten thousand dollars...I know that's a pretty high average, but this is only theoretical. If we have, let's say, fifty million people in this category, it gives us another point on the graph. Now if we draw a smooth curve through these three points we get what looks like a bell, right?" Flapper drew the line and held up the graph.

Boats looked at the graph and agreed. "It looks like a bell all right."

Flapper continued. "So most of the wage earners in the U.S. are represented by the middle part of this graph," he said, "and on either end we have a relatively few very poor, and a relatively few very rich. It's called a distribution curve. Now if you are president, the happiest situation for you is the case where a decision you make, or a program you plan, will help people on all parts of this curve. The reality is that on almost any issue, what you do is going to hurt somebody on some part of this curve or at the least help one group more than the other. Socrates would say if you are a politician, all your decisions would be based on what would help the large majority in the top of the bell. If you are a philosopher you might take a different approach...depending on your philosophy you might favor the very rich or the very poor. And guess what? Mister Count makes that the next item on the curriculum: 'Politics...The Progressive-Conservative Debate.' Are you following all this Booker T.?"

Boats said, "Yeah, I get it. If I'm president it's up to me to decide for whom the bell tolls, right?"

Flapper laughed loudly and said, "That's good, Booker T. That's exactly the point."

"But what about this Progressive-Conservative debate? Why is that in there?" Booker T. asked.

Flapper said, "Okay, now we're back to philosophy. The terms Progressive and Conservative refer to two different ways of approaching problems or situations...two different philosophies, you might say."

Flapper again held up the wealth distribution curve. "The simplest way to look at it is that the conservative philosophy would support decisions favoring the right side of this curve, while the progressive philosophy would favor the left. The debate is about which side is correct. Another way to look at it is that, in general, conservatives are satisfied with the way things are while progressives, or liberals as some people call them, would like to look for new approaches. The cynic would agree with Ambrose Bierce who, in his *Devil's Dictionary* put it this way: a conservative is a statesman who is enamored of existing evils, as distinguished from a liberal, who wishes to replace them with others." He laughed, then continued, "As I read this curriculum, what Count has in mind is that you spend a lot of time considering different issues from both points of view. The idea is that the president should clearly understand both philosophies, and make decisions accordingly."

Flapper stopped to think. Boats was attentive; he thought about decisions he had made, and was trying with difficulty to relate his experiences to what Flapper was talking about. He could not think of anything he had ever done that was not based on some emotion, anger near the top of the list.

Flapper continued. "The next item in the curriculum is economics. Economics is the science that deals with the management of resources, and the production of goods and services

"Management of resources is one of the most important things a president does. What can be more important than deciding how the nation's money will be spent? The people who study these things...the economists...like to divide the whole money pot into two parts: the armed forces, and everything else. They call it 'guns and butter' issues. The butter issue covers a lot of territory including education, welfare, health, housing, transportation, crime and punishment, communication, recreation, taxation, commerce..."

Boats held up both hands asking Flapper to stop. "Whoa, Flapper you're losing me...I'm beginning to see why it's a ten-year curriculum."

Flapper said, "Yeah, and also why he's giving you fifty years to master it. Look, Booker T., it's getting close to lunchtime, and we're not going to solve the evils of the state anytime soon. Why don't we knock off for a while, but I do want to continue the discussion. I'm beginning to feel like a twentieth century Socrates. Maybe I'll read up on my Plato. And, speaking of Greeks, did you know my first name is Homer?"

Boats said, “Was your dad an umpire?”
Flapper rapped him playfully on the head with a rolled up sheet of paper.

>>18<<

PERIL ON THE SEA

Sunday, July 29, 1945 . . .Day fourteen A.A.

2300...*Indianapolis* steamed comfortably at sixteen knots through a restless sea. A three-quarter moon winked in and out behind broken clouds. In the warm summer night men were sleeping scattered all around the open decks to escape the stygian heat of the regular sleeping compartments burdened with battle condition two...compartment hatches closed and dogged. There was no air conditioning.

Boats and Flapper sat on the fantail, deep in conversation. Flapper was philosophizing. "Money is the most important form of power," he said. "If you have enough, and use it wisely, you can accomplish almost anything. That's one of the intriguing parts of Count's plan . . .that section where he describes how the whole thing will be financed. He intends for his candidate to be entirely free of financial obligations to anybody...no campaign fundraising...no contributions from special interest groups. He supplies all the money through his trust funds."

Flapper paused briefly, then interrupted his train of thought to ask, "Does Count really have that much money?"

Boats shrugged. "All I know is what he told me, " he said. "I didn't see the evidence, but I got no reason to doubt Count."

"So you really believe him?" Flapper asked.

Boats may not have had a reason to doubt Count, but he could not deny his uncertainty. It wasn't that he thought Count would lie to him or play games with him. It had something to do with the amounts; Count was talking about billions of dollars. Boats, when he thought about money, thought 100 dollars was a large number. His uncertainty also stemmed from one of his mother's favorite refrains: 'son, don't ever count your chickens before they is hatched.' He answered Flapper's question truthfully, "I don't know," he said.

KA BOoOoOoOoOoOM!

Without warning, an ear-shattering explosion rocked the forward part of the ship. Boats and Flapper, 500 feet away, were thrown to the deck by the powerful blast.

KA BLOOOOOOOOOOM!

Before they could regain their feet or even utter a cry of dismay, a second, equally shattering blast rendered the warm night air. The great ship shuddered ominously, and rapidly began to lose way.

Two 48-knot wakeless torpedoes, fired from a range of just under a mile by Japanese submarine I-58, had bracketed officers' country.

Flapper shouted, "Booker T., are you all right?"

"I'm all right, Flapper. What the hell happened?"

"I think we've been torpedoed!"

"What should we do?"

"Grab some life jackets!"

Men gathered on the fantail in large numbers, all wondering the same thing. What to do? They would have to figure it out for themselves; all ship's communications had been destroyed, there would be no orders from above. The men were on their own, but for the moment they did not know it. There was great confusion, but no panic. The moon which, like a blinking spotlight, appeared and disappeared behind the broken clouds periodically relieved the darkness.

Unfamiliar and alarming sounds were coming from somewhere forward, a sure sign that the ship was in serious trouble. The first explosion had ripped away a large part of the ship's tender bow, but being propelled at sixteen knots, she continued her forward momentum, and thus fatally imbibed thousands of gallons of seawater. Almost immediately the men on the fantail felt the deck tilting forward at a rapidly increasing downward angle, and knew that within minutes the unthinkable would occur, and they would be in the water. It was never a question of abandoning ship…the ship was abandoning the men, and she seemed in a great hurry to do so.

Lives were saved from the experience of previous fighting ships. Survivors had brought the message back to ship designers and planners: in the chaos of a rapidly sinking ship, there is no time to look for life-saving equipment. So life rafts, life jackets, and floater nets were positioned to float free should the ship go down.

Flapper and Boats, amidst the noise and clamor of yelling men and a dying ship, suddenly found themselves swimming desperately through a thick film of oily water.

"Grab anything that floats, Booker T., we're gonna need it! And get as far away from the ship as you can...when she goes down there may be suction!"

"My God, Flapper, look at that! I think she's gonna fall on us!"

The fantail of *Indianapolis* loomed straight up over the men struggling in the water, as if they were on a sidewalk looking up at a skyscraper. One of the screws, free from watery impediment, was still turning. But the ship did not topple. Instead, without fanfare, she hesitated for a brief farewell, then, like an express elevator, descended quickly and disappeared forever into a two mile deep. Twelve minutes had elapsed since the torpedoes had struck.

Of her 1,200-man complement, nearly 900 were left bobbing on the surface. Some were afraid, a few were laughing and joking as if it were an elaborate high adventure game, many had suffered painful burns and various other crippling injuries; all were at the mercy of the sea.

Monday, July 30, 1945 . . .Day fifteen A.A.

0600...The rising sun was a welcome sight on the first day. The 900 men had been in the water for six hours, and they were cold. They were spread over a wide area because of wind, current, and the fact that the ship was moving when it began to sink, strewing men along its wake like children falling off a moving hay rack. No one knew how many had survived. Men isolated in small groups, out of sight in the valleys of ocean swells, thought they were the only ones alive. Some were on rafts and nets, but the vast majority of men were alive only because of the kapok life jackets which in the beginning suspended them in the water like two-legged corks, their chests at water level. Makeshift floats were fashioned by tying several life jackets together, in some cases around a wooden potato crate or an empty oil can. The most fortunate were those who found themselves on life rafts...these contained a small but vital supply of food and fresh water. Most of the men were without either.

Boats and Flapper were together in a group of 20 oily-faced swimmers who looked like minstrel singers. They were floating in a gently rolling sea with three-foot swells. Flapper attempted to organize the group.

"Come in close where you can hear me better," he shouted. "I'm Flapper Jackson, First Division Officer, and as near as I can tell, Senior Officer afloat." Flapper tried to make a mental note of the men who laughed. He felt responsible for the group. It was important to learn their strengths and weaknesses quickly; he knew about Boats, but not the others.

"I'm taking command of this group, and if you'll listen to me and do what I tell you, we'll all have a better chance to get out of this mess. There's no sense kidding ourselves, we're in a bad spot. But it could be worse, let's start with that. Nobody is shooting at us; the water is warm; we're directly in the shipping and flying lanes between Guam and Leyte, so there's a very good chance we'll be spotted and picked up soon. These kapok life jackets are the best the Navy has. They're designed to hold you up in the water for at least four days, and you know we're gonna get picked up before that." Not all the men were listening; some were in a state of shock from which they would not recover.

Flapper continued. "Now a few things to remember from boot camp. First, and the most important thing of all: *do not drink this water*. This is salt water and it is poisonous...do you hear that? This water is poisonous...no matter how thirsty you get...*do not drink this water***.** If you drink this water it will kill you, and...listen to this...it will be an ugly, rotten, disgusting death...you will go stark raving mad. Does everybody understand? *Do not drink this water...it is poison!*"

Flapper looked carefully at the men around him. He could tell from their eyes those for whom this was a wasted message. He continued. "Next: sharks..." Heads came up. "We may see sharks. Be as still as possible. Don't flail your arms and legs, that will only attract them to you. Sharks are not smart; if you stay perfectly still they will take you for a piece of floating driftwood. They have never seen a human before, remember that." Some of the men nodded; the thought of sharks brought chilling terror.

"Finally, our best chance is to remain close together. Don't swim off by yourself. Before this is over you may be tested to the limit of your endurance. Conserve your strength. Be determined. Take courage. Be strong. Make up your minds that you *will* survive. You are young, you have much to live for. Do not despair. Don't ever give up. Show that you have the guts to live. What do you say?"

Halfway through his exhortation, Flapper realized he was sounding like a football coach giving a pep talk...it stirred him to add a few additional appeals. But if he expected the men to shout, "Let's go" at the end of his speech, he was disappointed.

"How close is the nearest land?" One of the men asked.

Flapper thought a moment. "We left Guam Saturday morning," he said, "we've been traveling at about sixteen knots, so we're probably about five hundred miles from there, and another six hundred miles from Leyte where we were headed. I don't think there's anything but deep water in between."

"How come you know so much?" The hostile voice came from the edge of the group.

Navy discipline was deep-rooted, and most of the men were comforted by Flapper's voice of authority, but the wrenching experience of being snatched from familiar surroundings and cast in an instant into life-threatening uncertainty left some of the men resentful, and their officers became lightning rods of blame.

Flapper was startled by the question, but instinctively reacted to what he recognized as a challenge to his authority. He spoke as forcefully as he knew how. "I know so much because I am an officer, and I am in command here. There will be no challenging my authority. All our lives depend on your doing what I tell you to do...you are still in the Navy, and I demand that you never forget it. You must obey your officers."

For a while there was silence in the group as they pondered Flapper's words. Finally somebody, hoping for the help of a higher authority, asked, "Do you think we should pray?"

Flapper said, "It can't hurt. Can you lead us in the Lord's prayer?"

Noon...The mid-day tropical sun reflecting off the oil-slick water at 11 degrees north latitude was blinding and brutal. Many of the men were already suffering from blurred and distorted vision from the thick fuel oil that was impossible to keep out of their eyes, but ironically provided some protection to their sensitive skin. Suddenly shouts erupted; a plane had been sighted. Men waved and yelled as loudly as they could...in vain. The plane was too high, and gave no indication it had seen them. Reconnaissance flights over open ocean were not designed to look for men in the water, especially not for men who weren't even known to be missing. Still, sighting the plane gave reason for hope.

"Maybe he saw us and sent a rescue message."

"Do you think the *Indy* got off an S.O.S. before she went down?"

"Sure she did. She must have."

Shortly after the excitement of spotting the plane, the first shark appeared.

Terror swept the group.

"Stay calm, men, don't panic. Be still," Flapper said in a firm voice.

The menacing dorsal fin circled the group as if on a scouting mission. A man on the outer fringe began to cry loudly, "It's coming closer! It bumped my leg! It's after me! HELP! HELP!"

The man began to thrash in the water with his hands, trying to frighten away the shark. It was a fatal error. He screamed as the shark ripped into a flailing leg. Blood pooled around him. Instantly more sharks appeared, and the helpless sailor quickly disappeared in a melee of milling sharks. The remainder of the terrified group watched in grisly fascination as the gruesome slaughter unfolded before their horrified eyes.

Flapper called urgently: "Don't anybody move! Don't panic! Be still! Your life depends on it. All our lives depend on it. Don't move!"

Five hours later...1700 hours. Another plane was seen flying high in the sky. It was the third, but no one shouted or waved for fear of attracting sharks. Throughout the afternoon the dread dorsal fin had circled the pitiful group, which had pulled closer together after the grisly noontime spectacle.

"I'm thirsty, Flapper."

"We're all thirsty, Dyer. Don't think about it."

"How long can a man live without food and water, Flapper?"

"A long time. Maybe a week, maybe longer."

"If they're not gonna pick us up, do you think we could swim back to Guam?"

"No chance, Dyer. Conserve your energy. Just relax. Don't exert yourself."

"Should we say another prayer?"

Flapper had an idea. "Maybe we should sing 'The Navy Hymn,'" he said. "That's kind of a prayer. Do you remember it from boot camp?"

Flapper began to sing the familiar, and altogether appropriate hymn. The others joined in. They sang it five times.

Eternal Father strong to save
Whose arm doth bind the restless wave.
Who bids the mighty ocean deep
Its own eternal vigil keep.
O hear us as we cry to Thee
For those in peril on the sea.

Tuesday July 31,1945...Day sixteen A.A

0630...It had been a night of terror. They discovered that sleep was also an enemy for when they dozed, their faces dipped below the surface, and they were startled into wakefulness, choking and gasping for breath. So the cycle of desperation was almost complete: no food, no water, no protection, no sleep. What remained was hope, and for some an iron-willed determination not to die. After 30 hours in the water, hope was still strong, reinforced during the night by a flare fired from somewhere near. They were cheered by the presence of nearby rafts with signaling devices. The flare had been fired in response to the presence of a plane flying low enough to see its running lights. The sagging spirits of the floaters were enormously lifted by the candle glow of the Very pistol flare against the dark South Pacific night. Surely this would be seen. Soon their ordeal would be over. Daylight would bring resurrection.

But daylight brought only the bitter taste of the sea, the biting whip of the wind, stinging salt spray in their eyes, the cruel presence of sharks, and yet another notch of the torture rack...the kapok life jackets had noticeably lost buoyancy...their heads were closer to the water.

And then, the first hallucinations..."Look, look, for God's sake, look over there! It's an island! An island! Look...over there!" The sailor began to swim frantically in the direction he was pointing, but was quickly restrained by Flapper and Booker T.

"Hold it, Dyer, hold it, Dyer, not so fast, not so fast, let's be sure. Take it easy, if it really is an island, it won't go away."

"It *is* an island, Flapper. Can't you see it? Let me go. I'll show you where it is. Just follow me, I'll show you."

"I don't see it, Dyer. Does anybody else see it?"

Several shouts went up.

"I see it. I see it. It's over there."

One man spoke up in disgust. "I know that island," he scoffed. "My grandma sells ice cream there. Dyer is right, there is an island over there. That island used to be off the coast of Rhode Island, but now it's here. Except it's closed in December. There ain't no sense goin' there now, it's closed. Forget it."

"You hear that, Dyer? Blinky says it's closed," Flapper said. Then quietly aside, "Do you see it, Booker T.?"

"No, Flapper, I don't see it. Do you?"

"I thought I did, just for a minute."

Dyer began to shout again. "Did you guys see those flares last night? You know what that means don't ya? It means there's some rafts somewhere over there, and they're full of officers. How come all the fuckin' officers get to ride the rafts and we have to swim? Huh? How come?"

Other joined in. "Yeah. How come, Flapper? They probly got food and water too. How come, Flapper?" Some moved menacingly toward Flapper.

"Hold it, men. Flapper's here with us, how can you blame him?" Boats shouted.

One of the men bellowed, "Stay back, men, he's got a hand grenade."

From the outer edge of the group, Dyer was yelling, "You can have my life jacket, I'm headin' for that island, closed or not. You dummies can stay here if you want." He had stripped off his life jacket and swam furiously away.

Wednesday August 1, 1945...Day seventeen A.A.

Only 10 of the original 20 men remained as dawn came marking 54 hours in the water. Now their chins were in the water as the soggy life jackets continued to lose their buoyancy. Flapper was exhausted from fighting off an attacker who mistook him for a Japanese infantryman during the night. Boats was the strongest of the lot, which didn't say much for they were a feeble lot. During the morning two men drowned when their life jackets sank; they were too weak to remove them, and seemed beyond caring. By evening only six remained alive...they floated in silence, beyond hope.

Flapper gathered his strength for a final admonishment, his voice coming as a hoarse whisper through cracked and painful lips. "Booker T.," he said, "don't close your eyes. You must stay awake. There's still hope."

Thursday, August 2, 1945...Day eighteen A.A.

Boats was alone. It was morning after the fourth night in the water. Looking around he saw nothing but sea.

"Flapper!" he called in a small voice. There was no answer. Three times he repeated the plaintive cry, then lapsed into a stupor.

Shortly before noon, after 84 hours in the sea, without food or sweet water, Boats raised his head at the sound of an airplane motor, and found he was still capable of excitement as it was clear that the plane had seen him. The plane circled, and dropped a life raft close enough for him to reach after a great effort. With his last ounce of strength he pulled himself onto to the raft and sank into oblivion.

PART TWO

>> 19 <<

FLAPPER OF BREESE

Flapper Jackson was dead, he was sure of that...he had drowned in the Pacific Ocean on August 2, 1945. He remembered the water closing over his head and the feeling of peace after three and a half days of terror at the mercy of the sea following the midnight torpedoing and sinking of the heavy cruiser *Indianapolis.*

So if he was dead, where was he now? He could hear voices, but they seemed far away and muffled. He heard the soft, relaxing sound of a piano playing a familiar melody...it sounded like "Claire de Lune." Was he in heaven? He tried to open his eyes, but found it difficult, and gave it up. He became aware that he was lying down. He waited for something to happen, but nothing did. He slept. It was heaven.

Flapper lay on a starched white sheet covering a stiff mattress on the hospital ship *USS Mercy*...he had been there for four days while life dripped into his veins. When he finally opened his eyes at three in the morning he saw nothing but black night. He tried to sit up, and with difficulty managed to raise himself to a position where he was leaning on one elbow, but the effort was too much and he slumped back. He closed his eyes and tried to sort out a procession of thoughts marching across his consciousness.

He had died, of that he was certain, so what did it mean if he was lying here trying to understand what it meant? Was there life after death? Or did it mean he had been restored to life, that he had been resurrected? If that was the case, was it now his job to go out and perform miracles...to redeem souls? He waited for instructions. If he had any choice here he would prefer life after death, he had seen enough of life before death. He looked forward to what the next life had to offer. Would there be baseball?... Chopin?...Mozart?...the Casta Diva?...Peking Duck?...Ille de

Flotante?...Chilton County peaches?...Shalimar?

He awoke to bells and whistles; he heard people shouting..."It's over, the war is over!"

So it was resurrection. He sighed and wondered when he would receive his instructions about soul saving. Somehow he knew there would be no instructions...he would have to improvise. He began to think about what miracles he might perform. He sat up in bed, looked around the room, took a deep breath and smiled. It was his first miracle.

When Lt. Susan Land, U.S. Navy Nurse Corps, pushed aside the white curtain to look in on Flapper she was thrilled to see him sitting up and smiling. She quickly walked to the side of his bed, and planted a big wet kiss on his still cracked lips.

"Ouch!" said Flapper. "What you tryin' to do, Ethel? I haven't been back long enough to start thinkin' about stuff like that."

In answer, Susan kissed him again, this time more tenderly.

"Mmm," he said. "Nice to see you, angel."

Susan beamed. "The war is over, Homer," she said, "and you are alive. For a while I thought we had lost you."

"I died, Ethel. I don't know how I got here, but I can tell you for sure I was dead."

Susan humored him. It was not the first time she had heard these words from recovering casualties; and though all her medical training told her it was not physiologically possible to die and come back to life, she had heard the claim often enough to wonder. One thing she knew for sure was that when Flapper Jackson was delivered to the *Mercy* seven days earlier he was as near death as it was possible to be. That he was now sitting up smiling was another wonder to be added to the list of miraculous recoveries she had witnessed here in the war zone. If he said he had died, she would not contradict him; she was, after all, a Christian, but admittedly, here in the war zone, one with more than her share of unanswered prayers.

"You got here because your luck held out, and a Navy flying boat got to you just before a hammerhead shark. You were almost the last one to die, but Homer, the war is over, you are alive, and nobody has to die anymore." She kissed him again. The end of the war seemed to spawn a great interest in kissing.

Flapper shook his head. "Ethel, you must not have heard me," he said, "I did die...but I guess that doesn't matter now...How could the war end so soon? Last I knew we were getting ready to invade the home islands...and when are you gonna start calling me Flapper?"

Susan sighed. "Your name is Homer," she said. "It's here on your dog tags...Homer Jackson. Flapper sounds like something blowing in the wind, or what my mom was twenty years ago...and when are you going to start calling me Susan? See, it's right here on my dog tags."

"Susan, honey, how could the war end so soon?" It never occurred to him to ask who won.

Susan shook her head and said, "I don't know, Flapper, it takes a while for the news to filter down. All I *do* know is that the announcement came over the loudspeaker about twenty minutes ago, and it seems to be true. Imagine! It's another miracle. The war is over!"

It would take some time for Flapper, Susan, and all the others to assimilate the full meaning of those four little words...the war is over...but the initial reaction after overcoming stunned disbelief, here and everywhere on the winning side, was universal elation, exhilaration, and joy. A weight had been lifted, the prospect of violent death faded, the future was a bright horizon. Flapper lay back and began to think about what it meant when he suddenly remembered his floating shipmates. He sat bolt upright and cried, "What about Booker T.?"

Startled by his quick movement, Susan put a hand on his shoulder and said, "Easy, Flapper, take it easy...did you say, Booker T.?"

"Yes, Booker T., my friend from Peoria. I taught him math in high school, he was in the water near me. Is he here too?"

"No, Flapper, you were the only one brought here."

"But there must have been more, I couldn't be the only one, there were so many."

Flapper was right about that. That any of the 800 in the water survived was only because of a chance observation by an alert pilot of a high-flying scout plane. Flapper was the last one picked up, and he was brought to the *Mercy*, anchored off Mindanao, the others were taken to the naval hospital on Palau. Susan did not know about the close to 300 survivors taken to Palau, and tried to steer Flapper's thoughts away from the horrendous idea that he might be the sole survivor. "I think I met Booker T. that night at the Mogmog USO party in Ulithi," she said. "He was your student? I didn't know you were a teacher."

"I don't remember much of that night. Was I a friendly drunk?"

Susan laughed. She remembered the night well. "Not only friendly, but very funny," she said. "We had a lot of fun that night, too bad you don't remember. I tried to get you to lay off those Mogmog Mules, they're about ninety percent pure rum."

"Did I behave myself?"

Susan pouted in mock disapproval. "As well as could be expected," she said. "You taught mathematics?"

Flapper nodded. "I tried," he said. "...algebra, geometry, trigonometry, a little calculus. It's not so easy getting teenagers interested in math when there's football, basketball, girls, and boys, but I tried. What about you? Were you a nurse before the war?"

Susan smiled. "My dad is a country doctor," she said, "which means he treats horses and cows too. We lived in Ware, Missouri...down in the foothills of the Ozark Mountains. I helped him in the office when I was in high school; it seemed natural for me to take up nursing. I graduated from Barnes Hospital in St. Louis just in time for the war. I joined the Navy to see the world."

Flapper couldn't resist. "And what did you see?"

Susan responded, and Flapper joined in chorus, "I saw the sea."

They both laughed.

Susan sat on the edge of the bed and put her hand on Flapper's forehead, checking his temperature, but at the same time getting a feel for him.

Susan continued. "I picked up the *Mercy* in San Diego," she said. "I've been on her ever since...I did get to spend some time in Hawaii, and of course there was Ulithi; I guess a coral atoll counts as part of the world."

Flapper took Susan's hand, and looked into her hazel brown eyes. "Would you believe me if I told you I was from St. Louis?" he asked.

Susan looked at him suspiciously. It was not easy being a woman in the war zone. "Why shouldn't I believe you? With a face like yours, you couldn't fool a zoo. When's the last time you tried to tell a lie?"

Flapper put on what he hoped was a serious face. "The next time will be the first time," he lied.

Susan noticed a water glass slowly slide across a bedside table; the ship had started to move. Flapper noticed it too. They looked at each other. Susan stood up and said, "Listen, my grand survivor, we have things to talk about, but right now I think you better lie back and take it easy, you're not completely recovered by a long shot." He was still hooked up to tubes. "I'm going to see what's going on, it feels like we're moving." She kissed him lightly on the forehead and left.

Flapper lay back and closed his eyes, but he did not sleep right away. The full appreciation of the war's end would not reach him for months, and it would be years before his dreams were not punctuated by exploding shells and anguished cries. His mind was assaulted by questions. *How could the war end so abruptly? Am I the only survivor of the* Indianapolis *sinking? Has God saved me for a purpose? Is Booker T. in heaven? What will I tell Susan when she asks what will I do now that the war is over? What* will *I do?* It was time to plan a life. Where to start? He slept.

He slept for two days, and towards the end he dreamed. He dreamed of the landings at Tarawa, Peleliu, and Iwo Jima. He dreamed of his role as fire control spotter for the 8-inch naval cannons of the *Indianapolis*. His head echoed with shattering bedlam. He groaned in his sleep. Susan was by his side, watching, tending, nursing.

The *Mercy* was plowing a course for Hawaii through the recently troubled South Pacific Ocean, and after five days, Flapper was up and out on deck. The sea was calm, and the bright moon aimed a path across the dark water exactly to the spot by the rail where Susan and Flapper stood shoulder to shoulder. They were growing closer, but had yet to acknowledge it, each holding something back.

Susan spoke. "It was an atomic bomb," she said, "or rather it was two atomic bombs, one for Hiroshima and one for Nagasaki…over a hundred thousand people died."

Flapper shook his head in disbelief. "I don't understand how a single bomb could cause so much destruction," he said.

They were both silent for a while, imagining the scenes. Flapper began again. "I also don't understand why we would use such a weapon on civilian populations. And I…" He stopped talking as a sudden realization hit him. "Susan…I…" he stammered, "we…we carried that bomb from San Francisco."

He stood shaking his head at the memory of the high-speed, 5,000-mile dash of the *Indianapolis;* he even remembered the date they arrived at their destination of Tinian Island…July 26, 1945. His head was spinning; feelings of pride at the achievement zigzagged through his mind around thoughts of remorse for his personal culpability for so much human suffering. "Nobody knew what it was," he said. "They told us that every day we saved getting it to Tinian would shorten the war by that much. The best guess was it was some kind of bacterial warfare. I saw it. It was about as big as a fire plug." His voice cracked. "We didn't know."

Susan thought of the suffering as she listened to Flapper; then, feeling his distress, moved closer and put her hand on his arm. "It's not your fault," she said.

Flapper shook his head. "Why does there have to be killing?" he asked. "Why can't we live in peace?"

"We can," Susan said. "Now we can. Look at the lights."

The ship was steaming at night with all lights blazing, something it had never done before. After years of extraordinary precautions to seek invisibility at night on the sea, the *Mercy* was now free of that difficult and ominous burden.

"What will you do?" Flapper asked Susan, beating her to the punch, and trying to buy time for his own uncertain answers.

Around the globe the question resounded wherever the warriors gathered to celebrate or despair the end of hostilities. For most the answer was as easy as reveille in the morning…it had been on their minds and in their talk during many a long night, and in more than a few muddy holes-in-the-ground for as long as they had been over there. Get married, get a job, raise a family, be a citizen, build a community, have a life.

Susan hesitated. Flapper waited, wondering if she had heard the question. She had. And she knew exactly what she would do; she would go back to school and become a doctor. The thought had developed slowly as she watched and assisted in countless life-saving operations over the past three years on the hospital ship. At the same time she recognized, and would not deny another need; the primal urge to become a mother. She had always felt she would marry a doctor, but now she knew…Flapper was her man. Finally she shrugged. "Why don't we get married, Flapper," she blurted, "and then see what happens?"

She was looking out to sea when she said it, and Flapper, straining to catch the muted words, only heard the ending. "That's probably about all we can do right now," he said. "Wait and see what happens."

Susan turned to face him, and grasped his shoulders firmly. "I don't think you heard me, Flapper," she declaimed. "I said, why don't we get married?"

Flapper blinked. He stared down at Susan, only a few inches shorter than him. He grasped her shoulders, and they stood at arms length holding each other in tight grips. He started to speak, but stopped. Finally he managed to say in what sounded to him like a croak, "You mean to each other?"

She moved closer, put her arms around his waist, and leaned her head against his chest. "I want to spend my life with you, Flapper," she whispered. "This is a proposal."

Flapper brightened. "Well, why didn't you say so, Ethel?" he said. "Let's go find the captain."

Susan stepped back. Resisting the temptation to punch him in the jaw, she said, "Flapper, I'm serious."

Flapper was struggling with the idea of spending his life with someone. If she had just said, "Let's get married," it would have been better. It wasn't that he didn't like Susan...he liked her a lot. Who wouldn't? She was the most attractive woman he had ever known...smart, very pretty, with dark brown, shoulder-length hair, eyes like two chocolate drops, and a woman's body that never failed to turn a head for a second look. Flapper was most appreciative of that body. In fact, from the first time he saw her—from his hospital bed after Peleliu—and how she moved, he had thought, *If she had been a boy, she would have been a halfback* —his absolute highest rating. But spend his whole life with her? Flapper had been raised to be cautious about important decisions, to weigh the pros against the cons. He needed time to examine the implications. Because he liked Susan so much, it counted a lot that she was ready to commit her life to him, but it puzzled him that she was ready to do that with so little knowledge of him. Also, it occurred to him that he didn't know very much about her either.

"Susan, honey," he said, "how can you be sure you want to spend your whole life with me when you don't know that much about me?"

Susan was different from Flapper in one very important category, a potential source of future conflict: she was impulsive where he was cautious. Although she, like Flapper, was raised to carefully consider important decisions, the lesson didn't take. Something in her genes made her prone to quick judgments, and living with the consequences. In the case of Flapper, it was easy for her. He was good looking in a quirky sort of way, with a slightly crooked nose, wide set dark eyes, heavy eyebrows, a strong jaw, and good teeth. He would probably be bald on top before he was fifty, but he had a soft mat of chest hair that stirred something in her. He was fun loving, and certainly courageous. He was sensitive to the suffering of others, and for her the clinching argument, he was a teacher; he would make a good father.

"I know you are kind, sensitive, brave, funny, and good looking. What else do I need to know?"

Flapper looked at Susan, and saw exactly the same qualities. But there was more, and he suddenly had to tell her. "What if I told you I was a messenger of God?"

She laughed a pleasant, sexy laugh. "I'd say you were nuttier than a fruitcake," she said.

He did not laugh, and she backed up a step when she saw that he was serious. At least he looked like he was serious; she wasn't sure. He was right, she didn't know him. "Are you a religious nut?" she asked.

"I don't think so," he said, "but let me tell you a story. It goes back to my first landing at Tarawa. I don't know if anyone has ever tried to tell you what that landing was like and if they did…" He paused and looked at Susan who shook her head in the negative. "It was too awful," he continued, "I won't even try…so many died." He paused again, then said, "My point is, I felt invulnerable, and I was. I felt the same way at Peleliu and at Iwo Jima…like I had a special destiny to survive the war. Even though I took that Samurai sword whack on the head at Peleliu I never felt threatened or even in danger, and then look what happened when the Indy-Maru was sunk. I died. Susan, honey, I really did die. I can tell you what death is like…it is red fading into blue, and blue shading through azure to indigo. And quiet, tranquil, serene, soundless…not even any ringing in the ears." He paused, thinking about death. "And then I came back to life. At first I thought I was in the next world, or maybe even heaven, but then I heard somebody yell, 'The war is over,' and I knew I had been resurrected. I guess I don't have to tell you what happened the last time someone was resurrected."

Susan listened, waiting for more, but for the moment Flapper was finished talking. They were both quiet for a while. At length she laid her open palm on his cheek. "All right, Flapper," she said, "I will be your first disciple, and if you are really good I may even become an apostle, but this time things will be different. First, you have to marry me, but before that I have some questions."

"Shoot."

"Where were you born, what was the date, and was it in a manger?"

"I was born in Breese, Illinois on November 11, 1918, and I think it was in the front parlor of our home which, as far as I know, was never used as a manger."

Susan pondered. "Hmm. Flapper of Breese. It has a certain ring to it, and the date is not without some distinction. We may be onto something here."

In that moment Flapper knew he wanted to spend the rest of his life with this woman. He took her in his arms and kissed her long and passionately.

At length he pushed her gently away, and holding her at arms length, said, "Susan there's something else I think you should know."

She saw a different look in his eyes, and pulled back slightly. "What is it,

Flapper? You look so serious."

"My family has a Jewish background," he said.

Susan was startled. Growing up in the Ozarks, she had never known any Jews. The only thing she knew about Jews was what she had learned in her Catholic Sunday school, and though she had always been vaguely troubled that Jesus, the rock of Christianity, was a Jew, she never brooded over it, accepting the conventional wisdom that there was nothing unusual about it. Now she looked at Flapper and said, "Well, I guess that settles it. You are the second Messiah."

Then *she* turned serious. "But Flapper," she said, "I should tell you something too...my family background is Catholic."

>> 2 0<<

A NEW BEGINNING

The Pacific Ocean was true to its name over the next 10 days as the *Mercy* continued its unhurried journey over smooth water to the snug harbor called Pearl on the resplendent island of Oahu. By the time she passed Diamond Head, and eased into the narrow channel leading to the pearl, Susan and Flapper knew a lot more about each other. Flapper knew that Susan was wary of people who wanted to call her Sue or Suzy. He knew that she liked fresh strawberries, and that she had never heard of a date shake. He was amazed at how soft her body was, and at how it affected him. Susan knew that Flapper had been trying all his life to escape the name Homer, and had tested ten different nicknames including "Push" Jackson (which he refused to explain), before deciding that Flapper suited him best. He was thinking of writing to the state of Illinois for an official name change. She knew that he liked fried okra and Spike Jones. She was amazed at how hard his body was, and at how it affected her.

She learned that it was not always easy to tell whether he was serious or whether he was joking. He learned that he must be careful about his deadpan jokes because it was too easy to fool her. He tried to explain to her about baseball, but found the best he could offer was that during the season he lived in dread of missing the start of a 10 game winning streak.

Flushed with the excitement of a new life together, they resolved to put the past to rest, and to not look back. The resolve was easier said than done for it was not that easy, indeed it was not even possible, to erase the memories when almost 15 percent of their young lives had been spent in the foul, but at times undeniably glorious business of war. What was needed, and what they were blessed with, was time...time to frame their dreams.

Susan and Flapper sat near the edge of a cliff, looking down on the sparkling blue-green waters of Hanauma Bay, 10 miles east of Waikiki. The coral outlines beneath the water formed a purple mosaic against a dazzling green where the water covered soft sand. They had much to share from the bundle of mail each received after the *Mercy* docked. One of the many wonders of war-time organization was the Fleet Post Office in Hawaii, which somehow managed to keep track of hundreds of thousands of men and women scattered over the wide Pacific theater, and to ensure that they got their mail from home.

"Listen to this, Susan," said Flapper. "It's a poem my mother sent. It's called 'A New Beginning.'" He read it to her.

"There is always time for beginnings
when the dreamer awakes at last,
urgent with a deep sense of reality,
and arises from his sleep,
turning his mind outward from himself
to frame his dream in action.

Thus is created for all to see,
in some imperishable form, his soul's desire.
Thus he makes an act of faith and love,
and a spiritual hope because immortal is the deed.

Now is the time for our beginnings again.
May we be dedicated to the dreaming of the dream;
and may we awaken from slumbers now made restless with hope,
to harness our arts and our strengths
to every sacred opportunity."

When he finished reading he handed her the paper, and she read it to herself. Then she read it aloud to him. When she finished they sat quietly thinking about the words.

"Frame our dreams in action," said Susan. "What a lovely thought." Glancing again at the paper, she said, "By Arthur Graham. Do you know him, Flapper?"

Flapper nodded. "He's a Unitarian minister. Also he is a Red Sox fan."

Susan wrinkled her brow. "Is the poem about baseball?" she asked.

"Of course," he said.

Susan looked to see if he was serious. It seemed he was. "Anything else?" she asked.

"*Everything* else," he answered.

She took his hand and held it to her cheek. "I think we have a sacred opportunity, Flapper," she said. "There's nothing we can't do... Where do we start?"

Flapper and Susan had not been together long enough to know who would be the leader of their team. Susan began with the conventional approach that it was the man of the family who set the course. She assumed they would have children, and that she would be a housewife. She would put her dream of becoming a doctor aside. It was up to Flapper to bring home the bacon. Flapper would have said the same if asked.

Flapper considered the question. Where to start? "I need some time, Susan," he said. "I always thought I would go back to be a high school math teacher, but now I'm not sure. I did enjoy teaching, but if we're going to have a family... teachers don't make very much money... still, right now it's about the only skill I have. I don't know how to run a business, and I'm not sure I want to learn." He gazed at the hazy horizon.

Susan, steeped in a medical tradition, said, "Have you ever thought about becoming a doctor? I could be your nurse."

Flapper shook his head. "No, I never did," he said. "I wonder if I could. I wouldn't mind going back to school."

Susan said, "The government is going to pay people to go to school; I heard some doctors complaining about it. They said they paid for their own education, so why should others get it free, and also they didn't like the idea of more competition. One said we already have more doctors than we need."

"Is that true, Susan?" Flapper asked. "Do we have more doctors than we need?"

Susan shrugged. "I only know what it was like before the war," she said. "I don't know about the cities, but out in the country where we live, my dad is the only doctor for miles... one time he had to travel practically all night on a horse to deliver a baby." She paused, thinking about babies. "You know, Flapper," she said, "we're not the only ones thinking about babies. I think we'll see a pretty big jump in population when all the guys get back from the war. Also, a lot of the doctors we have now are getting old... I think there will be a big need for more doctors."

Flapper had a thought. "What about you, Susan? Why don't *you* become a doctor? Who says doctors can only be men? There must be some lady doctors aren't there? You're already a nurse, it should be easy for you."

When Flapper said that, a thought raced across Susan's mind...*I may even learn to love this guy.* She knew she would be a good doctor. She had assisted in numerous intricate, and sometimes ghastly surgical procedures in the war zone, and found she was not squeamish, and to boot, after witnessing some doctors in action, there were times when she thought she could do it better. "I could do it," she said, "but what about our family?"

The idea of raising a family was so far from Flapper's mind that he had to stop a moment to think about what it meant. Never for a moment did he think it was something he couldn't do. Flapper was a problem solver, which had become evident over the past several years on all those hostile South Pacific beaches. But the problem here was that before they started thinking about a family there was the urgent business of starting a career, or more accurately two careers. "We don't have to have children right away, do we?" he offered. "Maybe it would be better if we waited...Don't they teach you something about things like that in nursing school?"

Susan blushed. "We have to be awfully careful, Flapper," she said, "it's too easy to make babies." She sat thinking, then said, "I wonder what my dad would say if I told him I wanted to be a doctor?"

Flapper looked up. "I guess your parents don't know about us...will they be surprised?"

Susan smiled. "I wrote to them," she said, "but they probably didn't get the letter yet. They will be startled, but not surprised. I can just hear my dad when he reads the letter." Susan lowered her voice, imitating her father, "Well Mother, your daughter has decided it's time to get married."

Flapper laughed. "What's your father like?" he asked.

Susan did not hesitate. "My father is a man of very strong opinions," she said. "I'm sure it never entered his head that I might become a doctor instead of a nurse. It's not that he would be against it, it's just that he would never think of it. Women are nurses. Men are doctors. He likes things the way they have always been. He hated Roosevelt and doesn't seem to like Truman much better. Every letter I get from him has a new complaint."

Flapper's ears perked up when he heard that. "Uh oh," he said.

Susan looked at him and asked, "What?"

Flapper said, "My dad thought Franklin Roosevelt was the best thing that ever happened to this country, and he doesn't mind telling people why he thinks that. We may be in for some interesting discussions if they ever get together."

Flapper looked at Susan carefully as he suddenly realized it might be more important for him to know what Susan thought about Roosevelt than what her dad thought. For himself, he had been too busy getting his life organized to think much about politics. He had never found any reason to disagree with his father's sometimes-impassioned analysis of the day's news. "What do *you* think of Roosevelt?" he asked.

Susan said, "To tell the truth, Flapper, I never thought too much about him at all. My dad certainly talked about him enough, but when I was home those things didn't seem to have much to do with me so I didn't pay much attention to them."

"That's about how it is with me, too, Susan," said Flapper. "I voted for Roosevelt in 1940, but it was more because of my dad than because of any strong convictions of my own, although I do think he did a good job of bringing the country out of the Depression."

Susan said a bit sheepishly, "My dad thinks Roosevelt got us into the war."

Flapper shook his head. "I wonder why he thinks that? It was not even four years ago when some Jap planes were flying over where we are now sitting to hit Pearl Harbor...What does your mother think?"

"She doesn't argue with Dad, but I'm not sure she always agrees with him. I've seen her roll her eyes when he goes into a tirade, which he has been known to do."

Flapper laughed. "My mother doesn't mind a good argument," he said, "but I think she and Dad are pretty much in agreement on Roosevelt and the Democrats."

Finished with politics for the moment, Flapper had a new question. "Do you have brothers and sisters?" he asked.

Susan answered. "One brother...his name is David...he's about sixteen now. He'll be asking you some questions about the war, you can bet on that. But I also have some aunts and uncles I want you to meet, and especially I want you to meet my grandmother and grandfather; they are very special. The whole family lives down in the Ozarks. I am going to take you to a place where I guarantee if you think you were in heaven before, you will know it for sure when you get there." Susan's eyes sparkled as she thought of this enchanting place. "It's my grandma and grandpa's summer resort. They call it Cottage Farm." Susan's eyes shone with pleasure thinking of Cottage Farm. "It's on a high bluff looking out over a wide valley and an endless sky. It's like you're standing on a cloud looking down at a peaceful land." Then she added as an afterthought, "My grampa built the only privately owned Catholic church in the world up on that hill…the view is sensational."

Flapper was captivated at the moment with the enthusiasm he saw in Susan. He gazed at her admiringly and said, "Susan, honey, I think we may have a little piece of heaven right here. Look at that coral. Did you ever see green water like that? Why don't we just stay here and forget about everything else?"

Susan opened a picnic basket and took out some sandwiches and a thermos. "Even in heaven we have to eat," she said.

They munched sandwiches and looked out on Hanauma Bay. At one time, the bay was like Diamond Head—a dead volcano. But at Hanauma Bay it was different in that the sea had broken through the outer wall leaving the old crater filled with salt water. The well-protected bay that resulted left a peaceful beach, in stark contrast to the rolling surf of Waikiki, and the wild water that attacked the Kona side of the island.

Flapper and Susan, only days away from violence and uncertainty, allowed the healing power of warm sunshine, green mountains, soothing waters, and cool breezes to flow over them. They thrilled to the marvel of a color show beginning with multi-tiered rainbows in the green hills behind them, and ending with a 60 minute coda of brilliant hues capping the western horizon as the sun fell out of sight. Radiant color gave way to soft violet, which gradually faded into inky blackness, and finally to a night sky overflowing with an inverted bowl of twinkling points of light that Susan and Flapper, lying on their backs in the soft sand, felt close enough to touch. Flapper was moved to recite:

"To him who in the love of Nature
takes communion with her visible forms,
She speaks a various language.
For his lighter hours She has a voice of gladness,
and a smile, and eloquence of beauty,
and She glides into his darker musings
with a mild and healing sympathy
that steals away the sadness ere he is aware."

Susan squeezed his hand. "William Cullen Bryant," she said. "How lovely."

" 'Thanatopsis'," said Flapper. "I memorized it for Miss Winchell's tenth grade English class. I never forgot it. It must be some kind of genius when a poem about death says so much about life."

" 'A mild and healing sympathy'," Susan repeated. "Lovely."

They dozed on the beach, and as the warm sand gave way to the coolness of the night air, they clung to each other throughout the night.

The squawk of gulls, and the slanting rays of the early morning sun peeking over the glistening hills awakened Susan. She sat up and rubbed her eyes. They were alone on the beach; it was a moment she would treasure. Flapper was still asleep, breathing slowly and regularly, lying on his side, his right arm serving as pillow, his knees slightly bent. She watched him with the eyes of a nurse, sensing strength returning to his tortured body. She watched him with the eyes of a lover, feeling the sweetness of his essence. She was surprised at the length of his eyelashes, the size of his biceps, and how heavy his shoulder muscles appeared to be beneath some loose skin from his not totally restored body. She marveled at the patterns of a two-day beard growth; a whorl of stubble on his cheek reminded her of a corkscrew. Tears spilled down her cheeks. She lay down again carefully, trying not to wake him, wanting to watch him sleep. She wanted to see how every part of his face was organized, to know every blemish, every wrinkle. She peered at the pores in his skin, imagined herself slipping through one to get inside his brain, to find out what was going on in there. She wanted to be part of him, and she wanted to know why it mattered to her so much. She shuddered thinking she might love him more than he did her.

Like the flick of a switch Flapper's eyes clicked open, and he found himself looking straight into Susan's chocolate-drop eyes. They remained locked eye to eye without speaking for what seemed like an eternity. It was in fact long enough for a tiny land crab to scuttle between them, though neither seemed to notice the intrusion. Finally, his eyes narrowing ever so slightly, he reached out to cup her cheek with his palm and said, "Good morning, angel."

Later, breathless after a spirited swim, and playful shenanigans in the tranquil waters of the bay, they sat close to the water's edge feasting on juicy and sweet Hawaiian pineapple.

"Flapper, do you have brothers or sisters?" Susan asked, pineapple juice dripping from her chin.

Flapper nodded between bites. "I have an older brother, Jaybird," he said, "and a little sister, Sally...she's about ten years younger." He paused and said offhandedly, "Jaybird is an infantry lieutenant...he's been reported missing in action...somewhere in Italy."

Susan looked at Flapper. "You don't seem worried about him," she said.

Flapper was worried more than he would admit. He wanted to think he could bring Jaybird back by sheer willpower. He was in total denial of the possibility that he would never see his brother again. "Jaybird will be okay," he said simply.

Susan was startled to see a tear roll out of the corner of Flapper's eye. She took his hand, and held it to her cheek. "You loved him very much, didn't you?"

Flapper was quiet for a long time, struggling to gain control of his emotions. He guessed that love was as good a word as any to describe how he felt about Jaybird, but somehow it seemed inadequate. "Can I tell you a story about Jaybird?" he said at last.

"Of course," she said.

"Jaybird is five years older than me," he began. "In nineteen twenty-seven when I was nine years old we belonged to the Knothole Club in St. Louis. We could get in free to all the weekday baseball games at Sportsmans Park where the Cardinals and Browns play. Jaybird and me went to at least fifty games that summer, maybe more. We lived in South St. Louis, and every time we went to a game our mom would give us each ten cents which was enough for streetcar fare to and from the park, and some for peanuts. Jaybird always handled the money. One time he gave me a dime to buy peanuts, and I lost it. We had to walk home, which was almost ten miles across the city, so we didn't get home until way after dark. But Jaybird never got mad at me, and I was never scared because I knew Jaybird would take care of me. Jaybird was like that.

"The Cardinals won the National League Championship in nineteen twenty-six, and beat the Yankees in the World Series, but in nineteen twenty-seven they were having trouble beating Pittsburgh and the New York Giants. Nobody in the American League could beat the Yankees in nineteen twenty-seven because they had probably the best team anybody had ever seen...Babe Ruth and Lou Gehrig between them hit over a hundred home runs. The Browns were not a bad team that year...against the rest of the league they won about as many as they lost, but against the Yankees they were helpless. The Yanks beat them twenty-one straight times, and were going for twenty-two when we went to the game that afternoon. Jaybird told me to pay close attention that day because he had a feeling we were going to see something that had never happened before, and had a very good chance of never happening again. What we saw was a pitcher named Milton Gaston, a guy who had already lost to the Yankees twice, and had given up three home runs to Ruth. To think this skinny right-hander could beat the Yankees, and stop that losing streak was like thinking the Mississippi River could run north."

Flapper paused, smiling at the thought of Gaston taking the mound that day. Caught up in his story, he had almost forgotten that Susan was there. She waited patiently, watching his face, marveling at the intensity of his feeling for this almost 20-year-old event. Susan knew little of baseball, though she was not without athletic skills. With great effort she tried to concentrate on Flapper's story, sensing there was more to it than just a game.

Flapper continued. "Jaybird told me that anything is possible in baseball, and that I should understand that if anything is possible in baseball it would also be true that anything is possible outside of baseball because baseball is like life…somebody wins, somebody loses, some people never stop trying, and some people give up before they should. There is always hope that next year will be better." He picked up a pebble off the beach and threw it into the water with a force that startled Susan.

"Imagine, Susan, a fourteen-year-old kid teaching a nine-year-old kid about metaphor. That was Jaybird. He taught me some other things that day too. One was about taking advantage of the odds…he had such a strong feeling about what was going to happen that day that he bet our carfare on the Browns at ten to one odds with a fifteen-year-old bookie in the Knothole Section. He won a whole dollar when Milton Gaston did the impossible and beat the Yankees six to two, even though Ruth hit his fiftieth home run of the season that day. Jaybird said I should remember Milton Gaston because of his courage, persistence, and determination. Fifteen years later, just before he went away, he reminded me of that game, and told me that he thought baseball helped get America through the Depression."

Flapper's voice trailed off. He stood and threw a handful of pebbles into the water thinking of Jaybird struggling for survival somewhere in Italy, perhaps alone.

Susan came up behind him, putting her arms around his waist and her head against his back, but said nothing.

After a while they began a slow walk along the beach, holding hands tightly.

"Maybe you should be a philosopher," Susan said.

Flapper was quiet for a few steps, then said, "I think maybe I already am. It's hard not to be when you've seen as many stars as I have. The Pacific Ocean at night could be a classroom for philosophers. You've seen it, did it inspire you?"

Susan nodded. "It's awesome," she said, "makes you feel so insignificant. I always felt like I was in the presence of the Almighty…Is that philosophy or religion?"

"That's what I want to find out," Flapper said. "Booker T. and me sat on the fantail of the *Indianapolis* night after night after night talking about the difference between religion and philosophy. We were trying to understand the universe. One night Booker T. asked if I thought the Japs had the same God we do. It reminded me of high school football coaches praying to God to let them beat the other side's brains out." He paused trying to imagine God, in man's image, watching the games, trying to pick sides. "You wouldn't believe some of the things we talked about," he continued. "I was even trying to teach him about Plato, which is pretty funny considering what little I know about Plato. Listen to this: Plato had Socrates say nations will only be free of their evils when philosophers are kings or kings philosophers. Booker T. was studying to become a king." He chuckled.

"Okay," said Susan, "listen to this: first you become a philosopher, then king. But I don't think King Flapper will do…maybe Homer, Rex." She reflected with her hand on her chin, then said, "But somewhere in there we have to work in Savior; don't forget, you were resurrected."

Flapper shook his head. "No, I think I'll go straight for Emperor." he said, "I will require total and unquestioned obedience to my commands and edicts, and I like the sound of Flapper the First."

They walked on, he pleased with the thought of being Emperor, she already feeling like royalty. Soon they stopped, and gazed at the horizon with the offshore breeze in their faces.

"We gotta go back," he said.

"I know," she responded.

They walked some more.

>>21<<

WHO WON?

October 1, 1945...Day seventy-six A.A.

Philadelphia, U.S.A...Cradle of liberty. City of Brotherly Love.

As the big Greyhound bus crossed the bridge over the Schuylkill River and wheeled onto Market Street, Boats McCan caught sight of the statue of William Penn high atop Philadelphia City Hall marking the center of the city. He would have been surprised to know that at the turn of the century Billy Penn stood atop the highest structure in America. He wondered whether Count was thinking of liberty and brotherly love when he rented the safe deposit box here in Philadelphia. On the long bus ride from Peoria, Boats had had time to reflect on his life. After leaving the relative peace of Peoria only 16 months ago he had faced death three times...at Iwo Jima, at Okinawa, and in the Pacific Ocean. Three Purple Hearts. His enlistment had almost three years remaining, and before midnight he would be reporting to his new ship here at the Philadelphia Naval Shipyard, his 30-day survival leave ended.

Standing on the corner of Market and 10th Streets in downtown Philadelphia, Boats looked up at the sign that read: Philadelphia Savings Fund Society—founded 1816; he thought of the odd circumstance that found him in this storied city for two very different, but perhaps equally life-shaping reasons: the safe-deposit box and the ship.

He followed the young lady down the steps and into the massive bank vault. She led him through stacks and rows of drawers, finally stopping in a dimly lighted and windowless room. She pointed to a large double drawer and said, "There it is. Number nine. That box hasn't been opened for a long time." She looked at Boats curiously, then turned her key in the double lock.

"Thank you, ma'am," said Boats.

The lady smiled. "There's a table over there you can use," she said. "When you're finished just come back out, ring the bell, and I'll open the door."

"Thanks," said Boats. She left him alone.

Cautiously he turned the key in the lower of the two small locks, opened the door, and pulled out a large metal drawer with a hinged cover. He was surprised by the weight of it as he carried it to the table and sat down. The drawer contained envelopes of all sizes, and many different colors. In a box he found 200 glittering $20 gold pieces neatly aligned in 10 rows of 20 each. Lying on top was a long white envelope addressed in large block letters: BOOKER T. McCAN. He picked it up, and looked at it with rising excitement. Now he would learn what had happened to Count. When he returned to Peoria after convalescing in San Diego, he found the city dump turned into a construction site and Count gone. A letter addressed to Booker T. had been delivered to his South Peoria home soon after the war's end. The enigmatic note said only: Philadelphia Savings Fund Society.

Taking a lesson from his father, he removed a small knife from his pocket, carefully unfolded the blade, adroitly sliced open the envelope, and withdrew three sheets of folded yellow paper covered with handwriting neatly crafted in dark black ink. He leaned back in the chair and read.

August 14, 1945
Dear Booker T.,

While being caught up in the excitement over the end of the war, I am at the same time deeply troubled as I read today's news and listen to the accounts and commentaries on the radio. The world news summary in my newspaper reads: "World War II became a page in history last night." Then, at the bottom of the page, almost as a footnote, was this: "In the midst of the rejoicing it was disclosed by the Navy that the heavy cruiser Indianapolis had been sunk, presumably by an enemy submarine, shortly after she delivered an atomic bomb cargo to Guam. All 1,196 men aboard were casualties."

I am not concerned about your safety for I know you will survive, though I grieve for your suffering and that of your shipmates. I am mainly troubled by the presence on Earth of these weapons of devastation. In our justified elation at the end of this war we must not be fooled into thinking that the forces of evil, at home and abroad, have been totally removed from the Earth, and to our sorrow, it can only be a matter of time before such forces will also have the atomic weapons. But even if America remains the only power with the weapons, who is to say we will not use them foolishly, as indeed we may already have done?

I think God is troubled also. In my long experience I have never known Him to express displeasure so dramatically as in the destruction of your ship. God is not a meddler, but I think He felt that the enormity of visiting such cataclysms on innocent civilian populations required an overt sign of His displeasure and disapproval. It was a warning that was ignored if not totally misunderstood or more likely unrecognized. President Truman, in his radio message after the second bomb was exploded, demonstrated appalling disrespect for the Almighty when he told the American people, "It is an awful responsibility which has come to us. We thank God that it has come to us instead of to our enemies; and we pray that He may guide us to use it in His ways and for His purposes." Empty words from empty heads that shrink from their own responsibilities, and imply that God's ways and purposes include the slaughter of innocent children, women, and men. What kind of victory is it that causes people to look to the skies in fear? What kind of victory is it that causes a shopkeeper to put a sign in his window asking, WHO WON? I hear frantic cries for the immediate establishment of world government to control atomic weapons. It would of course be a democracy. I hear nothing from the generals.

But dear Booker T. you are not in Philadelphia to learn of my post-war impressions, which are as meaningless as all the rest in the warped historical perspective of five days. But one thing remains as clear today as it did to Socrates more than 2,000 years ago when crossbows threatened to end all wars due to their violence: STATES WILL NEVER HAVE REST FROM THEIR EVILS UNTIL PHILOSOPHERS ARE KINGS.

The School for Presidents will go forward, and 50 years from now you, Booker T. McCan, will be elected president of the United States. It's probably not necessary to caution you about announcing your intention to become a philosopher-king. For a candidate to proclaim such purpose is to invite ridicule. In the end it is more important to be a philosopher-king than to say you aspire to be a philosopher-king.

There is no better place for you to begin your preparation than Philadelphia where the United States Constitution was crafted. You will learn much from the debates and discussions of the delegates to the Constitutional Convention in 1789.

I will be in touch with you from time to time through your parents in Peoria.

For the present I am beginning a three-year world-wide search for your classmates in the School for Presidents, and to look for inspired teachers. I will visit all of the original 51 members of the United Nations. In particular I will go to Africa where the people are beginning to stir at the prospect of independence from the yokes of colonialism.

And so dear Booker T., until we meet again, I leave you with these words which I can only say are the closest thing to wisdom of which I am currently capable...keep your eyes on the stars, and your feet on the ground.

Friendly, Count.

Boats folded the paper and returned it to the box. His head swam with questions. What did it all mean? Who won? What did that mean? Philosophers? Kings? Evils of the State? What did any of it mean? He shook his head. How could any of this make sense to a 17-year-old? He needed Flapper. A painful thought. Flapper was gone. Davey was gone. Count was...where was Count? He stiffened his back.

Boats emerged into bright October sunshine on a busy Philadelphia street corner. People moved purposefully in all directions. A trolley clanged impatiently. He walked east on Market Street toward the Delaware River, thinking about Count's letter, oblivious to the bustle. Presently he came to an area where the lines of buildings on both sides of the street were interrupted by a wide village green extending several blocks in both directions. At one end of the green stood a handsome two-story brick colonial building distinguished by a clock tower, and topped by a steepled bell tower...Independence Hall. If buildings have personality, this one glowed with cool confidence. If buildings could speak, this one would tell of wisdom and folly, of determination and wit.

Crowds were gathered on both sides of the Hall listening to fevered orations from men standing on wooden boxes, as men had done for 200 years. Boats looked from one side to the other, and moved to the right, attracted by the large red, white, and blue placards bouncing over the crowd on long wooden poles. On one he read: HERITAGE, on another: TRADITION, on yet a third he saw: LEADERSHIP. The man was speaking loudly and passionately. Boats moved to the edge of the crowd and heard…

"…now is not the time to retreat from the ways of our ancestors…from tried and true measures that have made America great. Of course the world has changed…who would deny that atomic power is leading us into a bright new future? All the more reason to put that power into the hands of those who best know how to use it for the great benefit of all the people…FREE ENTERPRISE! GLORIOUS FREE ENTERPRISE!…embrace it my friends…cherish it—In the past it has sustained us, in the future it will ennoble us. The mongers of fear wring their hands chanting the song of woe…they bring great dishonor to the courageous men who vanquished the enemy in the cruelest of all wars when they look at the atomic destruction and ask 'who won?' Ladies and gentlemen, let there never be a doubt…America won!"

Great cheers erupted from the audience…matched by cheers from the crowd on the other side of the mall. Boats turned in that direction, and saw people enthusiastically pumping fists into the air. He moved to the left to learn what this was all about. As he moved from one side to the other in front of the amused Independence Hall he passed a man carrying a small hand-lettered sign, and an expression of gloom. The sign read: THE WORLD WILL END TOMORROW.

The signs on the left, though smaller and less colorful than the ones on the right, lacked nothing in spirit. Boats saw one sign that read: DEMOCRACY, another: PEOPLE, on a third: ATOMIC POWER TO THE PEOPLE. He listened…

"…we cannot, do you hear? Can not allow this awesome power of the atom to be left in the hands of the politicians and the generals, for if we do…mark my words and mark them well…it is the people who will suffer, as we always do. We are told of the wonders of a brave new world where atomic power will bring us cars that never have to be refueled, airplanes that cross the country in minutes, unlimited amounts of plastic and leisure time.

Do not be fooled, my friends...we know what leisure time means...it means no jobs, and no jobs mean degradation...is that what the founders of our country wanted? Freedom to suffer the insults and outrages of the wealthy and powerful? Is that why we fought two world wars? To be humbled by the arrogant authority of the rich? In spite of all the promises we see how the power of the atom has been used...to kill. Do you hear? The power of the atom has been used to kill. My friends, let us ask who indeed won this war. Did America win? Perhaps. Did humanity lose? Most certainly!"

The 17-year-old future president drifted back to the center, and stood for a while looking from left to right where the fevered speakers, spurred by their excited patrons, pursued the sacred arguments to ever higher planes of persuasive peroration. Boats turned to look at Independence Hall; the building beckoned. Two-story wings extended to the left and to the right of the soaring bell tower in the middle. Boats thought of the bell curve. Independence Hall by its very shape was a metaphor for public opinion in this land of opportunity, and the men who sat here those seven score and sixteen years before ensured that the opinion of the public, for the first time in the history of the world, mattered. Boats looked at the high windows and small door, and realized that he was standing at the back of the building.

>>22<<

AGERHOLM

The slender warship rested alongside the dock, bathed in dim light from shaded bulbs strung along overhead wires networking the 150 year-old Philadelphia Naval Shipyard, birthplace of the United States Navy. Boats stood on the pier looking up at the smooth gray wall of the ship's prow with its artistically sculpted cutwater, designed for speed. Massive anchors hugged the stem near where the sides and the deck came together. Six-inch hawsers, braided to cleats on the dock, held the ship in a tight embrace. Eight foot high white numbers, shaded in black, adorned the sides just below the anchors: 828. It was the *Agerholm,* recently built and launched here in Philadelphia, and soon-to-be radar picket for Destroyer Squadron One—DesRon One. At sea on the *Indianapolis* Boats had seen destroyers spread like a fan in the vanguard of powerful formations, clearing the way for their big sisters, the battleships, cruisers, tankers, and aircraft carriers. He remembered the words of Admiral Spruance: "Greyhounds of the fleet. You want to be a sailor? That's the place to do it." So what were they? Greyhounds or tin cans? It depended on where you were sitting.

Boats walked along the dock, extra shoes and the rest of his gear stuffed into the heavy sea bag slung over his shoulder. He mounted the wood and steel gangplank rigged amidships, paused at the top, faced the rear of the ship, and saluted the flag even though the colors had been struck at sunset. He then turned to face the watch officer, saluted, and said, "Request permission to come aboard, sir."

"Where the fuck you been, Mac?" From out of the shadows Booker T. saw a familiar face appear. He shook his head in disbelief, dropped his bag, and did two double takes…"Buck Fulton?"

"You got it, buddy. I saw yer name on the new personnel list. How come yer a day late? You can get brig time fer bein' AWOL, ya know."

Boats knew he was reporting two hours before the midnight deadline. He looked closely at his old friend for a sign that he was joking. It was not possible he had lost a day. Or was it? He said, "Come on, Buck, or is it still Bucks? Don't bullshit me. Today is October first, I ain't late. And what the hell are you doin' out here anyway? I'm reportin' for duty and you ain't the duty officer."

Buck Fulton, as tall as Boats, but not as muscular, wore what the Navy called an undress blue jumper, cut into a sharp V-neck in front, revealing a sparkling white T-shirt. Across the shoulders in back, a severely truncated cape, part of the one-piece construction, ended just below the shoulder blades. Only a well-proportioned few could wear this child-like uniform and maintain their dignity. In barrooms all around the world many a free-for-all had started when drunken sailors rose to defend the honor of their ridiculous bell-bottom trousers, infantile jumpers, and toy caps for which the Navy had never figured out a name better than what they were: white hats, a name also used generically for the men who had to wear them. Boats also noticed the insignia on Buck's left shoulder: the crossed quills and single chevron of a yeoman third class. They had a lot of catching up to do.

Buck said, "Hey man, this is a tin can, the Old Man is already aboard, the watch officer is up in the wardroom havin' some coffee and shootin' the shit with some of his buddies. We play it loose on this bucket…it ain't no goddammed cruiser or battleship. You got yer orders?"

Boats, wearing dress blues with precisely knotted navy-blue neckerchief, took a well-folded sheet of paper from his small chest pocket, and handed it over. Buck was right, this was not a cruiser. Boats remembered when he first went aboard the *Indianapolis*…he could still feel his wet feet after being dipped in the ocean by the playful deckhands during his transfer-at-sea. He looked around the narrow, silent deck, and out at the eerily quiet shipyard. He had the odd feeling that he and Buck Fulton were the only people in the world.

Buck took the paper and made a notation in the logbook. He then looked up at Boats and scanned the double row of colorful battle ribbons on his left breast. "What the hell you been doin', man?" he asked, his eyes widening. "Three Purple Hearts?"

Boats had lost contact with Buck Fulton shortly after that wondrous night in the Princess Kaialani Suite, but in the year since that ecstatic event he had thought of it often, especially while watching the circling sharks at eye level in the Philippine Sea. Boats looked at his friend wondering if he really wanted to know about those Purple Hearts. He remembered Flapper telling him that nobody who had not shared your combat experience really cared about it. "You been usin' yer tuxedo much lately?" he asked.

Buck smiled. "That was some night wasn't it? I had a few more like that after you left…'til my money ran out," he cut loose with a lusty hoot. "But hell," he said after recovering from his mirth, "what's the money for anyhow? After that I tried every which way to get assigned to a transport…them babies were floating gold mines…but they just kept me sittin' on my butt in Pearl 'til the war was over, and now they got me on this rust bucket. I'm workin' on some angles. Depends on how long we stay here in Philly." He paused, then added as an afterthought, "Oh, I did make a few bucks comin' back from Pearl. Did you know they was bringin' troops back on aircraft carriers? Two thousand troops on the *Saratoga*…yeah, I made a few bucks." He laughed. "Right now, I'm workin' on an early release. I'm thinkin' about headin' for Las Vegas. People do like to gamble. You know somethin' about that, don'tcha?"

Boats flushed, remembering the low ball game on the transport that carried him from San Francisco to Hawaii. He said, "I think that low ball game cured me, Buck. What about you? Do you ever get in the game?"

Buck nodded. "Once in a while," he said, "just to keep the feel of it. But like I told ya once, I look for the sure thing. If ya run the game, ya can't lose. That's more my style. But hell you can't make no money on a destroyer."

Boats asked, "So what's the deal on this baby? How long we gonna be here?"

Buck answered, "This little jewel is fresh outa the blocks…new ship, new crew, new paint job, new everything. What we gotta do is take her out and find out what makes her tick. I think the Navy got caught by surprise when the war ended so quick…they got a bunch of new ships and nobody to shoot at, so I guess we get to shoot at each other. They got guys figuring out what kind of games we can play with these brand new toys."

An officer appeared out of a dark inner passageway holding a coffee mug in one hand and a cigarette in the other. His starched garrison cap, cocked at a sharp angle almost touching his right eyebrow, carried the single silver bar of a junior grade lieutenant. "Well, what have we here?" he asked. "Fresh blood?"

Boats looked at him carefully, trying to decide if he was sober.

Buck Fulton said, "Mr. Alcorn, this is Mac, he's reporting for duty."

The officer, his cigarette temporarily stashed in the side of his mouth, put out his hand in a friendly way and said, "Welcome to the *Agerholm*, Mac, glad to have you aboard. Is this your first ship?"

Boats said, "No, sir, I was on the *Indianapolis*."

The lieutenant's eyes widened. "The *Indianapolis*!" he exclaimed. "Now there was a snake-bit ship if there ever was one…torpedoed a week before the war ended. Were you on her when she went down?"

"Yes, sir."

Alcorn shook his head. "Not many guys survived," he said. "What was it like?"

Boats immediately thought of Flapper and a lump formed in his throat. Then a flush of anger and resentment welled behind his ears. This person was asking in an offhand, and clearly uncaring manner to describe events that defied description. It wasn't that Boats did not want to talk about the experience, it was just that he did not want to talk about it in a casual way. Also, he sensed that to tell what it was like would be to trivialize it, and inevitably to make him sound like a hero, and he did not feel like a hero. He thought of Flapper as a hero…but these people would not understand. He looked at the lieutenant and then at Buck, both waiting expectantly for his answer. He hesitated. "If you don't mind, sir," he said, "I don't want to talk about it."

Oblivious to Booker T.'s feelings, the lieutenant said, "Why not? You're not the first guy to survive a sinking. What's the big deal?"

Boats said, "We were in the water for almost a week."

The lieutenant blinked and Buck stared, a glimmer of understanding dawning. There was an awkward silence. Finally Alcorn, unwilling, or unable, to abandon his jocularity said, "That's almost long enough to sprout gills." He laughed loudly at his own humor. The two sailors now stared at him in ill-disguised scorn.

Lieutenant Alcorn looked back at the two incredulous faces, cleared his throat, and said, "Yes, well, Fulton, maybe you better take this man to his billet." Then, as an afterthought he said, "By the way, Mac, did you know the *Indianapolis* carried the atomic bomb to Guam?"

Boats said, "Yes, sir, I read about it. At the time we didn't know what it was. And we carried it to Tinian, not Guam."

"Tinian," repeated the officer, not as a question.

"Yes, sir. Tinian," said Boats. "It's an overnight trip from Guam."

Buck led Boats, dragging his seabag, forward along the deck on the starboard side. He turned into an open hatch that led down a ladder and into a cramped compartment that featured a narrow center aisle bordered on both sides by double tiered sleeping racks. Dim light came from two wire-covered recessed deck bulbs on either end of the compartment. The hum of blowing air testified to the life of the ship. The sound of heavy breathing and loud snoring testified to the life of the men curled in the racks. The blowing air did not entirely eliminate the stale smell of burned tobacco and sweaty bodies. The two sailors moved forward through another open hatch into a larger, multi-functional compartment that served primarily as the crew mess hall, but was also used as an indoor movie theater, a lecture room, and as a battle dressing station should the need arise.

Buck sat down at one of the long mess tables, and motioned Boats to do the same. The compartment was dark in the corners and along the bulkheads, but some overhead lights were on near the center. Boats saw two poker games in progress, and a few men in various stages of undress reading books and magazines. Layers of cigarette smoke filled the air. Buck motioned with a head nod and said, "There's another sleeping compartment forward. I think you can find an empty rack up there for tonight, and then tomorrow you'll meet your chief and get a permanent assignment. Yer gonna be in the First Division." Buck looked at Boats and said, "You were in the water almost a week? Were you on a raft?"

Boats shook his head "No raft," he said. "Just life jackets."

"My God," said Buck. "No food or water?"

Boats shook his head and said, "The ship went down so fast…" He began to choke up as sounds of screaming men flooded his memory.

Buck patted his shoulder and said, "Jeez, I'm sorry, man."

Boats gathered himself and cleared his throat. "It's okay," he said. "It was just a…a…" he was searching for words that did not exist. "Oh, hell, I don't know." He was silent for a few moments, then asked, "Do you really want to hear about this?"

Buck shifted his position nervously. "Well, yeah," he said, "…that is, if you want to talk about it…would it make you feel better if you talked about it? It must have been awful."

Boats saw a different Buck Fulton than he had known before. A solicitous young man that caught Boats momentarily off-guard had replaced the brusque, devil-may-care Bucks. But Boats did not drop his guard easily.

"Don't ever take a drink of sweet water for granted, Bucks," he said.

Boats abruptly changed the subject. "Tell me what you been doin', Bucks. I see you got a rating…third class yeoman. Not bad. Keeps ya from workin',

I hear. Congratulations."

The yeoman rating was more or less the Navy equivalent of a secretary…filing, typing, and record keeping…many a grizzled deck hand and gunner's mate thought of it as women's work, and by saying so found it a good way to break the monotony of just plain drinking during long hard-knuckle nights in waterfront hangouts.

"Thanks, Mac," said Buck. "Yer right, it keeps me off the paint chipping details, and sometimes it even gets a little interesting. Learnin' how to keep books is gonna come in handy some day. I been workin' for the supply officer. You might be surprised at some of the things it takes to run a ship like this. Oh, yeah, damned interesting. The other day we had to give up two gallons of paint to get a crate of oranges."

Boats was curious. "You still pissed off at white folks?" he asked.

Buck pursed his lips, then rolled his upper lip under his lower teeth as he gazed into a far corner. He, like Boats, had learned to consider carefully what he said. "I guess I'll always be pissed off," he said, "but I've been surprised a few times. I'm almost ready to say there may be a few who ain't so bad. But that don't mean I'm ready to trust em'." He thought a moment, then added, "Maybe I don't trust nobody."

Boats picked up a newspaper that was lying on the table and read the headline…

U.S. SEIZES 21 BIG JAP BANKS AS MACARTHUR BREAKS UP EMPIRE'S FINANCIAL COMBINE

He thought about Count's safe deposit box in the Philadelphia Savings Fund Society, and wondered what MacArthur would find in the Japanese banks. His eyes then went to a subheading in the paper:

Yanks Find Stolen Gold In Jap Bank

Then he noticed an item about the atomic bomb and said, "I wonder if them Japs was building an A-bomb."

Buck said, "What?"

"An A-bomb," Boats repeated, "I wonder if them Japs was building an A-bomb. Listen to this." He read aloud.

"The Bing Crosby Foundation claims A-bomb defense found-Hollywood –

A simple practical defense against the atomic bomb was claimed

> *today by the Crosby Research Foundation which said it would hold on to its secret unless assured it would be used to make other nations play fair with the United States."*

Buck shook his head in disgust. "It's all a lot of bullshit," he said, "…this world is so fucked up…It makes me sick. We just finished a damn war…killed off I don't know how many million people…you'd think we could relax a bit, but oh no, now we got to worry about A-bombs and nations playing fair…it's bullshit, Mac…nobody plays fair…what's fair anyway?"

"You ain't worried about A-bombs?" Boats asked.

Buck sighed. "I'll tell ya one thing, Mac," he said, "…there wouldn't be a whole lot left of Peoria if they ever dropped one there. But what the hell, there ain't nothin' we can do about it, and I ain't one to worry much about things I can't do anything about. Anyway, I got more important fish to fry…Speakin' of fryin'," he laughed devilishly. "I'm gonna take you to a couple a spots down here in Philly that's gonna fry your hide, man. We ain't got time to worry about A-bombs…too many daisies to pick…did you know they got a street here called Broad Street? Yep, they sure as hell do, and it don't have nothin' to do with how wide the street is." Buck's loud laughing cackle got the attention of men all around the room.

Another item in the *Philadelphia Inquirer* caught Boats' eye. "Look at this, Buck," he said. Boats held the paper out and pointed to a side bar.

NAVY CUTS POINT SCORES REQUIRED FOR RELEASE

Reduction in points intended to release one third of its war-end strength by January 1

"What are points?" Boats asked.

Buck took the paper, and quickly scanned through the short article. "They're cuttin' enlisted men's points from forty-four to forty-one," he said. "Looks like they're in a big damn hurry to get guys out of uniform and back on bread lines. But it don't apply to yeomen. Just my luck, I'll probably rot on this damn ship."

Boats repeated his question. "What are points?"

Buck looked at Boats. "Nobody told you about the point system?" he queried. "You get points for a bunch of different shit…so many points for length of service…points for combat time. You get points for a wife and kids. Medals…with all them Purple Hearts, and that survival leave you probably got a whole bunch. A hell of a lot more than I got, that's for sure. I'll figure it out for you tomorrow."

Boats asked, "You gotta go back on watch?"

Buck nodded. "Yeah," he said, "I got a couple hours to go. Listen, I'll catch you in the morning, okay? We got breakfast from six-thirty to seven-thirty, and then eight o'clock muster on the quarterdeck. After that I'll see you get where yer supposed to be. And tomorrow night, get ready, babe, I'm takin' you to the Fragrant Moon."

>>23<<

MAGS

Maria Magaden was a beautiful young lady with smooth mahogany colored skin, high cheekbones, and deep chocolate brown eyes. She didn't think of herself as a whore, but by modern definition that's what she was. In gentler times she would have been a courtesan. She was intelligent, and not without hope. She had grown up in Center City Philadelphia without benefit or handicap, as the case may be, of mother or father. Eighteen years earlier, when the city was riding a wave of prosperity, she was discovered on a cold December morning, carefully wrapped in a warm blanket on the steps of the main entrance to the Thomas Jefferson University Hospital at 11th and Walnut. When, at 16, to her great surprise her own baby was born, she determined to keep the child, even though, like her mother, she was not sure who the father was.

Maria's family was in the Fragrant Moon Café on 7th Street, three blocks west of Independence Hall. The ladies called her Mags, and led by the example of Mother Porter, an 80-something former slave, were fiercely protective of her welfare, and that of her two-year-old son Frederick Douglass Magaden.

Mags was patiently explaining this to Booker T., wearing civilian clothes now that the war was over, as they sat at a small table in a smoky second floor parlor above the café. "I don't know why I'm telling you all this," she said. "...What did you say your name was?"

"Booker T. McCan, but why don't you call me Boats...So they take care of you, and this is your home. How long have you been here?"

"Oh, I've always been here," she answered.

"And you named your son Frederick Douglass. Do you know who Frederick Douglass was?"

Mags tossed her head proudly. "Of course I know," she said. "He worked to free the slaves. Mother Porter knew him. She told me all about him. And I know who Booker T. Washington was too. Do you know? And why don't you want to be called Booker T., Booker T.?"

Boats laughed. "Slow down, Mags," he said, "one question at a time, please...I knew someone who fought at Gettysburg in the Civil War...he told me about Frederick Douglass, and Harriet Tubman, and Sojourner Truth, and George Washington Carver, and Booker T. Washington, and W.E.B. DuBois, too. You ever hear of those people?"

Mags sat straighter, her eyes shining. "I know my history, Booker T. I graduated from high school just last summer. They got some good schools here in Philadelphia. Did you graduate from high school?"

Boats was startled to suddenly find himself on the defensive. "Well, I...well, not exactly. The truth is...no, I didn't. I joined the Navy after my second year. That's why they call me Boats." He paused, breathed deeply and said, "But I'm goin' to college when I get out of the Navy."

Mags raised her eyebrows, cocked her head, and smiled in an "oh, sure" expression. Boats saw the look, and said quickly before he even thought about it, "Don't look like that...it's true...I'm goin' to college. I have to because I'm gonna be president one day."

He was aghast when the words came out of his mouth, fighting the impulse to reach out and grab them before they reached Mags' ears, wondering why he felt it important to impress this strange young lady he had known for less than an hour. Once the words were out, he sheepishly lowered his eyes, not wanting to give the impression he was bragging. Thoughts of conversations with Count and Flapper raced through his mind. He thought of the School for Presidents, and for the first time since the torpedoes hit the *Indianapolis*, remembered the document he and Flapper had been studying.

Mags looked at him curiously, wondering what this odd and hopelessly serious young man was talking about. She asked, not unkindly, "President? President of what?"

Boats did not answer, thinking how ridiculous it sounded, but at the same time fingering a $20 gold piece in his pocket. He looked at Mags and she at him, both feeling a mystical pull that had caused each to reveal subdued and private thoughts to a person they had known only for minutes, in a setting not distinguished by lofty conversations. Boats finally said, "Never mind...it's nothin'. But I am goin' to college some day...when I get out of the Navy."

Mags asked, "How long you been in the Navy, Booker T.?"

"About a year and a half," he answered. "I got a couple of years to go on my enlistment."

"You don't sound like you're from Philadelphia."

"I'm from Peoria. You ever heard of it?"

Mags answered, "I heard Fibber McGee and Molly talk about it on the radio, but I didn't know it was a real place."

"It's a real place all right, and it's a long way from Philadelphia. In fact it's about as far away from the ocean as you can get. A lot of guys from Peoria join the Navy just to see the ocean. You must have seen the ocean. It's not that far from here is it?"

Mags shook her head. "I've never been to the shore," she said. "I've never been out of Philadelphia. What's the ocean like? I know it's big."

If anybody could describe what the ocean was like, Boats was the one. He had seen it, smelled it, tasted it, felt it, been wrapped in it; he had loved it, feared it, despised it; he had wondered at its vastness, its tranquillity, its fury, its terror, its majesty, and its mystery. Mags looked at him expectantly. Did she really want to know what it was like? Where should he begin? "The ocean." Boats formed a tent for his nose with his fingers, thumbs under his chin. "The ocean is big all right, probably a lot bigger than you can imagine; and it's deep...there's a place in the Pacific Ocean where the water is more than seven miles deep. The ocean is full of salt...if you drink seawater it will kill you. The ocean never stops moving, but it's not like a river where the water always moves in one direction. The ocean is full of life...dolphins, porpoises, whales, all kinds of fish...sharks, lots of sharks. Birds...one time we were hundreds of miles from land and an albatross landed on our fantail. Sometimes the ocean is as smooth as glass and sometimes, when the wind kicks up, it can form waves fifty feet high. Sometimes it's as blue as the sky, and other times, even in the middle of the day, it can be as black as midnight...Sometimes the moon is so bright you can see a rainbow at night; one time our ship ran right under a rainbow. On a clear night in the middle of the ocean you can see stars by the millions." As he said this, a tear spilled over the brim of his right eye and trickled down his cheek. Mags reached out with a small handkerchief and wiped it away. She had never seen this kind of emotion. She felt a tear of her own forming, and couldn't remember the last time that had happened.

Boats was surprised and embarrassed at his own emotions. "Sorry," he said, "I never did that before. I don't know what got into me. Sorry."

Mags waved it off. "It's okay," she said, "I never saw stars like that. I guess there's too much light in the city. Tell me about the stars." She marveled that the thought of stars could make a grown man cry.

Boats closed his eyes and conjured a warm, cloudless night where the nearest land was seven miles away, straight down. He shuddered at the thought of the last time he had seen the stars like that, when his chin was dipping into the water and his lifejacket was slowly losing its buoyancy. He shook his head and opened his eyes to see Mags again looking at him curiously. He said softly, "Some of the stars form pictures in the sky. You must have seen the Big Dipper."

"No." Mags shook her head.

"It's a group of seven stars shaped like a cup with a long curved handle. At different times of the year, the Dipper is turned up or flipped over, like it's filling or emptying; I think it's got something to do with how the Earth is turning." He paused. "…There's a group of four stars in the shape of a cross that you can only see in southern latitudes." He remembered when Flapper had pointed it out to him that dark night on the fantail of the *Indianapolis*, the night before they hit Okinawa…thinking of Flapper saddened him. He continued, his voice beginning to fade. "It's called the Southern Cross." Boats stopped again and stared at the floor, seeing the Southern Cross. Another tear rolled down his cheek. "It's very beautiful," he said softly.

He stopped talking and waited in some confusion as he felt a wave of emotion well in his chest, and roll into his throat. He stood up and turned away from Mags. When he felt her hand on his shoulder he was mortified to realize that he was actually crying, and that he couldn't stop. The nearest place to hide was Mags' shoulder, and she held him tightly as the long cloistered pathos of agonized death at sea burst out in choking sobs. It was for his brother Davey, for his friend Flapper, and the desperate men of the *Indianapolis*, for Sergeant Joe, and all the others on Iwo Jima, for the children on the beach at Okinawa, and for all the other innocents abroad in the world. People around the room stared and became very quiet; "Mood Indigo" filled the air.

Desperately Boats fought for control…remembering his surprise when he didn't cry at the news of Davey's death. Now his emotions betrayed him in a public spectacle that left him feeling drained and humiliated. Abruptly he pulled away from Mags, and with head held high walked resolutely toward the door with as much dignity as he could muster. Mags watched him for an uncertain moment, then followed quickly. She grabbed his hand before he reached the door and said, "Wait a minute, Booker T. I don't think we were finished talking."

Boats turned and looked at her, surprised at how tall she was, seeing her warm brown eyes at the level of his chin. "Are you wearing high heels?" he asked, feeling a little silly.

Mags lifted a slim ankle for him to see and said, "No, Mister Boats. Why don't you come back and sit down? I want to hear more about the stars."

"Is there somewhere else we can go?" asked Boats. "I feel kind of stupid."

"Why don't we go down to the café and have a cup of coffee? And maybe a Danish?"

Mags took his hand and led him down two flights of steps and into the high-ceilinged café where she found a small table in the back, near the kitchen. "You were talking about the Southern Cross," she said. "You said it was very beautiful."

"Look, I'm sorry, Mags. It's just that I saw so many people die..." His voice trailed off.

"Do you want to tell me about that?" she asked.

"No, I don't think so." He looked at her, seeing sympathy in her eyes. "You know your eyes are very beautiful too."

Mags felt blood rush to her cheeks. It was not the first time someone had said it to her, but it seemed the first time it was said in earnest. She briefly averted her gaze, then lifted her chin and looked hard at this extraordinary young man, who had seen so much. She wondered if she would ever see him smile.

Boats looked equally hard at her, narrowing his eyes to focus on her pupils. "Do you believe in God?" he asked.

It was not what she had expected to hear. Her quick answer was just as unexpected to him. "No," she said, without elaborating.

Boats waited for her to say more, but she did not. He could see she was thinking. He continued to wait. At length she said, "If there is a God he hasn't discovered Philadelphia." Her reward was a big smile she hoped would signal the end of his melancholy.

"When you're out there in the middle of the ocean, and looking up at all those stars, it's hard not to think about God," Boats said.

Mags said, "I go to church every Sunday, mostly because I like to sing in the choir, but when the preacher starts to deliver his message, I just don't get it. What he talks about...those Bible stories...all those sins...hellfire...heavenly bliss...I don't think that has anything to do with me...Do you think that makes me a bad person, Booker T.?"

Boats, when he was Booker T., remembered his friend Ma Jong, who had lived just around the corner at the Shanghai Tea House in South Peoria. In his young life, he had known whores he'd liked and whores he hadn't liked, but it had never occurred to him to judge them as good or bad. Boats was not about to pass judgment on a whore, especially one as enchanting as Mags, and certainly not because of her views on God. "What kind of a person are you?" he asked, genuinely interested.

Mags answered. "Mother Porter taught me not to lie and not to cheat," she said, "and..." she hesitated, considering the question seriously, "...and not to steal." She paused, "What difference does it make? Do you really care what kind of a person I am?"

Boats was startled by the question, finding himself wondering at the fact that he apparently *did* care, not only what kind of a person she was, but also what kind of life she lived, and what was going to happen to her. He sat quietly, wondering if it was really any of his business. He realized that his mind was wandering again to the black sands of Iwo Jima. The helpless victims on the beach...the indiscriminate shelling of men in pain lying on stretchers...his primal urge to help...to do something about it...to make a difference. He shook his head and looked at Mags, waiting patiently for his answer. "Have you ever felt pain?" he asked.

Her eyes widened and she threw up her hands. "I guess that answers my question. It was a dumb question. Why should you care what kind of a person I am?"

Boats scrambled to recover. "No, wait. I do care. I mean...I was thinking about a different kind of pain...I thought...I'm tryin' to know somethin' about you...if I knew how you felt about other people's suffering, it would help me see what kind of person you are. You know what I'm sayin'?"

Mags sniffed. "Huh. Now you're starting to talk like a Philadelphian. Okay, well look, I never saw anybody actually die, but sure, I've seen lots of suffering...I could take you to some places not too far from here where poor people are trying to live; not too far from Independence Hall either. You must have seen some of those guys sleeping on the street. How do I feel about it? It makes me very nervous because I know I'm not too far away from that life myself. You know what I'm sayin'?"

Boats had been lucky, and he was beginning to realize it. He had grown up with poverty all around him, but had never gone to bed hungry; his family was poor, but not penniless. It wasn't fair to ask Mags how she felt about other people's suffering when she was so close to her own suffering. He nodded; he knew.

"I'm no angel, Booker T....but my baby is." She smiled.

"How you gonna take care of him?" Booker T. asked. "Is this place run by the rackets?" He looked around the smoky, poorly lighted room…he saw people eating and drinking in what looked like a typical downtown café. A small piano combo was playing, and people were dancing. He saw a couple of tough-looking characters sitting at a long bar on one side of the room.

Mags looked surprised. "Rackets? What are you talking about?"

"In Peoria the houses are controlled by the Chicago mob," Boats said. "The girls have to go where they're told. They're like slaves almost. It's probably the same here in Philadelphia."

Mags furrowed her brow, and put her hand to her chin. "If it is, I don't think it has anything to do with me. All I know is I got a couple of sugar daddies who come down here from the Main Line once in a while. One time I went out there. You shoulda seen that house!"

Boats stood up. "So I guess you don't need no help from me. Listen, Mags, my ship is gettin' ready to head out, and I don't know if we'll even come back here, but maybe some day you might need some help. I'm gonna give you the address of my ma and pa in Peoria so you could contact me if you need help." He wrote the address on a paper napkin and handed it to her. "Okay?"

Mags looked at the paper, and then at Boats. She cocked her head and said, "You are a strange one, Mr. Booker T. Boats. Why does it matter to you what happens to me?"

Boats picked up a candle from the table and lighted a cigarette. Looking at the beautiful young woman through the flame, he said, "I like you…and I'm worried about the next Frederick Douglass."

He squeezed her hand and kissed her on the cheek, then turned and walked out the door. Mags watched him go, feeling a little confused, as if they had unfinished business. It was the first time she could remember when it seemed important that a man thought well of her. She opened her hand and was startled to find a gleaming $20 gold piece.

>> 24 <<

LIFE IS SHORT—ART IS LONG

September 19, 1946...St. Louis, Missouri

Homer and Susan Land Jackson sat in a large and well-lighted auditorium with 95 other newly-matriculated Washington University medical students, waiting for Chancellor Compton to enter the room, and deliver what they were told would be a welcoming address. Flapper was restless, and more than a little impatient. He was not entirely convinced that medical school was the right place for him, and he was anxious for the formal instruction to begin so he would know. He had had enough of indoctrination; he was ready for substance. Susan, on the other hand, was thrilled and excited, but she was worried about Flapper, knowing his doubts, and that he was here in large part because of her.

Flapper's thoughts drifted to the wedding ceremony held at Cottage Farm in Grampa Land's private Catholic church. Flapper had readily agreed to a Catholic wedding, knowing it was important to Susan and her family. For himself, he knew it would have little effect on his own search for religious and philosophical truth, and there was always the possibility that Christian theology might have something important to offer.

Arthur Holly Compton swept into the auditorium, black academic robe flowing, smiling at the polite applause of the benighted students who didn't know they were supposed to applaud until an older faculty member in the rear led the way. He removed his crushed velvet hat with red chevrons, and stood for a moment looking up at the novitiates assembled in a rising amphitheater before him. Compton was a scientific star, a Nobel Prize winning physicist. His discovery, and interpretation in 1923, of the change in wave length of scattered X-rays was a milestone in understanding atomic structure, pointing the way along the path that led, in less than two decades, to the splitting of the atom. He was awarded the Nobel Prize for Physics in 1927.

He was of average height, with dark penetrating eyes looking out from beneath bushy brows. He sported a trademark toothbrush mustache, and had the rugged good looks of a middle-aged movie star. He was a happy and greatly fulfilled man surveying the bright, intelligent faces looking back at him. He was motivated and inspired by a compassionate Christian humanism that led colleagues to describe him as a man to whom science was an intellectual adventure of compelling interest and beauty, but who also knew that the ultimate values of life are beyond science, and that the highest purpose of science itself is to elevate and enrich human existence. Compton was secure in his beliefs, and enthusiastically addressed the young people before him, many like Flapper and Susan, recently returned from war. He intended to make them understand what was important, and why they were here. Few present had any inkling of the role this man had played in developing the atomic bomb.

"Welcome to Washington University," he began. "You are an elite fraternity, and I congratulate you for the achievement of being here to begin what is sure to be the most exciting and fulfilling time of your young lives. You will learn from some of the finest professors in the world; listen carefully to what they say, watch carefully what they do. Study hard. Learn. You will find it is good for the body, good for the soul, and..." he paused, looked around the room from face to face, smiled, and said with a hand flourish, "good for Washington University." Nervous laughter arose from around the room.

Compton, speaking without notes, reached into his scholarly bag and brought forth a tale of ancient Greece...an era that had long captured his interest, and a subject he loved to expound upon. "Ladies and gentleman," he said, "I want to take this fugitive opportunity, early in your medical careers, to acquaint you with Hippocrates, who some consider to be one of the pantheon of Greek gods, but who Greek legend tells us lived more than two thousand years ago, some four hundred years before the birth of Christ, and who is generally recognized as the father of medicine. Perhaps you have heard of the Hippocratic Oath, which you will be asked to take before you graduate. You will be asked to examine this oath at various times in your curriculum, but I think it is appropriate and necessary here at the beginning for you to consider a singularly important part of it. I now quote from Hippocrates:

"Whatever things I see or hear concerning the life of men, in my attendance on the sick or even apart therefrom, which ought not to be noised abroad, I

will keep silence thereon, counting such things to be as sacred secrets.'"

He looked around the room, noting with satisfaction the nods of understanding, and the whispered comments. Susan leaned towards Flapper and said, "How can he remember so much?"

Flapper shrugged and whispered in Susan's ear. "You may not wish to noise this abroad, but I think you have about the cutest nose I ever saw." She gave him a playful punch in the ribs.

Compton continued. "But ladies and gentleman, there is more to Hippocrates than his famous charter of medical conduct." He turned to the wide chalkboard behind him and wrote in large block letters:

CORPUS HIPPOCRATICUM

He turned back to his audience and said, "The Hippocratic Collection, or Corpus Hippocraticum, was used as a textbook in medical schools well into the late nineteenth century, and though it is no longer part of the formal curriculum, there is yet something to be gained from it. For example, though you may scoff at the notion, there are still those who believe that disease is a punishment sent by God, and you can imagine that two thousand years ago such belief was almost universal. Let us look at one example: epilepsy. In those days epilepsy was called 'the sacred disease,' but Hippocrates wrote that 'every disease has its own nature, and arises from external causes.' Of course he didn't get that exactly right, but his main point that there was nothing sacred about epilepsy was on the mark. He also knew of the effect of food, occupation, and environment in causing disease.

"One more thing about Hippocrates…his aphorisms. The aphorisms are part of the Corpus Hippocraticum. Before Hippocrates, there was no such thing as an aphorism…he invented the term. Let me remind you: an aphorism is a brief statement of a fundamental truth. The first aphorism is the most famous, and one you may want to make a note of."

Once again he turned to the chalkboard and wrote in large letters:

LIFE IS SHORT,
ART IS LONG,
OPPORTUNITY FUGITIVE,
EXPERIMENTING DANGEROUS,
REASONING DIFFICULT

Susan and Flapper, along with the others, were taking notes as Compton turned back to the class. Flapper thought he saw some humor in these oddly worded statements, and leaned toward Susan with the whispered comment. "Love is delicious," he said, and received another playful punch for his trouble.

Professor Compton, a man who took life very seriously, looked from the board to the class and back again, allowing time for note-taking while examining the aphorisms in light of his own experience...his eyes settled on EXPERIMENTING DANGEROUS, and he wondered again at the wisdom of the Greeks.

He turned back to the class. "And now in conclusion," he said, "let me take this fugitive opportunity to share with you some of my own aphorisms, or at least what I hope are aphorisms...thoughts that have come to me over the years, which represent a distillation of ideas I have formed into what might be called a personal credo. I present these thoughts in all humility, hoping you may take from them what you find to be good, and if you are so inclined, to perhaps use them in the formation of your own guide for life."

He approached an easel that held a series of large white cardboard squares. He removed them one by one, reading aloud what was written on them.

> "Relying upon a faith that our universe is not a chaos, but an ordered cosmos,
>
> I believe that through sincere and courageous effort man can learn what is true.
>
> I believe that inherent in what is true is that which will serve creation in its highest form, which is humanity.
>
> I believe that truth shall make men free, free from the ills of the flesh and the spirit.
>
> I rely upon an unfolding knowledge of the truth to provide a solution for the problems and conflicts that vex humanity.
>
> I therefore dedicate myself to the task of seeking the truth fearlessly and zealously, and to the application of what knowledge I may gain for the establishment of a peaceful, just, and orderly civilization on Earth."

Compton removed the final cardboard square, and stood for a moment contemplating the class before delivering his final affirmation. "Ladies and gentlemen," he said, his voice rising in a burst of enthusiasm, "life is short, seize the hour. Let nothing distract your search for the truth. Washington

University offers you the fugitive opportunity to join the ranks of those scientists and healers who, following Hippocrates, have made it axiomatic that art is long. Do not fear to experiment dangerously. Develop your intellectual powers so that reasoning becomes that much less difficult. Go forth from this room and learn, so that the day will come when, with God's help, you will grasp the torch, and teach those who follow. Thank you for your attention."

Susan and Flapper stood with the others, applauding as Professor Compton concluded his welcoming address. They looked at each other, wondering what the other's reaction to this flaming oration would be. They were too young to be jaded, but given where they had been, the words seemed too highly polished, and had a tinny ring. Susan was the first to say so. "I don't know, Flapper," she said, "I think he's trying too hard."

Flapper agreed. "I have yet to hear a pep talk that wasn't boring. Of course, I never heard Rockne; maybe Professor Compton should have told us to go out and win one for the Gipper."

Susan laughed. "I guess we would have to agree, though, that old Hippocrates was onto something, although personally I intend to live a very long life. How about you?"

Flapper squeezed her hand. "It's our destiny," he said.

In the hall outside the lecture room they encountered a group of four students engaged in a spirited and noisy discussion. "Where does he get the moral authority to talk about establishment of a peaceful, just, and orderly civilization on Earth?" A small, thin young man with thick dark-rimmed glasses was speaking. His rising excitement could be heard above the buzz of normal conversation at some distance from where they were standing. "I mean, here is a man who built the atomic bomb, for Christ sake!"

"Who told you he built the atomic bomb?"

"It's coming out. It was in the newspapers. He's speaking all over the place; next Sunday at the Protestant Episcopal Church. Maybe he'll tell us what he means by an ordered cosmos." The student laughed derisively. "One year away from the slaughter of millions of people on the Earth, and he's talking about an ordered cosmos. If the rest of the professors here don't have more clues than he does, I'm getting out of here."

The other students looked at each other. A small crowd was gathering.

A young lady spoke up, "Wait a minute, Nelson," she said, "don't be so quick to judge. He couldn't have built that bomb by himself, don't you think he should have a chance to explain? Not everybody thinks the bomb was bad."

Nelson fairly shouted, "Not bad? How can anybody find something good about a weapon that wipes out cities in a single blast, and leaves the world cowering in terror?"

Susan and Flapper walked away and out into the sunshine.

Flapper asked, "Do you think he really was involved in building the bomb?"

Susan shrugged. "If he was, I wonder what he's doing here speaking to medical students?"

"Well, he *is* the Chancellor of the University," Flapper said. "And if I'm going to become a philosopher maybe I can learn something from him, like what kind of truth is he looking for? I wonder if it has anything to do with splitting the atom? If he's speaking at that church on Sunday, why don't we go and listen?"

>>25 <<

THE HOT OIL OF ACADEME

September 19, 1946... Urbana-Champaign, Illinois

Dean Daniel Dunn eyed with undisguised contempt the young man standing before him. "You think just because you served in the military you should be allowed to study at the University of Illinois?" he asked.

Booker T. McCan, standing at half attention, felt alone and vulnerable. He gulped, and with an effort looked hard at the bow-tied man in the three-piece suit sitting in the high-backed leather swivel chair. The man was regarding him with a scornful expression that caused a shiver to descend from the top of his head to his heels. It crossed his mind that his future might be in the hands of this ill-tempered man. Flustered, Booker T. was not sure whether an answer to the snotty question was required, and so remained silent. He had not expected hostility from the Dean of the College of Liberal Arts. His eyes moved beyond the dean to a long expanse of green grass crisscrossed with walking paths visible through the windows. Students were moving purposefully; tall oak and maple trees shimmered in the hot September sun. Booker T. thought about the circumstances that had brought him here; the unexpected early release from active naval service when the ship's wartime complement was cut in half...the point system that allowed him to make the early release list because of his three Purple Hearts.

Dean Dunn sat behind a massive mahogany desk with his back to latticed glass doors opening onto a balcony. The large room was high-ceilinged and emanated a feeling of space, comfort, if not opulence, and above all, to the myriad students who had trooped here over the years, intimidation. The room featured thick carpeted floors, long forest-green velvet drapes, floor to ceiling bookshelves covering all the walls and jammed with old books. It was a room for the centuries...an ivory tower. If the youths presently coming before him had faced whirling shrapnel and blazing bullets on Iwo Jima or anywhere else, it was of no concern to him; he had a college to run.

In the fall of 1946, close to eight million men and women returning from the war, anxious to put violence and terror behind them, each with a story to tell, besieged campuses across the country, eager to begin a new life. Many were the first in their families to go to college. Deans and department heads were overwhelmed...many took it badly. Much of the faculty had missed the war because of age or infirmity, and now, touched with vague and unfamiliar stirrings of guilt, they braced to rebuff the imminent invasion by manning the ramparts with the hot oil of academe: condescension, sarcasm, ridicule, and mockery.

The dean, as if suddenly remembering that his power was diminished while his quarry stood, rose from his chair and said, "Sit down, mister..." He ran his finger down a page. "...McCan, is it?"

"Yes, sir, McCan, sir." Booker T. took a low seat in front of the big desk. It appeared the dean wanted to deliver a lecture. Booker T. braced himself, and thought of Coach Schmidt, Lieutenant Allgood, and to his surprise, Colonel Nishi. Dean Dunn stood, but stayed behind the protection of his desk. Booker T. was jerked back from the caves of Iwo Jima by the raised voice of the Dean.

"Are you listening to me, McCan?"

"Yes, sir. Sorry, sir."

"Sorry is what your record is, McCan. And stop calling me 'sir'. Call me Dean Dunn or..." He cleared his throat, "Doctor Dunn...Look at this." Dean Dunn held up a sheet of paper. "You haven't even graduated from high school. What are you doing here anyway? Why are you wasting my time?"

Booker T. screwed up his courage. "I completed a G.E.D. course, and got a certificate," he said. "And I got a letter from the admissions office saying I could come. I'm on the G.I. bill."

Dean Dunn was indignant. He was more than indignant—he was outraged. He fumed, "G.I.bill? G.E.D.? God help us."

Booker T. was perplexed. "Did I do something wrong, sir?" he asked.

"Wrong? Wrong? Of course you did something wrong," the dean raged, "You came here when you have no business being here. What do you expect us to do with you?" The dean's fury was leading him into irrationality.

Booker T. looked up hopefully, and answered with a question of his own. "Teach me?"

Dean Dunn sat down heavily, striking his forehead with the open palm of his left hand. "But that's the whole point isn't it? How can we teach you when you don't have the brains to learn? This is the University of Illinois, Mr. McCan, we only take the best students here. We can't allow seats to be filled by...by..." he hesitated, searching for the pinnacle of disdain, wanting to wound. "...by..." He straightened his arm and pointed at Booker T. "...By you."

Booker T. was unfazed. "I have this letter from the admissions office," he said artlessly. He held up the letter.

The dean was burning. "You and ten thousand others just like you! This is intolerable! I won't have it! We're being asked to educate a bunch of cattle! First the war, now this! I'll speak to the governor!" He slammed his fist on the desk, and began pacing quickly behind it, his hands clasped behind his back.

Booker T. was bewildered. He sat in growing wonder at the theatrics of the man he was told by the receptionist would help him outline a course of study for his first semester at the University of Illinois at Urbana-Champaign, some 100 flat miles southeast of Peoria.

Dean Dunn wanted only to be left in peace to pursue his scholarly works. The idea of educating the masses was as abhorrent to him as it would have been to his revered Plato. He was not sympathetic to the sacrifices of the young men and women now confronting him. He saw them as rising above their rightful places in an otherwise orderly world. If he could not stop them from attending, there was nothing to prevent him from making it difficult.

"You will not last two months, McCan," the dean shouted. "Do you hear? Two months, no more!" He lowered his voice, startled and a little embarrassed at his own vehemence. He paced some more, waiting for his temper to cool.

At length he stopped, faced Booker T., and said in a firm voice, "You will begin with English Composition." He laughed. "It's a joke, McCan. Nobody knows how to write in this country, and look at you, I doubt if you even know how to spell, let alone know the difference between a verb and an adverb."

Booker T. remained silent. The dean was right about that.

Dean Dunn sighed, then continued, "English Composition, Biology, Chemistry, and Trigonometry. Fifteen hours of credit. Do you think you can handle that, McCan?" The dean sneered, "I give you two months, no more. Now leave me." The dean initialed a course schedule sheet, and pushed it across the desk with a look of distaste.

Booker T. looked at the sheet and frowned. He looked at the dean who had turned his back and was standing before the window. He took a step toward the dean and said tremulously, "Excuse me, sir, uh, I...uh, I mean...uh, excuse me, Dean."

The dean did not turn, and for a long moment did not answer. Booker T. waited. At length Dean Dunn spun on his heel and shouted, "What?"

Booker T. took a backward step. "Dean Dunn, sir, I…uh, this sheet says biology and chemistry, but I'm studying business and government, not science. I think there's a mistake."

Dean Dunn snatched the paper from Booker T.'s hand and sputtered, "There is a mistake all right, thank the Lord. But it's worse than I thought…if you can't even find the right college, you will be lucky to last one month…you, sir, are in the wrong college. In the College of Liberal Arts, everyone takes biology and chemistry. How can you call yourself educated without them? For the love of God, go…get out of my sight. I daresay the Dean of Business Administration will be equally unhappy to see you."

Dean Dunn was not the only one at the university determined to make things difficult for the multitude of new students. For years the faculty celebrated a tradition of rigid adherence to "high standards," which for many simply meant that they were miserly with grades of A. The biggest part of the faculty were reluctant to teach at all, preferring to spend their time on research, which for many meant searching musty libraries for clues to what earlier scholars had to say about subjects of enduring interest, such as the nature of the chemical bond, or the meaning of dreams, or, even better, the impact of one upon the other, or vice versa. The faculty, in general being of above average intelligence, had long ago perceived that the university reward system, unable to put a number on teaching quality, basically ignored it. Still, for some, love for their subjects was so strong that simply by talking of their passions, students learned by listening to their mumbled musings. And in spite of everything there were those teachers, it must be said, who provided true inspiration.

The professor gathered himself to his full height, somewhere on the nether side of 5 1/2 feet, and cleared his throat…a signal for quiet. He stood behind an ancient and scarred wooden lectern, eyeing the chattering class from the pit of a partially filled 200-seat amphitheater in front of a 20-foot wide blackboard. He was a slight man with dark brooding eyebrows, and a tuft of white hair on his head, who even as he regarded the ragged assemblage, was organizing a poem in a private section of his brain reserved only for him. It was a device he had perfected over the years…he looked forward to his lectures as a time when he often produced some of his best works. For some, a quiet time in early morning with the optimism of choiring birds and the pink sky of a hidden sunrise...for Lloyd Rhodewald, Professor of English Literature, an hour before a group of disinterested students who might only occasionally interrupt his deathless thoughts with foolish questions. As always he contemplated the meaning of life, and currently was slogging his poetic way through the significance of atomic power in the cosmic scheme.

The professor withdrew an unsharpened yellow wooden pencil from his shirt pocket and tapped the lectern, more as part of a ritual than a demand for silence; he was in no hurry to begin. He looked up at his first post-war class, wondering what they had seen, where they had been. He scanned the rising rows looking for eye contact, finding more than he expected. He noted missing arms and legs, eye patches, grimly determined faces. Before the semester ended he would have occasion to consider the cosmic significance of the fact that more than 20 percent of his class carried a lifetime burden of shrapnel fragments in their arms, legs, and backs. This was a class in English Composition. He would ask them to write of their experiences.

Gradually, and grudgingly, the class fell silent. Morning sunshine streamed through high windows around the top of the amphitheater illuminating myriad, sparkling dust particles aroused from summer calm. A student sneezed. The professor waited. Ninety-seven eyes focused on him. A scant 27 years before, following the war touted to end all wars, he had stood in this same spot looking at these same faces, so recently returned from ghastly old lands. Now, as then, he would offer them Walt Whitman.

He spoke from memory, focusing his eyes on a spot above and behind the top row.

"As I ponder'd in silence,
Returning upon my poems, considering, lingering long,
A Phantom arose before me with distrustful aspect,
Terrible in beauty, age, and power,
The genius of poets of old lands,
As to me directing like flame its eyes,
With finger pointing to many immortal songs,
And menacing voice, What singest thou? it said,
Know'st thou not there is but one theme for ever-enduring bards?
And that is the theme of War, the fortune of battles,
The making of perfect soldiers.
Be it so, then I answer'd, I too haughty Shade also sing war,

and a longer and greater one than any,
Waged in my book with varying fortune, with flight, advance and retreat,
victory deferr'd and wavering,
(Yet methinks certain, or as good as certain, at the last,) the field the world,
For life and death, for the Body and for the eternal Soul,
Lo, I too am come, chanting the chant of battles.
I above all promote brave soldiers."

The professor paused, and row by deliberate row, scanned every face in the room.

"I above all promote brave soldiers," he repeated.

In spite of himself, exposed before the class, the professor felt the single tear rolling down his cheek. Abruptly, as he had done in his middle age 27 years before, he turned and strode purposefully from the room, leaving the line hanging in the air...*I above all promote brave soldiers.*

Booker T., along with the others, caught off guard by the sudden plunge into substance, expecting the usual first session banalities, recovered too late to catch the unfamiliar cadences, the strange juxtaposition of words. He with the others, was left to ponder in silence the hanging phrase, *I above all promote brave soldiers.*

For a moment there was a hush, then nervous laughter, a flutter of conversation. The student-veterans looked around, wondering how the others were reacting. If they thought of themselves at all, even those decorated for valor, it was never as "brave." It was a poet's word...but wasn't that why they were here? To learn the poet's words?

The professor had left two stacks of paper. One was a book list, the other an assignment sheet. Booker T. scanned the book list, and noted at the top, *Leaves of Grass* by Walt Whitman. *The Red Badge of Courage* by Stephen Crane intrigued him. Noting *The Republic* of Plato he remembered Flapper. The list seemed long and menacing; the longest book he had ever read was *The Wizard of Oz.* He thought of Count. He thought of Dean Dunn and his "two months, no more." He looked at the assignment sheet. Assignment number one: From Walt Whitman's *Leaves of Grass* select any poem, and write a 500 to 1,000 word analysis, critique, or commentary. You may select more than one poem and compare them if you so choose.

Booker T. burned the hot midnight oil of academe, and fell asleep with Walt Whitman, beginning to understand why this man was celebrated. He awoke with a start and a stiff neck at 3 a.m., and refreshed with three hours sleep, began to write.

Dear Mags,

How are you? I am fine. I only been in college one day but I already learned some things that made me think of you. My first assignment was to read a poetry book and write a commentary about one of the poems. Here is the poem that made me think of you . . .

TO A COMMON PROSTITUTE

Be composed-be at ease with me- I am Walt Whitman, liberal
and lusty as Nature,
Not till the sun excludes you do I exclude you,
Not till the waters refuse to glisten for you and the leaves rustle
for you,
do my words refuse to glisten and rustle for you.
My girl I appoint with you an appointment,
and I charge you that you make preparations to be worthy to
meet me,
And I charge you that you be patient and perfect till I come.
Till then I salute you with a significant look that you do not
forget me.

That's what they want us to read in college. I hope you and Frederick Douglass are okay.

Your friend,
Booker T. McCan

P.S. I never did think you were common though.

Booker T. read the letter and smiled. He liked Mags, and he was beginning to like Walt Whitman. He picked up *Leaves of Grass* again and scanned through the pages, stopping now and then to jot down a phrase that caught his eye. Finally, as the morning sky brightened, he closed the book and sat thinking. He thought he understood much of what the poet said, but not everything. He was troubled by Book XXI—Drum-Taps. He began to write.

COMMENTS ON WALT WHITMAN
By Booker T. McCan English 101- Professor Rhodewald

I was quite amazed when I read the poem called *THE CENTENARIAN'S STORY.* First of all because I always thought poems had to have rhymes and second of all because it is a story told by a man over a hundred years old about General Washington's first battle against the British at Brooklyn in the Revolutionary War where he watched from a hill while twenty thousand British Red Coats made mincemeat out of two thousand young men from Maryland and Virginia. So its not really a poem but a story. But to me it was most amazing because I know a hundred year old man who told me about the battle of Gettysburg in the Civil War. They both told of young men being slaughtered and now I have seen the same thing and I wonder if when I become a hundred years old I will be telling some young man about the slaughter at Iwo Jima and if when he is a hundred years old he will tell somebody about the battle he was in. It's not that I don't like Mister Whitman's poems. It's just that I think he wants to make war look like something better than it is. When I first went off to war I felt that way too but when I saw how terrible it was at Iwo Jima I changed my mind. But maybe he changed his mind too. In the poem called *THE WOUND-DRESSER* which is also really a story he seems very sad and I know that feeling too although I never kissed any dead soldiers.

But I have to say that the poem *ETHIOPIA SALUTING THE COLORS* kind of made me mad because he tells about a hundred year old negro lady watching Sherman's army marching through Georgia and asks why she curtsies to the flags going by when anybody should know why and shouldn't have to make fun of her and call her wooly headed and hardly human. And to call her Ethiopian I think is an insult too because she probly came from the Gold Coast or the Ivory Coast.

>> 26 <<

MONEY AND VOTES

September 19, 1946... Washington, D.C.

The president of the United States sat behind his desk in the White House Oval Office, his hands clasped across his vest; to his left was Attorney General Tom Clark, to his right Administrative Assistant David K. Niles. Arrayed in a semi-circle in front of the desk were seven earnest-faced men who had come to speak to him about civil rights, and more specifically about the problems of Negroes in the United States.

President Truman eyed the group warily, and leaned forward in his chair. "Everybody seems to believe the president by himself can do anything he wishes on these matters," he said, "but the president is helpless unless he is backed by public opinion."

Walter White, Executive Secretary of the National Association for the Advancement of Colored People, and spokesman for the group nodded. "Mr. President," he said, "with all due respect, sir, the American public is appalled by the spectacle of lynch mobs…and if I may say so, sir, you must be aware that the image the United States would like to project as the Land of the Free is shattered in the United Nations, and all over the world, when they read of the cruelties and injustices. I have been asked in South America and in Africa if these stories are true. People ask: 'can this be America?'"

Truman had much on his mind, and was trying hard to concentrate on what the group spokesman was saying, finding it less compelling than the problem of getting Soviet troops to withdraw from Azerbaijan as Stalin had agreed to do at Yalta. He was vexed by the advice of some cabinet members that he must prepare for war with the Soviet Union. Also, he was galled by the temerity of Secretary of State James Byrnes, who continued to treat him as if he were a junior Senator who had cheated him out of the 1944 vice presidential nomination, and thus now occupied the president's chair which rightfully belonged to him, Byrnes. He was determined to ask for Byrnes' resignation.

The president heard White say, "...they dragged him off the bus and gouged his eyes out with a nightstick."

Truman, who had been slumping in his chair, sat up straight and said, "I'm sorry, Mr. White, but would you mind repeating that story? I think I missed something."

Walter White patiently retold the story of Isaac Woodward, a Negro soldier in uniform, accused by a white bus driver of being drunk and disorderly (although he did not drink), pulled off the bus by police in Batesburg, South Carolina, beaten and blinded by nightsticks jabbed in his eyes.

The president was horrified. "My God!" he exclaimed. "I had no idea it was as terrible as that! We've got to do something."

When David Niles suggested appointing a committee to investigate the entire subject of violation of civil liberties, and to recommend corrective action, Truman agreed immediately. He loved this way of doing business. He relished the power that allowed him to take quick action when it suited him, and to send the problem off to a committee when he wasn't quite sure what to do. He was not comfortable in the presence of Negro leaders. In fact he was never comfortable with any group he knew came from a different background than his own—white, Protestant, middle America; anyone who might raise an eyebrow when he referred to Negroes as niggers or coons, which he had been known to do. He did not trust women, other than his mother, wife, and daughter. He did not trust admirals or generals; he did not trust labor leaders, and he certainly did not trust Republicans. He was fiercely loyal to anyone who had helped him, including the Kansas City Democratic kingpin Tom Pendergast, of whom the appellation "notorious" was one of the kindest labels he received.

Truman venerated the U.S. Presidency, rarely saying "shit" in the Oval Office; Woodrow Wilson and Franklin D. Roosevelt were his heroes. He believed in fair and just treatment for all, in particular for U.S. citizens protected by that most sainted of documents, the U.S. Constitution. He recoiled at the images of Jews suffering in Nazi Germany. He thought he could work with Stalin who he called "Uncle Joe," but not to his face. He wanted people to like him. He thought the assembled group of Negro leaders seemed reasonable enough, but he would not have been surprised to find more than one to be a "smart-aleck" or "rabble rouser," as he had called Representative Adam Clayton Powell, Jr., the Negro congressman from New York. Powell had called Truman's wife "The last lady in the land," when Mrs. Truman had refused to boycott a tea given by the Daughters of the American Revolution in her honor, after the DAR had refused to allow Powell's wife, black pianist Hazel Scott, to perform in Constitution Hall, the same action that had caused Eleanor Roosevelt to resign from the DAR in protest.

With some impatience, Truman noted one of the group asking to be recognized. A tall pipe-thin man with skin the color of darkest ebony, white eyebrows, and a thatch of snow-white hair, stood and began to speak in a deep, rumbling, baritone voice. It was Count.

"Mr. President," he began, "with all due respect, sir, may I say that not only are conditions in the South worse for the Negro than you could have imagined, but any proposed change in these conditions will be met with massive resistance. With the Senate filibuster, no legislation designed to bring relief will be possible."

The president looked sharply at the black and white man standing before him, and said in his trademark biting style, "So what do you suggest, sir? Another Civil War? I am fully aware of the difficulties that face us in this matter. I will create this committee by executive order, and I will pay for it out of the president's contingency fund. What more can I do?"

As quickly as the words were out of his mouth he wanted to pull them back. He was not looking for suggestions, he had just agreed to formation of a committee to do that. At the present time he was prepared to do no more, and the thought crossed his mind that if these people pushed him too hard, he would drag his feet on the issue since he did not feel he owed them anything more than acknowledgment of their problems. After all it was only in the second Roosevelt election that any significant numbers of Negroes had voted Democratic, and he was skeptical of those reports anyway. Less than 100 years away from the Civil War, Negroes in the United States still voted for the party of Lincoln. Truman knew that, and so felt little political pressure to favor this group.

Count held the floor as Walter White started to answer Truman's rhetorical question. He waved White to silence with a hand gesture and said, "Mr. President, earlier you said, and we all perfectly understood, that the president is helpless unless he is backed by public opinion. With all due respect, sir, may I suggest that the president, with his bully pulpit, is in position to influence public opinion by speaking out on issues. We all know the burdens of office you carry, and the terrible responsibilities you bear, so may I say that we who are here to seek your support for our cause do not come empty handed, but with resources we are prepared to offer in support of your causes. May we assume one is to be elected president in 1948?"

Truman needed no introduction to power politics. He looked up with some amusement at the suggestion that this group could in any way aid his election plans. He knew of the Democratic move to nominate Eisenhower in 1948; he himself had spoken to Eisenhower about it. He had not announced any plans of his own to be a candidate, though as the party leader after the death of Roosevelt, feeling strong, healthy, and highly energized, he had no intention of stepping down without a fight. He looked from Count to Walter White and said, "Mr. White, I don't know who this man is, and I don't know if he speaks for himself or for your group, but would you please tell him that if I were to use the bully pulpit to speak out in support of your cause, a most certain result would be loss of Southern support, and almost certain defeat at the polls should I decide to run."

Count had not discussed his plans with the group before the meeting. In fact, before the meeting he did not have a plan, nor did the group, other than to call the president's attention to recent racial outrages, and to ask for his support in correcting injustices. No one present knew much about Count; he had shown up at Walter White's New York NAACP office soon after the war ended in the fall of 1945 announcing that he wanted to do his part in the Advancement. White had taken him in, impressed with his intense and earnest demeanor, to say nothing of his gift to the organization of $1 million. Count was viewed as something of an eccentric, but because of his apparently unlimited supply of money was more often referred to as a visionary.

Walter White had no idea what Count was thinking as he spoke to the president, but decided he would support him now, if for no other reason that there was virtually nothing to lose. "Mr. President," he said, "this man is Count, he is an investment banker, and he speaks with my full backing. I believe he understands, as we all do, the political difficulties you face in taking the courageous decision to support our cause. Is it not clear that the fact a president of the United States must face such difficulties in standing up for citizens' rights is perhaps the best indication that such action...standing up for citizens' rights...is needed to heal a great nation's festering wound?"

Truman was a practical man not much given to thinking of the problems he faced as wounds, festering or otherwise. Nothing registered in Truman's mind after White characterized Count as an investment banker. Truman now looked with interest at Count, noting that in spite of his ramrod straight posture, this man was in fact very old.

"So, Mr. Count," the president said. "Just what, may I ask, is the nature of the resources you are prepared to offer in support of my causes?"

"Money and votes," said Count without hesitation.

"Money and votes," Truman repeated. "I see. Money and votes." He began to tap his fingers on the desk in front of him, then he held them in front of his face, and then he tented his hands over his nose, thumbs under his chin, elbows on the desk, eyes staring at nothing...thinking about money and votes.

>> 27 <<

THE MORAL MEANING OF THE ATOMIC BOMB

Susan and Flapper sat in a pew at the Protestant Episcopal Church reading the order of service from a small printed sheet inserted in a hymnal. The sermon was entitled *The Moral Meaning of the Atomic Bomb.*

The sanctuary was packed with people, some sitting in the aisles, some standing in the back and on the sides. Susan and Flapper recognized Nelson sitting with a number of other students.

After hymns, prayers, and scripture, Arthur Holly Compton, impressive in his black academic gown, rose to speak. He greeted the crowd amiably and plunged immediately into his text.

"I believe that Christianity has the key to survival, and the good life in the modern world," he began. "I have so idealized Jesus that he has become for me the Son of God to unique degree. I follow Jesus' teaching that the basis of existence, life, and motivation, which I think of as a conscious power, holds for me, and for all other persons, the attitude of a wise and loving father…a kinship with the Creator…God." His voice broke slightly. He paused to collect himself.

He cleared his throat, looked out at the attentive audience, and smiled slightly from one side of his mouth. He continued. "The past five years," he said, "have held, for all of us, strange, unusual, and all too often, terrifying experiences we will carry with us forever. Let me tell you something of mine.

"You must know by now that in these years I was privileged to participate, along with men of unbounded courage and wisdom, in the great scientific endeavor that resulted in the release of previously unknown sources of enormous energy. Thankfully we found a way to use this energy to bring an end to the calamity that was World War II. I would give much if I could have you understand the thrill a scientist feels when he discovers something of the unknown, the nature of which previously could only have been guessed.

"In nineteen forty-one we knew from theory, and more importantly because it had been accomplished two years earlier by scientists in Germany, that it was possible to split the atom experimentally, and thus release large amounts of energy. A top-secret study was called for by the National Academy of Science to determine the feasibility of a project to convert the energy of the atom into a military weapon. We all knew this would not be an easy task…if it were even possible, nobody knew. Let me illustrate the dimension of the problem with an anecdote.

"Only the heavy elements uranium and plutonium were suitable, and neither was readily available in the necessary quantities; in fact, plutonium does not exist in nature, but must be manufactured. In nineteen forty, the cyclotron at Washington University, here in St. Louis, was kept in operation day and night, week after week after week for a year, to produce half a milligram of plutonium…about the size of a grain of salt. It was only enough to study the chemical properties of the element. It was then necessary to develop plans for construction of an engineering facility that was capable of producing the element in the pound quantities needed for bomb construction. This was done.

"It was not until…and how could I ever forget this date? December second, nineteen forty-two…Not quite a year after the Pearl Harbor attack, that we knew with certainty that the bomb was possible. That was the day at the University of Chicago Metallurgical Laboratory, when the first controlled chain nuclear reaction was accomplished. I emphasize 'controlled.' It was also the day that I, and my peace-loving colleagues, had to face ourselves in the mirror and ask: *is this something you can do in good conscience?* It was a difficult question for someone like me, raised by a Presbyterian minister father…a man of God…and a Mennonite mother who renounced war in any form. I found comfort in the Bible. In the Old Testament book of Nehemiah, we read that Nehemiah, a royal official in Babylon, learned of the distress of Jerusalem, and obtained a royal commission to rebuild the city. Despite violent opposition from Samaritans, Ammonites, and Arabs, he built the wall of Jerusalem with a weapon in one hand, and a trowel in the other *'for the people had a mind to work'* — so said Nehemiah.

"The search for truth sometimes leads us to Greek mythology. Daedalus, the Greek architect, learned from the gods the secret of making steel. With forge, hammer, and anvil, he fashioned a sword and gave it to King Minos of Crete. His neighbors said to him, *'but Daedalus, a sword will not bring us happiness, it will bring us strife.*' Daedalus smiled and answered, '*it is not my purpose to make you happy...I would make you great.*'

"You may find it hard to think of fissionable materials when fashioned into bombs as being a source of happiness. However this may be, if with such destructive weapons men are to survive, they must grow rapidly in human greatness. A new level of human understanding is needed. The reward for using the atom's power toward man's welfare is great and sure. The punishment for its misuse would seem to be death and destruction of the civilization that has been growing for a thousand years. These are the alternatives that atomic power, as the steel of Daedalus, presents to mankind. We are forced to grow to greater manhood.

"And so, atomic power is ours, and who can deny that it was God's will that we should have it? As we struggle with the task of using this new power for the good of man, inevitably there must result a growth of the human spirit...Let us pray."

Leaving the church, Flapper and Susan overheard Nelson, whose voice seemed to be amplified by a built-in megaphone, saying, "The gods must be having one big laugh...here we are stuck with the atomic bomb because somebody is comforted by apocryphal Old Testament stories, and inspired by Greek mythology. I'm surprised he didn't tell us they built it because they knew it would be so terrible it would be the end to wars."

The thought must have occurred to Compton, for he knew well the story of Alfred Nobel who in 1867 began to market "Nobel's Safety Powder"—better known as dynamite—an invention of nitroglycerin absorbed to a type of clay prevalent in northern Germany. Nobel went on to build a fortune from the manufacture of dynamite, smokeless powder, guns, shells, and aerial torpedoes. He then conceived the notion that his goal was peace that could be achieved by making war so horrible that no nation would consider waging one. He proclaimed, "*the day when two army corps can annihilate each other in one second, all civilized nations will recoil from war and discharge their troops.*" So said Alfred Nobel.

"I need to talk with Professor Compton," Flapper said to Susan. "I want to find out more about his feelings toward God. He seems so certain. He says the truth will make men free, and that he is dedicated to the search for truth...and yet when he talks about God he sounds like he has found the truth. Is the moral meaning of the atomic bomb that it's God's will we have it?"

Susan said, "I think he said it will result in growth of the human spirit.

But why don't you ask him?" She pointed to the church entrance where Compton was emerging.

Flapper started to walk towards Compton, coming down the church steps in a dark suit carrying his academic robe folded over one arm. Two men, one with a Speed Graphic flash bulb camera, got there first. Flapper heard one say, "Dr. Compton, I'm Mel Park from the *Post-Dispatch,* this is the first time you have spoken in public about the atomic bomb and I'd like to ask you some questions."

Compton, taken by surprise, took a step back, and looked with annoyance at the reporter just as the flash bulb popped. Before he could say anything, Mel Park asked his first question. "You know of course that your bombs killed and maimed close to a half million people, most of them innocent women and children, how do you feel about that?"

Compton looked at Mel Park as if he were a snake that had just risen up from the grass. His dark eyes flashed, and then faded as he struggled for an answer. His emotions had been in turmoil over this question during many sleepless nights since the end of the war, and he knew he was not alone in this torment. He had joined with many of his colleagues in discussions and proposals to limit, and even to end further research on the use of atomic power for military purposes, but he knew, with the certainty of a pi electron, that these matters had passed from the trembling fingers of the scientists to the sweaty hands of the politicians and generals. He thought of some of his friends who had turned away from physics in disgust, and who had taken up studies in biology. He thought of others who were eager to continue the weapon's work. He knew that the fusion of light elements would soon make the fission of heavy elements seem like the pop of a cap gun. He remembered the day in the summer of 1942 when the possibility was discussed that releasing atomic power from the nucleus might result in ignition of the Earth's oceans or atmosphere, and burn up the world. He harbored the hope remaining in Pandora's box, but dreaded the insects of suspicion, hatred, fear, and malice already released. He felt like Prometheus, chained to a rock by Zeus for stealing the fire from Olympus and presenting it to man as a gift...condemned to an eternity of agony as vultures tore at his liver.

"I feel like Prometheus," he said and walked quickly away.

Mel Park followed at a trot, and ripped away another small piece of the professor's liver with the shouted question: "Did Prometheus kill small children?"

>>28<<

NEVER AGAIN

Booker T. had long since passed Dean Dunn's dire prediction of how long he would last at the University of Illinois. The dean and the entire academic community were learning a few things from the returning veterans about the values of motivation, determination, and commitment in enhancing the learning process. The tide of knowledge was unexpectedly lifted as good teachers, with inspired performances of their own, rose to the bait of students eager to learn, well aware that in spite of everything, the teacher always learned more than the student. Now, halfway through the spring semester of 1947, Booker T. sat looking out the window of a second floor class room waiting for Professor Odin to convene the class…Political Science 102, better known as Poly Sci Two. Feeling very grown up at the age of 19, Booker T. took notice, for probably the first time in his life, of a panoply of crocuses, hyacinths, tulips, and flowering cherry trees. He was amazed at their beauty, and wondered if there were such things in Peoria. He thought of his spur-of-the moment decision to join the Naval Reserve Officers Training Corps program. Did he not have enough of the sea? Apparently not. It puzzled him. A catchy tune ran through his head…*I joined the Navy to see the world. And what did I see? I saw the sea.* Flapper Jackson's smiling face appeared in his mind then faded.

The professor tapped the podium. "Ladies and gentlemen," he said. "Good morning…I greet you with special pleasure this morning after six months of learning about the science of politics, or, if you prefer, the black art of politics." Snickers rippled through the class; an appreciative glance was cast from the professor. "Today," he continued, "we begin what you may have noted in your class syllabus is called…" He paused to look meaningfully at the class over his glasses. He cleared his throat and said, "…a special project." A buzz of chatter swept the room.

The professor smiled. "Ladies and gentlemen," he continued, "we live in turbulent times...portentous times." He looked at the young faces in front of him. So far, so good, he had their attention. "But surely times of great opportunity. An opportunity for us right here in this poor insignificant classroom to push back the frontiers of knowledge, to advance to a new level of understanding, to become part of the great and glorious history of scholarly endeavor that marks us civilized."

He noticed some slightly rolled eyes, and people glancing at their neighbors. He pushed on. "Ladies and gentlemen...you who have seen so much...you who have fought so well. You will know better if I tell you that fighting a war is easy, but ladies and gentlemen, with all due respect, that is what I am here to tell you. Fighting a war is easy," he paused, "compared to making a peace."

He paused again. The class waited. "A study of Political Science must in the end confront the truth of the von Clausewitz aphorism... *War is nothing more than the continuation of politics by other means*...and the Clemenceau corollary...*Peace is the continuation of war by other means*...and of course those other means are politics."

The professor was startled to hear some derisive cheers arise from the class. He nodded appreciatively.

"Your special project...at last I come to it..." More cheers. "Your special project is to assume the role of world leaders and devise a just and lasting peace for all nations...a just and lasting peace for all nations...political science may be needed." Nervous laughter and a few derisive snickers rippled through the class of 25 students.

"You will be the peacemakers. Bless you." He signaled the sign of the cross with an upraised hand, and was rewarded with a few hoots. He smiled and continued, "I will assign each of you to one of four groups. You will represent the victors in the recently ended triumph of good over evil. I refer to the British, the French, the Soviets, and of course, the Americans. I want you to put yourselves into the shoes of these people...consider the special circumstances that may only apply to your country...will you negotiate solely on the basis of your own interest, or will you yield to the common good? Do you trust the other side? Can you expect them to trust you?

"You will have four weeks to prepare for a two-day conference that I will convene in the ballroom of the student union building. It will be called the Champaign Conference on World Peace. Each group will bring to the table their own proposals for solutions to such problems as where or whether to establish zones of occupation in Germany; where to establish frontiers for the liberated eastern European countries of Poland, Bulgaria, Rumania, Austria, and Czechoslovakia; how to deal with the ancient ethnic animosities of the Balkan states; the role of the United Nations in establishing the state of Israel; should Germany and Japan be allowed to continue as sovereign nations and if so what, if any, is an appropriate level of reparations they should be required to pay to compensate for their aggression. You might consider the role of the United Nations in settling these questions. At the conference you will discuss and vote on proposals from the different groups. You will be guided by the knowledge that what you agree to at this conference may hold the seeds of World War III (and perhaps the end of the world) as the Treaty of Versailles held the seeds of World War II, or that if you are wise, you may forever shield Earth's children from the plague of war." He stopped speaking and looked up expectantly.

Hands went up. Professor Odin pointed to one.

"Why do you include the French? They were a defeated nation and did not contribute to the Nazi defeat."

Professor Odin nodded. "Yes. A very good question. The answer lies in the fact that historically, and for more than two centuries, France has always been one of the great powers. A stable Europe, if there can ever be such a thing, depends in no small degree on a strong France. Also to say that France did not contribute to the Nazi defeat is to overlook the heroic work of the French resistance in the country, and the Free French regiments outside."

"What about the Chinese? Why aren't they included?"

Once again the professor nodded. "Another good question," he said. "Perhaps a quarter of the world's population is Chinese. How can they be excluded from a world peace conference? The problem here is that for the moment we don't really know who speaks for the Chinese, because they are in the melancholy business of continuing politics by other means in that most grievous of human trials...civil war. The Western powers would no doubt be pleased to see Chiang Kai-shek and his Nationalists prevail, but from what we read it now appears that Mao Tse Tung's communists are on the rise, which is likely to make the Russians smile, or perhaps not.

"Speaking of communists, this is a good time to point out that you tyro peacemakers are presented here with a problem unique in history...the victors are divided; perhaps fatally at odds. We see on one side a major power, not to say an ally and comrade-in-arms, with a well established political system...communism...anathema to the other side; and of course, vice versa. In the beginning, Great Britain and France tolerated Hitler's mad excursions because they saw Russia as a greater threat, one that Hitler could blunt. But as events unfolded, and they were forced into an uneasy alliance, they found it expedient to shelve differences, never achieving the comfort of trust. No doubt the most often used phrase in communications between Churchill and Stalin was: 'your actions in this matter are intolerable.'

"But enough of this, it is time for me to make the assignments. I rank the victors in the order of their strengths…first the United States, second the Soviet Union, third Great Britain, fourth France. Accordingly, I assign leadership roles to students in order of their class rank." He consulted his grade book. "Miss Norton you are the Premier of France; Miss Sullivan you are the Prime Minister of Great Britain; Mr. Reali you are the Bolshevik leader of the Soviet Union; and…congratulations Mr. McCan…you are the president of the United States."

Booker T. raised his head in surprise as applause sprang up around the room. He stood and waved as if he had just won an election. The smiling class acted as though he just had. He was caught up in the game. He called for quiet with a wave of his hand. "My fellow Americans," he intoned. "Thank you for your support. This is something I have worked for all my life. I shall not fail." He sat down thinking of Count and Flapper.

The class cheered. Professor Odin beamed.

Four weeks later ersatz President McCan rose to address the assembled faux dignitaries, and not a few curious spectators at the Champaign Conference on World Peace. Standing next to his seat at the large round table, he spoke with occasional reference to a palm-sized piece of notepaper, hastily prepared as he listened to the presentations of the other three groups.

"My honorable and distinguished European colleagues," he began, "permit me to speak with all the candor I can muster. I have listened to your pitiful and stale proposals with growing impatience…For too many bloodstained and heartbreaking centuries the countries of Europe and the British Isles have squabbled like children over scraps of land, spheres of influence, affronts to honor, wounded pride, and on, and on, and on, and on. Like children also is the indifference to the consequences of your actions. What matter if fifteen, twenty…a hundred million people die? I ask you to stop for a moment to think about the agony of those huddled masses."

Booker T. paused for a long moment. He waited. Then he waited some more. All eyes in the room were riveted on him. Members of his own delegation looked at each other and smiled.

"Never again."

A late May thunderstorm was gathering, lightning flashed in the distance. The room lights flickered.

"The United States of America stands before the world in sole possession of the most powerful weapon the world has ever seen. The United States of America, in the dawn of this atomic age...at this time let the word go forth...stands ready to use this weapon to ensure that never again will people die in the puerile madness of misguided, misbegotten, misanthropic war." Again he waited.

"Never again."

The room was silent.

"If we could but look over the shoulders of our children's children's children's children as they read of noble and heroic deeds, would we not rejoice to know that the word war had disappeared from the lexicon? It is my intent to make a beginning...now, in the middle of the twentieth century...toward this goal.

"Is this foolish fantasy? Many may think so, but mark this well...if I alone hold the ultimate weapon, and I say it will be done who is there to dispute me?" He looked around the table seeking eye contact. Finding none he continued. "The United States of America offers a five point program."

Copies of the program were distributed. The delegates read:

MANDATE FOR WORLD PEACE

1.DISARMAMENT

a. Armies will be disbanded and their weapons destroyed.

b. Weapons and munitions factories will be destroyed.

c. Guns, ammunition, and all explosive devices held in private hands will be seized and destroyed.

d. Invention and development of new weapons will be prohibited.

2. HUMAN RIGHTS

a.Freedom of speech, assembly, religion, and freedom from fear and hunger are affirmed.

b. Full and gainful employment of all able-bodied persons is guaranteed.

c. Freedom from poverty is established.

d. The right to vote is established for all adults beginning at age eighteen.

3. COMMERCE
   a. All barriers to free trade throughout the world are removed.
   b. Freedom of the press is guaranteed.

4. INDEPENDENCE
   a. All countries of the world will be free and independent.
   b. Borders will be redrawn to reflect the natural distribution of populations and culture, with particular emphasis on Africa.

5. ADMINISTRATION
   a. The principle of World Government is established.
   b. The Constitution of the United States of America, amended as appropriate, will become the Constitution of the World.
   c. The United States of America will maintain a security force to ensure compliance.

Booker T. waited quietly, allowing everyone enough time to read the paper. He watched the initial reactions, noting a few smiles, a few frowns, but mostly surprise. At length he spoke. "It is a simple philosophy," he said, "…war is not possible without the instruments of war…peace is not possible without the instruments of peace." He sat down. After a short silence, a buzz of whispered conversation surged over the room.

The Prime Minister of Great Britain, Miss Sullivan, arose to speak, gamely attempting a Churchillian accent. "May I first offer congratulations to the distinguished president of the United States for a bold, nay, a breathless proposal that addresses with brilliant clarity and dazzling focus the grave and significant problems we face. His Majesty's Government stands of course shoulder to shoulder with our gallant North American allies in this noble and deserving quest for peace. Perhaps at this time my venerable colleague will be so kind as to provide clarification of certain points in the proposal. In particular, sir, I refer to points one and four. Pray tell me, sir, do you in fact mean there will be no, that is to say none at all, armies in the world? And do you realize, if I understand your intent, that with a bold stroke of the pen you have dissolved the British Empire upon which, you may recall, the sun never sets?"

President McCan, imposing in dark suit, white shirt, red white and blue tie, stood again. "It is not a proposal, sir, it is a mandate. There will be no, that is to say not any, armies in the world. And may I say to my esteemed friend and colleague…if, because of this mandate, the sun at long last sets on the British Empire, surely it must be clear that a new day is dawning for the tortured world."

Premier Reali-Stalin rose to speak for the Union of Soviet Socialist Republics. "Mr. President," he said, "we of the Soviet Union have devoted long hours in serious consideration of the aims of this conference. We are not amused by your ill-advised attempts to turn the conference into a joke. We come to this conference burdened with the overwhelming grief of more than fifteen million deaths…half of them civilian, suffered in the name of our sacred Motherland. At this time the Soviet Union has in the field the largest and most powerful land army in the world…more than ten million battle tested and loyal veterans…pledged to defend and protect. Do you expect us to disband this force in the hour of our triumph? How dare you suggest it?"

Once more Booker T. got to his feet. He glanced around the table, fixed his gaze on the Soviet Premier who had taken his seat, and sighed deeply. "We suggest nothing," he said. "We decree all. It is not a proposal," his voice began to rise, "it is not a suggestion…it is a mandate!" He banged the table with his fist. He lowered his voice, and added almost in a whisper, "For peace." He looked around at the startled faces.

"Do you not see?" he questioned. "It is precisely because of the millions of deaths that these measures are required. It is the last hope of…" his voice rose, "listen to me…the last hope…of our precious Earth. You have offered nothing but old, tired, failed, and benighted solutions…it will not do! It can not be! You may be angry at having your guns taken away. You may be outraged at losing your colonies…your possessions if you will. You may be furious at what you perceive as loss of sovereignty. You may cry Utopia in all your scorn. You may do all these things, but in the name of the tormented victims, and above all to the everlasting profit of the innocent…you will obey this mandate! You have no choice." He sat down.

Norton-DeGaulle rose to speak for France. "Monsieur President. The grand Republic of France, ever mindful of, and eternally grateful for, the sacrifices of the noble people of the United States in the cause of restoring and maintaining the proud French democracy, can, I am bound to say, never agree to place its fate in the hands of the non-French. We must control our own destiny. We must."

Reali-Stalin rose and said, "Mr. President, let me make it clear to you in the most direct way…the Soviet Union will not disband its army! Do you understand?"

Booker T. lighted a cigar and spoke from his chair. "What you fail to appreciate, sir," he said, "is that your position is weak, you have no clout, your army is obsolete. The Atomic Age has arrived and you speak of divisions, tanks and artillery. Pardon me if I laugh."

The room became very quiet. For several moments no one spoke, re-reading the mandate, thinking of the implications.

At length Professor Odin stood. He looked around the room. It was over. He said, "Never again."

>>29<<

THE PURPOSE OF MAN'S EXISTENCE

...lives of great men all remind us we can make our lives sublime, and departing leave behind us, footprints on the sands of time ...

Henry Wadsworth Longfellow—A PSALM OF LIFE

Arthur Holly Compton finished the final letter with a flourish and turned from the chalkboard to face his class, PHILOSOPHY 425—LIVES OF GREAT MEN. The class was comfortably small, only 15 students. He looked out over the heads of the fresh faces before him, only vaguely aware of their presence. He was thinking about some of the great men he knew and had known...Einstein, Fermi, Oppenheimer, Szilard, Neils Bohr. He cleared his throat. "Ladies and gentlemen," he began. He hesitated as if he was not sure he wanted to say what was written on the course outline lying before him on the wooden podium. He sighed. "The central question..." He plunged ahead, "The central question we will examine in this class is no less than simply this..." He cleared his throat, "...What is the purpose of man's existence?"

Never one to feel sheepish, he paused to look meaningfully at the class who were mostly agreed that for them the purpose of man's existence at this particular time in their lives could be easily summed up in a single word...graduation.

Compton avoided eye contact and continued. "Our approach will be to examine the nature of the goals that have inspired worthy and satisfying lives...the lives of great men."

Flapper, in the absence of Susan who was sitting in on a genetics course somewhere else on the campus, was not the only one present to think, *what about women?*

"What about women?" A young lady in the front row asked.

The great man was ready for the question. "Of course women. We use the term man or men in the generic sense, as in mankind...there is no intention to exclude women. The poet used men, not people, we will do the same. At the same time I would point out that over the centuries, for the most part it has been man, not woman, who has made the great discoveries, who has provided the profound insights, who has led the way. However, in all fairness, I should also say that where women have contributed, perhaps it is fair to say, allowed to contribute, it is all the more remarkable and memorable. Madame Curie comes to mind, and on our own campus here at Washington University, Dr.Gerty Cori who along with her husband, Karl, has made important discoveries in the field of biochemistry for which they were jointly awarded a Nobel prize only last year."

He paused to allow thoughts to percolate in his brain. He was slightly annoyed at the interruption. His approach to teaching was not that of Socrates, though he would speak of Socrates; he did not have time to tease out a truth using leading questions. He had settled on his own answers and conclusions, and he did not seek, nor did he expect to receive, any new insights from a group of undergraduates. His purpose here was to present his thoughts. If someone learned he would not object.

He continued. "It is from our understanding of the world that we must form our attitudes toward life. May we not say that in learning our relation to our world and to each other, which is the task of science, we are developing the aspect of our being that makes us distinctly human? To many of us it is the possibility of adding something to this understanding that makes the task of science seem worthwhile. And yet...and yet..." he paused, searching for the right words, "and yet we must admit that the ultimate values of life are beyond science, and that the highest purpose of science itself is to elevate and enrich human experience. And so we see the fusion of science and philosophy...before the term science was coined it was called Natural Philosophy...and we examine the goals that have inspired worthy and satisfying lives in the hope that we can find answers to the wistful question...What is the purpose of man's existence?"

Professor Compton strolled in front of the class allowing time for his words to sink in. Following two cross-room excursions, he picked up a compact forest green book from his lectern, and displayed it before the class.

"Our text for this course, which I am pleased to see you have with you, is *THE AUTOBIOGRAPHY OF SCIENCE*, compiled and edited by Forest Ray Moulton and Justus J. Schifferes. We will not limit ourselves to this text, but it will serve as a good point of departure. Also, since this is a one-semester course, which meets a total of only forty-five times, and since, you may have noticed, there are ninety-five different men and three women treated in this book it will be necessary to choose carefully those we will study and discuss...Let us begin...and where better than with Genesis?"

He picked up the 600-page text, and turned it over in his hand allowing time for the students to do the same. He opened it and read:

"Part one—Science is Born in Antiquity. No scientific explanation of the existence of the universe and the flesh-and-blood men who do the explaining has superseded the first four words of the Bible...*In the beginning, God...*"

Flapper's mind wandered...He was sitting on the fantail of the *Indianapolis* with his friend Booker T. McCan under a moonless night on a dark sea. Engulfed by an avalanche of stars, they had talked of God, and considered the concept of the infinite. They were struck by the irony that all this beauty would give way in the morning to the supreme ugliness of a take-no-prisoners assault on the Japanese home island of Okinawa...

"...For many centuries after their promulgation, some time after fifteen hundred B.C., the opening verses of the first of the five books of Moses gave what the wisest men of those times considered the most reasonable, and hence the most scientific account of creation. Hebrew was the language in which Genesis and other historical books of the Bible were compiled in Babylon twenty-five hundred years ago."

Professor Compton closed the book and began to recite from memory. *"In the beginning God created the heaven and the earth. And the earth was without form, and void; and darkness was upon the face of the deep. And the Spirit of God moved upon the face of the waters. And God said, Let there be light: and there was light."*

Compton stopped and looked around at his students, noting different reactions to what he appeared to believe was a profound insight he had just conveyed.

Flapper thought, *so that's it...God created the heaven and the earth...so the purpose of man's existence is to carry out God's will.* He raised his hand. Though not recognized, he spoke anyway.

"Professor Compton, with all due respect, sir, is this a course in religion or philosophy, or are they the same thing?"

Compton looked hard at the somehow older-than-he-looked man with the penetrating eyes, who had just asked the type of impertinent question that angered him most. He had endured much from his wartime colleagues in the

Manhattan Project because of his iron-willed Christian beliefs. He knew what they said about him…'wherever Compton was, God was not far away.' He knew his friend, the great Danish physicist Neils Bohr, considered his philosophy primitive. He did not care what they thought, he stood with Hegel, the acclaimed 19th century German philosopher, inspired by the Christian doctrine of the Holy Spirit and grounded in the faith that God has been revealed as truth and spirit, that man in receiving this revelation knows God, which is to say he knows absolute truth. He was all too familiar with the agnostic argument of T.H. Huxley, "Darwin's bulldog,"that there was no common ground between Christian theology and the requirements for scientific truth. He rejected it.

Compton continued to stare at Flapper, waiting for him to lower his eyes, but to his further annoyance, Flapper's gaze was unwavering. Compton looked down at his seating chart and said, "You are, ah," he ran his finger down the page, "ah…"

Flapper said, "Jackson, sir, Homer Jackson."

"Yes, I see…Jackson. Well now, Jackson, what is it you wanted to know?"

Flapper said, "I was surprised that we begin a study of the lives of great men with the Bible, I asked if religion and philosophy are the same."

Compton smiled condescendingly, and looked around the room at the other students to let them know he understood that they were not as dim-witted as this brazen person, and at the same time causing them to understand what kind of treatment they could expect if they asked unsolicited questions. Flapper waited. Compton spoke at last, not looking at Flapper. Being the academician he was, the concept of a simple answer was as alien to him as the possibility that mass and energy were unrelated. "The academic discipline of philosophy," he said, "in common with all disciplines, is based on certain principles and is organized into various branches. There is a branch of philosophy that is concerned with the origin and general structure of the universe…it is called cosmology. The cosmological argument, sometimes called the first-cause argument, asserts that the universe is composed wholly of entities such as planets, stars, and living things, not least man, and that the contingency of each entity demands the admission of an adequate external cause, which is God. The book of Genesis tells us that on the sixth day God created man, male and female, in his own image."

It occurred to Flapper and not a few of the others that the Bible had been written by man, and that the cosmological argument was circular, but nobody was prepared to bring it up at this time.

Compton swung around and glared at Flapper as if reading his thoughts; he remembered Neils Bohr scoffing at these ideas. "Now, if nobody objects," he said in his most sarcastic tone, "I would like to talk about Socrates."

"So then he tells us about Socrates, the first of his great men." Flapper and Susan, sitting over lunch at a table on the patio of the student union building, were each bursting with information to share about what they had learned that day. Susan listened patiently, sensing the excitement in Flapper's voice, waiting her turn.

"The central problem of philosophy changed after Socrates, from cosmology..." He stopped and looked at Susan. "Listen to these new words I learned," he gushed. "Cosmology...the branch of philosophy dealing with the origin and structure of the universe. Epistemology...isn't that a great word? Epistemology...the branch of philosophy that investigates the origin, nature, methods, and limits of human knowledge." Flapper paused and took a bite from a hamburger cooling on his plate while he thought about epistemology. White-chinned sparrows hopped under his feet, looking for crumbs.

"I wonder if there is a limit to human knowledge," he mused. "...Hey, you're all finished eating, how come I'm so slow?" Flapper began to chew furiously.

"You were talking," Susan said, not unkindly.

"Okay, I'm sorry. Your turn. Tell me about genetics."

Susan was momentarily quiet while she considered where to begin. "Did you know there are over three hundred thousand species of beetles on the Earth?" she asked.

Flapper looked up in surprise. "No kidding," he mumbled through a mouthful of french-fried potatoes.

Susan smiled at Flapper's surprise. "The professor," she continued, " a lady by the way...her name is Florence."

Flapper interrupted. "Professor Florence?" he asked.

Susan nodded. "Right. Geneva Florence," she said, "Professor Florence told the story...you'll like this, Flapper...She told the story about J.B.S. Haldane, the English biochemist and geneticist, who was once asked what the study of biology could tell us about the Almighty. Haldane replied, 'I'm not sure, except that He must be inordinately fond of beetles'."

The punch line caught Flapper with a mouthful of Coke that he could not entirely contain as he laughed appreciatively. "I wonder if Professor Compton knows that story," he said. "...That's wonderful, Susan...fond of beetles." He laughed some more.

Susan waited before continuing, beaming at Flapper, resisting the temptation to hug him. "Professor Florence talked about the origin of species," she said. "Darwin and Mendel. Do you know what a gene is, Flapper?"

It was June 1948. Susan and Flapper had just completed two years of the medical school curriculum...the basic sciences: anatomy, physiology, biochemistry, pharmacology, and pathology. They were poised to begin clinical training in the fall, but given the opportunity to pursue electives during the summer session they eagerly undertook studies in areas that had attracted their interests...Susan in genetics, Flapper in philosophy. Genes had been touched on in the biochemistry course, but only briefly because nobody knew what a gene was although there was pretty convincing evidence about what genes could do.

Flapper, still smiling about beetles, said, "I don't know what a gene is, but I know genes are mixed up in heredity."

Susan nodded. "Mendel pretty much proved that with his garden peas almost a hundred years ago," she said. "But what we are only now beginning to understand is the reason genes may be mixed up in heredity. And not only that," she continued, "but get this...before long we may even know something about the chemistry of genes."

Flapper noticed Susan's face flushed slightly with the excitement she felt. He did not resist the temptation to lean across the table and kiss her cheek.

Susan brushed breadcrumbs off her cheek and continued. "Do you remember when they talked about sickle cell anemia in the pathology course, and also in biochemistry class?"

Flapper remembered. "The red blood cells crumple into sickle shapes when they pass from the arteries to the veins," he said, "it occurs mostly in Africans."

Susan beamed. "Very good, Flapper," she patted his cheek in approval. "Now listen to this...it has just been discovered that the reason the red cells crumple is because something is wrong with the hemoglobin in those cells. In arterial blood, hemoglobin carries oxygen from the lungs to the various body tissues, the hemoglobin in venous blood does not have the oxygen, and in people with the sickle-cell trait the globin protein of the non-oxygenated hemoglobin molecule folds in a funny way, and causes the cell to collapse. Since the sickle-cell trait is inherited, it means the gene must have determined the difference in the globin."

Flapper was concentrating hard on what Susan was saying, trying to follow the argument. "So it means that genes determine the nature of proteins," he said.

Susan nodded. "Right," she said, "but it still doesn't tell us what a gene is. Now, get ready for this...I'm going to tell you about experiments that give some powerful clues about just what a gene is. Okay?"

Flapper took another bite from his hamburger and mumbled, "Okay, shoot."

"About twenty years ago," Susan began, "a British medical officer named Griffith isolated bacteria from the sputum of patients with lobar pneumonia...he found two types of pneumococcal colonies on his plates, one with a rough surface and one with a smooth surface. When he injected the two different types into mice he found that only the smooth colonies were virulent. Later, other investigators determined that the rough, non-virulent pneumococci could be transformed into smooth, virulent pneumococci by simply adding an extract from killed smooth colonies. Just four years ago, scientists at the Rockefeller Institute in New York showed that the transforming principle from the smooth bacteria was deoxyribonucleic acid—DNA. Professor Florence says it tells us that DNA is almost surely the genetic material."

Flapper understood and was appreciative. "I get it, Susan," he said, "I see why you're excited." Flapper thought about the experiments and said, "Imagine how that guy must have felt when he found out that only the smooth bacteria were virulent, and then to understand what it meant...wow! It looks like a good time to be involved in genetics research."

He saw a curious look come over Susan's face as he completed his sentence. "What?" he asked.

"That's what I want to do," said Susan, "you're reading my mind."

"You want to do research in genetics? What happened to medical school?" Flapper was puzzled.

Susan's eyes shone. "That's the beauty of it, Flapper," she said, "I can do both. They have an M.D.-Ph.D. program here, Professor Florence told me about it."

Flapper was momentarily dumfounded, but he quickly recovered, and fired a salvo of questions. "An M.D. *and* a Ph.D.? How long would it take? Why would you want both? Would the G.I. Bill pay for it?" Flapper's mind was working fast. Before Susan could answer he suddenly grasped what

Susan had in mind. "Wait a minute," he said. "...Of course...What a great idea...you get to study what you're really interested in and...and...what was it Professor Compton said?...He was off on another of his inspirational talks." Flapper lowered his voice in a mocking imitation of Compton, " 'The task of science is to learn our relation to the world and to each other. The possibility of adding to this understanding makes it seem worthwhile'."

Susan nodded enthusiastically. "Think of it, Flapper," she enthused, "...The chance to add something to the understanding. We don't just have to read about science, we can actually do science."

She paused momentarily then said, "You know, Flapper I really wonder about your Professor Compton. I don't understand how he can talk about science as the shrine of truth, and then stop doing science; I think that bomb has him confused. I think he is getting science and philosophy mixed up if he says the task of science is to learn our relation to the world and to each other."

Flapper agreed. "Right," he said, "he begins a course on the lives of great men with the creation story. But you know what? He's got me hooked on philosophy. If you're going for a Ph.D. in genetics, maybe I'll try for one in philosophy. Whaddaya think?"

Susan grinned. "I think," she said, " that there's going to be a lot of doctors hanging around our house." She held up a cup of Coca-Cola in toast, and they clunked cardboard cups to the new doctors.

>>30<<

TO SECURE THESE RIGHTS

Jerry Mulhane IV was a son of Dixie, born and raised in Pisgah, Alabama, a wide spot at the end of county road 88 where it ran into county road 58, up in Jackson County, about 40 miles from Chattanooga, Tennessee. There wasn't a whole lot to say about Pisgah, but whatever there was to say, Jerry didn't mind saying it because it was his home, and had been home to five generations of Mulhanes since his great-great-grandfather, the first Jerry Mulhane, had come there at the age of 20 from Protestant Northern Ireland in 1840 just ahead of the potato famine that killed over a million people. The Mulhanes were a family of warriors. The first Jerry, colonel of the Confederate infantry, died defending Lookout Mountain in 1863. His father, Jerry III, colonel of the United States infantry, survived a gas attack in the Argonne Forest in 1918, and he, the fourth Jerry Mulhane, born in 1920, got to be a major through a battlefield promotion in the heavy fighting around Pisa during the Italian campaign in 1944.

J-four, as he was known around Pisgah, came home from Italy a different man from the boy who left. For one thing he was having serious doubts about God and His place in the universe, although he still loved nothing more than a night of raucous singing of the old hymns with friends, along with a bottle of Jack Daniel's sour mash whiskey. Nothing lifted his spirits more than the loud and off-key harmony of the old favorites… "Bringing in the Sheep"; "Rock of Ages"; "Let Us Gather at the River"; "Swing Low, Sweet Chariot." After half a bottle of Jack Daniel's, "Onward Christian Soldiers" never failed to bring him to his feet with tears in his eyes. The "Battle Hymn of the Republic" was included reluctantly because it was simply a great song, but it didn't take long to look away from that baleful ballad to a foot-stamping, top of the lungs, nothing-held-back rendition of "Dixie." Old times there were not forgotten.

J-four loved Dixie, but after Italy he was ready to take a closer look. He couldn't get the image of those Buffalo Soldiers around Mount Pisano out of his head. This was not an easy thing for him...the first Jerry had owned slaves, and Jerrys junior, II, and III were Ku Klux Klan members. Following his daddy, before the war J-four himself had been a Klan member.

The Old Testament book of Deuteronomy told of Moses viewing the Promised Land from the summit of Mount Pisgah. When J-four came home to Pisgah, Alabama after the war, the first thing he did, recalling his eyeball to eyeball brush with mortality in Italy, was to marry Becky Blaine, his high school sweetheart. He couldn't see the promised land from Pisgah, but he knew where it was...a couple of hundred miles south, in Auburn, where before the war, at the Alabama Polytechnic Institute, he had been introduced to Mark Twain, O. Henry, Hemingway, Galsworthy, and Faulkner. He would be a writer.

J-four was not happy with the opening line. He ripped the paper from his typewriter, crushed it into a ball, and tossed it in a graceful arc at a corner wastebasket. Inserting a fresh piece of paper he quickly typed:

> THE BAMBINO AND THE BUFFALO SOLDIER
> By Jerry Mulhane IV
>
> It was quiet on the piazza, but not for long. Anxious fingers stroked triggers, and frightened eyes searched for targets across the wide cobble-stoned piazza with the fountain in the middle. On one side, the black fingers of A Company, 2nd Battalion, 370th Regimental Combat Team of the 92nd Infantry (Buffalo) Division. Their first taste of combat after what seemed like training that would never end.

J-four stopped, thought a moment, then x-ed out the last six words, and wrote instead, "what seemed like endless training." Still not right. He shifted in his seat, and looked out the window of the second-floor room thinking, *It shouldn't be this hard.* He could see students walking across the campus, cutting new paths that illustrated an ancient theorem...the shortest distance between two points is a straight line, not a winding walkway. Books and papers were piled high on both sides of his desk. He sighed, and reached for a small blue examination booklet from the top of a stack. He knew he should be grading these papers, but he had been putting it off. He wondered at his decision to accept a graduate assistantship, but he needed the extra money with the new baby and all. The G.I. Bill was good, and with the baby it was up to 150 dollars a month, but it still left them a little short. He would not complain. He could do this.

Stanley Gordon, another graduate student, approached shaking his head. "Look at this, J-four," he said. "Can you believe it?" He was holding a copy of the Birmingham News dated February 3, 1948. He pointed to the large black headlines:

TRUMAN TO SOUTH : CHANGE YOUR WAYS

"Can you believe it, J-four? First Hugo Black, now Truman...these are Klan brothers, how can they do this to us?" Stanley was incensed.

J-four took the paper, and read the sub-headline:

PRESIDENT SENDS SPECIAL MESSAGE ON CIVIL RIGHTS TO CONGRESS

He scanned down the page stopping at the words "sweeping ten-point agenda." He read:

"1. Establish a permanent Commission on Civil Rights, a Joint Congressional Committee on Civil Rights, and a Civil Rights Division in the Department of Justice;

2. Strengthen existing civil rights statutes;

3. Enact an anti lynching law;

4. Protect everyone's right to vote;

5. Create a permanent Fair Employment Practices Commission;

6. Prohibit discrimination in interstate transportation facilities;

7. Grant home-rule and suffrage in presidential elections for the District of Columbia;

8. Grant statehood for Hawaii and Alaska, and greater self-government for our island possessions;

9. Equalize the opportunities for all residents of the U.S. to become naturalized citizens;

10. Settle the evacuation claims of Japanese-Americans.

In addition, the president made two personal pledges. He promised to issue executive orders 1) to enforce an end to discrimination in the federal government and 2) to end segregation in the armed forces."

J-four looked up at Stanley Gordon. "Stanley, mah friend," he said, "this country is carryin' a whole lot of loose baggage."

Stanley was outraged. "What you talkin' 'bout, J-four? What's it got to do with baggage? Them Feds is tryin' to tell us how to run our lives again."

"There's gonna be trouble, Stanley."

"You kin say that ag'in, J-four. We let them get away with this, the next thing you know they'll be tellin' our children to go to thuh same schools as nigger kids. It ain't right, J-four. Why cain't they just leave us alone?"

"Stanley, you got some kids ah don't know about? You ain't even married…you been holdin' out on me?"

"Aw hell, J-four, you know what ah'm talkin' about."

There had been a time when J-four would have agreed with Stanley on most, if not all, of these sentiments, but the world was not as simple to him as it had been when he went off to fight for democracy. He was not outraged by Truman's Civil Rights message, in fact he thought it was, if anything, a bit tame. It occurred to him that it might have taken some courage for Truman to send such a message when he would need Southern votes in the upcoming presidential election. But right now J-four had other things on his mind. He resumed typing.

THE BAMBINO AND THE BUFFALO SOLDIER
By Jerry Mulhane IV

Small arms fire was crackling across the piazza as the veteran German SS troops took dead aim at the young Americans of the 92nd (Buffalo) Division in their first action since landing in Italy less than one month earlier.

J-four looked at what he had written, shook his head, replaced "was crackling" with "crackled," then sat back and sighed heavily.

Walter White, sitting in his NAACP Washington office, was not feeling as good about the message as he thought he should. It was a landmark message there was no doubt about that, one they had never been able to get Roosevelt to send, but he had the uneasy feeling it didn't go far enough. The president had been as good as his word though, appointing a Commission to study the problem and make recommendations, and he had to admit the president went an important step further than he had agreed at that Oval Office meeting 17 months earlier—he acted upon the recommendations. White wished the American people could read the report of the Commission or at least those parts that might be sure to get their attention. He knew that few Americans would fail to be moved by these words from the Declaration of Independence: *"Man is endowed by his Creator with certain inalienable rights. Among these are life, liberty, and the pursuit of happiness. To secure these rights, governments are instituted among men."* The Commission had entitled its report "To Secure These Rights" and White thought it was a report Jefferson and John Adams might have been proud of. His eyes blurred as he read the letter of transmittal:

> Mr. President:
>
> Your Committee has reviewed the American heritage and we have found in it again the great goals of human freedom and equality under just laws. We have surveyed the flaws in the nation's record and have found them to be serious. We have considered what government's appropriate role should be in securing our rights, and have concluded it must assume greater leadership.
>
> We believe that the time for action is now. Our recommendations for bringing the United States closer to its historic goal follow.

White marveled at the studied understatement, "serious flaws in the nation's record on human freedom"—Jefferson and Adams would have loved that. He smiled sardonically.

> THE BAMBINO AND THE BUFFALO SOLDIER
> By Jerry Muldane IV
>
> The patch on their shoulders showed a Black Buffalo reflecting the name Buffalo Soldiers given to them by the Plains Indians in 1867 when they wore Buffalo robes into battle to protect them from the cold on the western prairies. Now a chill November wind hit them as they faced the even more chilling prospect of German rifles and sub-machine guns across the piazza.

No. No. No. Still not right. He looked at the paper and thought, *Christ, I can't even spell my own name.*

Olin Johnston, Senior Senator from South Carolina, a state where only 10 percent of eligible voters cast ballots in the 1944 election, looked at the headlines, and shook his head in disgust. He addressed his friend and colleague Strom Thurmond, the Governor of South Carolina. "We got to take a stand heah, Strom," he said. "Ah mean, what's to be gained by givin' equal rights to someone with an artificial civilization that has been forced on him only a hundred fifty years ago?"

Strom Thurmond put a match to a South Carolina cigar, leaned back in his chair, inhaled deeply, and blew a thin stream of smoke toward the ceiling before he answered. "You got any ideas, Senatah?"

"The South stands alone, Guvnah. Abandoned by both parties in owra fight to keep the white and Nee-gro races apart. The Suthen people have theah pride you know. We not gonna submit tamely to havin' owra traditions made a political football for the benefit of political ass-pie-rants. We not gonna stand for it."

"You got any ideas, Senatah?"

Johnston was now on his feet, his face beginning to flush as he warmed to his theme. "The people of South Care-lina," he trumpeted, "and ah'm sure people all over the South, have a deep and abiding faith in the basic laws under which we and owra fellow Amare-cuns live and prospah. We revere the lettah, and oh yes, the spirit of the Amare-cun Constitution which guarantees owra rights as free citizens of these Yew-nited States."

Governor Thurmond looked impatiently at the Senator, now pacing back and forth. "Senatah," he said patiently, "ah know all that shit, but simmah down heah, and tell me now, Senatah,...you got any ideas?"

Johnston huffed. "Lemme tell you somethin', Guvnah." He pointed a finger at Thurmond who sat looking at him with a sardonic smile on his face. "They been takin' us for granted way too long, and ah think this may be just owra chance to do somethin' about it. Ah'm gonna start by boy-cottin' the president's speech at the Jefferson-Jackson Day dinnah in Washington next week."

Thurmond looked up in astonishment. "You tellin' me the Feds is tryin' to shove integration down owra throats, and all you gonna do is boycott Truman's speech?"

"Ah'm gonna rent a whole table right in front of the speaker's lectern, and then leave it empty with a big sign on it so he will know...THE SOUTH WILL RISE AGAIN, it will say."

Thurmond shook his head sadly. "That ain't gonna git it, Senatah," he said, "you might as well save yo' money. You is smart enough to know bettah, Senatah...listen to this, Senatah...The only way to do it is with votes. Votes, votes, votes...get it? We got at least ten States down heah and..." He stopped speaking as a blinding insight hit him. "That's it!" he said. "Senatah, ah got a idea. Listen to this..." he paused long enough to stand and walk to the middle of the room where he turned and pointed a bony finger at his friend the Senator. "What we got to do is form a new party. If the Republicans and the Democrats have abandoned us we can, by God, just as well abandon them."

Johnston looked in surprise at Governor Thurmond, standing with a pleased expression on his face, and blowing a series of thick and swirling smoke rings.

"Think about it, Senatah, " said Thurmond. "Without the South nobody can get enough votes to elect a president, and when that happens the House of Representatives decides. We don't need a Civil War, we use the democratic process. They got to give in to us." He began pacing with his hand on his chin as he thought about the possibilities.

THE BAMBINO AND THE BUFFALO SOLDIER
By Jerry Mulhane IV

The firing began with no warning. A handful of civilians, filling their jugs with fresh water from the fountain in the middle of the piazza, were caught in the crossfire. A mother with a baby in her arms began to run, but died in mid stride

J-four stared at the page for a long time. He stood and walked to the window. Through the tall pecan trees below, students alone, and sometimes in pairs, strolled slowly, and more often hurried to Coca-Colas at the student union building or to classes in Samford Hall. J-four's thoughts were of a far away place.

...he saw only the steel helmet of a black soldier sail high over the troubled piazza of an Italian village as the young warrior, oblivious to the clash and shock of unmerciful war, bent to gather up the wailing baby.

Bob Black, a tall, strikingly dark and handsome man, was principal of the Booker T. Washington Elementary School on the north side of Auburn. He sat behind the desk in his small office, a book opened in front of him, when he heard the knock on his door. He looked up in surprise, seeing the sand-haired, stocky white man come through the door. Anxiety quickly gave way to relief and happy recognition. He stood up, and hastened to greet an old friend and comrade-in-arms. "Major Jay," he said, "what brings you here, my man?"

"BB, you old buffalo," exclaimed J-four, as the two men embraced warmly in the middle of the room. Now they stood back, holding each other at arm length, and looking each other up and down. Black was a good six inches taller.

Mulhane smiled and said, "How are you, old friend? You been keepin' yo' head down?"

Black laughed and said, "Ah'm fine Major Jay, jus' fine. But whatchu doin' here?"

"Ah'm here to help," said Jerry Mulhane IV.

>> 31 <<

A SEWER OF IMBECILITY

We again state our belief that racial and religious minorities must have the right to live, the right to work, the right to vote, the full and equal protection of the law, on a basis of equality with all citizens as guaranteed by the Constitution. We again call upon the Congress to exert its full authority to the limit of its constitutional powers to assure and protect these rights.

...Civil rights plank, Democratic National Convention, Philadelphia, July 1948.

Hubert Humphrey, mayor of Minneapolis and a delegate from Minnesota, called it a sellout because it did not call for specific legislation.

H.L. Mencken, reporting for the *BALTIMORE SUN*, had this to say:

> *The Confederates, after two days in the doghouse, broke out on the floor of the Democratic National Convention tonight, and in an instant the hall was wild with yells, howls, bellows, whoops, and execrations. The delegation from Mississippi was seated despite its solemn vow to walk out unless the candidates for both president and vice president repudiated the Truman civil-rights program and promised to sin no more.*

Virgil Young was fed up, and ready to do something about it. He had seen it with his own eyes, though he could hardly believe what he had seen. He was in Poppy Jones' hardware store to buy some nails when this great commotion broke out, and the next thing he knew here was Joe Bob, Poppy's youngest son, punching this black-as-mother-midnight nigger, with the high-falutin' name of Malcolm, and shoving him against the paint cans in the window aisle. What Virgil couldn't believe, though he served as a witness when the sheriff finally got there, was that the nigger was actually fighting back. Not only was he fighting back, but Virgil saw with his own eyes when the nigger pulled a knife about the same time Joe Bob started after him with a crow bar. That was the signal for Virgil and two others to grab that savage from behind, and hang onto him before he could do any real damage with that knife. As it was he actually cut Joe Bob's arm, and for that he would have to pay.

Virgil had seen it coming. He had seen it in their eyes; these damn nigger soldiers, coming back from the war with these high falutin' ideas. He saw resentment in those eyes—those eyes that before the war wouldn't dare do more than look at the ground when you were telling them what to do. After the war, *his* war, the Great War, they didn't act that way when they came back. Now here they were, spreading the word that niggers had rights. What rights? They were niggers, they had to do what they were told, and be respectful.

Mencken sat in the steaming hot press section, not 20 feet from the podium, trying to digest a Philadelphia cheese steak while sharpening his pencils and his darts for the next outrageous affront to his sense of propriety. In the morning he had written:

> *The lodge of sorrow began at 8:50 with the entrance of color guards representing all branches of the armed forces. As soon as the flags were planted in the space before the speakers' stand, Lawrence Tibbett, the opera singer, was sent to the mike to sing "The Star-Spangled Banner." He made a dreadful mess of it.*

Mencken loosened his already loosened tie, adjusted the position of the cigar in the side of his mouth, and pulled the watch from its place in his vest pocket. Chairman Rayburn banged his gavel, and declared the convention adjourned. The watch declared it was 2:30 in the morning.

Truman and Barkley. It had taken 17 hours to get it done, and if he never saw another Liberty Bell it would be 17 hours too soon. His head vibrated with "The Missouri Waltz" and "My Old Kentucky Home" competing with the blaring trombones and rattling snare drums of "Dixie." He sighed and washed down three aspirin with a gulp of warm beer. He was still nettled at the Indian in full war-dress who leaped from a collection of artificial flowers in the shape of a bell that was hoisted down the platform after Truman's nomination. It took Barkley only a few minutes to immolate himself on the altar of patriotism in his acceptance speech, and Truman looked cocky in a white Palm Beach suit, and talked accordingly. In the whole show he saw not a trace of wit or humor, and if there was any aptness it came from the lobster and potato of Maine which they hung on their standard.

The story of the convention was the Dixiecrats.

> *The walkout of the Alabamians was carried out quietly...Alabama was taking to the bush, and part of Mississippi would join it.*

Truman and Barkley were nominated in the Philadelphia Civic Center on the University of Pennsylvania campus just across the Schuylkill River from Center City on July 15, 1948, some three weeks after the Republicans had nominated Thomas Dewey, Governor of New York, and Earl Warren, Governor of California, in the same place.

On July 17, two days after the Democratic convention ended, the States' Rights Party, to their displeasure known as Dixiecrats, convened in Birmingham, Alabama, and nominated South Carolina Governor Strom Thurmond for President, and Mississippi Governor Fielding Wright for Vice President. The Dixiecrats made no secret of the reason for their existence: "We stand for the segregation of the races and the racial integrity of every race."

Mencken was not amused:

> *The gallant Confederates who attempted a raid upon the late Democratic National Convention got a bad licking on the floor, but that licking did not dispose of them, nor even seriously punish them. What ails them now is a double handicap, both halves of it of southern origin. The first is to be found in the fact that when they got home all the worst frauds in the South rushed up to kiss them and have since hung around their necks. The second half springs out of the general northern assumption, unhappily well supported by recent history, that whatever originates in the South is half-idiotic, and hardly deserves to be heard. That assumption is bitterly resented by enlightened southerners, but the record is the record. The South, for years past, has been a sewer of imbecility.*

Truman did not waste any time; less than two weeks after he was nominated, Executive Order 9981 was issued from the Truman White House.

> *It is hereby declared to be the policy of the President that there shall be equality of treatment and opportunity for all persons in the armed services without regard to race, color, religion, or national origin.*

Not everybody got the message. The day after the order was issued on July 27, 1948, General Omar Bradley, Army Chief of Staff, who thought they were already doing all that, said, "The Army is not out to make any social reforms. The Army will put men of different races in different companies. It will change that policy when the nation as a whole changes it."

The Southern Senators, on the other hand, had no illusions about what it meant…it meant desegregation of the Armed Services. Nineteen of twenty-two Senators, led by Russell of Georgia issued a statement:

> *"we are fixed in our purpose to use every resource at our command to stop an upsetting march of the Federal Government into our way of life. This order is an unconditional surrender to the treasonable civil disobedience campaign organized by the Negroes."*

In March, Union leader A. Philip Randolph had formed the League for Non-Violent Civil Disobedience Against Military Segregation in protest of the omission of an anti-segregation clause in the Senate passed Selective Service Act scheduled to go into effect in August.

One by one, the grim-faced men, screened at the door by the Klexter (outer guard), solemnly filed into the semi-darkened, all-purpose room of the church basement, pausing inside the door to shake hands with Virgil Young, and say "KIGY, E.C. (Klansman, I greet you, Exalted Cyclops)," to which Virgil replied, "KLASP (Klannish Loyalty, A Sacred Privilege)." The room was arranged with a table in front flanked by two large flags, regal with their golden tassels, the stars and stripes of the United States on the left, the stars and bars of the Old Confederacy on the right. On the table a large candle flickered, causing the shadow of a golden crucifix to be cast on the wall behind the table where a large banner was hung. The banner was divided into three equal sections, the two outside sections crimson, the white center section containing a large black circle enclosing a black cross. Both the circle and the cross were edged in gold.

Thirty men took seats on metal folding chairs, arranged in five rows with an aisle in the middle, and waited for the Exalted Cyclops and his Terrors (officers) to make their entrance from the rear, and take their seats flanking the table facing the assembled membership. Presently they entered at a measured pace to the accompaniment of a scratchy record playing "The Old Rugged Cross." The officers wore shiny white satin ankle-length robes, belted at the waist with a white sash, and marked on the chest with a red blood-drop emblem. They were the Klaliff (vice president), the Kludd (chaplain), the Kligrapp (secretary), the Klabee (treasurer), and the Klokard (teacher of Klankraft). Leading the procession and carrying a small flaming cross, held high in front with both hands, was the NightHawk, in black robe, full-face mask, and tall black, inverted cone hat. The NightHawk, in addition to his job as custodian of the fiery cross, was in charge of new recruits presented to him by the Kleagle (organizer and recruiter), prior to their initiation. Tonight they would initiate five new members; Stanley Gordon was one.

"Ah heahby declare, the New Smyrna klavern of the Federated Ku Klux Klan of Alabama of the exalted Invisible Empire, Knights of the Ku Klux Klan, founded in eighteen sixty-seven by General Nathan Bedford Forrest, of evah honahd memry, to be in session." Virgil Young, Exalted Cyclops, banged a gavel on the table. "The Kludd will lead us in prayer. All rise."

"Dearly beloved, the Bible tells us, '*to those who are called, who are beloved in God the Father and kept safe for Jesus Christ: may mercy, peace, and love be yours in abundance.*' But you, beloved, must remember the predictions of the apostles of our Lord Jesus Christ; for they said to you: '*in the last time there will be scoffers, indulging their ungodly lusts*'. It is these worldly people, devoid of the Spirit, who are causing divisions. But you beloved build yourselves up on your most holy faith; pray in the Holy Spirit; keep yourselves in the love of God; look forward to the mercy of our Lord Jesus Christ that leads to eternal life. And have mercy on some who are wavering; save others by snatching them out of the fire; and have mercy on still others with fear, hating even the tunic defiled by their bodies. Now to him who is able to keep you from failing, and to make you stand without blemish in the presence of his glory with rejoicing, to the only God our Savior, through Jesus Christ our Lord, be glory, majesty, power, and authority, before all time and now and forever. Amen."

"Remain standing for the pledge of allegiance," Virgil commanded.

The Kladd (conductor of ceremonies) led the pledge of allegiance:

"Ah pledge allegiance to the flag, of the United States of America, and to the Republic for which it stands. One nation, under God, indivisible, with liberty and justice for all."

Virgil called for reports from the Kligrapp and the Klabee, who reminded the group that some had neglected to pay the 25 dollar annual membership fee. He then called again on the Kludd to read from the scriptures.

"Grace, mercy, and peace will be with us from God the Father and from Jesus Christ, the Heavenly Father's son, in truth and love. I will now read from the book of Revelation. *Blessed is the one who reads aloud the words of the prophecy, and blessed are those who hear and who keep what is written in it; for the time is near. And to the angel of the church in Smyrna write: These are the words of the first and the last, who was dead and came to life: I know your affliction and your poverty, even though you are rich. I know the slander on the part of those who say that they are Jews and are not, but are a synagogue of Satan. Do not fear what you are about to suffer. Beware, the devil is about to throw some of you into prison so that you may be tested, and for ten days you will have affliction. Be faithful until death, and I will give you the crown of life."*

The Kludd closed his Bible with a meaningful look at the crowd in front of him and took his seat.

The Exalted Cyclops stood, and walked behind the table where the light of the candle reflected off his face. "Amen. Amen. Amen," he said. "Be faithful until death, and I will give you the crown of life. Amen. Amen. Amen."

Virgil's chest swelled with pride as he looked out over his group. They were his klavern, and what did it matter if many of the faces were those of some of the sorriest bastards it had ever been his misfortune to come in contact with? They were his klavern, and he would make the most of them, in spite of themselves. "Klansmen, I greet you," he began. "We are heah tonight for a special reason…it is to deal with the new problems created by the latest attack on the suthen way of life by the so-called Fedral Govment in Washington. It was a black, black day when they announced the dee-segregation of the ahmed forces. Fust baseball, next the ahmed forces, ah don't even wantta think about what's next. Klansmen, listen to me…we have a solemn duty to protect our precious heritage. Do you heah me?"

They heard and responded with loud shouts. "We heah you, E.C.…You tell 'em, E.C.…Amen, E.C."

Virgil continued. "It is truly the synagogue of Satan that is behind this," he said. "The northen press and the radio call us racist for standin' up for the rights of our state. They say racist like it was a dirty word, but ah say to you, and ah say to them, and ah say to anyone who wants to listen, or don't even want to listen, ah say…see these hands," he held his hands high with palms facing the audience, "see this skin," he extended both index fingers, and pointed to his cheeks which were wrinkled and held a faint yellowish tint. "This skin is white, and if protectin' the integrity and the honor of the white race is racist then amen and hallelujah, we are racist and proud of it. Do you heah me?" The room rocked with raucous shouts and rebel yells.

Virgil waited patiently, savoring the wild exuberance of his eager klavern. After several minutes he began to wonder if they would ever quiet down. He held up his hands for quiet, and gained it only after several more minutes. At last he was able to continue; he had more points to make. "The Bible says it is all right for us to hate," he said, and was greeted with more shouted agreements. Again he had to wait for quiet. "Klansmen," he said, "listen to me…I want us all to be sure our hate is directed to the right place, and that place is not to the niggas who live among us, and who we know it is our custom to take care of. No, Klansmen, the truth is the niggas is nothin' but pawns in this game, and the real scoundrels heah is the satanic Jews, the oily papists, and the godless Communists. Does anybody heah doubt that there is a international conspiracy led by the Jew bankers to suppress our rights, and to force us into doin' things we know will destroy our way of life?…Where is our rights in this? Where, I ask you?"

Nobody had an answer, they waited for Virgil to tell them where. Virgil threw up his hands in frustration, he didn't have any answers either, but he thought he knew what needed to be done. "Klansmen," he said, "prepare yourselves. We will put up massive resistance. Massive resistance! Heed the Bible. Do not fear what you are about to suffer. You may be tested when the devil throws you into prison. Be faithful until death."

Virgil paused to pour water from a pitcher into a tall glass, and to take a long drink before he continued. He waited, the word death hanging in the air of the stuffy room. He drew a large red bandanna from his hip pocket, and wiped his sweaty brow. He felt a wave of dizziness, and steadied himself by grasping the edge of the table. He needed a drink, and not of water. From his other hip pocket he withdrew a palm-sized pewter flask, unscrewed the cap, and tilted it up for a long satisfying gulp. He wanted to walk out into the cool night air, but there was unfinished and important business that could not be postponed. "Now brother Klansmen," he said, "ah want to tell you about what ah saw at Poppy Jones' Hardware Store last Saturday."

Two days later, in a dark and secluded spot near the Coosa River, Malcolm and his wife, along with a friend and his wife, were executed by a firing squad. The coroner said that at least sixty bullets were pumped into the bodies of the four Negroes. No arrests were made. Folsom liberalism was being embraced by a majority of Alabamians, but nightriders in dented Fords still ruled the darkness.

>>32<<

MIZ SARAH AND THE TUSKEGEE COUNT

Jerry Mulhane IV bent over the old man's shoulder, and guided his ancient and trembling hand along the page. "Now Aaron," he said, "you practice writing that A, and I'll be back as soon as I see how Miz Sarah is doin' with her S's."

Genesis 23:1 *Sarah lived one hundred twenty-seven years; this was the length of Sarah's life.*

Miz Sarah was not that old, but she was old enough to remember the day they told her the war was over, and that they were free. Free to do what? She remembered that question too. She was 15 years old at the time, and had been layin' with the old master for three years. They had just taken her 18-month-old daughter from her. Free…To do what?

Miz Sarah was learning how to read and write. She wanted to read the Bible for herself before she died, and she was determined to live as long as her Bible namesake Sarah, wife of Abraham and mother of Isaac. Determined was a word that fit Miz Sarah well; when she learned about the adult education night classes starting at the Carver Elementary School, she knew the Lord was looking down on her and answering her prayers. She didn't know it would be this hard, but she was determined.

She looked up as her white teacher approached. She would have been more comfortable with a black teacher, but Miz Sarah would never say so. If Miz Sarah had learned nothing else in her almost 100 years, the lesson to make the best of what the Lord gives was the one she never forgot. She had also learned it was not fruitful to make judgments about people, but this did not prevent her from liking or disliking someone. This white teacher…he said to call him Jerry, but she would have to call him Mr. Jerry if she called him anything, was likable, and seemed friendly. He had asked her to tell him the most important lessons she had learned in her life. She thought about the request for several days before telling him that she had learned so many lessons that she might not live long enough to tell them all. Then she told him that she had just learned a new lesson. It was that the student and the teacher learn from each other, and it is not easy to tell who gains the most. Mr. Jerry wanted her to tell him about her life so he could put it in a book. She was agreeable to this because she believed in the Golden Rule, and if he was going to teach her how to read and write, it was easy enough for her to tell him what joys and sorrows she remembered from her life. She remembered everything, though it would not be possible to tell him all of it. She would teach him the sorrow songs and the jubilation songs, though she reckoned it was not songs so much that he was interested in. She would tell him about old master who had fathered her daughter, her two half-sisters and her half-brother. She would tell him about the times she had cried with her white mother, old master's wife.

THE FATHER OF HIS COUNTRY
By Sarah Lincoln, as told to Jerry Mulhane IV

Abraham Young was master of all he surveyed, and what he surveyed was a big, a very big, cotton plantation on land taken from the Creek Indians after General Andrew Jackson routed the Creeks in the Battle of Horseshoe Bend on the Tallapoosa River in 1814. The plantation was carved out of East Alabama pine forests around the time in 1819 when Alabama became the 22nd state in the Union.

Abraham Young liked to think of himself as a man of God. When God said to Noah "*Be fruitful and multiply*" Abraham Young heard the words, and knew God was speaking to him. When God said to Abraham, *"I will bless you, and I will make your offspring as numerous as the stars of heaven, and as the sand that is on the seashore,"* Abraham Young heard all he needed to hear.

Abraham Young fathered eight children by his own wife, but nobody knew the number of children that came from his unions with the black ladies he owned. If he needed assurance he got that from the Bible, too, in the Genesis story where Abraham is told by his wife to take an Egyptian slave girl. It was good business to him, and when his sons became old enough he made sure they contributed to the business.

> Abraham Young sold my mother, and used the money to pay a poor white field hand to go and fight for him in the war between the states so that he could stay on his plantation and obey God's command to be fruitful. It is only common sense to see that here in the middle of the 20th century, not even 100 years after the old master scattered his pollen, and his offspring did the same, over the flowers of his country, it is only common sense to see that here in the middle of the 20th century there is a good chance—a very good chance—that anyone living here in Tallapoosa County, Alabama, carries the blood of Abraham Young, and nine out of ten chances, the blood also of the black ladies he owned and pollinated.

Count stood on a shaded walkway in the middle of the Tuskegee Institute campus in the small, dusty town of Tuskegee, Alabama, 40 miles west of the Georgia state line, and a universe away from President Truman's office in Washington, D.C. He looked around at the stately brick buildings, noting with satisfaction the ivy growing on them. He turned to the marble monument showing a black man in a three-piece suit standing with one arm extended, palm up, and the other grasping a cloth partially covering the head of a Negro sitting on an Ashanti Chief's stool with a large book in his hand. Count read the inscription:

BOOKER T WASHINGTON
1856 1915
HE LIFTED THE VEIL OF IGNORANCE
FROM HIS PEOPLE AND POINTED
THE WAY TO PROGRESS THROUGH
EDUCATION AND INDUSTRY

This is the place. I will build it here. "This is the place. I will build it here." Count found himself giving voice to his thoughts as he stood looking at the Booker T. Washington monument.

"Build what?"

Count was startled from his reverie by the voice of a white-haired man, younger than himself of course—nobody was older than Count—who had been quietly standing next to him.

Count turned to look at the man, then returned his gaze to the monument and said, "The School. The School for Presidents."

The man turned to look closer at Count, and took a step back. He looked hard at Count who continued to gaze at Booker T. Washington.

Count spoke again, as much to himself as to the stranger next to him. "There's something wrong with the inscription," he said. "Veil of ignorance...what does it mean?"

The white-haired man turned back to the monument. "It means that we are strangers in a strange land," he said. "What are we doing here anyway?"

The two men stood for a long time, quietly looking at the statue of Booker T. Washington, considering the question hanging in the air like the scent of magnolia.

Presently the white-haired man stepped back, and once again turned to face Count. The two men looked into each other's chocolate brown eyes, and saw what they had never seen: Africa...the plain of Accra, the great market at Yammasoukro, the proud Ashanti chiefs, the matrilineal societies, the open doors.

The white-haired man extended his hand and introduced himself. "Gomillion," he said.

"Count," said Count, taking the offered hand in a firm grip. "You look like you belong here."

Gomillion nodded. "I am Dean of Students," he said, "...and you are an architect, here to build a school. A School for Presidents." His eyes twinkled.

Count smiled. "It's a dream I have," he said. "Do you have time to listen? Is there somewhere we can go to talk?" He paused, then asked, "Does your name have anything to do with money?"

Dean Gomillion laughed and responded with a question of his own. "Does yours?"

FREE AT LAST
By Sarah Lincoln, as told to Jerry Mulhane IV

When they told us we was free, we didn't know what to do so we didn't do nothin'. We kept right on workin' the fields and doing the cookin'. So nothin' much changed. Old master called everybody together, and told us that the war was over and the United Confederacy was no more. We couldn't tell whether he was happy about that or if he was sad. Two of his sons died in the war, and he was sad about that for sure. Then our white mother called the women together to talk to us. White mother was always good to us and we

> liked her. We did think of her as a mother…she was like one of us because we had a common enemy…old master. She told us we was free, and that we didn't have to stay on the plantation if we didn't want to, but they wanted us to stay because they thought of us as part of the family. The truth is, even when they owned us they didn't treat us too bad, especially white mother. Of course some of the boys got whipped now and then but most of the time it was because they did things they knew they wasn't supposed to do. Workin' on the plantation was hard, and nobody liked the overseer, but what else was we goin' to do? And we always had somethin' to eat. If you ever tried to sleep when your belly was callin' for somethin' to be put in it you will know it was no small thing to know you was goin' to git somethin' to eat. Some of the men talked about goin' North, and one or two actually did, but the women just stayed.
>
> One thing did change, and it made our lives so much better it was almost like a miracle. They let us build our own church. Old master let us use the land. He told us it wasn't right for him to give us the land, but that he would let us use it. At first, and for a long time, we had a white preacher who told us we were like children and must learn the words of God, and do what the Bible said or we would be condemned to live forever in Hell. Then one glorious Sunday morning, even though it was raining, another miracle happened…we got our own black preacher. His name was Moses Clayton, and he was a revelation. My oh my could that man preach. He told us about salvation and the Kingdom of Heaven and the Glory of Jesus Christ, and can't you just think how that made us feel. It made us want to sing and clap our hands and stomp our feet, and did we sing! We could even put some of the sorrow songs away and sing the songs of jubilation.

"My dream is that in fifty years this country will elect a Negro president, and I want to be sure he is properly prepared." Count was sipping iced-tea on the spacious back porch of Dean Gomillion's house on the Tuskegee Institute campus.

Dean Gomillion smiled. "So you want to start a School for Presidents," he said. "It's a grand idea, but not very practical I'm afraid, especially here in Tuskegee. You're not from the South are you?"

"I was," said Count. "...A long time ago. I went north with Harriet Tubman when I was about ten years old. My story is long and complicated," he said, pausing to remember.

Dean Gomillion's eyes narrowed as he looked more closely at Count. "Did you say Harriet Tubman?"

Count nodded. "Maybe you'll hear the whole story sometime, for now let's just say I ended up in Illinois. I came here to see the place that Booker T. Washington founded."

Dean Gomillion said, "Okay then...let me tell you something about Tuskegee." He sipped his iced-tea while he gathered his thoughts of where to start. "To say that we are an island in a sea of trouble would, I think, be to state the obvious. The white man tolerates us because he could not otherwise live with his guilt. The State of Alabama contributes five thousand giant dollars a year to our three million dollar budget, and considers that sufficient to give them the right to control our affairs. But whether from Alabama or not, you can be sure our affairs are controlled by white men. Tuskegee Institute is run by a Board of Directors that meets in New York City." Gomillion paused, "...Why do you think the Julius Rosenwald Fund of Chicago, and the Carnegie and Rockefeller Foundations of New York are interested in Tuskegee?"

Count found Gomillion looking at him, and realized he was waiting for an answer. Count considered the question briefly then answered with his own question, "Do you think they *are* interested in Tuskegee?" he asked.

Gomillion's eyes widened slightly as he quickly grasped the implications of the question. "Interested or not," he said, "they have set us up with a ten million dollar endowment that produces about five hundred thousand dollars a year for our operating budget," he offered, a touch of pride in his voice.

Count shrugged. Half a million dollars a year seemed to him a niggardly figure for the task at hand. He questioned, "And for that they control the Board of Directors, and call you to New York City for periodic accountings?"

Dean Gomillion was quiet. He was not comfortable with the idea of defending the white money givers, and it *had* occurred to him, it had occurred to him more than once, to question their motives and intentions. Gomillion decided he needed to know more about this old, but obviously vigorous, and it seemed, iconoclastic man who had just taken a shot at what the dean had always thought was one of Tuskegee's strengths.

"Who are you, anyway?" he asked.

Count did not answer quickly, realizing that it would not do to tell his whole improbable story to this man, or to anyone he did not know well enough to reward with the one thing he had in such abundance: money. Still, this man deserved an answer for he, Count, was after all a stranger here, and one who had dropped out of the sky with the outlandish claim that he was going to build a school.

"It's not important who I am," he answered, deflecting the question. "What matters is what I can do for you and for Tuskegee."

Gomillion waited for more, but for the moment there was no more. Finally he asked, "And what *can* you do for Tuskegee? Forgive me if I seem skeptical...we have so many needs."

Count nodded. "Your doubts are understandable," he said, "but let me ask you this: what could you do here at Tuskegee if you had all the money you needed?"

Gomillion shook his head. "No, Count," he said, "all the money in the world..." He stopped and thought a moment before continuing. "...Money could do a lot for us," he mused.

Count said, "Why don't you think about it...believe it or not, I am in a position to furnish you with what may be an unlimited supply of money."

Gomillion stared at Count, wondering if he was looking at a lunatic or a messiah.

SAVED BY SINGER

By Sarah Lincoln as told to Jerry Mulhane IV

Not too long after the end of the war a travelin' man came to the plantation. He was travelin' with a mule and a wagon, and he was sellin' a machine that even now when I think of it the only thing I can say is it was a miracle. It was a Singer sewing machine. Now that may not seem like much to anybody these days, but at that time it was just plain hard to believe what that machine could do. It could sew a seam in a minute that might take a half hour to do by hand, and it could do it better.

On that plantation all the clothes was made by hand stichin'. One of my jobs was to make dresses for the ladies, and shirts and pants for the men. When white mother saw what that machine could do she told old master to buy it, and don't make no fuss about it. So we got a sewing machine, and I learned how to make two dresses in one day that might otherwise take more than ten.

> Old master told us now that we was free we could go back to Africa if we wanted, and some did…to a land called Liberia. Or we could work the land and share the profits with him. He give us a piece of land we could call our own and grow our own cotton….it seemed like another miracle. That plantation was so big he divided it into many sections. We was only one of 10 different families that worked his land, and one of those families was white. My man Moses and me, we worked hard on that land, and we made us a family too. Four boys, it was God's blessing, and we gave them all Bible names—Matthew, Mark, Luke, and John, and we took the surname Lincoln to honor the man who made us free.
>
> Life was hard, but it was good. We had our church, we had our farm, we had our family, and I had my Singer sewing machine. I was making clothes to sell at the store in Youngville, and we was able to save some money even after paying old master his share. God was good to us, and we were thankful. Not everybody was so lucky. Some of the other families got themselves in debt so bad to the old master and his store that they was no better off than before when they was legal slaves. It was the sewing machine that saved us.

"It has been said that money is the root of all evil," Count said, "but it should be added that money is also the root of all good, and we might as well say that money is at the root of everything in between."

Gomillion shook his head. "If it were only that simple," he said. "I'm sorry to disagree with you, Count, but I'm afraid that the evil we see in the society all around us goes far beyond money. You would be amazed at how difficult it is to get people registered to vote here. Every year I try to get more of our faculty registered, but for every effort we make to exercise our constitutional rights, the white power structure in this county works harder and harder to prevent it. Money might be one way to do it, I don't doubt for a minute we could buy in, but I'm trying to make a point so everyone can vote. Let me tell you what we are up against here…In addition to the poll tax, it is necessary to find two registered white voters to endorse the applicant, then they have to answer questions about the Constitution, and the answers would be wrong even if the whole thing was recited from memory, which one of our history professors actually did…Forgive me if I seem discouraged."

"I understand your discouragement," said Count, "and I do not minimize the difficulties…the road to equality is long and hazardous…and paved with stones of ignorance." He stood and walked around his chair. "Would it be too much to expect our nation's capital, Washington, D.C. to set a positive example for the country?" he asked. "Shame on Washington!" he said. "In our nation's capital even today segregation rules…Negroes cannot be seated in public restaurants…it is a disgrace. In Constitution Hall, which is owned by the Daughters of the American Revolution, Negroes are not allowed to perform…it is a disgrace. In the same Constitution Hall where they can not perform, Negroes can attend performances with no restrictions on seating…it is insanity. In public theaters it is the opposite…Negroes may perform, but are not allowed to sit with whites…it is a disgrace. It is this kind of lunacy that makes our task more difficult. Still, we cannot give up. Is there any comfort knowing that future generations will look back on this period in American history in disbelief and shame?"

Gomillion shrugged. "That future is too far away for me to imagine," he said, "but you are right that we cannot give up, and I have to say I am cheered by some of the statements of our new governor, Folsom. But I have no illusions…we will be second class citizens as long as I am alive." He shrugged again and added, "That's probably too optimistic…we are third class citizens striving for second class status." He sighed and looked again at Count. "So tell me about this School for Presidents," he said.

Count brightened. "Yes," he said, "let me tell you about my plan…I have followed politics in this country for a long time, I have seen how presidents are chosen, and I think the country deserves something better, and more importantly the world deserves something better." He paused. "…You are an educated man, Professor Gomillion, let me ask how many United States presidents you can name from Lincoln…no, why don't we just start at the beginning…from Washington."

Gomillion waved his hand. "I am no historian," he said, "but let's see…Washington, Adams, Jefferson, Madison, Monroe…Adams again, Jackson, Polk…Buchanan, Lincoln, Johnson, Grant…Cleveland, Roosevelt, Wilson, Harding, Coolidge, Hoover, FDR, Truman…" He paused and looked at Count. "How did I do?"

Count smiled. "Impressive. You left out a few, but I'd say you did well enough, better than most, but my point here is not so much who were the presidents, but how did they get to be presidents…what qualifications did they bring to the job? I think you can see the reason for asking these questions at the present time. We have a president in the White House who was picked to be vice president almost by accident, and is there only because FDR died in office. President Truman, who I know is an honorable man, is learning his job while at the same time he controls weapons capable of destroying the world. I think it is time we change the constitution to reflect the current reality of these doomsday weapons. We can no longer accept as our leader anyone who is not trained to deal with the problems of the twentieth century and beyond. We have always had special institutions to train our generals and admirals, is it not time we did the same for our presidents?"

Gomillion shrugged while at the same time nodding his head from side to side. He said, "Nobody could deny the logic of your argument, but to implement such a plan..." His brow wrinkled as his thoughts raced. "Where to begin?"

Count reached into a briefcase he was carrying and withdrew a thin manuscript bound in a blue cover. He held it up and said, "We can begin with this. It is an outline of a ten-year curriculum designed to produce, in the finest Platonic tradition, a philosopher-king." He smiled triumphantly as he handed the document to the startled Dean Gomillion.

POLITICS AND SCHOOLS
By Sarah Lincoln as told to Jerry Mulhane

> There were more than sewing machine salesmen coming down from the North after the war ended. Old master called them carpetbaggers and scalawags, but I'm here to tell you them scalawags taught us some things that changed us from sheep to wolf in a hurry. Old master and the other white landowners began to worry that so many Negroes were leaving the land and moving west because we had been told that things were better in the west...the land was better and there were fewer people...we could start a new life.
>
> The problem for old master and the others was that if we all left there would be nobody to farm their land and pick their cotton. The scalawags helped us take advantage...it was the first time in our lives we ever was in position to make deals. Our men got to vote, and when the white men needed our votes they made promises in exchange for the votes, and the next thing we knew they was building schools for our children. It was no longer against the law to teach Negroes to read and write. We learned that when we had

something the white man needed it was like having money…he had to give us something in exchange for what he wanted from us. The scalawags told us this was called politics.

>>33<<

THE NUMBER ONE THREAT

June, 1951...St. Louis, Missouri

Secretary of Defense, and General of the Army, George C. Marshall stood on the stage behind the podium in the Washington University fieldhouse looking out at the graduates. He felt awful. His head hurt, and his chronic bronchitis made it difficult to breathe. But he had promised his friend Arthur Compton he would be here, and for Marshall a promise made was a promise kept. He knew his task was to inspire these young people, many of whom had been tempered in the cauldrons of World War II, and not a few of whom were about to be tested in the fires of Korea. He was pensive as he waited for his moment to begin. He had much on his mind less than two months after President Truman had fired MacArthur. Thinking of MacArthur saddened him. A brother officer for more than 50 years, doing what he did as well as anyone on earth...trying to win a war. MacArthur had lost his perspective. He was guilty of one of the most egregious sins in the code of military conduct: ignoring the dictates of his commander-in-chief. As Secretary of Defense it had been Marshall's duty to support the president's decision to relieve MacArthur, and to explain to a Senate investigating committee why it was necessary. It was necessary because to do otherwise would have been to risk World War III with the Soviet Union and Communist China as foes, a war the United States was in no position to fight except with atomic weapons, a thought that caused Marshall to shudder.

The MacArthur episode was the most difficult thing he had ever done, and the effort had drained him both physically and mentally. He was now 70 years old, and could not help wondering how he would be remembered...as the man who directed the destruction of Europe, or as the man who directed the reconstruction of Europe? As a warrior, or as a statesman? He was weary of war, but Korea was raging and once again he had to send young men to their deaths. Unlike Eisenhower, he found less and less to smile about.

Susan and Flapper sat side by side holding hands in the section closest to the front reserved for Ph.D. candidates. Patiently they waited their turn to march across the stage and receive their diplomas, basking in the warm glow of significant accomplishment. They would both receive two diplomas this day, one for Doctor of Medicine and one for Doctor of Philosophy, Susan in Biochemistry, Flapper in Philosophy. Bulging with new knowledge, they felt the exhilaration of achievement and the excitement of anticipation. Flapper the philosopher noted the irony of Marshall, with his years of accomplishment, approaching the end of his grand career, facing the sea of graduates, their fragile dreams filling the air.

Flapper, as usual, was providing commentary. "The most important man in the history of our country…a general from Virginia named George," he said.

"Washington?" asked Susan.

Flapper shook his head. "Look at him, Susan," he said, "General George Marshall from Virginia. He may be the most important man in the history of our country."

"He looks tired," Susan said and yawned.

zzzzzzzzzzzz zzzzzzzzzzzzz zzzzzzzzzzzzzzzzzzzzzzz

"…to have the nation maintain a respectable military posture at all times rests on a workable universal military training program…"

Flapper squirmed in his seat and leaned to whisper in Susan's ear. "Why is he talking to us about universal military training?" he asked.

Susan, like many of the graduates, was dozing in the presence of the final academic hurdle, the commencement address, no matter that it was being delivered by the most important man in the history of the country. She lurched at Flapper's question. "Huh?"

Flapper said, "Sorry, didn't mean to wake you up, go back to sleep, he's talking about the draft. Four years ago at the Harvard commencement he announced the European Recovery Plan, I was hoping we would get something important from him today."

zzzzzzzzzzzzzzzzzzzzzzzzzzzzzzzzzzzzzzzzzzzzz zzzzzzzzzz

"…we salute the courage and skill of the men fighting for our country in the bitter hills of a far away country—Korea. But let us clearly understand what is at stake in this conflict, for it is more than our country they fight for. In the long and bloody history of armed strife never before have nations gathered under the banner of an international organization for the noble purpose of combating lawless and naked aggression. The free nations of the world speak with a single voice and a common language to those who would impose alien philosophies on freedom loving people, and the message is as clear as a glass of Budweiser: stop your reckless adventurism."

Flapper shook his head, and looked around to see if others had heard what he thought he had heard: "clear as a glass of Budweiser." Apparently not...what he saw was mostly dazed expressions, and not a few closed eyes. He wondered if he had dozed off too. On the speaker's platform he noted a few smiles, and a frown from Arthur Compton. He thought about the fighting in Korea, and wondered briefly if there were any fire control officers on the beaches. He was conscious of an ever present ringing in his ears, the legacy of countless ear-splitting detonations; he thought it a small price to pay for an otherwise intact body, and had learned to live with it.

zzzzzzzzzzzzzzzzzzzzzzzzzzzzzzzz zzzzzzzzzzzzzzzz

"...Imagine if you can, a world in which the only beer is brewed by workers shackled under the yoke of a government calling itself Communist, but which in truth is no different from the brutal Fascists we have so recently defeated..."

It was warm in the fieldhouse and Flapper, slumped in his chair, was finding it difficult to focus on the words of the general. His mind wandered to the image of a frosty glass of Budweiser. He sat up straight and stared at the speaker with deliberately widened eyes.

"...Military preparedness is our only defense against the number one threat to freedom and democracy in the second half of the twentieth century...the threat of international communism."

June, 1951...Tuskegee, Alabama

"The number one threat to freedom and democracy in the United States in the second half of the twentieth century is unreasoned discrimination against groups and individuals because of differences in customs, religious beliefs, and, God help us, in different skin color."

Sadie Tanner Alexander, a Philadelphia lawyer, addressed the Tuskegee

Institute graduating class in an earnest and well-informed manner. Mrs. Alexander had worked more than 30 years for equal opportunity for Negroes, and even in Philadelphia, the nation's cradle of liberty, she found the task difficult and more often than not, discouraging. But she was not a quitter, and relished the opportunity to display her fighting spirit, and hopefully to inspire these young scholars to go forth and do their part to make the country a better place.

Mrs. Alexander was one of 15 Americans chosen to serve on the President's Committee on Civil Rights established by President Truman's executive order in December1946. Her text today drew extensively from the report of that committee.

"No fair-minded student of American history, or of world history, will deny to the United States a position of leadership in enlarging the range of human liberties and rights, in recognizing and stating the ideals of freedom and equality, and in steadily and loyally working to make these ideals…these sacred ideals…freedom and equality, a reality."

She paused, allowing her words to hang in the humid air. Looking out at her audience she saw shining, eager eyes, she saw hope. "Young scholars," she continued, "go forth with your new knowledge, go forth from this shrine of education, and become part of the sacred crusade to bring these ideals of freedom and equality to our people who have suffered so much."

Jerry Mulhane IV had come to believe in this sacred crusade. He sat listening to the small black lady on the stage, and reflecting on his apostasy from the traditions of his ancestors. During his graduate studies at API he had continued to work with Bob Black and his adult literacy class two nights a week at Carver Elementary School in Auburn. For J-four the issue was now clearly drawn, he could find no rational explanation for the brutal suppression of the Negro people, and he determined to do his part to make things better. When Bob Black told him of the new School for Presidents going up at Tuskegee Institute, only 20 miles away, he did not hesitate to investigate the opportunity, and to become part of it.

He remembered his first interview with the man known only as Count. Even now, sitting here as Assistant Professor of English Literature in the new school, he wondered at the grandness of the scheme. Count had a vision that transcended current problems, and he had the wherewithal to make the vision, if not a reality, then at the least, more than just a possibility. Count was wise enough to know that establishing the School for Presidents was the easy part, what he needed now was a staff of instructors to implement and expand the curriculum. After telling of his vision, Count said he would be very careful about selecting his staff, and he needed to know more about J-four than he could learn in a short interview. Could J-four put his thoughts on the project into the form of an essay?

THE AMERICAN DREAM
By Jerry Mulhane IV

There was a time in America when every little boy was encouraged to believe that he could grow up to be president...all it took was hard work. Hard work has always been recognized in America as the price for success...work hard enough and you can achieve anything...this is America, and that is the American dream. Work hard and you can grow up to be president. President of what? The senior class? The PTA? The American Can Company? Yes, all that, and as well, president of the United States...unless you happened to have the wrong skin color.

The irony of placing the School for Presidents on the Tuskegee Institute campus will not be lost on those who continue to view the Negro as inferior, but the wisdom of placing it there will be appreciated by future generations who will look back at the middle of the twentieth century and understand that this was the time, and Tuskegee in the state of Alabama was the place, where after more than two centuries, America stirred itself to correct the ugly flaw in its grand credo that "all men are created equal," and begin to truly recognize the worth of all its citizens. A time when the American dream at long last changed from a nightmare for many, to a shining prospect available to all.

Turning from the judgment of history to the reality of the present, it makes no difference what the project is, a person picked at random off the street could give you 10 reasons why it can't be done. In the case of the School for Presidents the question is not about the school itself which is close to completion, but rather about the goal of the school...is the goal to train men/women/people to be president of the United States, or is it to succeed in training a candidate, and having him/her elected to the presidency? Clearly the first goal is easier than the second, but in either case it is not difficult to find 10

> reasons why it can't be done. If the goal is to elect a Negro president of the United States the number of reasons it can't be done becomes a very large number.
>
> Conceding that it can't be done, can we find 10 reasons, indeed can we find any reasons why it is worth a try? Finding reasons why it is worth a try, it turns out, is as easy as finding reasons why it can't be done because for every "nay" there is a "what have we got to lose?"

"What have we got to lose?" Flapper looked around the room, and saw concern on all the faces except Susan's. Flapper popped another champagne cork, and began to refill glasses all around. Balloons and streamers festooned the room, and two wide banners crossed at the room-centered light fixture, and stretched from corner to corner. In bright red, white, and blue the banners read:

CONGRATULATIONS TO DOCTORS SUSAN AND HOMER

"Your lives?" The answer came at the same time from Flapper's mother, sitting on his left, and from Susan's father, standing to his right.

Flapper and Susan both laughed, happy that his mother and her father could at least agree on something. Flapper said, "Our lives? Come on, it's not like we're going to a war zone." Flapper's mother said, "Alabama may not be a war zone, but it's like a foreign country, and their justice system is primitive; they still lynch people down there. I don't think you know what you're getting into Homer."

"We've been to foreign countries before, Mother. We feel like we..." Flapper hesitated and looked at Susan. "...It sounds corny, I know, but we feel like this is a place where we..."

"Are needed." Susan finished his sentence.

Flapper nodded his head. "Right," he said. "A place where we are needed."

Flapper's mother said, "Well, it's nice to be needed, but it's so far away, and I think it's dangerous...you don't know what it was like for us when you were in the battle zones..." She choked on tears and could not continue.

Flapper moved to comfort her. "It will be all right, Mom," he said "...you'll see."

Susan's father joined the conversation. "I don't doubt they could use some good doctors in Alabama," he said, "but let's face it, Homer, there's plenty of need for more doctors right here in Missouri. For once I agree with Mrs. Jackson." He smiled, and raised his glass in the direction of Flapper's mother. "Alabama is too far away, and I'm not pleased about what's happening down there. From all I read they are still fighting the Civil War," he hesitated before adding, "...and maybe for good reason."

Susan's mother said, "Forgive us for being parents, Susan and Homer, but just because you are doctors four times over doesn't mean we can stop worrying about you. You will never stop being our children."

Susan put her hand on her mother's arm. "I know, Mother," she said, "but really you should try not to worry, there's more to this than going where we are needed. It's an opportunity for us both to do something we want to do."

Susan's father spoke again. "That's another thing I don't understand," he said. "You are both trained as physicians, and yet you are not going to practice medicine, you are going to teach."

Susan interrupted. "Dad," she said, "we may do both...don't forget we are interning at Lee County Hospital in Opelika."

Susan's father seemed not to hear. "I'm sorry, Homer," he said, "but teaching philosophy at a Nigrah college in Alabama strikes me as a big waste of time." He paused for a deep breath, which took the form of a sniff, and continued. "I might as well say it, Homer...teaching philosophy anywhere strikes me as a big waste of time."

"Dad!" Susan exclaimed. "Please!"

Flapper flushed at the rebuke, but quickly realized that there was no point in trying to explain himself; it was not the first time his father-in-law had questioned his purpose. To his great surprise his father, who until now had little to say about his philosophy studies, rose to his defense. "Excuse me, Dr. Land," he said, "allow me to explain." Hank Jackson, formerly Heinrich Myers, deep-shaft miner turned auto mechanic, rose from his chair and moved to stand next to his wife. He took her hand and said, "His mother and I have always had reason to be proud of our son, and if he chooses to teach philosophy in Alabama, or anywhere else, we would never presume to judge if it is a good thing or a bad thing, but of one thing we are certain...whatever Homer determines to do, somebody will benefit, and it will not be a waste of anybody's time...as for philosophy, I believe it is the noblest, and the most pure of human endeavors, and I can only express my great happiness and satisfaction that my son is able to spend his days in this pursuit of understanding. And what is more, to think he has the opportunity to teach what he has learned is beyond bliss." His voice choked and Flapper's mother patted his hand.

Dr. Land listened with growing agitation, and when Hank Jackson finished he scoffed, "Rubbish! Mawkish melodrama, cheap sentimentality. Rubbish, I tell you."

Susan was distressed, "Dad!" she exclaimed, and tried to stop her father from saying anymore, but his outrage was beyond control.

He raged on. "Anyone who thinks like that, and goes to live in Alabama is only asking for trouble," he pronounced. "And anyone who expects to teach coloreds about philosophy…what's the point? And let me tell you something else…I don't care if Harry Truman is from Missouri, he's a goddamn New Deal Democrat who wants to desegregate the whole country, and if I was from Alabama I'd be raising hell, too, about how the federal government is trampling all over states' rights."

The room became very quiet as even Dr. Land was abashed at his unplanned outburst.

Flapper's thoughts went back to his surprise and amazement when he saw the notice in the *Chronicle of Higher Education* announcing the School for Presidents, and soliciting applications for faculty positions in several disciplines including, to his unbounded joy, philosophy. It was like destiny calling, because of course it was not the first time he had heard of the School for Presidents. He remembered the night on the fantail of the *Indianapolis*, when Booker T. handed him the thin blue manuscript describing the curriculum. When he read the notice, and saw that the school was located at Tuskegee Institute he felt a thrill as if he were being touched by a signal from the director of the universe. Susan understood immediately, but her father was a different story. Flapper worked hard to explain what it all meant to him, but Doctor Land was unyielding in his judgment that the whole thing was nonsense and a total waste of time.

Flapper had never seen Susan so upset. She wanted family harmony, but had to endure bitter conflict. She shook with emotion as she addressed her father who stood defiantly in the center of the room ready to accept any challenge.

"Dad," she began, "…Dad…please…I…don't do this."

Dr. Land softened quickly, took Susan's hand and said, "I'm sorry, honey, I know it's your big day, but I had to say it…if Homer wants to throw himself into lost causes it's one thing, but when he drags you into it I think it's damned irresponsible."

"Dad, please," Susan pleaded, "…I'm not being dragged into

anything…why can't you understand? This is something we both want to do. You don't have to like it, but you must respect our right to determine the direction of our own lives…you must."

>>34<<

SWEET AUBURN

Heading south from St. Louis, Susan and Flapper, flushed with a sense of adventure, picked up state route three in Red Bud, Illinois and nosed along the eastern edge of the Mississippi River to Cairo, where they stopped for lunch at the KIM Cafe. Everything they owned was piled into the trunk and back seat of a forest green, two-door 1941 Pontiac sedan. They learned from the waitress that KIM stood for Kentucky, Illinois, and Missouri, three states that touched here at the confluence of the Ohio and Mississippi rivers. They also learned that it's not a good idea to order lobster in a river town where all they know how to cook is catfish, 1,500 miles from the nearest ocean. When they crossed the Ohio river into Kentucky, Flapper had the odd feeling that they had just leaped from the safety and comfort of a cozy airplane cabin into the uncertain and turbulent air of a strange and unfamiliar land, where water fountains and public restrooms were labeled WHITE or COLORED. When Susan reached for his hand he knew she, too, was feeling strangely disconnected.

Five hundred miles to go, through Jackson, Tennessee; nicking the northeast corner of Mississippi at Corinth, and into Alabama where they wondered at the oversize billboard greeting from the large smiling face, vaguely reminiscent of a horse.

WELCOME TO ALABAMA
JAMES E. (BIG JIM) FOLSOM, GOVERNOR
Y'ALL COME

They moved on through Birmingham and down to Auburn... *"Auburn, sweet Auburn, loveliest village of the plains"* ...straight into the heart of Dixie, and a new life. Flapper and Susan squeezed each other's hands, took deep breaths, checked their parachutes, and did not look back.

They bumped across the dusty railroad tracks in the oven-hot August air on North Gay Street in sweet Auburn, and headed up the hill toward Toomer's Corner in the center of town. Halfway up the hill Susan put her hand on Flapper's leg, and for reasons she did not try to understand picked this time to tell him something she had known since before they left St. Louis. "I'm pregnant," she said.

Flapper, intent on his driving, still not convinced the other drivers in this curious land were entirely reliable, heard the words and was instantly overwhelmed by a torrent of thoughts that threatened to drown him in hot, bubbling emotion. To his great surprise he said, while keeping his eyes on the street, "Our children will be born in Alabama."

Susan, struggling with her own emotions, and looking out at a store window sign that read EAGLE HARDWARE, to her great surprise found herself repeating Flapper's words, "Our children will be born in Alabama."

Flapper eased the car into an angled parking space at the top of the hill and cut the engine. He turned to look at Susan, and found her looking at him with wide, and he thought, perhaps a little frightened, eyes. They got out of the car, and walking hand in hand, soon found themselves on the Alabama Polytechnic Institute campus, where they sat on a shaded bench and began to unravel their tangled thoughts. The sudden realization of impending parenthood caught them both by surprise. They knew they should be happy at the prospect, but they were faintly uneasy and strangely apprehensive.

Flapper thought, but hesitated to say it, *I'm not sure I'm ready to share Susan.*

Susan thought, *I'm going to be a mother.*

Flapper turned his head slightly to look closer at Susan. She was dressed for travel in shorts, sandals, and T-shirt, her dark brown hair pulled back in a ponytail against the heat. Small beads of perspiration formed above her upper lip. She didn't look any different. "How do you feel?" he asked.

"Hot," she answered, then added, "A little stiff from the driving…maybe we could find a court and shoot a few hoops."

Flapper shifted to face her and said quickly, "No hoops for you, Dr. Jackson."

"Ping pong?" she offered. "I really could use some exercise."

Flapper said, "I don't think so."

They sat quietly for a while before Susan said, "It must have been the champagne."

Flapper said, "If it's a girl we'll call her Dixie…what do you think?"

Susan nodded. "Dixie Jackson," she said. "...Good. I like it." She paused. "If it's a boy, how about Homer Junior?"

Flapper shook his head vigorously from side to side. "Oh no, not in a thousand years," he said. "Why don't we name him after you. What do you think of Sue?"

Susan looked at him in astonishment. "A boy named Sue?"

"Why not? Anything is better than Homer."

Susan looked at Flapper, but he avoided her eyes. She knew he wasn't serious. She looked closer. She was pretty sure he wasn't serious. She changed the subject. "So," she said. "Here we are in the heart of Dixie. It does feel..." she paused, considering how it felt. "...Hot."

In the mid-August heat, the early afternoon sun blazing, the campus was empty except for a few maintenance men drowsily working around shrubs and flower gardens, and cleaning up around the messy magnolia trees. They sat near a fountain in front of the Ross Chemistry Laboratory, a stately three-story brick building with four tall Greek-style columns spread across its wide portico.

Susan sniffed the air, trying to place the faint odor. "Do you smell anything, Flapper?" she asked.

He nodded. "It smells like goats," he said.

Susan agreed. "Yes, goats," she said. "...It's butyric acid. That must be the chemistry building...unless there are some Gingko trees around here." She looked but saw only magnolia trees framing the square.

Susan had more than a passing interest in that chemistry building because in a little over a month she would be teaching biochemistry there. It had happened as suddenly and as unexpectedly as Flapper finding the notice about the School for Presidents in the *Chronicle of Higher Education.* It was a six-line ad in the Job Opportunities section at the back of *SCIENCE* magazine.

> *ASSISTANT PROFESSOR OF BIOCHEMISTRY — Tenure track position. Nine month appointment. Successful applicant will teach undergraduate and graduate biochemistry to pre-med and chemistry majors, and will be expected to initiate a research program. Salary commensurate with experience. Send curriculum vita and three letters of reference to Professor Achilles Demimelius, School of Chemistry, Alabama Polytechnic Institute, Auburn, Alabama.*

Susan was surprised to receive a job offer less than a month after submitting her application. So there it was. She would teach at API, and Flapper would teach at Tuskegee. They would live in Auburn; Flapper would commute to Tuskegee, only 20 miles away.

Susan stood up and said, "Flapper, let's go take a look."

Flapper was uncertain. He looked at Susan in a funny way and asked, "Is butyric acid good for Dixie Sue?"

Susan was on her feet and heading for Ross Hall, Flapper hustling to catch up. They found the doors open, but no one in sight. They entered a large airy lobby with wide corridors branching off left and right. Straight ahead were two broad staircases, one on the right going down, and one on the left going up. In the center of the lobby, two portable bulletin boards had been rolled in. Susan saw tacked to the boards long sheets of paper with names in alphabetical order followed by letters…mostly Fs, an occasional A, a few Bs, some Cs and Ds.

Susan said, "These are grade sheets for CHEM one oh two, Flapper, look at all those Fs."

Flapper was pondering a note pinned to the board across one of the grade sheets.

IF THE STUDENTS HAVEN'T LEARNED,
THE TEACHERS HAVEN'T TAUGHT

"Professor Bungler says it's not possible to teach a jackass."

Susan and Flapper were startled by a voice from behind. They turned to see a slight, dark-haired man in short khaki pants, polo shirt and sandals, wearing thick black-framed glasses, carrying a double armful of books and papers, and smiling broadly. "Sorry," he said, "didn't mean to startle you, but I saw you were looking at the example of student wisdom. Freshman chemistry grades are a sore point here at Auburn, a lot of people agree with that sign, including some professors, and not a few deans."

Flapper and Susan detected a slight accent in his speech, clearly he was not a native of Dixie.

"But look, you're new here, " he said, "can I help you with something?"

Susan became slightly flustered. She had not expected to meet anyone, and blanched at the prospect of meeting a new colleague, dressed as she was for travel, and wondering if her pregnancy showed.

Flapper apparently felt no such qualms, and before Susan could stop him said in his usual friendly and open manner, "Susan is the new biochemistry teacher here, we happened to be sitting out front, and decided to have a look at the building."

The dark-haired man looked at them in surprise, took a step back, started to place his books and papers on the floor, then dropped them in a heap. Enthusiastically he seized Susan's right hand, and began pumping it vigorously in exaggerated up and down motions. "Welcome, welcome," he said, "why didn't you say so? Welcome, Dr. Land. I am so happy to see you. We didn't expect you until next week, but never mind, here you are...I am so happy to see you."

Susan and Flapper smiled broadly. Caught off-guard by the sudden enthusiasm, they braced for a possible back pummeling. Susan tried to pull away, and managed to say, "Thank you, we're happy to be here...I think...you are?"

"I am...forgive me, I am Achilles Demimelius...and this is your husband?"

"Yes, this is my husband, Flapper Jackson. It's good to meet you Professor Demimelius. I'm sorry about barging in like this, we really didn't expect to meet anyone."

"Not at all, not at all, no need to apologize...none at all, I'm happy to see you. If you have time, let me get you a cup of coffee or perhaps you would prefer iced-tea, we can go to the faculty lounge in the student union building, it's just over there, we can have a little chat, maybe get to know each other a little...you must have many questions."

"Now looky heah, Virgil, it's time you pissy-assed boy scouts callin' yo-selves Klansmen either shit a log or git off the double damn pot, you heah me?"

Virgil Young was troubled that as he got older he was softening, and though he still thought of himself as tough, he had to admit he was afraid of the steely-eyed man who had just called him a boy scout. The man was Robert Fields, head of the National States Rights Party headquartered in Atlanta, an organization dedicated to cleansing the United States of "riff-raff and trash" by sending all Jews to Madagascar and all Negroes to Africa. "What do you want us to do, Mistah Fields?" he asked plaintively.

"Ah want you to have a plan, Virgil, how many times do ah have to tell you? This country bein' sucked dry by the mongrelized commie jew bankers, and all you do is go around killin' a few niggahs. It's pathetic, Virgil, you heah me? It's pathetic...Where are your bombers?"

Virgil squirmed in his chair. "We got to be awful careful, Mistah Fields," he said, "Ah think we got a FBI informer in our Klavern."

Fields was scornful. "Ah do believe you is afraid, Virgil, and it makes me sick, you heah? What is it you afraid of, Virgil? Goin' to jail?" He shook his head in disgust. "You better just give it up to some of your young blood, Virgil, don't you know the FBI don't give a shit? We got informers in the FBI…the FBI hates niggahs and jews as much as we do, and you worried about the FBI? Don't make me laugh, Virgil. Do you know while we sittin' heah right at this very moment, the courts is considerin' cases brought by the niggahs to make segregation against the law? Do ah have to remind you what that means, Virgil? Do you want to be forced to sit next to a smelly niggah on a bus or in a restaurant? Do you want your children and grandchildren goin' to the same school as niggahs?"

Virgil was indignant, "It ain't right, Mistah Fields. It ain't right. We got to do somethin'."

"Did I get that right? Your name is Flapper?" Flapper and Susan were walking with Professor Demimelius across the plaza in front of the chemistry building, on their way to the student union building. Flapper was suddenly aware that once again it might be to his advantage to change his name to something that did not require an explanation. It also occurred to him that anyone with a name like Achilles would have no trouble relating to some one named Homer.

"Yes…Flapper. Actually it's a nickname, but you probably guessed that. My real name is Homer…my dad was reading *The Odyssey* when I was born. I daresay you have some Greek in your background."

Professor Demimelius laughed heartily. "You might very well say that. I was born in Athens and came to America with my parents when I was ten years old."

"How long have you been at Auburn?" Flapper asked.

"Going on seventeen years, I came here in nineteen thirty-five."

Susan and Flapper took seats on a low overstuffed couch behind a large glass-topped coffee table. The professor sat across from them in a soft-cushioned chair. A white-coated student waiter took their iced-tea order.

"Well." The professor beamed at them across the table.

Susan felt a quick collegiality with the friendly professor, and was emboldened to ask a question that had been on her mind since the day she received the job offer. "Professor," she began, but he quickly interrupted her.

"Why don't you call me A. D.," he said, "that's pretty much what everyone calls me here. I think Achilles is too big a mouthful for my colleagues. I'll just call you Sue."

Susan wouldn't have minded calling him Achilles, but she was uncomfortable with easy familiarity, especially with a senior colleague she had known for only a few minutes. On the other hand, to continue calling him professor after he had asked not to be called that would be to deny him the respect she thought she owed him; also she was charmed by his modesty. Calling him by his initials was a good compromise; but she recoiled at being called Sue.

"A.D....Okay...A.D. But don't call me Sue, I prefer to be called Susan. Now, A.D....I have a question...I was surprised to receive the job offer so soon after I submitted my application...I thought you would ask me to come here for an interview. Can you tell me what happened?"

Professor Demimelius smiled. "That's easy," he said. "First, we were impressed by your experience, and by your academic record at a first-rank school like Washington University. Second, your letters of reference were excellent...your teachers appear to hold you in very high regard." He hesitated. "And finally," he hesitated once again, then said with a chuckle, "Yours was the only application we received." He laughed uproariously.

Flapper and Susan looked at each other, not sure they should join in the joke, not sure if it was a joke. They managed to smile weakly as they waited for Demimelius to regain his composure. When he did he had a question of his own. "And what about you, Sue? You must have had choices, why did you choose Auburn?"

Susan and Flapper both understood at once that it was a difficult, if not a grossly unfair question, because no matter how she answered, it would diminish her. It was a question that would never arise in a college noted for academic excellence, and that of course was the problem. Susan decided to go with the truth. "It was an opportunity sent from heaven," she said. "Flapper is going to teach at Tuskegee so we can stay together, and we both get to do what we are trained for."

Demimelius looked at Flapper with new interest and more than a little curiosity. "You're going to teach at Tuskegee? What will you teach?" he asked.

"Philosophy," said Flapper, and braced for the expected laugh or scornful remark.

Demimelius did not laugh, but he did smile, and it was a smile of pleasure and approval. “Philosophy!” he exclaimed. “You don’t say…philosophy.” He mulled it over in his mind. “Sometimes I like to think of myself as a philosopher…it’s one of the benefits of being a college professor…you may be teaching organic chemistry, but you can be a philosopher while doing it, and you get paid all the same.”

Demimelius laughed and allowed himself some philosophical thoughts, for the moment losing track of Susan and Flapper sitting across from him wondering if they should file him under the Arthur Compton School of Nutty Professors. “Imagine if Plato had known about organic chemistry!” he said. “Can’t you just see Socrates sitting with his students, trying to make them understand the poetry of a benzene ring and how it relates to the meaning of life.” He laughed again.

Susan interrupted his reverie. “Excuse me, A. D.,” she said, “do you teach organic chemistry?”

The professor started. “What?…Oh…Yes, I teach organic chemistry, and also biochemistry. At least I did teach biochemistry, but now that will change…now that you are here.” Again he unleashed a happy laugh.

“What’s it like?” Susan blurted.

Demimelius looked at her questioningly. “Well I love organic chemistry,” he answered, “the logic of it, the beauty of a Friedel-Krafts reaction, the endless variety of a Grignard…it would help if the students were better, but…”

Susan interrupted. “No, I mean…you’re not a native here, you’ve lived other places…what’s it like to live here in the South?”

Susan surprised herself with the question. She wasn’t sure where it came from or even what information she sought. Before he could answer she tried to recover by saying, “No, I’m sorry, forget about that question, it’s…it’s…it’s just that we don’t know anyone here, and we’ve heard and read so much, and these WHITE and COLORED signs are…I don’t know…they seem sort of threatening. I guess if you’re not used to them they are almost like a signal to beware.”

She looked at Flapper to see his reaction. She had not shared these thoughts with him, mostly because in fact it was the first time they had surfaced from her unconscious, and she was perplexed to hear the words coming out of her mouth.

Demimelius shrugged. “Nothing to be concerned about…it is a segregated society. Not unusual at all…many places in the world have such arrangements.”

Susan protested. "But this is America, our Constitution forbids it."

Demimelius frowned. "If that is true," he said, "it appears that here in the South local custom takes precedence over the Constitution." He shrugged and added, "The system seems to work well here."

Susan, like many other Americans, was not as well informed about the Constitution as she thought. Most Americans had the correct notion that the Constitution called for equal treatment for all citizens. What was less well appreciated, except in the South, was that the Supreme Court in 1896 had ruled that in the case of Negro Americans, separate accommodations, as long as they were equal, whatever that meant, were acceptable before the law.

Susan persisted, intent on pressing her new acquaintance for his views on racial segregation, ignoring her father's parting admonition to mind her own business. "But doesn't it bother you?"

Flapper interrupted, sensing by the professor's facial expression that this was a dangerous subject that should not be discussed with someone who all they knew about was that he taught organic chemistry. "Wait, Susan, " he said, "why don't we talk about something else?"

Demimelius interrupted Flapper. The smile was gone from his face. "I hope you have not come here to be a crusader, Sue," he said. "It would be a mistake. You should not underestimate the depth of feeling here on these matters."

Susan did not think of herself as a crusader, she had simply grown up with the Jeffersonian aphorism that "all men are created equal." She would be told here that in spite of his eloquence, Jefferson, who owned 200 slaves, did not for a moment consider Negroes to be equal to Whites. In any case, segregation was not at the top of her list of concerns at the moment, and she did not mind changing the subject. She looked carefully at Professor Demimelius wondering if he had just delivered a warning or a threat.

Flapper, too, heard what sounded vaguely like a threat, and instinctively felt constrained to support Susan. "We are not crusaders, Professor, but it is not in our nature to ignore what we might perceive as injustice."

Demimelius had seen it before. Yankees bent on bringing reform to what they regarded as a sick and malevolent society. It would lead to nothing but trouble, and he briefly considered advising them to go back to St. Louis, but reconsidered when he thought about having to teach biochemistry again. He was nearing 50 years old, and was still the junior member of the aging chemistry faculty, which meant when pressure from pre-medical students to teach biochemistry increased with the return of World War II veterans, he got stuck with the job. He sighed. In the aromatic world of Achilles Demimelius the cardinal injustice was his having to teach biochemistry. He smiled at the thought that Susan, true to Flapper's words, would rectify that injustice.

The conversation veered to a discussion between Susan and Demimelius about the makeup and organization of the API School of Chemistry, and what Susan might expect in the way of teaching assignments, committee work, and so on.

Flapper's mind wandered to his first meeting with the near mythical Count, scheduled for later in the week. Flapper, like Susan, had been hired without an interview, but he did not think it unusual under the circumstances. In his application letter he made the point that he had been teaching philosophy in the School for Presidents before the school even existed, and he felt a mystical attraction to the school.

>>35<<

TO CURE A CARBUNCLE

"So you are Flapper Jackson." Count extended his hand and exchanged a firm handshake with Flapper, so firm that it made Flapper wince with pain. "Booker T. spoke highly of you...I'm pleased to meet you."

They met near the statue of Booker T. Washington, on the Tuskegee Institute campus. Flapper looked hard at the legendary Count, trying to reassure himself that this man was real, and that he was not in the middle of a surrealistic dream. For the moment Flapper was speechless, recalling solemn discussions on the fantail of the *Indianapolis* with Booker T. McCan, who told of a stunningly wealthy hundred-year-old man living in a shanty in the middle of the Peoria city dump. Flapper tried to reconcile that image with the tall white-haired man in the dapper, dark three-piece suit who stood before him. He struggled for words..."Booker T. told me you lived in the city dump," he said. "Forgive me, but...you're not what I expected...I...I've never met a legend before."

Count laughed his booming, the world-is-tough-but-we-can-handle-it laugh. "Whoa, man," he said, "don't make me a legend before my time." He led Flapper to a nearby bench and said, "Why don't we sit down here and get to know each other a little better?"

Flapper sat and looked carefully at the reluctant legend. "Booker T. told me about you," he said. "I was never sure you were real...Booker T. seemed to have a great imagination. He said you picked him to become president of the United States...it sounded like a dream." Flapper paused as he thought of Booker T. struggling in the water. "...And now he's dead."

Count smiled and shook his head. "He's not dead. He survived."

Flapper was dumbfounded. "But...I...he...I thought..." He looked at Count in disbelief and confusion, remembering the last time he saw Booker T., his chin in the water, his eyes closed...the flickering, fading hope.

Count said, "Not only did he survive, but also he's off in Korea fighting another war...one war wasn't enough for him...he'll make a great president...it's his destiny."

Flapper tried to collect his thoughts. In the space of less than a minute he had been told that not only was Booker T. alive, but also he remained Count's number one choice for president. On top of that, Count had invoked the concept of destiny that he was all too familiar with; it was an abstraction that had sustained him through the bloody horror of three Pacific Island amphibious assaults. But his graduate studies in philosophy had brought him into close touch with what the most respected minds in Western civilization had to say about "free will," and the experience had left him with more questions than answers. When he confessed this to his doctoral studies committee, they pronounced him ready for graduation.

Flapper stood and walked away. He was stunned. Count sat watching for a moment, then followed, after noting the curious expression on Flapper's face. "Hey, man, I thought you knew," Count said as he came alongside the shuffling Flapper, "...I thought you knew."

Flapper, almost breathless, managed to say, "I didn't know...I thought he was dead." He recalled waking up on the *Mercy*...he remembered Susan telling him there were no other survivors. The thought occurred to him that Booker T. had been resurrected, as he had.

"Have you seen him?" Flapper asked.

"He's an officer on a destroyer in the Pacific Fleet," said Count. "He cuts a fine figure in his dress blues...he'll make a great president."

Flapper was stunned. "Booker T. is an officer? How did it happen?"

Count told Flapper about the return of Booker T., his enrollment at the University of Illinois, his graduation with honors, his commission through the Naval ROTC program, and his assignment to the *USS Agerholm* in the Pacific Fleet.

Flapper was nonplused. "I never went back to Peoria after I returned," he said. "We were in school a hundred miles apart at the same time, and didn't know it." He shook his head. Then he brightened and said, "But this is wonderful news...Booker T. alive, and a naval officer! I would love to talk with him...graduated with honors...fantastic! You're right, Count, Booker T. is special...I can't wait to tell Susan."

Thinking of Susan brought him up short. He had to talk with Count about something that was on his mind.

Count beamed as he watched Flapper's reaction to the news about Booker

T. Then he noticed the quick change of expression. "Is something wrong?" he asked.

Flapper looked up quickly. "What?"

"All of a sudden you look worried. What is it?" asked Count.

Flapper was not sure how to express a concern that had slowly worked its way into his consciousness. "Susan is pregnant," he said.

"Well then, congratulations," said Count, once more beaming. "I take it Susan is your wife...how soon is the blessed event?" He grasped Flapper's hand.

"She's in her first trimester, the baby is due sometime in March," Flapper said. "I'm concerned about raising the child in a segregated society."

Count stopped shaking Flapper's hand, but retained his firm grip as he looked into Flapper's anxious eyes. "Yes, I see," he said. He released the hand, and returned to the bench where he sat quietly for a few moments considering his response. Count had seen and experienced prejudice and discrimination all his long life; he knew with dazzling clarity that here in Alabama, in the middle of the 20th century, to say that the life of a Negro was precarious was a flagrant understatement. Tuskegee Institute might seem a beacon of light in a sea of darkness, but it would shine only as long as the white power structure perceived it as run by "white man's niggers," also known as "good niggers," as indeed they viewed Booker T. Washington himself. Count might speak of destiny, but he had not gotten this far without a steel-willed practicality. He might speak of prayer, but he had learned long ago that man had to solve his own problems. He had a vision, and he had the financial resources to advance his causes, but he could not do it alone. He needed people fired with his dream, and if he were to pull it off here in the heart of Dixie, these people would need extraordinary courage as well. He thought Flapper was one of those people. Flapper was concerned about raising his child in a segregated society. It was precisely the reason Count determined to build the School for Presidents here in Tuskegee. Sadie Tanner said the number one threat to freedom and democracy in the second half of the 20th century was unreasoned discrimination against groups of people different from the majority. What better place to face that threat than here in Macon County, Alabama, where the threads of discrimination were so much a part of the fabric of society that most people would have been surprised to be told the garment was flawed.

Count's thoughts went back to the night he sat with Booker T. McCan in the middle of the Peoria city dump. The night he conceived the idea; the night the vision came to him. He was not thinking about threats to freedom and democracy at that time, it was much simpler than that. It was just that he knew the post-war world would become increasingly complex and would require leaders with special training to deal with the problems intelligently…and this was B.A.B…Before Atomic Bombs. His was a global vision, not tied to particular causes or even to political agendas. The country and the world needed trained leaders…if the curriculum was properly crafted, and implemented with care and imagination, the result could only make the world a better place; he would settle for that.

As for Flapper, always introspective, he was surprised at his reaction to impending fatherhood. From the day Susan gave him the news, he had become more cautious in everything he did. He drove more slowly. He checked the rearview mirror. He quit cigarettes and took up a pipe. He jumped at loud noises. He was solicitous of Susan. Feeling immortal at Peleliu and Iwo Jima, he felt vulnerable in Opelika and Notasulga. He reexamined his reasons for coming here—they went back to the image of Booker T.'s brother Davey heroically manning a machine gun on the bridge of the *Oklahoma* at Pearl Harbor. He remembered the black Marine sergeant who saved his life at Peleliu, of Booker T. himself fearlessly joining the assault at Iwo Jima, of stories about black U.S. war veterans in South Carolina, required to sit in the back of buses in deference to white German prisoners-of-war. He had lied to Achilles Demimelius—he was a crusader. If he was honest with himself, he had to admit that he came to Alabama to continue the fight against injustice begun for him on the South Pacific beaches, where he had the support of 8-inch guns. Here in Alabama he was armed only with the force of ideas. And now the extra factor in the equation: a new life to consider. When it was only he and Susan it was an exciting carefree adventure, but now there would be Dixie Sue.

"It had to be here," Count said, not looking at Flapper.

Flapper, looking straight ahead, his eyes focused on nothing in particular, nodded. "I know," he whispered.

"When it becomes known there will be a great outcry," Count said.

Flapper nodded again. "Yes," he said. Then the realization and a quick glance, "You planned it this way, didn't you?"

Count turned to Flapper with a smile and said, "To cure a carbuncle, you got to attack the core."

"There may be violence," said Flapper.

Count nodded. "I have considered it," he said.

Count considered it a near certainty. He knew the history of Tuskegee Institute, how it had been born in 1881, the child of murder, intimidation, and political expediency. How, in 1871, after brutally driving an elected Negro state representative and his family bleeding and fleeing for their lives from the county, the white power structure had been taken aback by the mass exodus of their black work force, and scrambling to recover, had agreed to seek money from the state to establish a black normal school at Tuskegee. It was always understood that good relations between the races depended on the political behavior of blacks who had been corrupted after the Civil War, "the difficulties of 1861," by the evil teaching of base and selfish men, and led astray by meddlesome and designing persons. Count knew, with the certainty of a dynamite cap, that the only difference between then and now was better weapons.

Dean Gomillion had contributed the wisdom that to make the true purpose of the school known would be to invite ridicule, if not crippling resistance from the white power structure. Better, he said, to give it the bland and unthreatening title "School of Sociology." But Count saw this as a continuation of a failed policy, and rejected the approach. He favored the revolutionary idea of facing the problem head on. He planned to use local, regional, and in the end, national newspapers and magazines to announce and explain the program. It had not escaped his notice that news coverage might in the end be useful in gaining acceptance of the concept. In this he was relying on the basic goodness and good sense of the American populace.

He fretted at the prospect that his scheme would almost surely be the cause of suffering and indeed death. He could only hope that the innocent would be spared, but he had the uneasy feeling that would not be the case. He was not concerned for his own life except for thoughts of what would happen to the program once he was gone. It was important for him to have potential leaders in place, and the sooner the better. With Jerry Mulhane IV and Flapper Jackson he thought he had two, though he was fully aware that an integrated faculty was yet another source of irritation to the inflamed outlook of certain groups eager to disrupt. He looked forward to the return of Booker T. McCan.

Count looked carefully at Flapper, and saw a troubled countenance. He placed his hand on Flapper's shoulder. "Flapper, my friend," he said, "your courage under fire is well known to me from my talks with Booker T., and I would feel more confident facing this action with you at my side, but I do appreciate your family concerns and I will understand if you choose to withdraw."

Flapper knew he could not make a decision without discussing it with Susan. He thought of her impulsive nature, and sensed she would favor joining the fight, but it also occurred to him that she, like himself, might be thinking differently now that she was carrying Dixie Sue.

Count's hand was still on Flapper's shoulder and Flapper now placed his own hand on top of Count's. "This is my fight too, Count, " he said, "but I must speak with Susan."

The discussion whether to remain in Alabama was over before it even started. Susan scoffed at the idea of leaving Alabama in the face of adversity. Her clinching argument went something like this: "What is this compared to fighting in the South Pacific? Can you imagine telling Dixie Sue we left because we were afraid? I don't think so."

Flapper was not surprised at Susan's reaction, but it did not lessen his concern. He found himself looking closely at white shopkeepers, truck drivers, people on the street, and most especially policemen carrying guns, wondering how they would react to the knowledge that a School for Presidents was underway at Tuskegee. He found it hard to laugh at bumper stickers displaying confederate battle flags, and proclaiming THE SOUTH WILL RISE AGAIN, and in small letters, the sub-heading SAVE YOUR CONFEDERATE MONEY.

He was still shaken by his experience at the Lee County courthouse in Opelika when he and Susan registered to vote. The ancient registrar, a wizened old man whose neck appeared to have shrunk away from his shirt collar, in a creaky voice had asked him, "How far'd yawl go in school?" Flapper answered that he had a Ph.D. The ancient looked at him without a trace of humor and asked, "Didja go to college?" Asked about his military service Flapper had to spell the word Navy for the man. He could only imagine what prospective Negro voters might have to endure to become registered voters.

If Flapper had known, as Count did, the history of black-white relations in this part of Alabama, it would not have eased his mind. Flapper Jackson, decorated war veteran, found himself in a new war zone where the rules of the game were unwritten, the participants were unaware, and there were no medals awarded.

Jerry Mulhane IV, decorated war veteran, knew all the unwritten rules, and over a glass of sour mash whiskey in his and Becky's small kitchen, was explaining, in his soft north Alabama drawl, a few to Flapper and Susan. "There is no such thing as vertical segregation," he said, "except, of course, in state liquor stores. It's okay for Whites and Negroes to eat in the same room as long as they don't sit down. If they took all the chairs out of restaurants, libraries, and schools...well, maybe not schools, there's an unholy fear amongst most white Southerners about sending their children to the same schools as Negroes. Hell, there's still a lot of folks down here who don't hold with sending Negroes to school at all."

He paused for a drink. "As a matter of fact," he said, "you might be surprised to know there's a whole lot of white folks here who don't know how to read or write."

"I have an idea that registrar at the Lee County court house is right on the edge of literacy," Flapper said, "I had to spell Navy for him."

From the first moment when Count introduced them Flapper knew he was going to like Jerry Mulhane IV. Apart from Flapper's natural tendency to like people in general, this man had a rumpled appearance and an easy smile that generated a comfortable feeling in Flapper. For his part, Flapper's strong grip and serious eyes favorably impressed J-Four, but he had not entirely overcome his deeply felt suspicion of anyone coming from the North. J-Four and Flapper would have occasion to discuss these feelings over many a glass in the days and months ahead. Neither man was inclined to talk much about their war experiences, nor to inquire about the other's, and, but for Count informing each separately, might have waited a long time to learn how alike they were in this regard.

"Okay, here's another one for you," J-four continued. "Negroes have to sit in the balconies of movie theaters unless one is carrying a white baby, then it's okay for her to sit with the white folks...'course plenty of those white folks been nursed by black mammies...don't try to make any logic out of all this. Speaking of movies, did yawl happen to see that movie with the three Roberts—Young, Mitchum, and Ryan?"

Susan and Flapper were enthusiastic moviegoers, and knew immediately what J-four was referring to. It was the movie *Crossfire*, a clumsy, but at the time revolutionary, attempt by Hollywood to deal with the subject of antisemitism, and to a lesser extent, anticatholicism. In the early years following World War II, America was looking for a new enemy, and although ethnic, religious, and racial prejudices were candidates, they never stood much of a chance against the more visible "red menace"...international communism.

"We liked it," said Susan. "What did you think of it?"

"It shows a pretty good example of blind and unreasoned hatred," said J-four. "But when Robert Young gives his sermon on prejudice, and how his grandfather was murdered on the street just because he was Irish and Catholic, I couldn't help wondering why they didn't have anything to say about how Negroes are treated in this country."

Susan asked, "What about you, J-Four, you grew up here in the South, why don't you have any prejudices?"

J-Four had a quick answer for that question. "Oh I have my share of prejudices," he said, "but I've managed to shed the one about black skin, or at least I think I have. It's because of what I saw in Italy," he said simply. Susan and Flapper waited while J-Four thought about what more, if anything, he wanted to say about what he had seen in Italy. First, he had to get over the ear-splitting din that always assaulted his head when Italy came to mind. It occurred to him that Flapper knew that sound, and when he looked at Flapper he felt an odd telepathic signal that Flapper was hearing the same thing.

When J-four mentioned Italy, Flapper immediately knew what he was talking about, and his own mind conjured images of desperate men, engulfed in a cacophony of pain-threshold noise, facing each other across blistered no-man's lands. He also thought of his brother Jaybird.

J-four said with a slight shrug of his shoulders, "It was a simple conclusion…if Negroes could stand up to the gut-ripping terror of a Panzer assault, they were the equal of any man on earth and deserved to be treated accordingly. Flapper understands that."

Flapper nodded and said to no one in particular, "Are we the only ones who see it?"

J-four responded, "We're not the only ones, though it may seem like it sometimes…you musta read about Truman's special message to Congress on civil rights, and of course the desegregation of the armed forces. Those acts stirred up a lot of fuss down here. Most of the white folks are convinced that if Negroes get equal rights, especially voting rights, they will be overwhelmed, and once the Negro gets in power it is assumed they will treat the Whites as bad or worse than the Whites been treatin' them. The idea of a totally integrated society terrifies them, so they make a lot of noise about states' rights, conveniently forgetting about what's called 'the difficulties of eighteen sixty-one' that was supposed to settle that issue once and for all.

"It's just too soon after those difficulties…there's still Confederate veterans alive, and they tell stories that glorify the slaughter…you probably didn't know that Robert E. Lee's birthday is a holiday in the state of Alabama and that the Confederate battle flag flies higher than the stars and stripes over the state house in Montgomery. I bet you even think John Philip Sousa wrote 'the Stars and Stripes Forever'...down here it's called 'the Stars and Bars Forever'. I think it'll be another one, maybe two hundred years before people of all colors are treated the same in this country, and even that may be too optimistic. But that don't keep me from thinkin' we have an opportunity here in the middle of the twentieth century to make a start. That's one reason I decided to hitch on to Count's outrageous idea of a School for Presidents."

J-four took a deep breath, and a gulp of sour mash. "Sorry," he said, "I didn't mean to preach."

Flapper said, "So you think it's an outrageous idea?"

J-four looked at him and said, "Don't you?"

From the first time Booker T. told him on the *Indianapolis* about the School for Presidents Flapper knew it was an outrageous idea, but at the same time he was captivated by the grandness of the vision. His recent scholarly adventures, in particular his study of Plato, had only strengthened his agreement with the foundation of Count's scheme; the wise should lead and the leaders should be wise. Wisdom required knowledge, but knowledge was useless without understanding; it was possible to know everything but understand nothing. "Of course it's an outrageous idea, that's what gives it its charm," Flapper said.

Becky Muldane, J-four's wife, now joined the conversation. "But why did he put the school here in Tuskegee where he knew it would be greeted with resentment and hostility?"

Flapper smiled. "Maybe we should stop calling him Count, and start calling him Socrates," he said. "What he's doing here is the same thing Socrates did in Athens twenty-five hundred years ago...corrupting the youth to rebel against a chaotic and wasteful society. Of course in the end the angry mob claimed Socrates' life, but his legacy has endured."

J-four chuckled to himself, giggled, then laughed aloud. The others looked at him curiously.

"What's so funny, J-four?" his wife asked.

"I was just thinking the University of Georgia is located in Athens, maybe Count should have put his school there."

Flapper felt a warm glow as he looked around the table at Susan and his new friends, J-four and Becky. With several ounces of good Kentucky bourbon circulating through his system, whatever intractable problems might loom beyond the walls of Becky's cozy kitchen were put aside as he gathered up the table cloth and flung it around his shoulders like a Roman toga or a Greek philosopher's robe. He took a stance in the middle of the room, his head thrown back, his right arm grasping his left shoulder. "I am Socrates," he said, "I seek truth…let no man enter here who does not know geometry."

Susan laughed and said, "Pi R squared…can I come in?"

J-four held up his hand. "Hold it right there," he said. "In Alabama pie are round, cornbread are squared."

Soon after that they were all on their feet, arm-in-arm, singing "Rock of Ages" in four-part, fractured harmony. Susan was almost sure she heard J-four in the second verse sing, "crocked for ages."

Less than five miles away at the Rebel Yell roadhouse, on route 29 between Auburn and Tuskegee, not too far from Chewacla State Park, Virgil Young dropped a shot glass of whiskey into a stein of beer, and proceeded to drink the entire contents in one long 10-gulp draught to the delight and admiration of his five glassy-eyed companions.

"Yee-ha, Virgil," shouted Stanley Gordon, pummeling the sputtering Virgil on the back.

The high-pitched rebel yell went largely unnoticed in the general melee of the dimly lit, smoke-filled roadhouse where a high-volume jukebox played somebody-done-somebody-wrong-songs when there wasn't a guitar-picking singer and a drummer pounding out a live performance on the elevated stage.

After three boilermakers, Virgil was as happy as it was possible for him to be. He could still hold his own with these young bucks even though he was just past 50 years old. Now that he had their attention he would entertain them. He motioned for them to gather closer, which they eagerly did, knowing Virgil's reputation as a story teller. "These two niggahs," he began, "the Jones brothers, had just stole a pig, and was drivin' down the highway when they saw the blinking lights of a po-leese roadblock up ahead. They knew they was in trouble so they tried to hide the pig in the backseat by puttin' a hat and coat on it. When the po-leese stopped them the cop looked in with his flashlight and said 'What's yo' niggah names?' The driver said, 'Isaiah Jones, suh', the other one said 'Isaac Jones, suh'. Then the patrolman looked in the back seat at the pig and said, 'What's yo' name, niggah?' and the pig let out a big OINK."

Virgil was laughing with the others, and held up his hand to let them know there was more.

"So then thuh officer looked back inta thuh front seat and said, 'Where you headed, niggah?' and the driver said, 'We headin' fo' our momma's house, suh.' The officer said, 'Okay, but you bettah get yo' black ass down to the garage and git that right headlight fixed, you heah?' The niggah said, 'Yes, suh' and drove off. After they left the officer turned to his buddy and said, 'Ya know, that OINK Jones is thuh ugliest niggah ah evah saw."

Virgil basked in the riotous laughter of his appreciative audience.

Joe Bob Jones was laughing as loud as anyone and said, "Them Jones boys was pretty smart, Virgil, like all us Joneses."

Virgil's smile quickly turned to a scowl. "Yeah, that's the trouble with niggahs these days, they is gettin' too smart for theah own damn good. Maybe it's time we done give 'em a little reminder of where they is and who they is."

"What you got in mind, Virgil?"

"What ah got in mind is we find us a big ole buck niggah, and we cut off his balls." He looked around the table, his eyes glittering, his teeth showing through a tight grin. The others shrunk back at the thought and looked at Virgil with a mixture of fear and awe.

"You evah done that, Virgil? That'll teach 'em all right."

Virgil curled his lip and narrowed his eyes. "You damn right ah done it," he said. He grasped the neck of an empty beer bottle and held it up. "And this is what ah done it with." He smashed the bottle against the side of the table and brandished the jagged edges before the glittering eyes and wide-mouthed grins of his inebriated companions.

>> 36 <<

AGAIN

"COUNTERBATTERY! COUNTERBATTERY!"

The destroyer was straddled by gunfire coming from somewhere high on a looming desolate headland, gray brown in the sunless gloom of a winter morning in a forbidding land. A different war, a different place, deadly as always...the sea war in Korea.

"Counterbattery, coordinates zero four able..."

"RIGHT FULL RUDDER! ALL AHEAD FLANK! LET'S GET THE HELL OUT OF HERE!"

The sleek ship shot forward and heeled to starboard as an artillery shell exploded, leaving a 100-foot geyser of oily saltwater rising in its wake. It was like a fly avoiding a swatter. Captain Jack S. Ross reacted instinctively to the perceived danger, and felt his knees buckle at the realization that he was jumping from the sizzling pan of shore battery bombardment into the blistering blaze of a magnetic minefield.

Wonsan Harbor, North Korea...a classic training model for countless future gunnery exercises, but in frigid February, 1952, at 39 degrees north latitude, a nightmare for fragile destroyers and minesweepers called on for the dirty business of getting in close to unmask the batteries and clear the mines.

The beautiful city of Wonsan, principal seaport of North Korea on the relatively tideless Sea of Japan, was a transportation hub for north-south truck traffic, and for east-west road and rail lines connecting to the capital city, Pyongyang. It embraced an industrial complex, including a 4,000,000 square foot petroleum refinery that somehow continued to function despite a deluge of 50,000 naval shells in the first six months alone of the longest siege in modern American naval history, February 1951 to July 1953.

The voice radio crackled in the wheelhouse of the *Agerholm.* "Brass Hat,

Brass Hat, this is Monte Carlo. Over."

The junior officer of the deck, Ensign Booker T. McCan, triggered the key on the hand-held phone and said, "Monte Carlo, this is Brass Hat. Over."

"Brass Hat, this is Monte Carlo, please explain your movements. Over."

Ensign McCan was not sure how to reply to this request; all he knew was that they were executing radical movements, and that the captain seemed to have lost his cool. He could see without his binoculars the faint outline of the heavy cruiser *Toledo,* flagship of Task Force 95, several miles out to sea. The admiral was obviously observing the action, and not seeing what he had expected. The *Agerholm* was on a shore bombardment mission designed by Flag operations officers to accomplish two things. First, to hit the Wonsan airfield with a barrage of five-inch fragmentation shells; second, to discover and eliminate shore batteries. The drill, as they had practiced it on San Clemente Island off the coast of southern California, was to target counterbattery fire as quickly as possible and eliminate it with concentrated fire from all three 5-inch, .38 caliber gun turrets. In reality, here at Wonsan, the captain gave his gunners no chance to respond to the hostile fire, but ran like a startled jackrabbit at the first flash of enemy guns. From this moment the sobriquet Rabbit Ross was added to Big Jack S. by those several officers and men who wondered how such a man had ascended to command one of the proud greyhounds of the fleet.

Booker T. looked inquiringly at Lieutenant Cooley, officer of the deck, who had just stuck his cold head into the wheelhouse from the wing of the bridge. Cooley rolled his eyes, shrugged his shoulders, and said through chattering teeth, "Tell them we are taking evasive action."

Booker T. did not hesitate. "Monte Carlo, this is Brass Hat. We are taking evasive action. Over."

"Brass Hat, this is Monte Carlo." The staff officer, miles from the action, was calm and famously unconcerned. "My radar has you on collision course with Little Eva and a string of chestnuts. Please adjust...on the double...Monte Carlo himself says to get your rusty butt back on station and resume your firing mission. Over."

"Monte Carlo, this is Brass Hat. Roger. Out."

"Brass Hat, this is Monte Carlo. Can we get a willco on that? Over."

Little Eva was the code name for a small barren island called Hwangto Do, only 3,000 yards from shore, occupied by U.S. Marines and naval personnel as a shore fire control spotting station. Chestnuts were acoustic mines. Booker T. delivered the message to the OOD who consulted the captain staring ahead into an icy wind on the starboard wing of the bridge. It was beginning to snow.

Cooley, his foul weather jacket pulled up around his ears, quickly returned to the wheelhouse, and said in a calm and controlled voice, "The Oh Oh D has the con. All stop."

"The Oh Oh D has the con. All stop, aye aye, sir." The engine order telegraph man repeated, then executed the command, pulling the engine handles to the straight upright position accompanied by a musical *chiiiiing*! The answering *chiing chiing* came quickly.

"Engine room answers all stop, sir." The ship continued to move ahead, but at a much reduced speed; steam relief valves began to hiss and sputter as the superheated steam from four boilers, diverted from its turbine driving task, sought an outlet different from blowing up the boilers. A phone in the back of the wheelhouse rang insistently.

"Bridge, aye," Booker T. answered, and quickly pulled the phone away from his ear as a loud and angry voice came blasting through the line and echoed through the wheelhouse.

"This is the chief engineer! Can somebody tell me what the floody buck is going on up there? Don't you hass-oles know we've got five hundred pounds of live steam down here tryin' to find somewhere to go? Is somebody trying to scuttle this buckin fucket? Who the tuck am I falkin' to anyway?"

Booker T. wondered if he was in the middle of a nightmare. The ship was threatened by shellfire, a minefield, running aground, a flustered captain, abominable weather, and now by its own machinery. A cool head was desperately needed.

Lieutenant Cooley grabbed the phone. "Throw her in reverse, Squid," he said, "we're tryin' to get our bearings up here." He hung up the phone and said, "All back full." The ship, still moving forward, began to shudder and shake, and slowly, but with increasing momentum, to move in reverse.

Cooley was navigating by the seat of his pants, caught in restricted waters, the hilly Kalma Pando peninsula on one side, the small inner harbor islands of Tae Do and Hwangto Do on the other, and not knowing his exact position, only his trained-eye sense of distance to go by. "All ahead one third," he called to the engine order telegraph man, and to the helmsman, "rudder amidships, steady as you go. What's your heading, Boats? Lemme see that chart, Dawg, and get me a bearing on Square Head and Little Eva."

"Steady on course one zero five, sir," the helmsman called out.

"Very well," said Cooley, "right standard rudder." He stepped to the starboard wing of the bridge looking for obstacles.

Dawg McCan they called him, he wasn't sure why, except that all the junior officers were given nicknames soon after they came aboard—names of animals, an *Agerholm* tradition. Ensign Booker T. McCan, with an unacknowledged wink and nod to Dean Dunn as he crossed the stage to receive his magna cum laude diploma, had graduated from the University of Illinois on a cold December day, and two weeks later had boarded a U.S. Navy C-47 for an island hopping, (Oahu, Midway, Wake, Honshu, Kyushu), seemingly endless, 10,000 mile journey over the vast Pacific to join his ship in Japan. Six months earlier, June 25, 1950, thousands of well-armed and dangerous young soldiers carrying the battle flags, whistles and bugles of the Republic of North Korea had swarmed across the 38th parallel, and attacked the ill-prepared and unsuspecting Republic of South Korea. The United States, under the drums and banners of the five-year-old United Nations, had been quick to respond. It was called a "police action." Six million people would die before a truce could be reached. It seemed impossible to end it.

Booker T. crossed from the port to the starboard wing and approached "Antelope" Cooley. "Okay Lope, here's the dope," he said. "Little Eva is one three five, Square Head is at three one five, and Curly Locks is zero four five. That puts us right about here." He pointed to a spot on the navigational chart Cooley held in his hand.

The helmsman's urgent voice declared, "Rudder is right standard, passing one eight zero, sir."

Cooley responded, "Very well. Come to course three zero zero. All ahead standard, make turns for twelve knots. As soon as we steady up, Dawg, I want a course at twelve knots to get us back on firing station."

Cooley now turned to the sound-powered telephone man, "Alert the main battery," he said. "Tell them to stand by to resume firing."

At that moment, Captain Ross approached. "Ahh now, Mister Cooley, can you now tell me what is now…ahh…happening to my ship?"

"Yes, sir. We are coming around to resume our firing position. I believe that was the order from Monte Carlo, sir." Lieutenant Cooley began to salute, but noting the captain's snarling visage thought better of it.

"Yes, well Monte Carlo is not here taking hostile fire, is he? He and his pussy-footing staff are sitting three miles out to sea smoking cigarettes, drinking coffee, and playing acey-deucy. We are sitting ducks for those shore batteries and there's no way in God's hell we can eliminate them with our five-inch pop guns. They fire and then roll back into their caves before we can get a shot off. I have a responsibility here for two hundred and fifty men and a damned expensive piece of naval architecture." The captain, all his personal boilers on the line, was blowing off steam. He would not disobey the admiral's orders, but there was nothing to keep him from expressing his frustrations. He stalked the wheelhouse before the mostly averted eyes of the general quarters crew, embarrassed by their whining leader.

"Steady on course three zero zero, sir."

"On station in five minutes at this course. Good guess, Lope," Booker T. said, looking up from the chart.

"Okay, lemme talk to Lieutenant Odell in the main battery director," Cooley said to his phone man.

"Main battery, this is the bridge. Put Lieutenant Odell on the line." The phone man took off his headset, and handed it to Cooley who took it and held one earpiece to the side of his head without putting on the whole set.

"Bridge, this is Odell in main battery. What's up?" Cooley triggered a button, and spoke into the mouthpiece. "Moose, this is Lope. We're coming back into firing position, did you get those coordinates on the counterbattery before we scrambled?"

"Affirmative, Lope, they're plugged in. What happened anyway? We were about to let 'em have it."

"I'll tell you later. Right now I want you to hit that spot with everything you've got. Give 'em a rapid-fire barrage, about sixty rounds, one forward turret and the after turret. Let's see what happens. Maybe we can uncover a few more sleeping beauties so hold your other forward turret in reserve in case another battery unmasks. You can crank 'em out whenever yer ready, okay?"

"Roger, Lope. Stand by for a blast."

Momentarily the ship coasted to a near stop, and the five-inch batteries opened up with an ear-shattering barrage that cleaved a generous chunk out of the North Korean hillside, and at the same time numbed the senses of the bridge personnel.

Booker T., like most, but not all, of the others had plugged cotton into his ears. He stood on the port wing of the bridge alongside the captain and the OOD, all three scanning the scene with high-powered binoculars. The ship was moving slowly, 1,500 yards off the beach, on a course parallel to the hilly finger of the Kalma Pando peninsula behind which lay the city of Wonsan.

Attracted to the action on the port side, little attention was paid to the danger developing on the starboard side, and the urgent warning calls coming over the voice radio circuit in the wheelhouse were drowned out by the crash of the five-inch guns. Spotters on the small harbor island of Hwangto Do, now 4,000 yards off the starboard quarter of the *Agerholm*, were frantically trying to alert the firing ship to the threat of a blind-side attack from a high-speed torpedo boat rapidly closing the gap on the rear of the unsuspecting ship.

At the point-blank range of 1,500 yards, the boat released two long lance torpedoes, deadly at 10,000 yards, but next to useless at short range because there was no time for the projectiles to arm their firing mechanisms. The *Agerholm* was spared disaster, but not humiliation, by the inexperience of the Korean boat crew as one of the dud torpedoes struck and severely damaged the starboard propeller and rudder.

By allowing itself to be so victimized in a surprise attack, the *Agerholm*, in spite of endless hours of mind-numbing training, showed its own inexperience. The book on naval tactics had many Cardinal Rules, one that even a Peoria street fighter knew from common sense: never leave your butt uncovered.

In the clamor and thrill of the continuing salvos, only the helmsman, unable to maintain his course, was immediately aware that something was wrong, but it was only short moments before everyone knew as the ship, propelled unevenly by the undamaged port screw, veered crazily to the right. The quick-thinking Lope Cooley, still in tactical and emotional control, began to issue orders. First to the phone man, "Tell main battery to cease firing." He moved quickly through the wheelhouse to the starboard wing of the bridge to see where the ship was heading, noting as he passed that the helmsman was frantically spinning the wheel in a futile effort to bring the ship back on course. He did not need to be told that the ship had lost steering control, even if he did not know why. What he did know was that he might be able to maintain a heading by judicious use of his port and starboard engines.

"Well, you can guess what happened next. Ol' Lope is callin' starboard ahead, port back, and Squid is on the horn from the engine room tryin' to find out fut the wuck's goin' on, Monte Carlo is squawkin' at us on the TBS, Rabbit Ross is runnin' around in circles, just like the ship because the starboard screw and steering gear are out...." Booker T. paused to suppress his own sotted giggle, and to revel at the raucous laughter of his drinking buddies,

Moose Odell and Spider Snyder, also known as Jimbo.

Now they could laugh. In the event they were as confused and bewildered as all the rest. The indignity of a 10 day, 500 mile tow through the Sea of Japan to the snug harbor of Sasebo, on the southern Japanese home island of Kyushu, was fresh in their minds, but they were free, young, resilient, and not inclined to brood. The psychic invoice of the tow would be presented shortly by colleagues; officers of their sister ship *Parks*, still basking in the glow of the glorious tow. Bad enough to be towed by a tug, humiliating to be at the mercy of a rival. The *Agerholm* now lay in a floating drydock undergoing emergency repairs here in Sasebo harbor. The officers and men had time on their hands.

Booker T. stood in his bare feet, a half empty bottle of Asahi beer in his hand, looking foolish in a black silk kimono that reached only to his knees. Moose and Spider were sitting cross-legged on thin bamboo mats in the company of three winsome young Japanese ladies who were laughing and giggling along with the men though they had only the vaguest notion why. It was Mother McCree's Shamrock Teahouse, a 10 minute taxi ride from the quay. Halfway up the looming promontory protecting the harbor from the open sea, and strategically placed to afford a stunning view of Sasebo harbor, almost as good as the fragrant harbor of Hong Kong.

Of all the mamasans, in all the teahouses, in all the ports-of-call of the still flattened, but rapidly recovering Japan of 1952, Mother McCree, her soft black hair streaked with silver dye, was the clear choice of the easy-come-easy-go tin can sailors of the United States seventh fleet who happily handed her a month's pay, and a sack full of soap for a few days frolic at the Shamrock. Mother McCree had learned English from a chief boatswain's mate named O'Roark soon after the war, and her Irish brogue only added to her natural charm. She was partial to destroyer men, and boatswain's mates in particular, though she tolerated officers. She would not allow carrier, cruiser, or battleship sailors into her house. For one thing she found them arrogant and disrespectful, for another, she had seen too many fights between them and her beloved destroyer men. She often said, "Sure and the *real* men are ridin' the cans." She was tough, but sentimental. Once when she threatened to call the shore patrol to keep some carrier sailors out, one of them said, "Fuck you anyway, Mamasan." She replied, "Sure and yer ass is flied lice if you try it, boobsan."

Group singing was part of the nightly agenda at the Shamrock, the more Irish songs the better. All the girls had Irish names. Even now, Moose Odell, in a fine Irish tenor, was beginning to serenade his lovely lady of the evening who lowered her eyes and blushed in embarrassment.

"*I'll take you home again, Kathleen,*" he sang. Moose was the only one who knew the words, but the others, including the ladies, hummed along and joined in where they could. When it ended, with a few damp eyes, Spider Snyder jumped to his feet, and said loudly, "Spider's gonna walk." Spider, like his buddies, clad only in a silk kimono, cast all modesty aside, and began to walk around the room on his hands to the great astonishment of the ladies. His face covered with silk, he crooned an off-key and upside down rendition of "When Irish Eyes are Smiling." Mother McCree, entering the room with a tray full of fried rice fixings, put down her tray next to the hibachi pot centered in the circle of the group, pushed Spider over and quickly secured the kimono sash just above his knees. She then stood and said, "Okay, now Spider walk." The room rocked with laughter.

The rice paper door slid open, and a head appeared shouting, "Hey, you guys are havin' too much fun, I'm comin' in." He started through the door with yet another pretty girl in tow who was pulling back, and trying to break away. They recognized an officer from the *Parks* though they didn't know his name. Moose Odell jumped to his feet and started with balled fists toward the intruder. "You guys think you can tow anything you want?" he bellowed.

Belligerence was part of the destroyer man package. Personality changes often began when a man, sensing the power of the ship, first crossed the quarterdeck and became part of it. On liberty with a few ounces of alcohol in his blood, his courage up in the presence of spirited camaraderie, a man might erupt in unpredictable and sometimes violent ways. Mother McCree knew this, and made it the basis for one of her rules: personnel from different ships were not allowed in the same room. She rushed to put herself between the men, trying to head off the confrontation: the walls were thin, and not built to withstand flailing bodies.

Reaching up to place outstretched palms on the chests of both men, each at least a foot taller than her, she said, in a voice of authority, "No fighting in Shamrock, darlin's, you wanna fight, you gotta go."

The *Parks* officer looked through bleary eyes at the tiny mamasan, then at the fogged images of Moose Odell, Dawg McCan, and Spider Snyder who had collapsed in a heap. He shook his head uncertainly, and began to laugh loudly, drunkenly, and derisively. "Well if it ain't the saggy Aggies!" He laughed some more and said, "I suppose you sports will be needin' a tow back to the ship." He laughed loud and long. Moose lunged forward, spun the man around, clamped him in a powerful bear hug, and gave him a bum's rush towards the door. But this man was one step from collapse, and Moose found himself holding a limp rag before he reached the door. Released from the angry grip, the man slumped insensible to the floor. Laughter erupted all around the room, and the festive mood continued as if nothing had happened.

To the tune of "She'll be Comin' Round the Mountain When She Comes," alternate verses sung in Japanese by the ladies, and blurred English by the men, the merriment accelerated. That neither group understood the other's language allowed the ultimate in free expression, the women unaware of the men's lewd lyrics, and the men unaware that the shapes of their eyes, the sizes of their noses, and the amount of their body hair, to say nothing of their perceived zaniness, were being ridiculed, one melodious verse after another. Both groups were consumed in their own private laughter.

On the morning of the third day, exhausted from their labors, they rested. Mother McCree was cheerful, serving hot coffee, and providing steaming water-to-the-neck baths. "Come on darlin's, eight o'clock muster on the poop deck." She cackled at her own joke. Booker T. had never been so pampered. He felt like a king, and marveled at these warm and friendly people he had hated so much those few short years ago. He found himself giving money, just as he had done in Philadelphia, to forlorn and legless veterans sitting with beggar's cups on bridges and street corners; he noted that the stale urine smelled the same. He looked closely at their faces, seeing hopelessness and despair, remembering the malevolence and defiance at Iwo Jima. At one point he thought he recognized Colonel Nishi, but was met with a blank stare and an extended cup when he spoke to the man in English. He was only mildly surprised, standing on a Sasebo street corner, to hear the swirl of bagpipes, thinking it no more improbable to see the Canadian Black Watch marching to an Asian war than it was for Booker T. McCan to be standing on a street corner in Sasebo, Japan. Of greater interest was that no crowds gathered to see the colorful spectacle of tall, red plaid-kilted drummers twirling their sticks, and steely-eyed pipers piping their pipes, followed by rank after rank of grim-faced, lock-step infantry. Japanese eyes turned away.

Booker T. mounted the gangway preparatory to boarding the *Agerholm*. Reaching the top he turned to salute the colors before requesting permission to board the ship. It was a ritual that he had executed hundreds of times before, so many times in fact that the simple gesture had lost much, if not all, of its meaning. But today, on this sunny morning in April, returning from two days of unrestrained liberty at the Shamrock Teahouse, Booker T. stood facing the colors snapping in the wind on the fantail of his ship, thinking of Mother McCree and her doll collection. Was there any connection between Old Glory, symbol of liberty, and Mother McCree, purveyor of liberty?

"Wake up, Dawg." A loud voice stirred Booker T. from his reverie. "You gonna stand there daydreaming? Or are you comin' aboard?" The officer of the deck, Ensign Alsop, called to him. Booker T. sheepishly completed his salute to the colors and came aboard, avoiding the curious glance of Ensign Alsop. He headed straight for his compartment in the forward part of the ship, and was pleased to find a large pile of mail deposited on his sleeping rack. Sorting through the pile he felt a small thrill when he found a letter from Count. It had been almost seven years since he had heard from his old friend and mentor. He remembered reading Count's letter in that Philadelphia Bank vault. In the letter Count had said he would keep in touch, Booker T. had thought it would be more often than every seven years. He had also wondered more than once if Count was still alive.

April 1, 1952
Dear Booker T.,

Greetings from Tuskegee. Alabama. At long last I have news for you. The School for Presidents is alive and well, and functioning in the land of cotton. If this comes as a surprise to you let me explain. A new beginning is underway in the land of the free and the home of the brave, and I might add, in the heart of Dixie. The dreamer that is the country has awakened at last, urgent with a deep sense of reality, the sense that separate water fountains for white and colored is unworthy of a nation that would call itself great. We can thank two people...first Branch Rickey...if Baseball is integrated could the Country lag behind? Second, Harry Truman...if the Armed Forces are integrated can even the most rabid segregationist fail to take notice?

There is a lesson here, Booker T., and it is this...in a country of more than a hundred million people, a single person can make a difference...a single person can lead the way. Prepare yourself Booker T., your destiny is to lead the country into the 21st century. Your parents have told me of your accomplishments at the University of Illinois and of becoming an officer in the United States Navy. Congratulations, I am proud of you.

I will be in touch.
Friendly,
Count
P.S. Your friend Flapper Jackson sends greetings. He is a Professor of Philosophy in the School for Presidents.

Booker T. sat quietly on the edge of his bunk, holding Count's letter in his hand, and staring at the floor. Flapper was alive? He pinched himself to be sure *he* was alive. At length he stood up and stretched his muscles. He climbed the ladder to the main deck, and walked to the fo'c'stle where he stood for a long time in the eyes of the ship, looking out at the busy Sasebo harbor, a stiff Japanese breeze blowing in his face. The news was stunning and Booker T. would like to share it with someone, but how could he? He was close to his officer shipmates to be sure, especially Moose and Spider, but close enough to talk about this? He needed Flapper. Seven years...

The agony returned. The vision of Flapper, water creeping over his chin, flooded his mind. "There's still hope...There's still hope..."

O hear us as we cry to thee for those in peril on the sea.

>> 37 <<

TEMPEST AND STORM

Arrowneter Grant was tired, but she was not ready to give up. She was working two jobs to support her three children and her middle-aged mother. She lived in the Washington public housing project on the northeast side of Auburn, and she rode the bus to the Lee County Hospital 10 miles away in Opelika where she had the high-sounding title of Nurse's Aid. What it meant was she cleaned the bedpans, mopped up the blood after birth and death, and in general handled all the dirty work that the white nurses viewed with aversion. But she did not complain; it would never occur to Arrowneter Grant to complain. Whatever she was asked to do could not be worse than the alternative of being without work and on the public dole as some of her friends in the Washington project were. A hospital job put her on a higher level of achievement than the most commonly held job of maid to the white folks in town—she would endure any tribulation to hold the job.

Susan liked her from the start; something about her shy, disarming smile, and the way she moved. She emanated a quiet dignity, almost a nobility, that Susan found strangely enchanting; in an earlier life she might have been an Ashanti Queen Mother. She was large and hefty, but curiously graceful and surprisingly agile. Though in her mid-20s she retained the facial contours of a young teenager. The white nurses, though highly appreciative of her skills and reliability, viewed her with some confusion because, for reasons beyond their comprehension, they always felt vaguely patronized by her.

Arrowneter was also attracted to Susan. She had never seen a lady doctor before, and was emboldened one day to approach Susan in a hospital corridor with a question that had been gnawing at her for a long time.

"Excuse me, ma'am." Susan heard the soft, insistent voice from behind and turned to face Arrowneter, lumpy in a blue hospital scrub suit.

Susan saw uncertainty and fear in Arrowneter's eyes, but noted that her chin was tilted up. “Can I help you?” she asked.

“I been told, ma’am, that you is a doctor,” Arrowneter said softly.

Susan smiled. “Yes,” she answered, “I am a doctor. Is there something I can do for you?”

Arrowneter lowered her eyes. “It’s my boy, Jamie,” she said, “…he got the spells.”

Susan was not sure she heard correctly. “You have a sick boy?” she asked.

“Yes, ma’am, Jamie got the spells. Can you help him?”

“I don’t know,” Susan answered. “I don’t know what you mean by spells. What seems to be the matter with him?”

“He falls down and shakes, and sometimes he turn blue. Preacher say the Devil is in him, but Jamie’s only four years old and he’s a sweet boy. They ain’t no Devil in him.”

“How long has he been doing this?” Susan asked.

“Started a couple of months ago. It got me awful worried, ma’am…ah don’t know what to do. Can you help?”

“Have you taken him to see a doctor?”

“No, ma’am.”

“It sure *sounds* like epilepsy,” Flapper said after Susan related her experience with Arrowneter, and asked his opinion of her preliminary diagnosis. They were driving from the hospital back to their small apartment in Auburn. Susan was in the driver’s seat.

“What are you going to do?” he asked.

“She asked for my help, Flapper. She’s desperate. I want to help her. I need to examine that boy.”

Flapper was puzzled. “Why didn’t she take him to a doctor?” he asked

“I think she was afraid,” answered Susan. “Also I don’t think she trusts doctors, especially white doctors…I think it took some courage for her to approach me.”

Flapper mused. “Epilepsy…The sacred disease. Does she believe it’s a punishment from God?”

Susan shook her head. “I don’t think so,” she said. “Her preacher told her the Devil was in the child, but she rejected that idea. She said he’s a sweet, four-year-old boy.”

“Any family history of the disease?” asked Flapper

“I don’t know…listen, Flapper, why don’t we go see him right now?”

Flapper was agreeable. “You’re the driver,” he said, “do you know how to get there?"

"She gave me directions…it's on the north side of town, close to the high school."

Flapper said, "J-four says they have a pretty good school system for Negroes here in Auburn, all things considered. Of course they don't get as much money as the White schools, but according to J-four they do a good job with what they have."

Flapper was speaking as they crossed to the other side of the railroad tracks. Rays from the late afternoon sun slanted through scattered loblolly pine trees. The air was heavy with warm, clinging humidity, and behind them, unnoticed in the southeast, a line of thunderclouds was moving quickly in their direction.

Flapper pointed to a building they were passing. "There's the elementary school," he said. "J-four comes here twice a week to help in the adult education classes. They're teaching people to read and write. What would you say if I told you I'm thinking about joining him?" He looked at Susan and noticed an odd expression on her face. "Are you okay?" he asked.

She smiled. "I just got a boot from Dixie Sue; he might grow up to be a football player."

Flapper said, "Maybe you should let me drive."

"No, I'm okay," said Susan. "We're almost there…see those buildings?" She pointed to a group of buildings.

The Washington housing project, built by WPA labor in 1936, was a series of four, two-story brick buildings arranged in a square around a central courtyard where children were playing as Susan, small black medical bag in hand, and Flapper, looked for Arrowneter's door. Approaching the door, they became aware that the sky had darkened, and that a brisk, hot wind had picked up. Arrowneter's apartment, like all the others, consisted of a small living room, two bedrooms, a kitchen, and a bathroom. Arrowneter considered herself lucky to have a corner apartment on the first floor although sometimes her upstairs neighbors were too noisy. Even though it was crowded with the three children and her mother, Arrowneter was proud of her neatly kept apartment, and happily welcomed Susan and Flapper.

"Welcome to mah home, Dr. Susan and…" Arrowneter looked at Flapper and then back at Susan.

Susan said, "This is my husband, he is also a doctor. His name is Flapper."

Arrowneter again looked at Flapper, "Dr. Flapper?" she said. "Ah'm so glad to see you…welcome to mah home." She looked out the door, and noting dark rapidly moving clouds, said, "Umm umm, look like they fixin' to be a storm." She stepped outside and called to her two daughters, eight and six years old, to come inside, then turned back to Susan and Flapper. "Now yawl come on in and sit down, let me git you some ice tea or maybe yawl would like some lemonade?" She looked at Susan. "My oh my, Dr. Susan," she said, "it do look like that baby is fixin' to come on out just about anytime soon." Arrowneter introduced her mother, then went to one of the bedrooms to get her son.

Flapper and Susan were sitting on a soft sofa when Susan stood up suddenly. "Flapper," she said, "my water just broke."

Flapper jumped up in alarm. "Are you sure?" he exclaimed. "It's too soon, isn't it?"

Susan felt water running down her leg, and looked at Flapper in confusion and anxiety. Flapper, too, was confused. The doctors Jackson were caught entirely off-guard, and stood looking at each other, waiting for the other to do something when Arrowneter returned.

Arrowneter saw the startled looks of Susan and Flapper. She did not need to be told what was happening. She calmly led Susan to a straight-backed chair. "Now you sit right down here, honey," she said, "and don't you worry...everything goin' to be just fine."

Flapper started for the door. "We have to get her to the hospital," he said.

But there would be no hospital today. When Flapper opened the door he was hit by a torrent of water and a howling wind, the leading edge of a destructive storm system spawning numerous funnel clouds packing whirlwinds exceeding 150 miles per hour, and shattering everything in their path. Flapper got the door closed as a bolt of lightning illuminated the courtyard. A quickly following crash of thunder told him how close the storm was. He turned to face a room gone dark as all electric power to the area was lost in the advance of the violent weather. Flapper had faced darkness and deafening noise before, but in the presence of death not birth.

Arrowneter was cool. In her young life she, too, had faced adversity, and delivering a baby in the Washington housing project held no fears for her; she had done it before, but not in a howling storm without electricity. She quickly took charge, and began to issue directives with the sureness of a master sergeant. Her mother was dispatched to a bedroom with the children and orders to tell them it was all a game. Power outages were nothing new here; she was prepared with a supply of candles.

Arrowneter led Susan into the other bedroom and said, "The first thing is we got to get you an enema." Holding a lighted candle, she rummaged in the closet, and found what she was looking for: a hot water bottle with a long rubber tube attached. She handed it to Flapper and said, "Fill this with warm water in the kitchen, and see if you can get some water boiling, we need to sterilize some towels…thank the Lord we got a gas stove."

Three hours later, by flickering candle light with the storm still raging, Nurse's Aid Arrowneter Grant, with Dr. Flapper Jackson's jittery help, delivered Susan and Flapper's first child, a squirming and squalling baby girl they named Tempest. Thirty minutes after that she delivered Susan and Flapper's second child, a squirming and squalling baby boy they named Storm.

Ten days later, Susan's mother stepped off the train at the Opelika station, and was met by Flapper who greeted her with a big smile and a sigh of relief. "Welcome to Alabama, Mother Land, am I ever glad to see you."

"You look tired, Flapper, have you been getting enough sleep lately?" She laughed.

Flapper slumped and said, "I haven't slept for a week, does it show?" He picked up her suitcase and began walking to the parking lot.

"How is Susan holding up?" Mother Land asked.

Flapper smiled. "Susan is Susan," he said, "solid as a rock just like always. You have a remarkable daughter, Mother Land."

"And now two remarkable grandchildren…born in Alabama. I can't wait to see them. Are they okay?"

"In my doctor's opinion, all bodily functions are normal…when you tickle their feet their toes curl; they sleep, they fill up at their mother's milk stations, they burp, they eliminate. They wail, they gurgle, they smile a little; they look out at the world with great curiosity; they are tiny, soft, and cuddly; their fingers and toes are so small and perfectly formed it is truly miraculous. When their tiny hands grasp my fingers, one on the left, one on the right, it sends a thrill from my toes to the top of my head which feels a few feet higher than it really is…it is like they are saying, 'Help me Daddy'. In short, they are beautiful and precious, and quite wonderful."

Mother Land beamed. "I see," she said. "Well it's too bad you don't like them." She held Flapper's arm and gave it a little squeeze. Approaching the car, Mother Land said, "It seems awfully warm, is it always like this in March?"

Flapper said, "You're used to the cold, this is not too bad…in summer it's an oven. But spring comes early here in the land of cotton…did you notice the hyacinth, daffodils and azalea? The dogwood blossoms are about finished but they were beautiful."

"We were just getting crocuses when I left. It's been a long cold winter." Mother Land paused, she had something on her mind. "Flapper," she said, "this is probably a dumb question, but do they have a Catholic church here? We have to think about the baptism."

Still struggling with his personal theology, and with everything else that was happening, baptism had never crossed Flapper's mind. Not only had Susan never mentioned baptism, but as far as he knew, in the almost seven years they had been married, except for the marriage ceremony itself, and Arthur Compton's exegesis on the moral meaning of the atomic bomb, neither of them had ever been inside a church of any kind. He was embarrassed to say he did not know if Auburn, Opelika, or Tuskegee had a Catholic church.

But of course they did, and the following Sunday at Saint Paul's Catholic Church in Auburn, Alabama, Tempest and Storm Jackson, two weeks old, received the gift of the Holy Spirit, and were relieved of both original and actual sin, thus paving their way for entrance into the Kingdom of God. Mother Land was pleased, and Susan was happy that her mother was pleased. Flapper was introspective as usual, his philosopher's mind ruminating on the concept of actual sin perpetrated by a two-week-old child.

>>38<<

EXECUTE TO FOLLOW

Lieutenant Junior Grade Booker T. McCan felt his shoulders tighten as the racing destroyer accelerated to an exorbitant thirty-two knots. The deck plates beneath his feet began to vibrate in a most alarming manner; the comfortable hum of the hurrying ship shifted to a high-pitched whine approaching a muffled roar. Hunched over a glowing radar screen in the smoky, and tightly arranged Combat Information Center of the *Agerholm*, the butt of a dying cigar clamped between the back molars in the right corner of his mouth, he stole a glance at Chief Muldoon standing to his right. The chief electronics technician, a commanding six feet three inches tall with a lavish black beard and eyes to match, was muttering dark epithets under his breath. Booker T. noted that it was the first time he had ever seen the chief with his tie loosened.

The oversized, clear Plexiglas operational board, lighted from behind, and spread across the entire front of the small, equipment-stuffed room, told the story: *Agerholm*, in position two of a five destroyer column headed due north, aimed toward the top of the board; ahead at 10,000 yards, and rapidly closing, two aircraft carriers, a heavy cruiser, and their eight-destroyer screen. Two men wearing headphones, and holding tattered cloth rags in one hand and grease pencils in the other, were trying to accurately display the rapidly changing formations based on range and bearing information coming to them from the men at the radar screens. One of the men was writing with his left hand, the other with his right; Booker T. made a mental note to suggest the two exchange positions for greater efficiency in the future, if there was to be future. The future seemed very much in doubt as he assessed the present situation. It was a high-speed night torpedo attack, a desperate gambit in war, an outrageous risk in peace. It was like five Mac trucks racing bumper-to-bumper at 90 miles per hour executing quick synchronized turns triggered by hand signals; it was a training exercise.

Officer of the Deck Lope Cooley straddled the combing separating the wheelhouse from the port wing of the bridge, squinting into the wind and salt spray trying to make out the foaming wake trailing the fantail of the *Parks*, only 500 yards away, traveling at 32 knots; a distance the ship could cover in 25 seconds. The drill called for darkened ship, and on a cloudy night it meant that the world for Lope Cooley had shrunk to the dimensions of the soft glow over the helmsman's wheel, and the bubbling fluorescence of the churning water, only seconds ahead of him.

Cooley understood that 300 shipmates' lives were in his hands at this moment, and that the time to execute a 30-degree starboard turn to unmask the torpedo batteries was imminent. He marveled at the audacity of the tactical scheme—five speeding destroyers in a tight line each firing five torpedoes at an approaching "enemy" formation meant that were this an actual combat situation, as the torpedo spreads fanned out, more than two miles of ocean would be blanketed with 25 underwater missiles that should reach their targets in less than a minute. Captain Jack S. Ross, standing near Cooley, pulled the foul weather jacket collar up around his ears, and pondered yet again the grim fate that had handed him command of a Seventh Fleet destroyer under a squadron commander who never tired of playing with his ships as if they were toys under a Christmas tree. Cooley saw the plan as audacious; Ross knew it was reckless.

"Headlight, Headlight, this is Vigil King. Standby to execute…shackle, able charlie dog, unshackle…turn." The voice crackled over the loudspeaker in CIC, and simultaneously in the wheelhouse where Junior Officer of the Deck Ensign Mouse Alsop manned the tactical voice radio circuit.

Booker T. scrambled for the shackle code manual and quickly called out, "It's a starboard turn to zero three five." He handed the manual to Chief Muldoon. Muldoon scanned the page and said, "Confirm. Tell the bridge CIC confirms from Vigil King, standby to execute zero three five turn…that's a turn to starboard." He spoke to the sound-powered telephone man who relayed the message to the bridge.

Tension mounted in the Combat Information Center as they waited for the signal to execute the turn. The six enlisted men and two officers on duty were experienced and confident, but not one of them had ever before faced the challenge of a high-speed night torpedo attack in close formation. What made them squirm was the tight spacing—destroyer men were always uneasy operating at 500 yards distance from a neighboring ship even in bright sunshine and sensible speed. In the black night of the present situation where the bridge crew could only hope that the other ships knew what they were doing, the CIC men were in the paradoxical position of being the "eyes of the ship" with their glimmering radar scopes, but blind to anything more than the confining dimensions of the close-packed room they hoped would not become a coffin. Heavy on their minds was the too recent incident, also in a training drill, where a destroyer had failed to turn at a prearranged time, and been run down and sliced in two by a heavy cruiser. The hard-driving admirals and squadron commodores, in the name of combat readiness, never forgetting the disaster at Savo Island during the World War II battle of Guadalcanal, did not hesitate to put their men in the most hazardous situations they could conjure up. Booker T., jittery now like all the others, mused if such grand strategy might have applications for him when he became president.

The radio crackled again, "Headlight, this is Vigil King…execute to follow…turn…shackle, able charlie dog, unshackle."

In the brief pause Chief Muldoon shouted, "HE'S CHANGED THE SIGNAL TO A PORT TURN!"

"Standby…execute"

"Right standard rudder," Lope Cooley called out to the helmsman.

"Right standard rudder, aye aye, sir…rudder is right standard, passing zero one zero, sir."

"Very well. Steady on course zero three five."

"Steady on course zero three five, aye aye, sir…passing zero two zero."

"Alert torpedo batteries. We are approaching firing course zero three five." Cooley spoke calmly to the sound-powered telephone man standing at his elbow.

Captain Ross was shouting into Cooley's ear. "I heard turn zero three five, not zero three five turn, why did you come right?"

Cooley was calm. "The original standby was for a turn to the right…we would have to come around 265 degrees left to reach zero three five. I figured the final signal was a mistake."

Cooley was correct, but not all the ships saw it that way…two turned left, two turned right, and one, in total confusion, continued on course and did not turn at all. CIC was in turmoil trying to figure out what happened with ships on the radarscopes heading in all directions like the vectors in a Roman candle.

In the inky blackness surrounding the bridge, Cooley and the captain were not immediately aware that anything had gone wrong. The 35 degree turn changed the formation from a column to a line so the foaming wake of the *Parks*, carrying the flag of Commodore Benjamin Katz, a.k.a. Vigil King, the only other ship to execute the right turn, was now coming from 35 degrees off the port bow instead of dead ahead. Cooley was grateful for the reduced burden; it was no longer a concern that slight differences in speed could put his ship in contact with ships fore and aft in the column. He prepared to signal the torpedo batteries.

On the flagship bridge the commodore was fuming. His formation was in disarray because a single word had been placed before, rather than after, the designated three number heading. The drill had revealed a weak, and potentially fatal flaw in the audacious, not to say reckless, plans. A further weakness was the commodore himself. The muddled circumstances called for a composed leader to restore order; the commodore succumbed to uncontrolled rage. He was consumed by thoughts of who he could hang for the offense, knowing that Admiral Pride, task group commander in the cruiser *Helena*, was likely at this moment making black marks in his book on the performance of Destroyer Squadron One, and considering changing the squadron call sign from Headlight to Taillight and Katz's personal call from Vigil King to Trance Queen. He was rescued for the moment by his chief of staff, the in-fact Vigil King, who called a halt to the exercise by ordering all ships to turn on their running lights, reduce speed to a sensible twelve knots, and prepare to form a column with 1,000 yard distance, *Parks* in the van.

Forty minutes later normal watch sections were restored, and officers and men, coming off the general quarters ordeal, began to unwind. Nobody stopped to tabulate how many thousand barrels of fuel oil were expended over the East China Sea in this fruitless exercise, but neither was there ever any question that the U.S. was prepared to go to war wherever the need arose to guard its access to the world's oil pools needed to supply the fuel for the exercise.

Cruising the East China Sea, Lt.(j.g.) B.T. McCan had more than high-speed night torpedo attacks on his mind; he had homework. He was being supplied with a steady stream of notes, essays, and assignments from the School for Presidents, the most recent dealing with diplomacy. He sat at the gently rolling wardroom table examining the assignment sheet, and organizing a response in his head before putting anything on paper. To his embarrassment the word had gotten out amongst the officers about his ambition to become president of the United States; it was not possible to have any secrets on a small closely knit ship such as a destroyer. At first he denied it, but when mail continued to arrive with the neatly etched return address "School for Presidents," he decided to plead guilty, and invited his fellow officers to contribute their ideas on how best to run the country from the Oval Office. In the beginning what he got were sly and dry comments along with a full complement of not always friendly sarcasm, but as time went on he was surprised to find some of his friends offering serious and sometimes reasonable ideas. More than once on long, eventless night bridge watches Booker T., now a fully qualified underway watch officer, found himself in deep discussions with his Junior Officer of the Deck Ensign Mouse Alsop. Ensign Alsop once offered the observation that it was no more unjust that there had never been a Negro president than that there had never been a president from the great state of Texas, his home.

"What you up to, Dawg? Another note from the White House?" Moose Odell pulled up a chair at the wardroom table and sat down with a cup of bad coffee, and a two-month-old copy of *TIME*.

"It's an exercise in diplomacy, Moose, this job may not be as easy as it looks."

Moose put down his magazine. "You want to tell me about it?"

Booker T. looked at him to be sure he was serious. Moose Odell was from California, and after almost two years of shared experiences on and off the ship, had developed into one of Booker T.'s most valued friends, in no small part because he always showed a sincere and genuine interest in Booker T. and his improbable goals.

Booker T. shrugged. "You want to be my Secretary of State?" he asked.

"Sure, I got nothing better to do," said Moose. "What's the problem?"

Booker T. picked up his assignment sheet, glanced over it again, then looked at his friend Moose, thinking of how to summarize what was documented on the single-spaced, fully-covered sheet of paper, into a brief and informative statement of the problem. "Okay," he said, "In a nutshell here it is...should the atomic bomb be used as a diplomatic tool?"

Moose looked surprised. He sat nodding his head in a short up and down rocking motion as if he was in agreement with himself on what he was thinking. He uttered a muffled "hmm" to let Booker T. know he was considering an answer, knowing that whatever he said the Dawg would have a rebuttal.

Booker T., the *Agerholm* Dawg, sat watching his friend Moose ponder the question, and decided to elaborate with some background information. "It's a drill, Moose, an exercise...just like this damn high-speed night torpedo attack. I'm supposed to pretend I'm vice president of a country at war, and the president dies suddenly, so in an instant and without any warning I become president and commander-in-chief. The first thing I learn before the dead president is even buried is that scientists in our country are developing a bomb so powerful it can destroy an entire city, and maybe more...if I'm president what do I do with this weapon? I guess we don't need to pretend we don't know that this is what Truman faced when Roosevelt died in 1945. The School for Presidents is asking what I would do if I became president under those circumstances."

Moose nodded his head and said, "Well, we know what Truman did...he certainly didn't use it as a diplomatic tool...more like a bludgeon, but he saved an awful lot of lives by using it...can you imagine how many people would have died if we had invaded the home islands?"

"That's what everybody thinks," Booker T. reflected, "but I'm getting some information from the School that tells me Japan was ready to surrender anyway, and the A-bombs were only used to scare the Russians. Some diplomacy...kill two hundred thousand civilians to scare the Russians into allowing free elections in Poland, Hungary, and Czechoslovakia, and they just thumb their noses at us anyway; some of our own military leaders are saying it was barbaric."

"Maybe we should just go ahead and drop the bomb on Russia," Moose offered. "Get it over with once and for all...I don't think they even have a navy...we're stronger than they are, why do we have to sit around and listen to all their shit?"

Booker T. looked at his friend Moose Odell, and thought of Bus Taylor the neighborhood bully from so many years ago on the streets of south Peoria. "You know something, Moose?" he said, "That is exactly the problem...do we use the threat of the bomb to get them to do what we want or does the threat have the exact opposite result that we want...does it force them into building a bigger bomb? If a bully threatens to beat your brains out, what do you do?"

Moose looked at Booker T. with a curious expression on his face. "Are you telling me the U.S. is a bully?"

Booker T. had the sinking feeling that it was exactly what he was telling Moose. "We might not think so," he said, "but what do you suppose the Russians think? It turns out that some of our highest officials in the State Department, and in the War Department...even Secretary of War Stimson...after the war ended, said we should share our secrets with the

Russians to build trust, and avoid a nuclear arms race that could destroy the world."

Moose sniffed. "I guess that's why Senator McCarthy is holding hearings…those guys were probably communists."

Booker T. said, "I wonder…Tell me something, Moose…what do you think is the number one threat to freedom and democracy in the second half of the twentieth century?"

Moose drained the remains of his coffee and grimaced. "Whoo, man," he said, "that stuff is bitter." He looked at Booker T. "Come on, Dawg," he said, "what kind of a question is that? Ain't that why we're out here practicing night torpedo runs? It's the damn communists…what else?"

Booker T. stared vacantly at the starboard porthole. "Maybe it's the damn bomb," he said.

>>39<<

ANDREIA

ANDREIA (Greek): manly courage

A full page announcement in the *Tuskegee News* was the opening salvo. The same advertisement also appeared in the *Lee County Bulletin* published in Auburn, the *Montgomery Advertiser*, the *Alabama Journal,* and the *Birmingham News.*

TUSKEGEE INSTITUTE
SCHOOL FOR PRESIDENTS
PRESENTS THE FIRST IN A SERIES OF PUBLIC FORUMS

ON MANLY COURAGE
A Greek Dialogue

WHERE — CARNEGIE HALL, TUSKEGEE INSTITUTE CAMPUS
WHEN — SATURDAY, SEPTEMBER 10, 1952 8 P.M.

PUBLIC INVITED

Virgil Young was confused. He didn't know whether to be amused or to be pissed off. The idea that manly courage could in any way be connected with Tuskegee Institute made him laugh. The idea that anyone associated with Tuskegee Institute would have the nerve to talk about manly courage in public pissed him off; he took it as a personal affront. Virgil felt good when he was angry, it didn't suit him to be amused; he even felt vaguely uncomfortable laughing at nigger jokes, so it didn't take long to resolve his confusion—he would be pissed off. It was just another example of the niggers getting out of place again. He still didn't know why they had ever allowed a place like Tuskegee Institute to exist; it was just asking for trouble to educate niggers. In fact, Virgil was not convinced that higher education was good for anybody. He didn't need it for his business and he was doing all right, wasn't he? One good thing about Auburn he had to admit though was the football games. Sometimes he even wished they could get a good nigger halfback in to play against Georgia or Georgia Tech.

Virgil ran a construction business in Tallasee, and business was good—the Folsom administration had proved easy pickings for a little under-the-table encouragement in awarding state contracts, and Virgil had all the right connections for getting his share of the rivers of money flowing from post-war Washington. It seemed like they couldn't wait to build four-lane highways all over the South. Virgil rubbed his hands thinking of those beautiful highways. If it weren't for the Feds pushing for equal rights for niggers he might even be a happy man, although he doubted it. It gave him some feeling of satisfaction to know he that could always find something to make him mad. He was happy to be angry.

The telephone rang. Virgil picked it up on the fifth ring; he liked to keep people waiting. "Yeah?"

"Virgil, did you see that big ad in the *News* about a public forum on courage at Tuskegee?" It was Joe Bob Jones.

"Yeah, I seen it...what about it, Joe Bob?"

"Is them niggahs startin' a School for Presidents? What the hell they talkin' 'bout, Virgil?"

"Ah seen that, Joe Bob," said Virgil, " and you know what? I think them niggers is done lost they cotton pickin' minds, but I'll tell you what else, Joe Bob...why don't you just see what y'all can find out about it. Call Stanley Gordon over there at Auburn; ah reckon he might could find out somethin' if he don't know somethin' already. Ah'd think it was kinda funny if it wan't so goddamn pathetic. Them damn niggahs thinking' they know somethin' about manly courage? We might just fire up a little surprise for 'em...see how brave they is."

Joe Bob guffawed. "That's purty good, Virgil," he said, "...fire up a surprise...Hee hee haw."

Dean Gomillion introduced the program. The large auditorium, with 12-foot high windows on both sides, was not completely filled, but more than 100 curious students, faculty, and visitors were in attendance, attracted by the title, and by rumors spread around the campus that something special was going to happen here tonight. The audience was racially mixed. Susan and Becky were there, as was Achilles Demimelius and a friend from the Auburn Chemistry faculty he had dragged along; Demimelius eager for anything Greek. Dion McKeen, head of the API Department of Philosophy had made the trip with three of his students.

Dean Gomillion walked onto the stage dressed as a citizen of Athens might have appeared in 450 B.C. wearing sandals, and what looked to a 20th century audience like a white bed sheet slung over one shoulder leaving the other shoulder bare. He looked out at the assemblage with some satisfaction—it gave him a warm feeling to see the young faces, eager to learn. He was also pleased to see the number of older faculty, many with their wives; it reminded him that true academics never tired of learning, indeed had dedicated their lives to learning. He would begin by giving a short history of Plato's Greece.

"Ladies and gentlemen," he began, "welcome to the first of what I hope will be many evenings of enjoyment and learning as we begin the new academic year with an exciting new program presented by the Tuskegee Institute School for Presidents. If you haven't heard of the School for Presidents it is because the School is new to Tuskegee, and no formal announcements about it have been made. Be assured you will hear more about the Tuskegee School for Presidents. But for now let me just tell you that the aim of the School is neatly summarized in a quotation from Plato that has been taken as the school motto...you will see it written on your programs."

Gomillion read the motto aloud, *"Until philosophers are kings or kings philosophers, States will never have rest from their evils."*

Gomillion looked around the room at the assembled group, taking satisfaction in their smiling nods and whispered asides. "So you see," he continued, "it is entirely appropriate that we introduce the School for Presidents with a dialogue from ancient Greece...I ask you now to imagine that you are a citizen of Athens four hundred and fifty years before the birth of Jesus Christ."

Without warning the doors at the back of the auditorium burst open, and twenty ghostly figures in white satin robes wearing conical head-pieces and white full-face masks with dark eye holes marched silently into the room taking up positions along the sides and back of the auditorium. They stood with arms folded across their chests peering out at the startled and wide-eyed assemblage. Outside and clearly visible through the windows on both sides of the building, 10-foot high flaming crosses burned.

Dean Gomillion hesitated only for a moment, and continued his introduction even as the robed and hooded figures were taking their places.

"...Before the birth of Jesus Christ..." he repeated. "...Jesus Christ! . . ." he said, as he saw the giant crosses flame up outside the building.

"Ladies and gentlemen," he paused, "...and late arriving guests." He paused again. "...The topic of tonight's dialogue is manly courage." He looked purposely from side to side at the mute and portentous figures standing near the windows. He waited as murmurs went though the audience.

" In ancient Greece," Gomillion continued, "we know that manly courage was important, as it has been throughout history, and as it is today. We also know that many if not most of the ideas that form the very foundation of Western civilization originated in ancient Greece." He held up a cautionary finger. "But lest we overly romanticize these Greeks, let us take note that Socrates, greatest of the Greek philosophers, were he alive today, would be the first to point out that not all the ideas of ancient Greece were felicitous...they did, after all, invent war and slavery. But let us talk of Plato. In 386 B.C. just thirteen years after the untimely death of his great teacher, Socrates, a man called Plato set up a school of philosophy in an olive grove on the outskirts of Athens at a place called Academy. The importance and influence of that school may be appreciated by noting that now, more than two thousand years later, those engaged in teaching all over the Western world are called academics."

Gomillion, in spite of the ominous presence of the white-robed intruders lining the walls of the auditorium, was enjoying himself. "And so fellow academicians, ladies and gentlemen," he said, "I come at last to the introduction of tonight's program...a dialogue on manly courage as documented by Plato from recollections of his days as a young man listening to the conversations of his mentor, Socrates. Granted that it was important in ancient Greece as it is today, the question posed by Socrates and examined here tonight is...what do we mean when we speak of manly courage?

"Once again, I ask you to imagine that you are a citizen of Athens four hundred and fifty years before the birth of Christ...It is a warm summer day in Athens, Socrates is sitting under the olive trees surrounded by his students...but today is a special day, they have visitors. A middle-aged man worried about the education of his son, and two generals...highly esteemed heroes of the wars between the Greek city-states of Athens and Sparta. One, call him Laches, is now head of the army...he has a firmly held view of what courage is. The other, Nicias, has become the democratically elected president of Athens…he, too, has a strong opinion about what courage is, but it is not the same as that of Laches. Socrates will listen to both men, then lead a discussion directed toward reaching a consensus."

Gomillion paused to make a point about Socrates before continuing. "You should know this about Socrates," he said, "with apologies to those present…you know who you are…Socrates was not a weak-kneed, flabby academic…before he retired to become a stonemason and philosopher he was a rock-hard Greek warrior, famed for his strength, physical endurance, and bravery in the most demanding kind of combat ever invented…the hoplomachia…the skill of fighting in heavy armor. Our word macho comes from the Greek machia, meaning to fight. If Socrates spoke of courage, his listeners, not least the generals, knew he was not unfamiliar with the topic."

Virgil Young, invisible in his Klan robes, to his great surprise, found himself interested in what the nigger was saying. Things were not working out as he had planned, though in truth he had not planned much further than appearing here to scare the hell out of some ignorant niggers. But these people did not seem in the least afraid of him and his men, it was almost as if indeed they were invisible. He was amazed and shocked to see that whites and niggers were sitting together in the audience, and he was disgusted to see some white women sitting next to nigger men. And now he was even more amazed to see two white men in military uniform, including an impressive array of medals pinned to the jackets of both, walking down the center aisle toward the stage followed by a tall, slim, half-dressed nigger in another bed sheet.

Dean Gomillion moved forward to greet the men walking down the aisle, and as they mounted the steps to the stage he assumed the role of an Athenian citizen and initiated the dialogue. "Greetings General Laches and President Nicias," he said, "I am very much in your debt for coming here today. It is more than kind of you to honor the request of a humble citizen that seeks nothing more than the welfare of his son, for where but from you could I find the type of advice needed to make the most important decision of my son's life…should he be trained in the hoplomachia?"

Flapper, in his dress khakis with lieutenant's shoulder boards and peaked cap adorned with the eagle and crossed anchors of the United States Navy Officer Corps, was taking the part of President Nicias. He was the first to speak. "Greetings to you as well, citizen Lysimachus," he said, "it is a pleasure for me to be here. I will waste no time in providing an answer to your question whether your son should study the hoplomachia. I answer most assuredly, yes; my reasons are several. Can anyone doubt that the hoplomachia is useful when ranks are formed in that most artistic, and at the same time dire disposition, the phalanx? And is it not true that the hoplomachia is even more useful when ranks are broken? Beyond its proven value in the field, the study of this manly art can only enhance the general interest in military studies, of which I venture no one would disagree is only to the good. Verily, these studies are nothing less than the gymnastics of war, and should in all cases be included in the curriculum of youth."

Flapper turned with a flourish and a sweeping bow, hat in hand, toward J-four taking the part of General Laches. "I would now be pleased," he said, "to hear the opinion of the admirable General Laches as to the question you have posed."

J-four, as General Laches, looking distinguished in U.S. Army dress greens with the golden oak leaves of a major on his shoulders and shirt collar, stepped forward, and in a forceful, painfully-rehearsed, though somehow comically accented voice said emphatically, "Ah speak from mah own experience on this matter, citizen Lysimachus, and ah tell you in the plainest way ah know how that the hoplomachia is useless and ridiculous, it makes the coward rash and headlong, and it subjects the courageous to offensive and invidious remarks out of envy. If we look to the great masters of arms, the Spartans, we find that they totally ignore the hoplomachia because it is neither a science nor an art."

J-four paused to clear his throat and gather his thoughts. "...Now you see, Lysimachus, that President Nicias and I have very different opinions on the question you pose regarding the education of your son, and though ah see the confusion in your eyes let me counsel that before you despair of learning a proper answer to your most worthy question you should know that you, and indeed all of us, are most fortunate that with us today is a man noted for his abilities to tease the truth from the most difficult disputations, and that man is none other than the person you see before you here...the notable and for all ah know, the noble Athenian...Socrates. If we are to find the truth today we can do no better than turn to Socrates to show us the way...is it not so President Nicias?"

Flapper once more removed his cap and affected a sweeping bow. "Let Socrates show us the way," he said.

Virgil Young had heard enough. As Count/Socrates stepped forward on the stage and began to speak, Virgil, trailed by his followers, began a slow walk from his position on the side of the auditorium to the front, where he passed those in the first row, and turned up the center aisle headed for the rear entrance. As the last man reached the door he stopped, placed a plastic bag on the floor and ripped it open with a six-inch switchblade knife to reveal a large, steaming, and very pungent, horse turd. The man then picked up the bag, swung it in an arc, like a man pitching a softball, and to the accompaniment of shouts and screams from the audience, let it fly in a high arc towards the stage where it landed with a sickening splat at the feet of Count/Socrates who stood firm and resolute against the outrage even as fragments of wet horse manure stained his white costume.

The assemblage was in turmoil. As individuals their rage was tempered by a chilling anxiety of what would come next. As a group they were ready to be led on a furious charge against the forces of evil. They looked to the stage where Count stood, flanked by his fellow thespians, holding both hands in the air signaling for quiet.

"What is courage?" he said, in his deep and resonant voice. He repeated above the buzz of voices. "What is courage?" Slowly the audience quieted. For a few moments there was silence in the hall as the audience watched Count standing firm, head high, arms upraised.

"What is courage?" Count/Socrates repeated.

Someone in the audience thought they knew, and began a slow, rhythmic clap that was quickly picked up by the rest who, in a spasm of recognition, were suddenly on their collective feet applauding vigorously and shouting wildly.

Count did not understand at first, then did, but went into immediate denial, shaking his head and trying to quiet the crowd with hand gestures. It only spurred them to increase the volume.

On the lawn outside the hall, Virgil and his men stopped long enough to look through the tall windows and listen to the commotion inside.

"Why is they clappin' and yellin', Virgil?" Joe Bob Jones asked.

"Because that theah skinny niggah done stood his ground when somebody threw some horseshit at him," Virgil answered in disgust.

Stanley Gordon, standing between Virgil and Joe Bob, said, "Ah read that at some battles in the war between the states, the Confederates refused to shoot a Union soldier if he showed special courage…did you know that, Virgil?"

Virgil nodded. "Ah knew that, Stanley," he replied, "but ah also know what Stonewall Jackson said about it; he said, 'Kill the brave first and the cowards will run away'.That niggah is gonna pay."

J-four, who, along with Flapper and Dean Gomillion, had instinctively ducked for cover when they saw the missile headed for the stage, suddenly realized that Count/Socrates was giving him a cue. The show would go on. He moved to stand next to Socrates, and began to speak his lines. He had to repeat them several times before at last the audience was willing to give up the spontaneous outburst, and settle back to listen to the dialogue. Many would later admit that what followed had either disappeared from their memory or had never at any time entered their head.

"Socrates," said Laches/J-four, "ah think ah know the answer to that question. Surely it is not difficult to see that a man of courage is one who does not run away, but remains at his post and fights against the enemy." The audience erupted again, enthusiastically endorsing this definition of courage.

Socrates ducked his head slightly, and a small grimace crossed his face. "Forgive me, good Laches," he said, "for I see that I have asked the question badly which has caused you to answer badly. Let me try again to put the question in a way that will allow us to consider what is the common quality which is called courage that includes all the various uses of the term when applied to both pleasure and pain, fears and desires, disease and poverty, and indeed to politics."

Laches responded easily. "Well then," he said, "if ah am to speak of the universal nature which pervades all the various uses you have mentioned ah should say that courage is a sort of endurance of the soul."

Socrates nodded. "This is well spoken, Laches," he said, "but I must remark that it seems to me that not every kind of endurance should be deemed courage. Let me tell you my reasons. I am sure, worthy Laches, that you would consider courage to be a noble quality."

"Most certainly, Socrates."

"And you would say that a wise endurance is also good and noble?"

"It is true."

"But what would you say of a foolish endurance? Is it not evil and hurtful and is anything noble which is evil and hurtful?"

Before Laches could answer, Flapper/Nicias stepped forward. "Allow me to enter the discussion, Socrates," he said, "for I have been thinking that both you Socrates, and you Laches, are not defining courage in the right way. Courage is the knowledge of that which inspires fear or confidence in war, or in anything. Every man is good in that in which he is wise, and bad in that in which he is unwise, and therefore if the brave man is good, he is also wise."

Socrates responded. "Do you hear him, Laches? He appears to mean that courage is a sort of wisdom. But surely, Nicias, you do not mean to say that courage is the wisdom to play the flute, the lyre, or God forgive us, the tuba?"

Laches interrupted. "Pardon me, Socrates," he said, "but this Nicias, President of Athens, is unaccountably speaking as a silly child for surely courage is one thing and wisdom quite another."

Socrates gave a small hand gesture of caution. "Ah but good Laches, " he said, "is it not better for us to instruct him rather than abuse him?"

Nicias spoke indignantly. "Having been proved to speak nonsense himself, Laches wants to prove I have been doing the same."

Socrates said, "Very true, Nicias, but I am sorry to tell you that you *have* been talking nonsense as I shall endeavor to show. Now let me ask, do you mean to affirm that courage is the knowledge of the grounds of hope and fear?"

"I do," said Nicias.

Socrates continued, "But clearly, justice, temperance and the like are all parts of virtue as well as of courage, and as for fear…fear is not of the present nor of the past, but is of the future and expected evil…"

A thunderous and shocking *CRASH!* accompanied by the sound of tinkling glass brought a sudden end to the performance as a large brick smashed through one of the side windows. The future and expected evil had come unexpectedly soon. Confusion and turmoil gripped the audience as all heads swivelled toward the smashed window, preventing them from noticing that Count/Socrates had been shot.

Count was saved from more serious injury by the poor aim of Virgil Young who was going for the kill. A .38 caliber slug in the leg is not what most people would consider a laughing matter, but that, alternating between teeth grinding pain, was what Count was doing as he sat on the stage watching the red blood stain spread across his white costume and obliterate the brown smudges remaining from the earlier episode.

A shout arose from the churning crowd. "…Socrates has been shot!"

Flapper was already tending the downed Count, ripping strips from Socrates' costume and using them to stop the bleeding. The bullet appeared to have passed cleanly through the left upper thigh.

J-four, though unarmed, quickly reverted to combat mode, running for the exit, intent on finding the would-be assassin. Fortunately for him the robed Klansmen were in their cars and pickup trucks, and on their way out of the parking lot by the time he got through the door. He ran after them a short distance in the forlorn hope he might catch a glimpse of a face in the parking lot lights. Stopping at the curb, he looked around to see if anything had been dropped in their hasty exit. He reached down to pick up a pencil he saw lying in the road. Holding it up to the light he saw writing on it...**API-HIS**.

At the Lee County Hospital, Count was resting easily and still laughing. Gathered around the bed were Susan and Flapper, J-four, and Becky, all concerned about Count's wound of course, but equally if not increasingly worried about his mental state. And yet they had all seen it before, men in combat laughing that their wounds were no more serious than a bullet in an arm or leg. But this was not combat. Or was it?

"Now, Socrates, are you going to tell us what is so funny about getting shot in the leg?" Susan asked.

Count laughed some more. "It's the first time I've been shit at and shot at in the same day," he said and erupted in more laughter, this time joined by the others. "...one of my old army buddies," he continued, "used to wake up every morning and say he felt like he had been shot at and missed, and shit at and hit." Once again, they all laughed together.

"I hope nobody's watchin' this," said J-four, "they'll think we've lost our minds."

Count became serious. "But I'm laughin' at somethin' else here too," he said. "Don't you see?...They have played right into our hands. It couldn't have been better if I had handed them a script. The only way to defeat them is by raising the public outrage against their cowardly, bullying tactics to the level where people will say, 'ENOUGH!' They are doomed by their dim-wittedness. Hoist by their own petard." He chortled. "But listen," he continued, "It's important that we get maximum publicity from this incident, we need the whole country to know what happened last night in Tuskegee. J-four, can you handle that?"

J-four nodded. "Sure, Count," he said, "ah'll write it up and see if ah can get some national magazines interested. Of course the problem is that nobody got killed, it may not be sensational enough for them. There were some local reporters there and some pictures were taken, but as local news goes this is pretty tame...KLAN HARASSES PUBLIC MEETING...so what?"

"So what will you do, J-four?" asked Flapper.

"Ah think ah know how to juice it up, Flapper," said J-four, "just leave it to me."

J-four changed the subject. "But let me show y'all somethin' ah found outside the hall where Count was shot," he said, "somethin' that gives me an idea. Look at this." He held up the pencil he had found in the parking lot after the Klan departure. "Ah have a pretty good idea where this came from, and if ah'm right..." He hesitated. "...Ah think it might help if we knew exactly who it was hiding behind those masks."

"Be careful, J-four," Count said. "They may be stupid, but they are also deadly dangerous, and don't imagine you can look to law enforcement for help here."

J-four nodded understanding to Count. "What would you say if ah joined the local klavern?" he asked.

Flapper asked, "How would that help, J-four?"

"It might help to have somebody inside so we'd know what they're planning," J-four answered.

"You're right about that, J-four," said Count. "But I'm not so sure it ought to be you...they saw you up on that stage, you may already have a price on your head."

> KLAN SPLATTERS, SHOOTS, SOCRATES
> By Jerry Mulhane IV
>
> Tuskegee, Alabama, September 10, 1952...Socrates was shot in the leg last night by the Ku Klux Klan as he led a discussion on Manly Courage at a public forum held on the campus of Tuskegee Institute. The shooting came after 20 robed and masked Klansmen stood silently inside the auditorium menacing the sizable audience while, clearly visible through high windows on both sides of the hall, flaming crosses lighted the night. Prior to the shooting Socrates was splattered with horse manure in a demonstration of Klan courage. The Greek dialogue was the first public presentation of the new School for Presidents recently established at Tuskegee Institute.

Walter White read it in the *Washington Post* while drinking morning coffee in his NAACP office outside Washington, D.C. Bucks Fulton read it in the *New York Times* while waiting for a train in Penn Station across from Madison Square Garden in New York City. Mother Land read it in the *St. Louis Post-Dispatch* while drinking iced-tea on her front porch near a dusty road in

Ware, Missouri. Three months later, following a mail transfer-at-sea in the choppy Sea of Japan from the fleet aircraft carrier *USS Oriskany*, Lieutenant Junior Grade Booker T. McCan read it in *TIME* magazine while sitting in the rolling wardroom of the Geary-class destroyer *USS Agerholm.*

>>40<<

DON'T EVEN SPIT

December 1954. The truce in Korea was holding after 16 months, but the Chinese Communists from the mainland and the Chinese Nationalists, evicted from the mainland in 1949, now operating out of their primary bases on the island of Formosa, and from a string of small islands up and down the China coast, were still hammering at each other with aircraft, ships, and artillery. The world watched nervously, knowing that the nuclear power of the Soviet Union on one side, and the United States of America on the other, loomed behind the Chinese struggle. The young United Nations worked for a solution to the two-China problem that currently excluded nearly a billion people on the Chinese mainland from representation in the world body.

December 1954. The other number one threat to freedom and democracy in the second half of the 20th century was quivering from the judicial hit administered in October by the United States Supreme Court. In a 5-4 vote the court erased "separate but equal" from the land of the free and the home of the brave, and made it against the law to separate school children on the basis of race. Supreme Court Justice Felix Frankfurter said the sudden death of Chief Justice Roy Vinson, who had previously blocked consideration of the issue, was his first convincing evidence for the existence of God.

New Year's Day 1955. Booker T. was learning how to write; Count had sent him a diary.

Saturday, January 1, 1955
1st day — 364 days follow
New Year's Day
At sea in the Formosa Straits aboard the United States Ship Agerholm.

A few notes on the state of the world as we start the spanking new year of 1955. The Korean War has long since been fought to an inconclusion, the Indo China situation has been settled for the moment, so now we find ourselves again involved in the so-called "cold war" between the ominous forces of the Russian and Chinese versions of Communism, and our own system of free enterprise. Red China is trying desperately, though so far unsuccessfully, to be recognized by the United Nations. They have vowed to take the Island of Formosa, and with it the forces of Chiang Kai Chek and his Nationalist Chinese. The president of the United States has stated that the U.S. Seventh Fleet will prevent such an act of aggression. So we find ourselves 12 miles off the coast of China watching for any sign of an invasion attempt by the Red Chinese. What we would do if we detected such an attempt I do not know. Though we are closer to the trouble spot than anybody, I have no doubt that the average citizen back in the States is more informed on the situation than we are. Most of our information comes from newspapers and magazines. I do know that we have orders not to shoot unless fired upon first for fear of touching off World War III.

Sunday, January 2, 1955
2nd day — 363 days follow

Standing into Kaohsiung harbor this morning to fuel from the Cimarron, I was struck by the sound of church music coming from amplifiers on the beach. The plural is used correctly for there were at least three different sources. All in all it made quite a confused racket, but the fact remains that it is Sunday and people are going to church, even in Formosa.

Chinese Nationalist ensigns were in abundant display. I sometimes wonder whether these people are really patriotic or whether they're just putting up a front. The Chinese are a mysterious people, it's hard to tell. Nothing mysterious about the little kids clustering about the ship on little homemade rafts — they're hungry. When I become president I will see to it that they are fed.

Completed fueling and returned to patrol.

Monday, January 3, 1955
3rd day — 362 days follow
The only significance a day has now is that Wednesday we will go into port and stay for a week. A week in port for a tin can sailor is like manna from heaven...anything to escape the interminable, unpredictable movement of the ship.

Tuesday, January 4, 1955
4th day — 361 days to follow
The ship is like a great coiled monster, waiting for an opportunity to reach out and crack you in the shins or smack you on the head at the slightest provocation.

Wednesday, January 5, 1955
5th day —360 days to follow
Stood into Kaohsiung harbor at first light. COMDESRON ONE shifted his pennant from the Parks, and we settled down between buoys 9 & 10 to a week or so of busy upkeep, along with the job of training about 50 Chinese in the mysteries of how a destroyer operates. The Chinese seem to be very good students, smart, alert, and eager to learn.

One thing about Kaohsiung, there is never any problem about liberty boats, there are always anywhere from two to a dozen small bum boats ready to paddle you ashore for 5 yuan, about 30 cents at the legal exchange rate of 15 Taiwan(another name for Formosa) yuan for one American dollar. In the bars you can get anywhere from 27 to 29 to 1 depending on the size of the bill and how well they know you.

Kaohsiung, Formosa in 1955 was by far the largest city on the southern part of the island. The island, a very large island, 250 miles long and a third as wide, had been settled by refugees from China more than 300 years earlier, so in 1949 when Chiang Kai Chek's Nationalist army fell apart before the superior numbers and leadership of Mao Tse Tung's Communists, Chiang did not even ask if he could bring his ragged and tattered crowd across the 100 mile straits to the sanctuary of the beautiful island. Like MacArthur he vowed to return, and left small garrisons on many of the tiny islands close to the coastal mainland. In defiance of the larger world, which was of the opinion that the United States should not meddle in China's internal struggles, the U.S. continued to provide aid and comfort to Chiang Kai Chek.

When Booker T. and his mates went ashore in Kaohsiung they found a smelly frontier town with dusty, rutted streets, and swarming crowds of people in funny-looking hats dodging clouds of bicycles and rickshas. The air was filled with loud and unnatural sounds—the nasal whine of Vaughan Monroe singing "Ghost Riders in the Sky" blasting from loud speakers rigged over rickety wooden buildings. Nobody knew for sure how many people were here, but half a million and growing would have been a reasonable guess in the first month of 1955. They came because the deep-water harbor and seaport was like a bubbling fountain of opportunity. Ships from around the world came, bringing the material needed to construct a new city, nation, region, and world.

Booker T., his feet on solid if alien ground after 14 days of relentless and unpredictable motion, stood watching a street vendor dispense wonton and steaming noodles…there seemed to be a lesson here…he was struggling to understand. His comrades urged him to stop dallying, there was drinking to be done and girls to seek out.

Upon entering the Blue Moon Café and Gin Parlor at two o'clock on a Wednesday afternoon they were greeted with shrieks of joy by sloe-eyed beauties in high-collared, form-fitting, ankle-length silk gowns, slit on both sides well above shapely knees. Spider Snyder, Moose Odell, and the ever-serious Dawg McCan were stunned by the reception. They expected to be welcomed, but something here was beyond the ordinary. They had been here before, of course, but it had been a long time ago, almost a year. As always, language was a problem. Some of the girls knew a few fragments of English, but the sailors were totally and hopelessly ignorant of Chinese. Moose Odell, never one to talk much in any case, made no attempt to communicate in words, but simply put an arm around the slim waist of his hastily selected choice, and swept her onto the dance floor. Four girls remained, crowding close to Spider and Dawg, their heads only reaching the shoulders of the enchanted men. Dawg scanned the smiling turned-up faces, and found them virtually indistinguishable—they were all young and they were all beautiful. He wanted to scoop them up in a large embrace; he felt a strong urge to take care of them, to shield them from harm. Spider and Dawg looked at each other, shaking their heads and rolling their eyes in wondrous delight…if this wasn't heaven then what was? They both gathered a girl on each arm, and began to swing and sway around the dance floor accompanied by Nat "King" Cole singing "Unforgettable."

Thursday, January 6, 1955
6th day — 359 days follow
It's nice to renew old friends in Kaohsiung, and the B-girls are just as charming as ever.

Kaohsiung is a town of many contrasts. Most of the people are poor to the point of being destitute, but they seem to survive. A small percentage, on the other hand, is extremely wealthy. It's not too difficult to see how a population of this kind could be swayed by Communist propaganda. The Mayor and his henchmen seem to have a dirty finger in every pie. When I become president things will be different.

The wardroom was bustling with conversation. A long table, secured to the deck in a permanent athwartships position, was spread with a sparkling white linen cloth; ten places were set with heavy silver utensils, and a starched white napkin rolled and secured in a silver napkin ring. The normal ship's complement of 19 officers meant that the usual routine was to eat lunch and dinner in two 45-minute shifts, but with the commodore and his staff of two line officers aboard in addition to the division doctor and the division chaplain, it became necessary to eat in three shifts. Also, they were carrying a Chinese officer in training, and on top of this they had taken on two journalists for a week-long assignment in the straits—Forrest Edwards of the Associated Press and Greg McGregor of the *New York Times.* Dawg McCan and his drinking buddies wondered if this meant things were more serious out there in the straits than their own eyes and experience may have indicated, especially when the journalists admitted they did not mind being thought of as war correspondents. What war? Dawg and his mates would have been astounded to know of deadly serious discussions presently underway in the Eisenhower White House over the question of nuclear strikes against Mao's Chinese should they attempt to cross the Formosa straits in force.

Commodore Katz, a four-stripe Navy Captain, Vigil King himself, sat at the head of the table looking contentedly and proprietarily around at the three-stripe Commander Ross, captain of the *Agerholm,* on his right, the two-and-a-half stripe Lieutenant Commander Green, his Chief of Staff, on his left, the two civilian journalists, and the collection of two-stripe lieutenants, one-and-a-half stripe lieutenant junior grades, and single stripe Ensigns falling away to his left and right like rungs of a descending ladder. Commodore Katz had relaxed the dress code here on the edge of troubled waters. He wanted to be known as a man who recognized what was important and what was not—no ties for his officers in Kaohsiung harbor. The commodore could never overcome his lifelong dim feelings of inadequacy resulting from his less-than-heroic stature; he hated being looked down on by lesser ranks, but he took comfort in the Eagles on his shirt collar, and the thought that if he could get these men—these peculiar men—to perform adequately, if not heroically, in the days and nights ahead, there might, there just might, be a Rear Admiral's two stars in his future. He sometimes fretted that, for unknown, and to his mind unfair reasons, Navy brass would not allow him to wear the single star of a Commodore since being in command of an eight destroyer squadron earned him the honor of being at least called Commodore. And Commodore he would be. He tapped the water goblet with his spoon.

Vigil King looked to the opposite end of the table, trying to get the attention of Lieutenant Guthrie, Division Chaplain, who was deep in animated conversation with Lieutenant Sifford, M.D., Division Doctor. The commodore was momentarily stunned when he heard Dr. Sifford's raspy voice rise above the buzz of other conversations, and indeed bring all talk to a quivering halt with the words, "Why, Padre, that makes you a pimp."

Chaplain Guthrie, immediately aware of the silence and the surprised, puzzled, and to his everlasting humiliation, amused faces looking at him, felt blood rushing to his face as if in response to a cry for help. Padre Guthrie, trying to steady himself, hoping he would not pass out, became vaguely aware of the commodore's words floating across the broad expanse of white tablecloth calling his name in what sounded like a compelling and urgent demand…"Padre, Padre."

Guthrie looked across at the commodore in confusion, half expecting to be told to go stand in the corner. But the commodore, a man of little humor, was intent on sticking to protocol. "Padre, will you please give us the blessing?" he said.

Mercifully, the padre thought, the faces turned away from him, and heads bowed in anticipation of his spiritual and sanctifying words. He cleared his throat hoping it would also clear his head, but all he could think of was the doctor in an angelic pose, and sporting an impish grin, sitting to his right.

"Dear God," he began…and was stopped by a muffled chortle. Abruptly, he fled the room.

Dr. Sifford explained. "Before he became a minister of God, he was a taxi driver in New Orleans."

Commodore Katz scowled at the doctor. The commodore had a lengthy hate list, but near the top was a disorderly wardroom mess, and this was not the first time Dr. Sifford had disturbed the wardroom peace. The commodore glared at the grinning doctor thinking, *Maybe I should have him go stand in the corner... if he continues to act like an adolescent I should treat him like one.*

The doctor, in spite of all efforts to inform, refused to take his assignment seriously. In his loud and annoying voice he had repeatedly made it known that when his two-year reserve hitch was up he intended to return to civilian practice as quickly as the archaic system would allow. He insisted that the presence of a medical doctor on the roster of a destroyer squadron was a colossal waste of time, money, and talent. In his view, men at the peak of their strength and resiliency had little need for a doctor, a pharmacist's mate could dispense antibiotics to treat venereal diseases as well as a doctor, maybe better. Also, in case anyone had questions, he held photographic evidence that pharmacist's mates could perform emergency appendectomies, and splint broken bones as well as anyone.

Booker T., sitting on the forward side of the table near the end opposite the commodore, watched as the commodore dispensed with the blessing, and signaled the three hovering white-jacketed and white-gloved mess orderlies to begin serving. The new, non-segregated Navy continued to reserve the steward's mate billet for Negroes and Filipinos, to the veiled discomfort of Booker T.

Booker T. heard the conversation turn to the subject of Esther Williams. Conspicuously displayed on the forward wardroom bulkhead was a large framed and autographed photograph of the Hollywood bathing beauty in a suitably provocative pose, smiling invitingly. Forrest Edwards of the Associated Press was curious. "Esther Williams?" he questioned, directing the query to the empty space between the table and the picture, "Is there a story here?" He looked around for a likely narrator. The young officers stared nervously at their plates, not anxious to talk about Esther in the presence of stern authority. If the war correspondent wanted to hear about Esther in the sanctity of the Blue Moon Café and Gin Parlor they would happily oblige, but not at the commodore's mess.

Dr. Sifford had no such compunction; on the contrary, he relished yet another opportunity to tweak the stuffy, would-be admiral. He spoke up in his usual high-volume voice. "It's a long story, scribe," he intoned, "but I'll make it short...the Aggies stole Esther from the Canucks in Hong Kong, and if they don't watch their butts they're gonna lose her to *Chainsaw* or one of those other buckets." He smiled sweetly at the commodore and raised his eyebrows to Forrest Edwards in an "any questions?" gesture.

Edwards, noting the scowling commodore, and the nervous laughter from around the table decided to accept the irreverent doctor's flippant account for the moment, and move on to perhaps more acceptable topics. "I see," he said by way of closing the Esther story, to the great relief of some of the young officers who knew the commodore would not be amused at the harrowing account of the after-midnight assault on the Canadian destroyer in Hong Kong harbor. Not that they weren't proud of their accomplishment—when the Canadian ship had steamed past them in the harbor blatantly flying the Esther pennant, they felt the honor of the entire U.S. Seventh Fleet was at stake, and theirs to uphold.

"Captain Katz," Edwards began. "Do you have any information about what's happening up in the Tachen Islands?"

The commodore knew that the Tachen Islands, along with Amoy, Quemoy, Matsu, and a few other tiny islands, were lonely and forlorn outposts sprinkled along the China coast, and foolishly left garrisoned by Chiang Kai Chek's Nationalists in the ever more hopeless dream that they would someday return triumphant to the mainland. It was clear to him, and to anyone else who took the time to examine the situation, that the Communists could dislodge the Nationalists from these encampments anytime they chose to do so. Recently they had unleashed a thunderous artillery barrage across the narrow channel separating the islands from the mainland, apparently having decided that it was time to clear the Tachens of hostile forces. This is what the commodore knew, and clearly Forrest Edwards of the Associated Press was sitting at his mess asking this inane question because he knew it too. They had been told, and seemed to believe, that what was at stake was the start of World War III.

Booker T. did not hear the commodore's answer, his mind drifted to the previous day's events at the Blue Moon Café and Gin Parlor. After the initial excited greetings, it developed that the reason for the more spirited than usual reception was because one of the girls believed the father of her infant child had returned. It was not an irrational belief, the *Agerholm* had been to Kaohsiung before; the timing was right. Booker T. thought about the consequences all over the Far East, indeed all over the world, of unleashing young and virile men—soldiers and sailors—on exotic, not unwilling, and often lonely young women deprived of their generation's corresponding male population by the consequences of uncompromising world war. He pondered the irony of men called on to kill the enemy, now cast in the role of male provider for the enemies' women. Was this some kind of whimsical cosmic scheme to maintain the population balance?

Booker T. was aroused from his reverie by the sound of a loud voice saying, "Don't even spit in that direction!" Followed by an explosion of laughter all around the table. Booker T. knew the story, he had been on the bridge when Lope Cooley approached Captain Ross with the intelligence that lookouts had reported that the large ship they had been tracking by radar appeared to be a Russian cruiser...did the captain wish to train the main battery in that direction? The captain's deathless reply—not likely to appear in naval texts along with "damn the torpedoes, full speed ahead," or "don't give up the ship"—"don't even spit in that direction."

Booker T. remembered more about that eventful day, and wondered who would tell the visiting journalists about what Gulliver in his travels must have felt when engulfed by the Lilliputians. Booker T.'s diary entry for that day read:

> *December 27*
> *361st day — 4 days to follow*
> *The day is almost too good to be true— bright sunshine and hardly a ripple on the water. Chinese fishermen confirm it, they are out en masse but good. The horizon is a forest of sails, we can count over 300, and they extend for about 5 miles on the radar scope. All in all we estimate that their numbers extend well into the thousands. We have been forewarned that any invasion attempt on Formosa would be mounted in a Junk fleet, and it becomes increasingly apparent why this is so. We also realize that if we were called upon to try and stop this horde we would be as helpless as a man trying to repel an army of ants. It is not a very comforting thought.*
>
> *Spent most of the afternoon firing small arms off the fantail, .45 pistol and Thompson sub machine gun. Spent the rest of the day trying to get my ears to hear normally again.*
>
> *Do they expect me to shoot those people?*

Booker T. was genuinely troubled by the poverty and general air of desperate survival he saw all around. Even the people populating the junk fleet. The ship had slowed to a respectful five knots threading its way through the junk maze; they passed close enough to see clearly that, far from being vessels of war, these decaying wooden craft were indeed homes to entire families. He was haunted by the unsmiling, beseeching faces of men, women, and children turned anxiously up to them as they passed.

Those people have been there forever; do they care if the government is communist, capitalist, or anarchist? Have they ever stood on dry land? When I become president will it matter to them?

Will it matter to anyone?

>>41<<

THE SYSTEM STINKS

J-four walked up the familiar wide stairway to the second floor of Samford Hall on the API campus, and went directly to the large room known as "the cave"; it was the place where the API history and literature graduate students hung out. J-four worked his way around temporary partitions, overflowing trash cans, dusty and torn sofas, half-empty bags of potato chips, an occasional apple core, and a maze of ancient and battered wooden desks piled high with books and papers. It was hard to imagine that from this chaos emerged some quite respectable scholarly works…like orchids growing on the slopes of a volcano.

J-four found Stanley Gordon sitting at his desk in a corner cubicle with large windows looking out in two directions, the choice spot occupied by only the most senior grad student; Stanley looked up in surprise as J-four appeared.

"What you doin' here, J-four?" Stanley greeted him icily.

Stanley and J-four had never been close friends, but they had shared the graduate student experience from close range for four years so they knew each other well. Stanley was a history major, specializing in the American Civil War; he was also an unreconstructed Rebel…J-four knew him well.

"You missin' a pencil, Stanley?" J-four held up the orange and blue pencil that he had found two nights before in the Tuskegee parking lot.

Stanley's eyes focused on J-four's chin as he took the pencil offered. He turned it over in his hands a few times while he considered the implications, and what he should say to J-four. At length he decided to let J-four do the talking. He stared at the pencil for a time then slowly brought his eyes up to meet J-four's steady gaze.

J-four said, "You lookin' to get the Red Badge of Courage, Stanley?"

Stanley flushed at the thought of Stephen Crane's classic Civil War story of the southern boy who ran away, and then returned to face the Yankee guns. "Ah didn't know they were goin' to shoot him, J-four," he said.

J-four took a seat. "Let me tell you somethin', Stanley," he said. Stanley turned nervously in his chair and looked out the window. Stanley Gordon, ten years younger than J-four, had just turned 17 when the first A-bomb exploded over Hiroshima, and so in his college years found himself immersed in a sea of veterans. He soon learned that there seemed to be a direct correlation between the amount of violent action a veteran had seen, and his inclination to talk about it. He knew that J-four preferred writing above talking, but here was J-four preparing to give him a lecture.

"Ah don't know if ah want to hear this, J-four, ah saw you up on that stage. It looks to me like you is on one side, and ah is on the other. You gonna tell me why ah should be a niggah-lover which it looks to me like what you is?"

"Let me tell you somethin', Stanley," J-four repeated. Stung by the appellation nigger-lover, he was suddenly very angry at Stanley Gordon, and with some difficulty resisted the urge to grab him and shake him.

J-four took a deep breath, trying to ease his rage. "First of all, Stanley," he said, "you bettah git this straight, and you bettah not evah forget it...What ah love is this country...nobody loves Dixie more than Jerry Mulhane the fourth, you heah me, Stanley? Mulhane the fourth...do you know what that means, Stanley? It means I'm the fifth generation carryin' the same name...it means mah family has lived heah for ovah one hundred years, and you bettah know somethin' else, Stanley, the first Jerry Mulhane, mah great-granddaddy, was a colonel of Confederate infantry, and died defendin' Lookout Mountain. Mah granddaddy, mah daddy, and me was membahs of the Ku Klux Klan before you was even out of diapers, so you better think about who you talkin' to when you start callin' me a niggah-lover, you heah me, Stanley? You listenin' to me, Stanley?"

J-four was venting a full head of steaming rage, and would not allow interruptions for unwelcome answers to rhetorical questions. "And another thing, Stanley," he continued, "before you start yappin' and makin' judgments about other people's likes, you bettah make sure you got the moral authority to say anything about anything...it don't require a whole lot of courage to take pot shots in the night at a man who is ovah a hundred years old...ah'm not happy about this, Stanley."

Stanley was not easily overcome, but now he looked at J-four in surprise, suspicion, and a hint of new appreciation. "Ah never knew you was in the

Klan, J-four," he said. "What klavern you belong to? And how come you workin' with them niggahs over in Tuskegee?"

J-four frowned. "That really ain't none of your business, now is it, Stanley?" he said. "Ah got reasons for what ah do, and if ah want you or anybody else to know what them reasons are ah'll be sure to tell you, now won't ah, Stanley?"

Stanley Gordon, like J-four, came from a long line of Klan members. Stanley's great-grandfather had been present in 1873 in Eufala, Alabama when a group of recently freed slaves, encouraged by the Republican party to think they could register to vote, were gunned down by white Democrats no longer licensed to kill Union soldiers. But Stanley, unlike J-four, had not seen the Buffalo Soldiers in action, and so had found no reason to question the wisdom of his ascendants. The history of the South made perfect sense to Stanley. Long before the Revolutionary War, Southern planters imported black labor from West Africa to work the tobacco and cotton fields. Stanley knew that these people were bought and sold like horses and cattle, but he had concluded from his studies that the Negroes brought to ports like Charleston and Savannah in the 18th century were simply the losers in tribal warfare battles in their native Africa. Stanley was of the opinion that these people were destined to be slaves wherever they lived, and it was clear to him that they were better off being slaves in the American South.

Stanley had in fact taken these thoughts a step further, in his mind even the word slave was not such a bad thing, certainly not bad in the context of what he knew about 19th century Alabama. What was so terrible about a life where in return for a day's work, a hard day's work to be sure, but who in life didn't work hard, a man or woman got a roof to sleep under and food to eat. Why even the great founders of the country, Washington and Jefferson, Madison and Monroe, owned slaves, and considered the Negro to be an inferior being—and there was nothing in the constitution proscribing the institution. Stanley Gordon, student of history that he was, knew about James Henry Hammond of South Carolina who, on the floor of the United States House of Representatives in 1836 affirmed his belief that, "slavery, regulated as it was in the South, produced the highest toned, the purest, best organization of society that ever had existed on the face of the earth." Stanley dreamed of how wonderful it would have been to live in those halcyon days. And finally, the clinching argument for Stanley, the Bible, in the book of Exodus, sanctified slavery. The first laws God gave to Moses and the Israelites on Mount Sinai, following the Ten Commandments, concerned the treatment of slaves.

Stanley Gordon, the thinking man's Klansman, was still amazed that in 1861 the North had been willing to sacrifice hundreds of thousands of lives for the so-called benefit of the so-called slaves that as near as he could tell from his studies, and from what people had told him from first-hand experience, would have preferred to just be left alone. He also knew about the arguments for preserving the Union which were even more mystifying to him than freeing the so-called slaves. He would have thought the North would be happy to just let the South go its own way. He was of the opinion that Abraham Lincoln was a wisecracking madman. He thought the idea of an independent South was as good or better here in the middle of the 20th century as it was in 1861, and he was not alone in his hope that it still might come about if they continued to push for it. He held Strom Thurmond of South Carolina in high esteem.

J-four knew all this about Stanley, and did not even consider trying to convince him otherwise because not only did he know it, but he also understood it, and more, he had not come all the way to entirely disagreeing with it. But J-four had seen enough of killing, and he had been profoundly moved by the manly courage of Sergeant Bob Black, and the rest of the Buffalo Soldiers as well as by the simple dignity of Miz Sarah. He knew the difference between the sleep-tossed, conscience-tortured nights of his pre-war Klan days, and the untroubled slumber of his post-war East Alabama Council on Human Rights' days.

"Stanley," J-four said, "let me ask you somethin'." Stanley looked at J-four, but said nothing. "Stanley, do you believe in the Bible?"

Stanley sat up straight and tried to look angelic as he answered, "Yes ah do."

"Can you recite the Ten Commandments?"

"Ah believe ah can. Yes, suh."

"Well then, Stanley," said J-four, "you must know about the commandment that says, thou shalt not kill. Stanley, there is a word for people who say they believe in the Bible, and then do not do what the Bible tells them to do. Do you know what that word is?"

Stanley squirmed in his chair. It was a hot day, and he wiped sweat from his brow, not all of which was due to the temperature. "Ah nevah killed nobody, J-four," he said.

J-four scoffed. "Stanley," he said, "you know as well as ah do that accessory to murder is a crime."

Stanley squirmed some more, evading J-four's gaze.

J-four continued. "Okay, Stanley, let's say ah believe that you nevah killed anybody; but what ah'm not hearin' from you is that you *wouldn't* kill anybody, and Stanley, if you don't tell me that, and you *do* tell me you believe in the Bible, ah see some inconsistencies here, do you see what ah mean?"

Stanley continued to squirm, still not answering and still looking out the window.

J-four was relentless. "What ah want to tell you, Stanley," he said, "is to consider very carefully the company you are keepin' because...listen to this, Stanley...are you listenin' to me, Stanley?" Stanley turned in his chair and looked at J-four.

J-four continued. "If a group is organized to protest government action that they do not agree with they might be called patriots, but if a group's only reason for existence, Stanley, is to harass, intimidate, mutilate, and kill law-abiding citizens, they are called thugs, Stanley. You hear what ah'm sayin', Stanley? The word is thugs. Now, Stanley, ah don't think you or me has any doubt about which category the Ku Klux Klan falls in, now do we, Stanley?"

Stanley was mixed up. He knew that J-four was right, and he knew that J-four had the moral authority to say these things, but the idea of a freely integrated society terrified him. "What are we gonna do, J-four?" he asked. "The niggahs already outnumbah us, are we supposed to just let 'em take ovah?"

J-four sighed. He looked at Stanley wondering if there was any hope that this forlorn figure could be led away from violence and made to see a better way. He knew it required a giant leap of understanding that Negroes were real people with the same hopes and fears that Stanley harbored, but he also knew that it was fruitless to point this out to Stanley; he would have to learn it on his own, and J-four was under no illusions that he ever would. "Ah'll tell you what, Stanley," he said, "...you are an intelligent young man, you are a student of history, and you are goin' to be a teacher. Why don't you step back from all this Klan talk about Jews and Communists and mongrelization, and try to think about things in a logical, rational way. If you do that ah think you will see there is no chance the Negroes are about to take over anything here in the South. And Stanley, remember this, the Negroes are Christians, just like you. Do what the Bible tells you."

Stanley was listening, but he was not comforted. J-four made it sound too easy. He remembered something. "What about this School for Presidents, J-four?" he asked. "What's that all about?"

J-four had known it was only a matter of time before he would be asked to explain the School for Presidents to somebody like Stanley Gordon. He also knew it would be virtually impossible to make Stanley understand. Still, Stanley was a student of history, maybe there was a chance...at the same time, J-four thought it more than likely that Stanley did not think of history as a guide for future action. "Stanley," he said, "do you think history has anything to tell us about how to approach present and future problems in society?"

"Well sure, J-four, " Stanley replied, "everybody knows that history repeats itself, what's that got to do with it?"

"What does history tell us about the way this country chooses its presidents, Stanley?"

Stanley did a quick inventory of U.S. presidents and how they came to office. He found some wide gaps in his memory. "Ah'd have to look some of that up, J-four," he said, then added as an afterthought, "Some of em', like Truman, got there because the president died." This thought reminded him of other presidential replacements. "Then there was Tyler who replaced Harrison in 1840 after only a month in office...whatever Harrison believed, Tyler believed just the opposite...the Civil War might have come twenty years earlier if Harrison had lived."

J-four nodded. "There's your answer, Stanley, " he said, "there is a need in this country for a school that teaches how to be president."

Stanley agreed. "Ah reckon you got that right, J-four," he said, "ah cain't think of a decent president we've had outside of Washington and maybe Jefferson though ah ain't too sure about him, but then ah sort of liked Andrew Jackson. What we really need is for the South to just split off and be an independent country. Why do we have to stay together with them damn Yankees? They got their ways, we got ours. It's like we hogtied together and we cain't move a muscle without them pullin' in the opposite direction. It makes me sick."

J-four thought of the yawning canyon between Count, and what he believed, on one side, and Stanley, with his unbending convictions on the other. Was he, J-four, the only one who could see the merits of the arguments on both sides? Was there any possibility of building a bridge where the two sides might meet in the middle to look for common ground? In 1861 the two sides had tried to bludgeon the other into submission, and here in 1952 it was clear that Stanley was willing, maybe even eager, to unleash the cannons again.

J-four sneezed. "Bless you," said Stanley.

"Thank you…Stanley, do you love Jesus?"

"Of course ah do, J-four, what kind of a question is that?"

"Do you remember what Jesus said in his Sermon on the Mount?"

Stanley began again to squirm in his chair. "Well ah…some."

J-four smiled. "Maybe it's time you went back and read your Bible, Stanley," he said, " you'll find it in the book of Matthew. Among other things, there are the nine beatitudes…listen to this one, Stanley…'Blessed are the peacemakers, for they will be called the children of God'…Do you believe that, Stanley?"

Stanley blushed. J-four continued. "…You said you believed in the Bible, Stanley," he said.

"Ah do believe in the Bible, J-four…How come you doin' this to me?"

"Stanley, mah friend," J-four replied, "ah'm just tryin' to get you to see straight heah. If ah remembah, you do a whole lot of prayin' and Bible readin' in some of those Klan meetings. Am ah right, Stanley?"

"So what am ah supposed to do, J-four?"

"You know what ah think, Stanley? Ah think you ought to just go on off to law school, and be a politician…you don't like what the fedral govment's doin', you can be a Congressman…see if that don't give you a chance to do somethin' about it. But one thing ah want you to acknowledge right heah and now, Stanley…the Ku Klux Klan is evil. Do you agree with me on that, Stanley?

Stanley was not ready to do that. "J-four, ah got some friends in the Klan…some good ole boys ah don't think are evil…we…" He stopped and looked at J-four. "A politician, you say?"

"Do you believe in democracy, Stanley?"

"Of course ah do, J-four. Ah like to think of mahself as a patriot." He sat straighter.

J-four nodded. "Of course you are, Stanley," he said, "and bein' a patriot you ought to know then that in a democratic system, politics is the proper way to get things changed. You musta read that Alabama Senator John Sparkman, from up in Huntsville, has been nominated by the Democratic party to run for vice president of the United States."

"Ah did read that, J-four, and ah'm proud for the state of Alabama, but ah'm not sure ah trust Senatah Sparkman, or Senatah Lister Hill either for that matter. Neither one of them joined the Dixiecrats in 1948, and they both refused to walk out of the convention with Handy Ellis and the rest of the Alabama delegation in protest over Truman's civil rights plank." Stanley paused then remembered something else. "...Ah didn't vote for Jim Folsom either...ah think that's why we're havin' so much trouble with the niggahs...our political leaders are encouragin' them to think they got all these rights includin' votin' rights and...oh hell, J-four, it's jist a damn mess...ah think we done elected ourselves some communists."

J-four held up his hand. "Wait a minute, Stanley," he said, "did you evah stop to think that Senators Sparkman and Hill was doin' what they thought best for the people of Alabama? They knew they couldn't git nothin' done if they walked out on the system...it's easy for people like Strom Thurmond and Handy Ellis who ain't in Washington to make all that noise. Politics is deal makin', and if Alabama needs federal money to build roads and dams and such, our Senators need to be there to make sure we get what's comin' to us."

"Ah don't like it, J-four. The system stinks."

"There's more than one system goin' around here, Stanley, and they all stink one way or another. I guess what smells like horse shit to one might smell like roses to somebody else, and speakin' of horse shit, can you tell me the name of your Exalted Cyclops?"

Stanley looked at J-four suspiciously. "Why you wanna know that, J-four? You know ah'm not allowed to tell you."

J-four said, "Ah'd like to talk to him, find out somethin' about the way he thinks. Ah might just think about joinin' your klavern."

Stanley was puzzled. "Wait a minute, J-four," he said, "you just got through sayin' the Klan was evil."

"Ah said it was evil, Stanley, ah didn't say it was bad."

>> 42 <<

THE SYSTEM STINKS — II

Susan turned away from the large chalkboard to address her class of 15 students. They were a mixed group—twelve fourth-year undergraduates, two first-year graduate students, and one precocious third-year undergraduate, a young lady who had quickly demonstrated a level of intelligence superior to her 14 male peers. One of the graduate students was from India, the other from Japan. Susan marveled at a social system that would go to war to prevent black African students from sharing a classroom with Whites, but did not even blink when a black Indian from Madras matriculated. Also it was only seven years since the Japanese were considered the yellow peril, yet their presence on the API campus went unquestioned. Susan was surprised and strangely ill at ease when she found Nagasato Nichida on her class roll. It was too soon after treating the casualties of fanatical Japanese resistance for her to see him initially for what he was—a shy young man with the courage to seek an education while trying to learn a new language in a strange land. Flapper suggested they invite him to dinner, and the young man rewarded them by teaching Susan how to prepare a delicious, country-style sukiyaki.

Susan addressed the class. "Now class," she said, "we only have a few minutes before the bell rings...are there any questions about the mid-term examination which, let me remind you, will be held in this room on Saturday morning at nine a.m. Don't forget to bring your blue examination booklets...Yes, Marylou?"

Several hands had gone up, but Susan recognized Marylou Coker, following the "ladies first" custom, but also knowing that Marylou would probably have a pertinent, and possibly an interesting question. Not this time.

"Dr. Jackson, will there be any questions on the exam about the names of scientists who made certain discoveries?"

It was a point Susan had talked about before. She acknowledged that it was more important to know the path of carbon in photosynthesis than to know the name of the man who devised and implemented the research strategy that established the pathway, but she wanted the students to recognize that new knowledge did not drop from the sky like raindrops; somebody had to do the work. The students were well aware of her position on this, but like students eternal, even the better students like Marylou Coker, they inevitably looked for opportunities to ease their study burdens. For her part, Susan, like teachers eternal, was not prepared to say precisely what questions would appear on the exam. She considered an examination as more a teaching than a testing tool.

Susan frowned. "Marylou," she said with an edge of impatience in her voice, "I think you know my position on that...if you know that Newton discovered gravity, why shouldn't you know that Calvin discovered how carbon dioxide gets converted to sugar in photosynthesis?"

"What's gravity?" asked Marylou bringing a big laugh from all her male admirers. Susan laughed too.

Other hands were up; Susan pointed to one. "Yes, Norman?"

"Dr. Jackson, do we need to know all the structural formulas in the Krebs cycle and the glycolytic pathway?"

Susan smiled indulgently. "Norman," she said, "this is a chemistry course, you know, how else can you understand how these things work? But listen, I don't want you spending a lot of time trying to memorize formulas, it's more important for you to understand the significance of these pathways. But I have to admit that sometimes you do have to memorize. Do you have a question, Sam?"

"Yes, ma'am. What about oxidative phosphorylation?"

"What about it, Sam?"

"Do we have to know where all the electrons are going?"

Susan sighed. The twins were six months old, she was sleep-deprived and tired. Anybody who thought having twins was only twice as much work might have been surprised to learn that it was more like a factor of ten. Flapper had done what he could, but feeding was a job only Susan could do, and with two it was exhausting. They had been fortunate to get Arrowneter to help on a part-time basis, and she had been rock solid in her support, but with her own family and her job at the hospital, her time with them was limited. When Susan had asked if she could recommend anyone to help in the care of the twins, Arrowneter said she wouldn't trust anyone but herself to do that since she took the circumstances under which they were born as a signal from God that one of her earthly tasks was to look after these children. At first she even refused payment, but Susan and Flapper prevailed in that short discussion.

Susan had only a few more weeks before completing her internship at the Lee County Hospital, and was looking forward to the extra time that would give her. The way she felt right now she thought she would just use it to sleep. But at the moment she had to deal with her biochemistry class. She was mildly annoyed at the questions because they reinforced her belief that the students' primary interest was in making a good grade on the examination rather than learning and understanding the subject matter, as she hoped they would do.

Susan sighed again. "Sam," she said, "do you think it's possible to understand oxidative phosphorylation without knowing where the electrons are going?"

"Well, ma'am," said Sam with a sidelong glance to Marylou Coker, "with all due respect, ma'am, ah'm not sure ah could understand oxidative phosphorylation even if ah knew where every one of them little bitty electrons was goin'." Everyone, including Susan, had a good laugh at that candid observation.

Another student vied for attention. "Excuse me, Dr. Jackson," he said, "but ah wonder if you could be a little more clear on this question of structural formulas, you say you don't want us to memorize them, but then you say sometimes we have to. Excuse me, ma'am, but ah...do you see mah problem heah, ma'am?"

Susan nodded. "Yes, I see your problem, Norman. Let me try to clarify what I'm getting at here. First of all, and this is something I've talked about often...when you finish this course I want you to have a good idea of the chemical reactions that go on in the cells of your body, and how these reactions are coordinated to produce the fuel that runs your metabolic engine. It's only a beginning course in biochemistry so you're not expected to be experts, but there are some things you should know. The exact structural formulas are not crucial, they can always be found in the textbook, but you should know the difference between a tricarboxylic acid and a dicarboxylic acid, between a reducing sugar and an amino acid, between a protein and a triglyceride...things like that. You should certainly know why adenosine triphosphate is more important to your body than adenosine diphosphate. Does that help any? I do wish it was not necessary for you to have grades...that you could just learn because you wanted to know."

"Why don't you just give us all A's then none of us would have to worry about grades?"

The question was asked in jest, but only half in jest; some of the students through their snickers, looked hopefully at Susan just before the bell rang.

The students sat quietly in place, waiting for Susan to dismiss them. Susan thought about the question and it gave her an idea. "Maybe I will, " she said, "but I would advise you to study for the exam. Class dismissed."

The students, except for Marylou Coker, cleared the room quickly. Marylou approached Susan as she gathered her notes spread out on a large desk at the front of the room. "Excuse me, Dr. Jackson," she said softly.

Susan looked up. "Yes, Marylou," she said, "can I help you?"

Marylou hesitated, then said, "Dr. Jackson…" She faltered.

"What is it, Marylou? Is something wrong?"

The shy Marylou blushed and looked at the floor. "No, no," she said, "…Ah just wanted to say that ah…ah really like this course, and ah was wonderin' if…if you had any special research projects in the laboratory ah could help with."

Susan was momentarily speechless. She was unprepared for the sudden thrill she experienced when Marylou became the first student to approach her for extracurricular guidance. She resisted the temptation to give Marylou Coker a big hug. Suddenly, and without warning, an entire new horizon opened before Susan's startled consciousness. It was not the same as giving birth to Tempest and Storm, but she felt some of the same emotions—a new scholar was born right before her wondering eyes. Her mind raced at the possibilities, she felt blood rushing to her head as if in answer to an emergency call for more brainpower.

Marylou stood hopefully, watching Susan's reaction to her question. She noted with surprise the sudden flush in Susan's cheeks, and wondered what it meant. When she enrolled in this class it had simply been to fulfill a requirement for the premedical curriculum, it had never been her intention to pursue it beyond that. She expected to learn the usual something, and she was only mildly curious in the beginning, but she had been fired with elation when she learned about enzymes and that the B vitamins were essential for certain enzymes to function. She wanted more.

For her part, with everything else that currently filled her life, Susan had put any thoughts of research far back in the vaults of her mind, though she had been touched by the contagion in the fertile laboratories of the Washington University School of Medicine. But here was a student, and a superior student at that, asking to do a research project with her. How could she refuse?

She found her voice at last. "I'll tell you the truth, Marylou," she said, "...right now I don't have any research projects going, but if you'll give me a little time to think about it, and look into the possibilities, I might be able to come up with something, okay?"

Marylou was pleased. "Sure, Dr. Jackson," she said, "that'll be just fine. Thank you."

Close to noon, Susan was hungry. It was Flapper's day to be home with the twins, and she had to do an afternoon shift at the hospital emergency room. She felt like taking a nap. She stopped to look in on Achilles Demimelius who sat coatless and tieless at his office desk facing the door, munching a sandwich and reading a book at the same time. Four straight-back chairs were arranged in an arc before his desk. A warm late October breeze stirred the curtains lazily behind him. Through the second-floor windows Susan could see students moving across the quadrangle below. An electric fan whirred and clanked periodically from its site on the floor near the corner of the spacious room. Susan noticed that the fan had worked itself around so that it was in fact blowing warm air, and not a few small dustballs, against the wall. A scent of acetone was in the air. On the wall was a giant, dusty, chart labeled in large letters THE PERIODIC TABLE OF THE ELEMENTS.

Demimelius looked up and smiled as Susan came through the open door after a perfunctory knock. "Ah Susan," he said, "do come in. How good to see you." He closed the book he was reading and rose to greet her. Holding a half-eaten sandwich in one hand, he said, "You look a little tired, is everything all right? Come sit down."

Susan sat and slumped in a chair. "I could use a nap, A.D.," she said.

Demimelius looked at her sympathetically and asked, "How much longer do you have at the hospital?"

Susan sighed. "About six weeks," she said, "but don't worry, I'll make it. Listen, A.D., the reason I came to see you is that one of my students asked about doing a special research project, and I wanted to find out if the department has any money to support things like that."

Demimelius sat on one of the chairs near Susan. He was obviously pleased at the prospect of a student research project, but he also knew that research was not a universally admired pursuit in the API School of Chemistry. "Well," he began, " the first thing you should know is that our dean is not too crazy about research...I once heard him call it adult play, but don't let that worry you too much, he hasn't prohibited research, at least not yet. What we usually do is squeeze a little out of the teaching budget, and mostly use standard reagents from the regular student laboratories. Do you have a particular project in mind?"

Susan shook her head. "The truth is," she said, "this kind of took me by surprise. But to answer your question, I do have a few ideas that have been sort of sloshing around in the back of my head." She smiled and continued, "I'd like to grow bacteria and isolate some DNA. Before I left Washington U. I got to work in Professor Kornberg's laboratory where they were studying an enzyme involved in the synthesis of DNA. It was very exciting."

Demimelius smiled; he loved enzymes. "We don't have too much equipment here," he said, "I don't know if we have what you might need for enzyme work." He thought a moment, then said, "You might be able to get some money from the graduate school, they have a small fund to support research. I think there is a deadline for receipt of proposals…it's a campus-wide competition. It seems like most of the money goes to the School of Agriculture, but you could try."

"Maybe I will."

Demimelius changed the subject. "How is old Socrates getting along?" he asked.

Susan smiled. "Okay I think," she answered. "He's still a bit sore, but back on his feet; back to work too…quite amazing for a man his age. Got himself a silver-knobbed mahogany cane…I think it's part walking stick and part weapon; he is fearless."

Demimelius nodded. "He taught us something about courage all right," he said. "He must be a tough old bird. Are they planning anymore Greek dialogues?"

"As a matter of fact they are," Susan replied. "Flapper told me the next one will be called 'What is Justice?'"

"Ah yes," said Demimelius, "the Greek holy trinity…What is truth? What is beauty? What is justice? I wonder if the Klan will be there for that one…they learned something about courage from old Socrates, they could use a lesson in justice. Do you know when it's scheduled?"

"I don't think they have a date yet," Susan replied. "Will you go?"

Demimelius took a bite from his sandwich. "I wouldn't miss it," he mumbled through the crumbs.

Susan looked at him sharply. "You're not afraid of the Klan?" she asked. "I remember what you told us about not trying to be a crusader. If you're willing to sit down with Negroes in a public place in the presence of the

Klan, it occurs to me you're not exactly practicing what you preached to us."

Demimelius shrugged. "Well said, Susan, and the answer is...maybe you can tell Socrates...I learned something about courage at that forum. It probably sounds corny, but there it is. You may be surprised to know that I also joined the East Alabama Council on Human Relations. I have surprised even myself."

The East Alabama Council on Human Relations was a nascent organization formed in answer to the White Citizens Councils that were spreading across the South. Even though the Human Relations Council preached a non-violent approach to improving race relations, the battle lines were drawn; it was hard to be neutral on the subject in mid-20th century Alabama.

Susan stood up preparing to leave. "That's very interesting, A.D.," she said, "and I'd like to talk about it some more, but I really have to go. I'm due at the Lee County Hospital in about thirty minutes, and I have to take the bus since our rusty Pontiac is in the shop for repairs of some kind or other. Thanks for the information about research money, maybe we can talk some more about that sometime too."

Flapper looked at his watch for the 50th time in the past thirty minutes. He paced back and forth across the echoing wooden floor in the living room-dining room of the two-bedroom apartment he, Susan, and the twins occupied on the edge of the API campus. The apartments were converted Army barracks, and were situated in the middle of a grove of pine trees. It was after 10 p.m., way after ten, dark in the absence of street lights, and softly silent from the carpet of pine needles—Susan was more than an hour late. Flapper wouldn't admit to himself, but she was more than two hours late. It was not like her to be late. The twins were under control...fed, bathed, and happy, but not asleep. At almost seven months they were mobile and mischievous, he dared not let them out of his sight. At the moment they were playing with wooden blocks on the floor. They each seemed to enjoy the other's company.

When he called the hospital at ten he was told that she had left a little after eight, her usual time. He stared at the telephone; why didn't it ring? He lifted the receiver to make sure there was a dialtone. Where was she? Where was Susan? It was impossible for Susan to be two hours late unless something bad had happened. He felt more helpless than he had ever felt in his life, even when mortar shells were exploding all around him. It was unbearable. He felt terror. *Dear God*...he briefly considered prayer. If she walked through that door in another moment he would never let her out of his sight again. Never. Their life together flashed through his mind...the *Mercy*...Hanauma

Bay.

The ringing phone gave him a start. He picked it up before the second ring. "Susan!" he shouted into the mouthpiece.

It was J-four. "Easy man, easy," he said. "Susan is okay." J-four tried to be reassuring.

Flapper was speechless.

"Flapper, can you hear me? Susan is okay...She's in jail."

Flapper recovered his voice. "Is that you, J-four?" he asked. "What did you say? Jail? How do you know Susan is in jail? How can Susan be in jail? Is this a joke?"

J-four answered slowly. "Flapper," he said, "...simmer down. They gave her one phone call and she called me because she knew you didn't have a car, and that you couldn't leave the twins. Ah'm goin' over there and bail her out. Ah'll get her back in about an hour. Just hang on...she's okay."

Flapper was relieved but confused. "But why is she in jail?" he asked.

"She refused to move from the colored section in the bus...they arrested her and took her to jail. The system stinks, Flapper, but that's the law in Alabama."

Ten days later Susan stood looking up at Judge John Saunders, stern and forbidding in his black robes; remote behind the fortress of the judge's bench in the Lee County courtroom in Opelika, Alabama. Standing next to her was her attorney, Morris Maloney, warning her not to be defiant. Flapper, J-four, and Becky sat together on polished long benches in the yawning room's spectator section, pondering the harsh power of the law. Flapper could not escape thinking about Socrates' question..."what is justice?" A handful of other curious onlookers were scattered mostly along the back rows near the wide double doors. Flapper had hoped to see a kindly, old, white-haired judge. What he saw was black. A black-haired, black-robed, brooding, bushy-browed, middle-aged, dark-visaged white-faced man burdened with what appeared to be a permanent scowl.

Morning sun streamed through high windows exposing a blizzard of dust particles. Judge Saunders took a large red handkerchief from his pocket, wiped his brow, began to speak, then sneezed. "Bless you," said Morris Maloney. The judge glared at Maloney, then, in a surprisingly high-pitched voice began the proceedings. "Miz Jackson," he said while looking at a sheet of paper he held in his hand, "you are charged with two violations of the laws of Alabama...first, creation of a public nuisance by refusing to leave the colored section of a public bus. How do you plead?"

"Guilty, your honor," Susan said quietly.

Morris Maloney said, "Your honor, could ah say a word here?"

"Go ahead, counselor."

"Your honor, mah client is new to this part of the country…she was trained as a doctor and a scientist in St. Louis, Missouri. Now your honor, we know that ignorance of the law is not an acceptable excuse, but your honor she was not aware that she was breaking a law, and we respectfully ask for the court's indulgence in this matter."

Judge Saunders looked at the sheet of paper on his bench as Maloney spoke. It was not clear if he heard anything the attorney said. When Maloney finished speaking he stood with Susan waiting for the judge's response. Slowly Judge Saunders pushed the paper aside. His eyes rose to briefly meet Susan's, then shifted to Attorney Maloney standing uncertainly at her side. The judge laced his fingers together in front of his mouth with his elbows propped on the bench. Slowly he moved his finger-entwined hands down under his chin and fixed Susan with an icy stare. "You are makin' a very weak argument heah, counselor," he said. "Accordin' to this heah charge sheet, Miz Jackson was advised by the arrestin' officer that she was breakin' the law, and she still refused to move. Miz Jackson, could you tell the court why you deliberately refused to obey this Alabama law?"

Susan, dressed in a two-piece navy blue suit with a white silk scarf around her neck, was dangerously beautiful as she faced the cold-eyed judge. Nervously she cleared her throat and began to speak. "Your honor," she said, "I was just coming off the afternoon shift in the emergency room of the Lee County Hospital, I was with a friend and a…a…a colleague, who had been assisting me in the emergency room. We were both catching the bus to Auburn…my car was in the garage for repairs…she happened to be colored…we were talking about some of the patients who had come to the emergency room that afternoon, and how we treated them. There was one case in particular…a boy who had broken his leg in a football game. The next thing I knew the bus driver was ordering me to move into the white section of the bus. My colleague and I were not finished talking, and that's what I told the bus driver. When he insisted I move I thought it was extremely rude, and I just refused."

Judge Saunders' eyes widened slightly when Susan spoke of the broken leg; any mention of football always got his attention. He leaned forward in his chair to get a better look at Susan. "This, ah…this…you say…colleague?

You have a colored colleague? You sure you usin' the right word here, Miz Jackson?"

Susan was sure. "Yes, your honor," she said, "I believe I am. This lady is a trusted assistant in the emergency room...she does not have all the formal education, but if she did she could be as good a doctor as there is...she delivered both of my babies...with very little help I might add."

The judge looked at Susan with widened eyes, which quickly narrowed to slits. Blood rushed to his cheeks; it was as if she had told him her uncle was a monkey. "What do you mean she delivered your babies?" he thundered. "Ah find that disgustin', Miz Jackson, and ah'll thank you to watch your tongue in this courtroom or ah'll find you in contempt."

Susan started to respond, but stopped when nudged by her attorney.

The judge cleared his throat and drank from a water glass on his bench trying to collect himself from the outrage he had just heard. He could only imagine the details of what this pretty lady had told him, and tried with some difficulty to put it out of his mind. He picked up the second charge sheet. "There is a second charge heah," he said, " . . .possession of an illegal substance. You were found to be carryin' a package of bar-bitch-yoo-rates, Miz Jackson. How do you plead to that?"

Morris Maloney stepped forward. "Your honor, sir," he said, "my client is a doctor...she is permitted to carry prescription drugs. She pleads not guilty to this charge."

"But she was carryin' the drugs, wasn't she?" queried the judge then continued, "Miz Jackson, why were you carryin' these drugs?"

Maloney started to speak, but Susan interrupted him. "Your honor," she said, "they were for my friend and colleague, Arrowneter Grant...her young son has epilepsy. Barbiturates are the drug of choice in the treatment of epilepsy, your honor."

A supercilious smile crept onto Judge Saunders' face. He nodded knowingly. "Epilepsy is it?" he sneered, then added, "If ah'm not mistaken Miz Jackson, these bar-bitch-yoo-rates are used for other things too, are they not?"

"Yes, your honor," said Susan, "they can also be used to help sleep, and sometimes they are used to help in labor."

The judge nodded. "Yes, well now, Miz Jackson, can you tell me if you are licensed to practice medicine in the state of Alabama?"

Susan sensed immediately that she was in trouble. *What is justice?* flashed across her mind as it continued to do with Flapper, watching the proceedings with rising apprehension and frustration at what he correctly perceived as a virulently hostile judge. He wanted to leap to Susan's defense, he wanted to shout...here is a woman who only wants to help other people....He writhed in his seat to the point where J-four, sitting next to him, tried to calm him by putting a hand on his leg.

"Your honor," said Susan, "I am completing a residency at the Lee County Hospital, I expect to be licensed within a few weeks."

Judge Saunders sighed impatiently, and pointed a bony finger at Susan. "But at the present time, Miz Jackson," he said, "you are not a licensed physician in the state of Alabama, and so are guilty of the charge...possession of an illegal substance...is that not correct, Miz Jackson?"

"Technically..." Susan began, but the judge cut her off.

"Is that not correct, Miz Jackson?"

Susan had to admit that it was correct, she was guilty of the charge.

Judge Saunders, looking satisfied, if not pleased, gathered the papers lying before him, picked up his gavel, and apparently speaking to the air at the top of the courtroom said, "The defendant has pleaded guilty to the charges. Court is adjourned until two p.m. at which time ah will pass sentence." He slammed down the gavel, rose and left the room.

Susan was dazed. In her entire life she could not recall a single instance where she had been accused of any wrongdoing. She was a combat veteran, a wife and mother, a doctor, a teacher, and now...a criminal. She watched, dreamlike, as the judge strode from the room. A uniformed policeman touched her arm, and began to lead her from the room; she was in custody. She looked around in alarm, and saw Flapper trying to reach her, but being restrained by a court warden. She looked questioningly at her attorney walking beside her. She searched for her voice, trying to suppress her sense of panic. "What will happen?" she managed to say.

Morris Maloney tried to reassure her though he knew of Judge Saunder's reputation as a strict disciplinarian. Still, he thought there was a chance the judge would be lenient...it was hard to imagine he would be hard on Susan considering all the circumstances.

In the event, the judge delivered a stern lecture, and sentenced Susan to two years in prison. Then, after savoring a gasp from Susan, and a muffled "no" from Flapper, he suspended the sentence, placed her on probation, and fined her $250 and court costs.

>>43<<

THE BURNING QUESTION MARK

The twins were asleep. Susan and Flapper sat on the grass in the velvet darkness under the pine trees outside their apartment. Two days after the courtroom ordeal neither had recovered their usual sense of well-being; nor would they.

"We can't stay here," said Flapper.

"But neither can we leave," responded Susan.

"It's a dangerous place for people like us, Susan, your dad was right."

Susan sniffed. "Well," she said, "we knew that right from the start, didn't we?" She was quiet for a few moments thinking about their circumstances; they had been in Alabama just a little over 15 months. Her father had warned them about coming here, to be sure, but Susan knew after her encounter with the menacing Judge Saunders that her father's dire predictions fell short of the ominous reality of this place. It was a place where violence might be rewarded and peaceful humanitarianism might be punished; it was an upside down world. But she was not ready to admit this to her father, she in fact was energized by the whole topsy-turvy society where sunshine and shadow mixed so seamlessly. "... I'm not ready to go back and tell him so, Flapper," she said. "The last time I felt so needed was on the *Mercy*. Do you know there is not a single Negro doctor in Auburn...or Opelika either, for all I know."

Flapper persisted. "Well," he said, "our staying won't change that, will it?" He reached for Susan's hand in the darkness. "Susan, honey," he said, "I thought I would have a heart attack when that judge sentenced you to two years in prison...I'm scared, Susan...we are totally at the mercy of people like that judge...what would we have done if he hadn't suspended that sentence?"

Susan had considered that question and she knew the answer. "We would have made the best of it," she said, "just as we always do. They can knock us down, Flapper, but we always get up."

Flapper said, "J-four thinks there were one or two Klan goons in that courtroom. We can't fight them, Susan…and what about the twins? Do you think they're safe? We could leave tomorrow…We could leave right now."

Susan did not respond right away. She sat quietly, letting Flapper's words hang in the air. She knew he wanted to stay and fight; so did she. If anything, the experience with Judge Saunders had strengthened her resolve, but she loved Flapper for his concern. She knew he was suffering from worry about the safety of the family; she also knew that if they left, the burden of remorse would be difficult to bear, and they would have a lifetime to think about it. The easy solution would be for her to quietly withdraw into the tranquil shell of teaching biochemistry and raising her children; after all, she was under court-ordered probation, nobody would question her motives if she did that. But she had tested the water of civil rights activism, no matter how inadvertently, and found it…and found it…what was the word?…Thrilling. Flapper was in it up to his ears with his high-profile position on the faculty of an all-black college; for the first time she understood what he felt. She moved closer to him and reached for his hand.

"Susan, I…" he began.

She interrupted. "I know," she said. He put his arm around her shoulder and she lay her head on his chest. He stroked her soft brown hair.

For some time, even before the incident, an idea had been percolating in her head. "I want to start a clinic," she whispered. "There is a desperate need."

Flapper melted. Tears welled in his eyes. "Susan, honey," he began, "I…I…dear God, I love you so much." He held her as tightly as he could without hurting her. She was so precious.

J-four unfolded the morning *Montgomery Advertiser* just delivered to his door; the two-inch headline proclaimed a simple message:

EISENHOWER

The sub-headlines told the rest of the story:

62-YEAR-OLD IKE BECOMES 34TH PRESIDENT
LANDSLIDE VICTORIES IN 39 STATES
SOUTH SLIPS BUT HOLDS SOLID FOR DEMOCRATS

J-four shook his head in wonder. He was not surprised that Eisenhower had won; he was not surprised at any of it. He was pondering the grasp of the solid South. Following the Civil War, Lincoln Republicans had rammed reconstruction down the throats of the white South and the South had voted Democratic ever since. J-four found it revealing that southern Negroes had perceived the switch in party philosophies almost 20 years ago when they stopped voting (when they could vote) Republican. In contrast, white southern voters were still giving Democratic candidates winning margins even though the drift of the Republican grand old party was clearly more representative of southern views. The GOP had no civil rights plank in the party platform; Eisenhower was entirely indifferent to Negro problems. Stevenson, the Democratic candidate on the other hand, as governor had desegregated the Illinois National Guard, and anybody who listened to what he had to say would quickly see he was a fervent advocate of civil rights at all levels. Much to the discomfort of northern supporters, Stevenson did not hesitate to point out that the South was not the only place in the country where Negroes were treated badly even if it was the most obvious. But in November 1952 here was the solid South once again blindly pulling the Democratic lever. J-four shook his head in wonder.

Susan and Flapper, on a rainy Wednesday morning, were also pondering the election of the first Republican president in 20 years. Flapper said, "I wonder what Socrates will think about this. I don't think he will be pleased...presidents are supposed to be philosophers, not warriors."

Susan nodded solemnly and said, "I think the country missed a good chance by passing up Stevenson...remember what he said about the stars?...'I have loved the stars too fondly to be fearful of the night'. Eisenhower said...'I shall go to Korea'...I wonder what Ike thinks about the stars?"

Flapper mumbled an incoherent reply as he picked up from the spattered floor a small piece of buttered and jellied toast fired from a highchair by eight-month-old Tempest Jackson who was looking down from her throne with great curiosity wondering where that sweet and gooey stuff had gone. Storm Jackson, in his own highchair, was also looking down, wondering what his sister found so interesting.

"Did you know Stevenson was a lifelong Unitarian?" Susan said in a voice Flapper noted was more casual than he thought she intended it to be.

Flapper replied, "I don't think I knew that...I thought I read somewhere that he belonged to the Presbyterian Church."

Susan said, "I was looking at an old *Newsweek* in the faculty lounge;

there was an article that said he was a lifelong Unitarian in his hometown of Bloomington, but joined the Presbyterian Church after he became governor of Illinois and moved to the state capitol in Springfield. The Unitarians were upset about it."

Flapper responded, "He probably did it to get votes...I don't think there are all that many Unitarians around the country, except maybe in New England, and these days it's probably a bad idea for a guy running for president not to be a Christian, unless of course he's Catholic. I don't know which would be worse...to be a Catholic or a Unitarian...probably Catholic, the country has had Unitarian presidents before."

Susan nodded. "That's what the Unitarians were upset about...they said he did it to get votes." Susan had more than a casual interest in Unitarianism; she had been thinking about the religious education of the twins. "Flapper," she said, "What do you know about Unitarianism? I remember the poem 'A New Beginning'...written by a Unitarian minister, you said."

Flapper smiled. "Arthur Graham," he said, "...the Red Sox fan." He thought a moment, then said, "I guess I never told you...our family joined the Unitarian church after we moved to St. Louis when I was a kid and my dad was trying to escape Judaism. The Unitarians are a feisty lot. They don't have any fixed dogma, and they don't hold with the Christian idea of the Holy Trinity. Even so, there are a few Unitarians I know who still like to think of themselves as Christians. Religions in general seem to get people confused...I didn't know you were interested."

Susan put down the newspaper she was reading. "Flapper," she said, "I've been thinking a lot about religion lately...especially how it relates to these two little sweetpeas. You know I've never been all that comfortable with Catholicism...I don't want our children to grow up with all the guilt and anxieties I had. When I was eight years old a nun told me I was a sinner, and if I didn't behave I would go to Hell...I never did stop worrying about it; I still dream about it sometimes. I don't want these two to go through that. Look at them, Flapper, they are so adorable."

Flapper looked. What he saw was elfin innocence, Susan's dark eyes, his own dark hair, jelly-smeared, chubby cheeks. What he felt was warmth, pleasure, happiness, and a nagging concern that it was his job to provide for these pixies, and to protect them from evil now and forevermore. But Susan was right, they were adorable. He looked at Susan...*she* was adorable. He wanted to freeze the moment. He stood up and kissed Tempest and Storm on top of their soft brown heads, then walked over and kissed Susan in the same place. He then sat down and said, "So what do you want to do?"

"Well," said Susan, "I think they should have religious education, but...I don't know...that's why I was asking about Unitarians...I thought that if Stevenson likes it maybe it's something worth looking into. Is there a Unitarian Church here in Auburn?"

Flapper shrugged. "I don't know," he said, "I'll ask J-four; he'll know. Unitarians...they are pesky bunch...if the cross is the symbol for Christianity, the question mark is the symbol of Unitarianism...I guess that's what you get with a non-dogmatic church...lots of questions. I once heard it said that given the choice between going to heaven or joining a discussion group about going to heaven, a good Unitarian would unhesitatingly choose the latter. There is also the story about the Unitarian vigilantes who substituted the burning question mark for the burning cross."

Susan laughed. "A religion where you have to provide your own answers? No wonder there aren't many members."

The Auburn Unitarian Fellowship was gathering at its regular meeting place, and at its regular time...10 o'clock Sunday morning in the Alabama National Guard armory. Folding chairs were set up on one end of the basketball court that doubled as a drill space, or maybe it was the other way around. In any case, not many chairs were needed because the membership consisted of only 20 families, as well as two single men and one single woman. Flapper and Susan, after some hesitation, had left the twins with a teenage girl who was in charge of the nursery. They felt isolated, exposed, and a bit cool sitting on the free-throw line in the drafty gymnasium waiting for the service to begin. Music from a scratchy record floated past their curious ears...a jazz clarinet riffing around a vaguely familiar tune. Susan looked at Flapper questioningly. Flapper shrugged and looked at the printed program. In large letters at the top he saw:

TO QUESTION IS THE ANSWER

Below that was the meditation:

Beyond the bright searchlights of science,
Out of sight of the windows of sense,
Old riddles still bid us defiance,
Old questions of Why and of Whence
William Cecil Dampier

Flapper then noted what was listed as the "Address"...*no sermon for the Unitarians,* he thought.

DARWIN'S BULLDOG:
SCIENCE VERSUS RELIGION IN 19TH CENTURY ENGLAND

Ref.—Apes, Angels, and Victorians — Darwin, Huxley, and Evolution
By William Irvine

Dion McKeen, head of the API Philosophy Department, spiritual leader of the Auburn Unitarian Fellowship, and speaker of the day, approached the battered wooden lectern at the end of the free-throw lane. Seeing him standing under the folded up backboard Susan had an odd feeling recalling ornate and sacred altars she had kneeled before. She wondered if his words would rebound, and how many times she would hear them.

McKeen did not waste any time getting into his topic. "His name was Thomas Henry Huxley," he began. "He was born above a butcher shop, the seventh of eight children, in Ealing, Middlesex, England in eighteen twenty-five, six years before Charles Darwin embarked on *H.M.S. Beagle*. His formal schooling ended after two years when he was ten years old, yet he became a polymath. When he died in eighteen ninety-five he had been associated with, and in many cases was president of the following scientific organizations in the United Kingdom...the Royal Society, the Linnean Society, the Zoological Society, the Royal College of Surgeons, the Odontological Society, the Physiological Society, The Royal Irish Academy, the Royal Medico-Chirurgical Society, the Dublin Botanical and Zoological Societies, the Cambridge and Glasgow Philosophical Societies, the Royal College of Surgeons of Ireland, the Geological Society, the Paleontographical Society, the Ethnological Society, and the British Association for the Advancement of Science. He was an honorary member of more than fifty scientific societies around the world including the American Academy of Arts and Sciences, the American Philosophical Society, and the New York Academy of Sciences. He was generally recognized as the most influential scientist of the century.

"Charles Darwin was hardly the first to imagine that man had evolved from lower species, it was an idea that was a hot topic for scientific discussion in the middle of the nineteenth century, and you can bet that Huxley was in on the debate. Though his own work included the observation of significant relationships between embryonic stages of widely differing animal groups, he was in fact one of the skeptics until he read Darwin's book, *The Origin of*

Species, published in eighteen fifty-nine. Huxley was overwhelmed by the force of the evidence Darwin had accumulated, and soon became an enthusiastic and forceful advocate of Darwin's thesis that man had evolved from lower forms of animal life. In the spirited public debate over the merits of the book, and more to the point, over the challenge posed to contemporary religious beliefs, Huxley was in the forefront. He was happy to be called 'Darwin's Bulldog'; Darwin himself preferring to let the book and others speak for him.

"When the British Association for the Advancement of Science met at Oxford in June of eighteen sixty, only six months after publication of the *Origin of Species,* Huxley found himself on the platform facing a boisterous and hostile audience of over seven hundred, including ladies with fluttering handkerchiefs on a hot afternoon. Curiously for a scientific meeting, a large contingent of clergymen had come to hear the Bishop of Oxford, Samuel Wilberforce, put the lie to Darwin's outrageous theory. The clergymen knew all too well, as proclaimed by Archbishop James Ussher, that creation of man and all the animals had occurred on Sunday, October twenty-third, four thousand and four B.C., at ten o'clock in the morning."

Susan and Flapper joined in the general laughter.

McKeen beamed at the response and continued. "Bishop Wilberforce, known to undergraduates as 'Soapy Sam,' enthusiastically attacked Darwinism to the delight of his audience, and it turned out, to Huxley as well, who recognized that the bishop did not really know what he was talking about. In the end, the bishop blundered...carried away by his success, he turned to Huxley and said, 'and so, dear sir, I beg you to tell me, was it through your grandmother or through your grandfather that you are descended from a monkey?'

"Following thunderous applause when the bishop sat down, the audience called loudly for Huxley to reply, which he did. In a careful and solemn style he explained key points of Darwin's thesis, pointed out errors in the bishop's presentation, then in a grave and dignified manner addressed the bishop directly, as the bishop in the end had addressed him: 'Lord Bishop, with due respect, sir, if the question is put to me would I rather have a miserable ape for a grandfather or a man highly endowed by nature and possessed of great means of influence, and yet employs those faculties and that influence for the mere purpose of introducing ridicule into a grave scientific discussion...I unhesitatingly affirm my preference for the ape.' The audience dissolved in laughter and cheered Huxley loudly."

The Auburn Unitarians laughed and cheered loudly as well—to Susan's great surprise—she had always thought religious gatherings were meant to be occasions for grave and sober reflection.

McKeen now added a footnote to the famous Huxley rebuttal. "The debate of course had only begun," he said, "and as anyone who reads the current letters to the editor of the Birmingham News knows, shows no signs of letting up." He looked up at a few uttered agreements, smiled and continued. "Some four years after Huxley put himself on the side of the apes, Benjamin Disraeli, later to become Prime Minister, in a speech at Oxford, proclaimed, 'The question is this: is man an ape or an angel? My Lord, I am on the side of the angels.'...Today some would say it is possible to take both sides."

McKeen then did turn the mood to one of sober reflection, with an account of Huxley's response to the crisis of grief he and his wife suffered when their adored four-year-old son died suddenly from scarlet fever. A letter of sympathy from the chaplain of Westminster Abbey affirmed that he, the Right Reverend Thomas Kingsley, could not face the loss of a loved one without the assurance of meeting that person in the next life. Huxley replied with a long letter, and here McKeen read excerpts from the letter.

> *"My convictions, positive and negative, on the matters of which you speak, are of long and slow growth and are firmly rooted. But the great blow, which fell upon me, seemed to stir them to their foundation, and had I lived a couple of centuries earlier I could have fancied a devil scoffing at me and them — and asking me what profit it was to have stripped myself of the hopes and consolations of the mass of mankind? To which my only reply was and is — Oh devil! truth is better than much profit. I have searched over the grounds of my belief, and if wife and child and name and fame were all lost to me one after the other as the penalty, still I will not lie...Science seems to me to teach in the highest and strongest manner the great truth which is embodied in the Christian conception of entire surrender to the will of God. Sit down before the fact as a little child, be prepared to give up every preconceived notion, follow humbly wherever and to whatever abysses nature leads, or you shall learn nothing."*

Susan heard nothing after the mention of the crisis of grief, and found herself trying to suppress sobs as McKeen quoted Huxley describing the cold body with the tangled golden hair who had only a week previous been romping in delight and joy. When McKeen began to read from Huxley's letter to the Queens' Chaplain, Susan headed for the nursery to be sure Tempest and Storm were all right. She found them crawling happily around the room with two other precious creepers. She returned to her seat next to Flapper just in time to hear a white-haired lady in a front row seat ask, "So Professor McKeen, if we can take no solace in a better life to come what are we left with?"

McKeen replied without hesitation. "If the prospect of a better life to come is soothing to you, Mary, do not hesitate to take solace in it; there is no convincing evidence to deny it. Huxley's point is: neither do we have evidence to support it. If you accept the prospect, you are a theist; if you deny the prospect, you are an atheist. Both positions demand the religion of faith. Huxley invented the word agnostic to define his own position, which was simply that he did not see scientific evidence to support either theism or atheism."

"And what is the Unitarian position?" a voice from the rear asked.

McKeen responded. "It is a matter of individual choice. If I recall correctly, the last numbers I saw showed that more than half the Unitarians polled chose the theistic position, but rejected the idea of a messiah."

"Only half? You mean most Unitarians are godless atheists?" The voice from the rear was indignant.

McKeen smiled indulgently at this unrecognized visitor and said, "I suppose you could say that, if you wanted to be redundant. But don't forget this...to be agnostic does not deny the existence of God, it simply begs the question."

The voice was not finished. "What about Jesus?"

McKeen had a ready answer for that. "Unitarians join a long list of distinguished Americans in denying the divinity of Jesus," he answered. "The founding fathers were almost universally in this group...Franklin, Washington, Adams, Jefferson, Madison. Jefferson almost lost the 1799 presidential election because of his strong opinions on the subject. He was viciously attacked by clerics for his anti-Christian views, and fought back by declaring he was against all tyranny including that of the mind, which he saw the clerics guilty of. Madison and Jefferson made sure separation of church and state, as well as freedom of religion, were included in the Bill of Rights of the U.S. Constitution."

The voice from the rear had heard enough—the voice and the legs beneath it headed for the door.

The white-haired lady in the front row asked, "But how can you lead a moral life if you don't believe in God?"

McKeen answered, "That's easy, Mary, you can practice the lessons of the Sermon on the Mount without believing in God...love thy neighbor as thyself does not require credulity."

McKeen waited for further questions, and finding none, went on to his closing anecdote. "Let me tell you about the prayer test," he said. "Some Victorian scientists proposed to experimentally test the power of prayer, and by implication to prove the existence of God. They chose a group of patients suffering from a disease of known mortality rate, and made them the object of special healing prayers by a designated group of the faithful. If there was a reduced mortality rate after three to five years it might be concluded that God had heeded the prayers and had interceded on behalf of the sick. If this seems preposterous to us today we may be equally amazed to know it sparked a raging debate in the Victorian England of the eighteen seventies. The clerics were cornered, but not dumfounded...they had all manner of ripostes, including one that basically the experiment had already been done by Sisters of Mercy who routinely prayed for the health of their patients, and it was only necessary to check the records of their recovery rates. The proposed test ultimately foundered on the shoals of the scientific requirement for a control group, and the Christian repugnancy *not* to pray for such a group.

"One can only wonder at the number of people who have conducted their personal prayer test, and how lives have been influenced accordingly. Think of the people whose prayers were answered when Bobby Thompson beat the Dodgers last year with the miraculous ninth inning homer called 'the shot heard round the world.' But on the other side there were those Dodger fans praying that he would not hit that homer. Can we conclude that God is a Giant fan? Or is it that God being a Democrat, added up the requests and found the weight in favor of the Giants? Or could it be that it is all a hat full of nonsense? To question is the answer."

>>44<<

CHINA NIGHT

Dawg McCan became a tourist after first declining the opportunity of a 50 mile bus trip south from Sasebo to Nagasaki to view the atomic bomb damage, uncomfortable with vague feelings of personal responsibility, and repelled by the idea of viewing a human tragedy as entertainment. But the Navy, true to its promise, was bent on showing him more than the edge of the world—an all-expense paid, fun-filled trip to the wonders of the war-devastated Orient. He sailed the seas—the Sea of Japan, the East China Sea, the South China Sea, theAndaman Sea. He sailed the straits—the Straits of Formosa, the Straits of Singapore, the Straits of Malacca, the wondrous, boulevard-narrow Straits of Shimoneseki. He sailed the wide and expansive bays—Manila Bay, Tokyo Bay. The Palawan Passage, the Irrawaddy Delta. He became a shellback at 107° east of Greenwich near Pulau-Pulau Lingga. Hong Kong, Singapore, and Rangoon were relatively undamaged; Tokyo, Yokahama, Manila, and Kaohsiung were not; Macau was untouched. He smelled the odors, he listened to the sounds, he saw the people.

And at last Okinawa. Now it was peaceful, and they called it Buckner Bay, named for the Army commanding general killed by an exploding shell during the final and bloodiest battle of the Pacific war—Okinawa. When Booker T. was here before it was called Nakagusuku Wan, and it was a cauldron of death. The island now occupied a strategic spot in the United States Far East defense perimeter against the perceived Chinese communist evils. For four weeks the *Agerholm* had been engaged in patrols 12 miles off the coast of China, up and down the Formosa straits, dodging fishing boats, and looking for invasion fleets. Now they were coming to Okinawa for refueling, and a few days of rest and relaxation. Booker T. trembled with emotion when he remembered the children on the beach. He never learned the fate of the beautiful little girl who often appeared in his dreams and haunted his memories. They told him that no children, dead or alive, had been reported on the beach. It was a blank wall, but the thought of suffering children clouded his thoughts.

Moose Odell and Dawg McCan crossed the quarterdeck, and saluted the officer of the deck smartly. "Request permission to leave the ship, sir," they said, almost in unison. Spider Snyder, a heavy .45 caliber service pistol hanging on his hip, gave a half-hearted salute in return and said, "What kind of buddies are you? Goin' on liberty without old Spider. Who's gonna show you what to do?"

Moose put his arm over Spider's shoulder in a friendly way and said, "Let's just call it a reconnaissance mission, Spider. We'll just scout around a little, get an idea what's out there. We wouldn't go on a serious liberty without the Spiderman, would we?"

"Okay," said Spider, "but you guys stay out of trouble, you hear?"

Moose and Dawg walked together, listing slightly to port, up the long wooden dock, and wondered at the crowds of people coming toward them; servicemen stationed on the island, bringing their families for a Sunday afternoon outing to visit the destroyer and submarine tied up to the dock. Booker T. and his shipmate were trying to escape the ship; the people were trying to escape the island. At the end of the dock Moose and Dawg caught a bus that headed up a dusty, meandering, hilly road to the Officers' Club on the edge of the Air Force base.

Deep-water sailors were like iron filings to the magnetic field of grain alcohol, taboo aboard ship, sanctioned on land, exalted in the service clubs. The finest French champagne was available here at the Officers' Club for two dollars a bottle. Moose and Dawg were not interested in champagne. They asked for a fifth of Jack Daniel's sour mash whiskey, two shot glasses, and two steins of beer. They sat at a patio table with a fine view of the bay, and began some serious drinking. A toast to their first liberty in three weeks...a shot of whiskey washed down with a draught of beer got them off to a good start. For Dawg McCan at the advanced age of 27, drinking, as with everything else, was not an activity to be engaged in casually. He knew exactly how much whisky and beer were required to get him in the mellow mood he craved. Half a bottle of Jack Daniel's and six bottles of Asahi beer were just about right; more than that made him cantankerous and combative. It was different with Moose. His mellow mood was short-lived, followed quickly by belligerence, and soon thereafter by insentience. It was not easy for a dog and a spider to carry a moose, but they had managed it on more than one weighty occasion.

The services also encouraged gambling, seeing it as an innocent diversion for men with time on their hands; the club was festooned with slot machines. Dawg and Moose began playing the nickel machines with indifferent success. Near them were two mellow Air Force second lieutenants playing a quarter machine.

"You swabs ridin' that can ain'tcha?"

"Howdja know?" Moose looked at them suspiciously.

"You ain't pale enough for the sub." They laughed. "You been out in the straits ain'tcha?"

Moose bristled. "What's it to you flyboy? You some kind of commie spy or somethin'?"

"Cool it, Boats, we been there too."

"Wad'ja do, swim?" Moose snorted.

"We flew."

"Did your arms get tired?" Moose giggled.

"We're in P two-V's. We're up and down that fuckin' coast five times a week. One week, days, the next week, nights. Gets pretty damn old. Rocks and Junks in the daytime, nothin' but black at night. Except when we buzz you shitbirds. Our skipper loves to do that." They laughed again.

Booker T. spoke up. "If that was you who illuminated us on the midwatch last week, yer lucky you didn't get yer ass shot off."

"That was us." They laughed uproariously.

Booker T. remembered. The ship had been steaming under increased state of readiness condition three, one step below general quarters. The main battery was manned, and the whole crew was on a one in three watch, a schedule that reduced them to hollow-eyed zombies if continued for more than a very few days. Booker T. had relieved the junior officer of the deck at 15 minutes before midnight on a moonless and cloudy night. The faint glow from shaded lights on the helm, engine order telegraph, and binnacle contrasted with the inky blackness of the night. The world seemed far away as the ship, with two boilers on the line, steamed north at a leisurely 12 knots, rolling gently in the calm sea. There was little breeze, and it was an altogether pleasant night to be on deck. The soft swish of the water as the bow of the ship sliced through it was soothing. Booker T. and Lope Cooley were on the wing of the bridge quietly discussing their mission while watching the phosphorescent glow of thousands of sea creatures stirred up by the turbulence, when suddenly, without warning, the entire ship was bathed in light bright as day; it was as if someone had flipped the switch for a giant spotlight. Before they had time to react, striker Perkins on the sound powered phones reported, "CIC says there's a P two-V Neptune in the vicinity asking us to identify ourselves."

Lope Cooley was shaken, confused, and angry. He shouted, "Tell those assholes to turn out that goddamn light before we shoot it out." The plane had flown on, and the incident was over as quickly as it had started, but not before Cooley had roasted the Combat Information Center for not picking up the plane on radar. They hadn't picked it up because the air search radar didn't work, and nobody knew how to fix it.

All this flashed through Booker T.'s mind as he watched the two Air Force shavetails having a laugh at his expense.

"I'll let you in on a little secret though, Boats." The lieutenant was laughing so hard he could barely get the words out. "Our skipper thought you were a Russian cruiser." Tears of glee covered his cheeks.

Booker T. joined in the laughter. "What would he have done if it *was* a Russian cruiser?"

"Probably shit his pants." Hoots of laughter.

Moose joined in. "Last week one of our lookouts reported what looked like a light cruiser on the horizon, and when I asked the captain if he wanted to train the main battery in that direction he said, 'Don't even spit in that direction'." Guffaws.

Booker T. turned serious. "That light cruiser turned out to be a British merchantman...said they were hauling soy beans from Shanghai to Rotterdam. That same day we spotted another Limey carting timber from Foochow to Shanghai. I wish somebody would explain to me how it is that the Chinks are our enemies, the Limeys are our friends, and the Limeys and Chinks are doing business. I don't get it."

"We're not supposed to get it, Boats. We just keep the fuckin' ships and planes runnin', and let the fuckin' brass do the thinkin'."

The other lieutenant chimed in. "Are you kiddin' me, Al? Them fuckers don't know no more than we do. The other day a bird colonel tried to tell me why we were out here, and he got so screwed up I finally asked him if he knew what Shinola was and he said, 'That's a bunch of shit'." Roars of laughter.

After an interval, Booker T. asked, "Can you guys tell us how to get to The Teahouse of the August Moon?"

The two lieutenants looked at each other, and shook their heads. "I don't think you wanna go there, Boats, that's a jarhead hangout."

Booker T. said, "I ain't afraid of no jarheads."

"How'd you know about that place anyhow?"

"A mamasan up in Sasebo told me about it."

"She probably didn't know about them jarheads...they don't like nobody hornin' in on their fun, especially swab jockies."

Booker T. laughed. "It's a free country, ain't it? How do we get there?"

They bounced over the hilly, dusty road in an Air Force jeep; the lieutenants in front, Moose and Booker T. in the back.

"We just gonna drop you off in front, that's as close as we wanna get to that damn place. You sure you wanna go there?"

"We're sure," said Booker T. "We ain't afraid of no jarheads, right Moose?" Moose grinned.

The Air Force lieutenant shook his head. "Gettin' back is your own problem," he said. "There's a bus that runs from Naha to the base, but it ain't very regular."

Booker T. and Moose were not worried about getting back; they would find a way. The ship was not scheduled to leave until the day after tomorrow. In the meantime they had to check out this teahouse that Mother McCree had told them about. Thinking about her, Booker T. began humming the tune that always went with her image. Moose picked it up, and to the surprise of the Air Force lieutenants, loud and boisterous singing rose from the back seat. They heard, *"Sure I love the dear silver that shines in your hair, and I love the sweet face that's all wrinkled with care..."*

Navy and Air Force collaboration was never better as the shavetails joined in the chorus. *"Oh God bless you and keep you...Mother McCree."*

Naha was the capital of Okinawa and the largest city on the island. The place where they dropped Dawg and Moose was on the outskirts of the city on a quiet, dimly lighted street corner. Their blood flowing with 190 proof ethyl alcohol, their wits dimmed to the level of alcohol lamps, they were oblivious to the wretchedness of the indomitable people living behind the manifold thin walls within range of their ugly American voices. They looked up at a paint-peeling sign featuring flickering neon light tubes...TEAHOUSE OF THE AUGUST MOON.

They stepped onto the sagging porch of a flimsy-looking wooden building, and heard music coming from behind the fragile walls—that nasal twang again, Vaughn Monroe, "Ghost Riders in the Sky." They entered a low-ceilinged, dimly lighted room with booths lining the walls, a bar on one end, and a small dance floor in the middle. The music was coming from a small black radio. There were a few couples dancing but the floor was not crowded. Booker T. saw two Okinawan girls with bleached-blond hair.

Moose and Dawg ordered beers from the bar, and sat in an empty booth near the door. Soon they were approached by a bantam, wrinkled old lady wearing sparkling white socks in toe-thonged slippers and an elegant black kimono. She bowed and said, "You wanta girl, okay?"

Booker T. stood, returned the bow, and asked, "Are you Mamasan Shigetsu? Mother McCree from Sasebo told us to come here."

The old lady looked at them suspiciously. "How I trust you, sailor boysan?"

Booker T. took a small jade pendant from his pocket, and handed it to the old lady. She looked at it, fingered it carefully, then looked up and smiled a gap-toothed smile. "You gonna wait here, sailor boysan," she said. She began to shuffle away then stopped, and looked back at Booker T. "Today you lucky day, sailor boysan..."

Soon she returned with two girls. One sat next to Moose. "My name Peaches," she said. "You gonna be long-timer, honey?"

Half a foot taller than Mamasan Shigetsu, her eyes cast down in shyness, stood the other girl. "This very special girl, sailor boysan," said the mamasan, addressing Booker T. "Her ancestor Ryuku Kings...she no come here before. You treat her nice, okay? Her name Heidi. You treat her nice, okay?"

"What's her real name, Mamasan, and why does she limp?" Booker T. asked.

"Real name Hideko, she hurt in war. She no speak English. She from royal family...you treat her nice, okay?" The old lady shuffled off leaving the young girl standing alone.

Booker T. got up and took the girl's hand. Next he put his finger under her chin and gently lifted. Slowly her eyes came up to meet his. She was *that* beautiful. She was a royal princess. He felt the blood rush to his face. He tried to speak, but no words came. Her eyes widened when she looked at him. He felt her relax, and she smiled so sweetly he thought he would dissolve. They began to sway to "Mood Indigo," and moved to the dance floor, clinging tightly to each other as the world disappeared.

They danced in silence for an eternity, their eyes closed, their minds groping for each other. At length Booker T. sensed she was tiring, and they sat at the booth. She took a spent match from the ashtray, and began to draw on the paper table covering. Booker T. watched in fascination as she drew a round face with two crossed eyes and a tongue sticking out. Next she drew two vertical lines, crossed them with two horizontal lines and made an X in the middle square. She looked impishly at him, handed him the matchstick, and giggled at his astonishment.

"But you must speak to me," Booker T. stammered. She did not understand.

"I remember you from the beach. You saved my life the day my little brother was killed. I could never forget you."

He did not understand. But he knew he must understand. He jumped to his feet.

"Don't let her leave, Moose. I'm gonna get the mamasan so I can find out what she's saying."

He was only gone a few minutes, but it was long enough for trouble to brew. When he returned with Mamasan Shigetsu in tow, he found a big red-faced Marine standing next to the table talking to Hideko who was shrinking from him in confusion.

"Who's the new gal, Mamasan? And how come you fix her up with these swab jockies?"

"Get lost, jarhead, I fix who I want."

"Izzat so? Since when you gettin' so high and mighty?" The big Marine stood menacingly over the small but implacable mamasan.

"You make trouble, you gonna see M.P.'s plenty quick, okay? Go peddle a fish, jarhead."

The Marine stared at the diminutive mamasan uncertainly, swore under his breath, and walked away, grumbling to himself.

"Mamasan, tell me what she is saying. I must know," said Booker T.

Hideko repeated what she had said about Booker T. saving her life on the beach. Then she told how, when the shelling stopped, a Japanese soldier risked his life by carrying her off the beach to a hospital unit where she was cared for. The soldier was later killed, as were all the other soldiers defending the beach area. For three months the killing continued. The explosions terrified her and her family. They fled to the north end of the island along with many other civilians, but they could not escape entirely. She had seen much death. When the war ended, they returned to their home, but it was destroyed, and they had to rebuild it. The family was poor. Her father was a fisherman, but his boat was ruined so he could not fish. He tried to farm, but it was difficult. She could not help because of her damaged leg. Her brother had been killed on the beach so there was no one else. Now she was old enough to work in a teahouse; she wanted to earn some money to help her family.

As she translated this story, Mamasan Shigetsu grew more and more sad, and at the end she was crying freely. Everyone was touched by the tragic tale, an archetype of civilian suffering for Okinawa, and the world. More than 100,000 civilians had died here in a three-month frenzy of violence.

Booker T. listened in awe, confused by unfamiliar feelings, guilt near the top of the list, as he watched the beautiful young girl tell her story.

"Ask her if I can meet her family," he said, suddenly feeling that this enchanting maiden...this royal princess...was put on earth for him to take care of.

Mamasan Shigetsu looked at him as if he were crazy. "Why you wanna meet her family? They no like Americans. They have plenty good life before Americans come. Americans kill their son, wreck their home and boat."

Booker T. knew it was true. He also knew he could not leave her. She inspired unknown emotions he wanted to explore. He engaged in wild fantasy. He imagined himself living on the island as a native, learning the language, helping her father build a boat, learning to be a fisherman. He imagined taking her with him on the ship; he would smuggle her aboard in a seabag, his shipmates would help. He would take her back to the States; she would learn his language, they would live happily ever after.

His fantasy was interrupted by a sudden quiet; the music had stopped. He heard a voice from the radio say, "This is P.J. your D.J. on Armed Forces radio Okinawa. The time, for you civilians, is three a.m.... for you Air Force good buddies, it's zero three hundred hours...for you Navy swabs, welcome to six bells on the midwatch...and for all you jarheads out there, listen up now...the small hand is on three and the big hand is on twelve."

Booker T. laughed just as the big red-faced Marine was passing the booth.

"You think that's funny do you? You nigger bastard." He towered over the booth, his face a mask of hate.

Booker T. recognized the signs of big trouble. This was a trained killer, drunk, mean, and hostile. It occurred to Booker T. that if his earthly destiny was to take care of the fair Hideko, this would be his first opportunity, not counting the beach. He did not hesitate. He sprang to his feet, emptied his glass in the Marine's face, then kicked him in the kneecap. Next he brought his knee into the jarhead's groin, and when the Marine bent in pain lifted his knee under the stricken man's chin. The big Marine fell backward onto the floor with a crash.

Booker T. grabbed Hideko by the hand, and rushed for the door. Two other Marines tried to stop them, but were quickly engaged by Moose Odell who never backed away from a good fight. They were out the door and into the street in an instant. He knew there was not much time before the Marines would be after them. Hideko pointed to a side street, and they headed for it. He quickly realized that she could not keep up because of her damaged leg. He lifted her onto his back, and ran piggyback style hardly aware she was there. He could hear the Marines shouting behind them.

Hideko, feather-light on his back, directed him into alleys and dark biways, making it easy to escape the angry Marines. Booker T. thought about Moose, and hoped he was all right. Now, the danger past, he stopped to catch his breath. They stood somewhere in total darkness, alone in the universe.

She took his hand, and they began to walk slowly.

They walked for a long time…away from the sleeping city and into the countryside. She was taking him to a special place. He felt at peace with her near him. Perhaps he had it wrong. Perhaps his destiny was for her to take care of him.

They sat near the edge of a cliff that dropped 200 feet straight down to a sandy beach. Holding hands, they felt the darkness slowly disappear. The sky lightened to a soft blue, then through the miracle of pink, orange, red, violet, and deep purple. Shafts of light reflected from high clouds and held them in awe. It did not matter that they spoke different languages, words would have been an intrusion; they moved closer. She laid her head on his chest; his arm encircled her shoulder and held her tightly. She felt warm and safe. For a long time they were quiet.

She began to hum, then shyly, and almost inaudibly to sing. "*Shee ee nano yo roo, Shee ee nano yo roo o ooo…*" — "China Night." A beautiful and poignant love song he had heard often at Mother McCree's Teahouse. He did not know what the words meant, but knew they spoke of a tragic lost love. He had seen Mother McCree's girls tremble with emotion as they sang the haunting melody. Never had he heard it expressed more beautifully…slight nuances, catches in her throat, singing sobs. He was stunned by a wellspring of feeling, and deeply touched.

When she finished there was a long silence again, as Booker T. sorted through his emotions, wondering at the unfamiliar feelings. He felt compelled to communicate to her through song as she had to him. Knowing the words would have no meaning for her, he searched his mind for a melody that would convey the warmth and tenderness he felt for her. He began to sing softly,

"*Sure I love the dear silver that shines in your hair, and I love the sweet face that's all wrinkled with care... Oh, God love you and keep you, Mother McCree."*

He sang it slowly and quietly, with as much feeling as he could. When he finished, she looked deep into his eyes. Tears welled, and began to run down her cheeks, first in a single stream, then in a cascade. She began to sob, and then to weep without restraint. Now they were both weeping. Together they mourned the centuries of unkindness, injustice, and cruelty. They cried for the desperate hopelessness of their circumstances and for the whole world as well.

They lamented until exhausted, then, as the sun rose, they slept.

>>45<<

THE VOICE FROM THE REAR

The voice from the rear belonged to Stanley Gordon, and Stanley was steaming as he headed for the exit. Stanley had been attracted to the Unitarian meeting by the notice in the *Lee County Bulletin* and by a certain curiosity when he had learned that J-four was a member of the Auburn Unitarian Fellowship. But what he had heard and seen here today left him bull-red angry. There was J-four, sitting next to the nigger they called Socrates; there was that white trash woman who had been arrested for sitting in the nigger section of the public bus, and there was the head of the API Philosophy Department telling everybody it was okay to be a godless atheist.

Stanley couldn't wait to tell Virgil Young, who he knew for a certainty could be found this bright Sunday morning at the Southern Baptist Church in Tallassee, on the Talapoosa river, over in Elmore County, about 30 miles away. If he hurried he might catch the last part of the sermon, which he also knew for a certainty would have something to say about God's love and the ultimate destination of sinners. Stanley felt vaguely unclean leaving the Unitarians, and hoped for a small redemption from the Baptists. Stanley honked impatiently at some Sunday morning drivers on the narrow highway, and finally skidded to a stop in the church parking lot just in time to see Virgil shaking hands with the parson at the church door. Stanley jumped out of his car and rushed up the steps to confront Virgil.

"Virgil," he said breathlessly, "am ah evah glad to see you. Can we go somewhere and talk?" Stanley was slightly out of breath from the fast pace of his driving, and his curious tendency to hyperventilate when he was excited.

Virgil looked at him from narrowed eyes; he was suspicious of Stanley because of his association with API. Virgil had a healthy mistrust for all things academic, and there was something about Stanley he couldn't put his finger on that made him doubly wary. He had never seen Stanley so agitated.

"Now slow down heah, Stanley," he said, "you actin' like you done seen the Lord Jesus Christ his self on this fine Sunday mornin'. What is it that's troublin' you, son?"

Stanley looked around at the flock of people coming out of the handsome brick church, with the soaring white steeple topped by a splendid white cross, and felt a cleansing need to enter the sanctuary. "Virgil, " he said, "can we go inside and talk? Ah think this is important."

Stanley, followed by Virgil, entered the now empty church and sat in a wooden pew somewhere near the middle of the room. Stanley admired the stained glass windows on the side and behind the pulpit. He actually crossed himself and made a small genuflection toward the altar before he entered the pew, something he could never recall having done in his entire life.

Virgil, coming behind, eyed him suspiciously, and made a mental note to ask Stanley if he was a goddamned Catholic. "Now, Stanley," he said, "what's this all about? You actin' mighty strange, boy."

"Virgil, ah just come from a meetin' in Auburn that you would not believe unless you was there like ah was."

"You gonna tell me what it was?"

"It was the Unitarians."

Virgil was puzzled. He was not sure he had heard right. "What's that, Stanley?"

"They call themselves a religion, but they don't believe in God.Virgil, ah heard em' say it with mah own ears. And Jesus, too."

"Stanley, you sure you all right?"

"Honest to God, Virgil, they said in their religion it's okay to not believe in God."

Virgil was mildly interested, but not excited. He knew there were people who didn't believe in God. One of his uncles one time admitted to him that he wasn't all that sure about the Virgin Birth; of course, that was after he had half a bottle of moonshine whiskey in him. The thought of whiskey caused him to touch his back pocket to be sure his hip flask was were it was supposed to be. "Now, Stanley," he said, "ah know, and ah think most ever body else knows, maybe except you, that there are people who don't believe in God...did you ever hear of Hindus and Mohammedans? Ah'm not that worried about people like that...the way ah look at it, it's just that much more room in heaven for people like you and me. Stanley boy, did you bust yo' ass rushin' all the way over here from Auburn just to tell me there is people who don't believe in God?"

"But, Virgil," Stanley protested, "the worst part of it was they was sittin' down together in that room with some niggahs, includin' that Socrates you put a bullet into a couple of months ago, which reminds me...I forgot to tell you before...that theah niggah, that Socrates, is over a hundred years old."

Virgil sat up straight. He could tolerate people not believing in God, that was their own funeral, but an integrated religious service in this part of Alabama, *his* part of Alabama, was something else. He sat still for a moment as Stanley watched him closely...waiting...expecting...hoping, for the type of violent outburst Virgil was famous for. This was in fact the main reason Stanley had rushed to bring his shocking report to Virgil as quickly as he could. When he probed his own beliefs deep enough, which he had done one time, he found himself mildly indifferent to the idea of an unsegregated society, but he was fatally enthralled by the passion such a concept aroused in Virgil. Sometimes he thought that a lot of his Klan brethren felt the same way; they were just in it to see how violent Virgil Young could get.

Virgil took the flask from his back pocket and lifted a long draught. Wiping his mouth with the back of his sleeve, he turned his gaze to Stanley and said, in a half whisper. "You done right to tell me, Stanley. This is serious." He paused. "...A hundred years old, you say?"

Stanley was alert to the menace in Virgil's whispered comment. Stanley's relationship to Virgil contained no small element of fear. Virgil was a commanding presence when he stood up—tall and thin, with arrow-straight posture, coal-black hair without a hint of gray even in his mid-fifties; dark eyes peering out from under bushy black eyebrows, large powerful hands. Virgil sat, apparently lost in thought, leaving Stanley wondering if he ought to get up and leave now that he had delivered his message. Stanley looked at the large stained glass window above and behind the pulpit, noting an angel, probably a guardian angel he thought, looking down on a pastoral scene showing sheep and children. To the side of the pulpit, in large white letters on a black message board, Stanley saw posted the scripture lesson: Matthew 19:24.

"What was the sermon about today?" Stanley blurted. As the words slipped out of his mouth he wanted them back because temerity was not part of his game, especially with Virgil, and he had no wish to intrude on Virgil's thoughts when he was clearly submerged in hatching a devilish scheme to inform the Unitarians. It was the first time he had ever tried to engage Virgil in a conversation.

Virgil was deep in thought, to be sure, but it had nothing to do with the

Unitarians. He first considered the prospect of being over 100 years old, but those thoughts were soon buried in a sexual fantasy involving the preacher's fine wife, who had a penchant for tight blouses and sweaters. Virgil thought of himself as a free man, just coming off the end of his third marriage, and any woman who displayed herself like that preacher's wife he thought of as fair game for his manly pursuits. He wasn't sure exactly how many children he had scattered around the county, or the world for that matter; he remembered high times in 1918 France, but it was not a matter of great concern to him. Born in 1898, Virgil was an authentic chip off the old Abraham Young, his grandpa, block.

Virgil looked up and said, "What?...The sermon?...It was the eye of the needle sermon."

It was Stanley's turn to ask what. "What?"

Virgil snorted. "This preacher likes to talk about poverty. Once or twice a year he tells us it's easier for a camel to pass through the eye of a needle than for a rich man to enter the kingdom of God. He wants us to give all our money to the poor, which as near as ah can tell means either the church or the niggahs...We fixin' to get rid of this preacher." He took another swig from his flask.

Seeing that Virgil was talkative, Stanley was emboldened to ask, "You worried about enterin' the kingdom of God, Virgil?"

Virgil Young was riding high in the saddle. He was overflowing with the things he liked best...sex, violence, and booze, in no particular order. Virgil was not introspective, but Stanley's question triggered a thought that pleased him a great deal; he turned it over in his mind, wondering if it was profound. "You know somethin', Stanley?" he said, "Sometimes ah think ah may already be theah." His loud, cackling heehaw startled Stanley.

Stanley had another question. "Virgil," he said, "did you mean to kill that hundred-year-old niggah?"

Virgil drew in his breath sharply and flared his nostrils. "Yes ah did, Stanley," he said, "and ah would have too, if ah'd had one less shot of that good ole rot gut whiskey in mah belly." He guffawed even louder.

"What you gonna do 'bout them Unitarians, Virgil?" Stanley was eager to get the news.

Virgil knew what he was going to do, but he was in no hurry to tell Stanley, who he considered a novice still wet behind the ears with no combat experience, and no idea how to talk or act in the presence of an Exalted Cyclops like himself. Stanley would have been shocked to know that Virgil considered him a snitch and a tattletale for bringing him the information about the Unitarians even though he gave the appearance of welcoming the news. That was the problem for Virgil—he hated to be in the position of having to respond to this kind of intelligence, but when presented to him as it was, he was left with little choice. He had to do something or appear soft. "Stanley boy," he said, "have you ever heard of dynamite Dan Dooley?"

>>46<<

SOME THINGS ARE MORE IMPORTANT

"I'm sorry, McCan..." The lieutenant commander paused, looked up from his desk and smirked. "Actually I'm not sorry at all," he continued. "I'm glad. I'm glad I can keep you from wrecking your life. You are plumb off your rocker, McCan. You want to marry an Okinawan B-girl you have only known one day? You expect me to approve it?"

Booker T. stood before the *Agerholm's* Executive Officer, Lt. Commander Hayes Dorr, who liked to be called Barney. Barney Dorr had been called on to consider many an odd request from his young and quirky officers here in the exotic, post-two-wars Far East. The free, easy, and hopelessly naive young men with money in their pockets were often too easy prey for all manner of scam artists, often involving pretty women. Barney Dorr happily assumed the role of a stern father to his spirited young officer corps. This was not the first time a starry-eyed youth had appeared before him to say he had found the girl of his dreams. But with Booker T. McCan, Barney had the feeling it was different. His story was certainly different; his outlandish tale about a girl on the landing beach accompanied by his claim of destiny calling. How was he expected to believe that? And even if it was true, it was no reason to marry her. And yet here was McCan with his unshakable resolve. The exec understood at once that there was no point in attempting to persuade McCan he was making a mistake; at the same time there was no need to even try, this one would be resolved in the simplest possible way—the ship was leaving the next day, and they would not be coming back. Besides, he had no authority to approve marriage to a foreign national.

Booker T., for his part did not really expect approval, either official or unofficial, from Barney Dorr or from anyone else on the ship for that matter, not even Moose or Spider. How could anyone understand his feelings for this young woman? How could he explain? What were the odds of him finding the young girl on the invasion beach after 10 years? It had to be more than mere chance. It was destiny. The exec had looked at him in disbelief, and Booker T. thought, disgust when he presented his request. He knew it was a longshot request, but it was one he had to make. The XO was looking at him now with an expression of amusement that Booker T. found difficult to assimilate. He felt a surge of anger originating somewhere in his chest. He began to speak, but stopped himself, and spinning on his heel, abruptly left the compartment.

Booker T. walked slowly toward the after part of the ship, frantically searching for an answer to the dilemma; the ship would be underway in less than 24 hours. What he felt for Hideko was so powerful, and had hit him with such unexpected force that he knew if he gave her up his life would be forever empty and without meaning. It was as if in her he could correct the wrongs of generations; he could heal centuries of wounds. He must find a way; a way to share her life, a way for her to become part of his life. It was his destiny to bring happiness to her life—to protect her from evil. Now. Always.

Following the end of the first dog watch, six hours and some 50 miles out of their berth alongside the dock in Buckner Bay, Dawg McCan saluted perfunctorily, said with unusual conviction, "I stand relieved," and left the bridge. Descending the ladder to the main deck he noted yet another gorgeous sunset. He stopped in the wardroom for a cup of strong coffee, went to his narrow compartment in the forward part of the ship where he picked up a carefully organized rubberized hand bag, then headed for the fantail. Moving along the outside walkway on the port side of the ship, he collected two kapok life jackets from a raft secured to a bulkhead along the way. Reaching the empty fantail area, he hesitated only briefly to don one of the life jackets, then calmly slipped over the side and bobbed in the destroyer's wake, watching the ship fade from his life at a brisk 15 knots. With a surge of exhilaration he turned and began a slow paddle toward the island he knew was just over the horizon, where the Ryuku Princess waited for him.

Feeling very small, but far from insignificant in the vast firmament, Booker T. began to hum the familiar tune, then to sing the words softly, and at last, exuberantly...

"oh hear us as we cry to Thee,
for those in peril on the sea."

Then he shouted the words that he had refrained from saying to Barney Door or anybody else until now…"Some things are more important than being president of the United States."

>>47<<

GOD IS A WAG

Count lifted a glass of port, and offered a green olive to his dinner guest, Miz Sarah Lincoln. "To your very good health, Miz Sarah," he said, "and to the next one hundred years."

Sarah smiled shyly. "Thank you, Count, " she said, "you make me feel young again."

Count smiled back. "That's my job, Sarah," he said, "to make people feel young, and especially to make you feel young." They clinked glasses.

J-four had wasted no time in introducing Miz Sarah to Count…it was an inspired decision; Count and Sarah had much to share besides their longevity. Miz Sarah had outlived her husband, and all of her four sons, as well as three of her 20 grandchildren. She had recently become a great-great-great-grandmother. Her mind was as sharp as ever, she still made clothes for the little ones, and in spite of the numbers, she was able, with occasional prompting, to keep track of the names and ages of her extended family, many of whom still lived in the area. She lived with one of her granddaughters in a small house on the north edge of Auburn. She was thrilled with the recently minted television industry, which brought the world into her living room. She had taken to ending her day with the late night Jack Paar show and a glass of beer. Her advice to the young bride one of her great-great grandsons had recently brought to her: drink a glass of beer before bed to make you sleep well, and listen to Helen Trent and Young Doctor Malone, sponsored by Oxydol and Rinso, on daytime radio.

When Count came to call, she donned a perky red beret and stepped out, feeling like a teenager. "Count," she said, "did you ever think maybe the Lord had something special in mind for us when He allowed us to live over a hundred years?"

Count had been convinced of that for a very long time. He was trying his best to fulfill what he thought was his special destiny—formation and implementation of the School for Presidents. He was wondering if the Lord intended him to live another 50 years to see Booker T. McCan serve as the first Negro president of the United States. "Sarah, my love," he said, "that's exactly what I have been thinking for a long time, and the longer I live the more convinced I am."

They sat quietly for a long time, sipping their port and remembering…Count hoping she had forgotten. Sarah had not forgotten. At length she asked the question Count had been expecting. "Why didn't you come back?"

Count shifted in his seat, reached for another green olive, then said quietly, not looking at Sarah, "Girl, I did come back, soon after the war ended, but I couldn't stay after I saw you was with another man…and you looked happy. I watched to be sure. You *was* happy, I had no doubt of it. You didn't need to see me."

Sarah nodded. "It's true," she said. "I *was* happy. My man Moses was a man of God…he was a good man and a good father, bless his soul, but I never forgot you, Count." She squeezed his hand and repeated, "I never forgot you."

Another long silence ensued. Finally, Sarah spoke in a voice so soft Count had to lean closer to hear, "We had a little girl, you and I…she was so beautiful."

Count was stunned. When she said it he knew immediately it was authentic; a torrent of memories flooded his brain…desperate and reckless meetings on dark and stormy nights…fierce young love untrammeled by hopelessness. To learn after all these years that he was a father struck him like a hammer. Upon leaving Alabama after the war he had gone west, all the way to California to seek and as it happened, to find his fortune. He had never married. And now here was lovely Sarah, his first, and truly his only love, four score and seven years later, telling him he was a father. The thought was overwhelming; tears rolled down his cheeks. He was speechless.

Sarah looked at him and smiled. She placed her palm on his cheek. "I named her Mercy. They took her from me after a year and a half. She was so beautiful." Now Sarah's eyes misted.

Count moved to hold Miz Sarah close, trying to erase the injustices of the countless generations. He tried to imagine the beauty of his infant daughter…his daughter…their daughter. He thought of the beauty and grace of the young Sarah; she danced in his mind's eye. He held her close. He began to speak…hesitated…then asked, "Do you know…" The words caught in his throat.

"What happened to her?" Sarah knew. She spoke slowly and haltingly, remembering the sad events of so many years ago. "She died young…in her first childbirth…Old master took her…she was just twelve…she's gone to a better place, praise the Lord."

Count and Sarah sat close together during a long silence…holding hands…imagining the agony of their daughter Mercy. At length Count asked, "Did the baby live?" Until this moment in his long life Count had rarely thought of his own mortality, but suddenly it seemed important to know if he had any descendants.

Sarah said, "It was a baby girl, she lived to have children of her own…you and I have heirs living in this county, my man, but I don't think they would be very happy to know it."

Count was suddenly amused and chuckled softly at the notion that some of his blood might flow in the veins of certain white supremacists in the vicinity. He glanced at Sarah who was smiling broadly now. A thought crossed his mind that caused him to laugh aloud, and with his usual gusto. "That's the answer, Sarah my sweet." He slapped his leg. "God is a wag. He can't wait to see the look on their faces when they find out, and he gave us long life so we could share in the joke." He laughed merrily. Sarah laughed with him. They drank more port.

Sarah had something else on her mind. "I'd like to go back," she said. "Back to Africa." She, of course, had never been to Africa, but in some mystical way she had never left.

It was not a new idea for Count, he had considered it seriously enough to do some research on the subject. He had no recollection of his own father or mother, but in his youth he had listened to enough tales from the elders around late night fires to know that his ancestors had heard the Ashanti drums and war-horns along the sub-Saharan West African coast known these days as the Gold Coast, but in bygone days was called the Slave Coast. He knew that Portuguese traders had taken the first slaves from this region 50 years before Columbus discovered America. The Portuguese were the first, but when it was found that gold and diamonds were abundant there, it was not long before competition arose from the Swedes, Danes, Dutch, English, Germans, and French. He also knew that slavery had been a business there; the slave traders did not seize the property, they exchanged European goods (guns were popular, so was salt) for able-bodied men and women. The Ashanti themselves practiced a peculiar form of slavery—slaves were allowed to own property, they could marry and have families, they had most of the rights of free men, with the large proviso that when human sacrifices were required, as they were in certain funeral ceremonies, slaves were the chosen ones.

"My people were the Ebba," Sarah said wistfully.

"Do you know anything about them?" Count asked.

"Only what the elders remembered. They lived near a great river. They believed in great spirits...they believed in living peacefully."

Count said, "My people were the Ashanti. Each village had a chief who settled disputes. When the chief died they believed his soul survived and resided in the stool he sat on during his life. Each village had a stool house to preserve the spirits of dead chiefs. The souls of all Ashanti were believed to occupy what was known as the Golden Stool of the Ashanti, which was a sacred icon that nobody was allowed to sit on. Christian missionaries came in the early seventeenth century trying to save the infidels."

"Did they succeed?"

Count laughed softly. "They probably got a few converts," he said, "but the Ashanti were perfectly happy with their own religion, the souls of their ancestors were all around them, why should they believe some wild tales about a savior and a God in three parts? One thing was sure though, the missionaries were a hardy lot. Can you imagine what it was like coming to a land where it was boiling hot the year round so close to the equator, where malaria, yellow fever, and sleeping sickness were endemic? Those missionaries must have thought they had been sent to Hell."

"I'd still like to go," said Sarah. "I'd like to see it with my own eyes. I'd like to know what it's like to be in a land where I can look people in the eye and feel like I'm equal. It would be like I had been resurrected."

"We'll go," said Count. He looked closely at Sarah, who was dreaming of a Promised Land, her Christian beliefs floating to the top of a stew of religious confusion. "We'll go."

>>48<<

ZENG-TZU

Floating on his back in the gently rolling waters of the northern Philippine Sea, 800 miles almost due north of where the *Indianapolis* went down, Booker T. reflected on his life...past, present, and future. He pictured himself as one of those novelty toys he had seen in a Hong Kong shop window—a receptacle in the form of a long-necked bird, balanced between filling and emptying. For the first 27 years of his life he had been filling with facts and with fiction, doing his best to distinguish the difference. He was not yet near the point where what he had learned would tip and flow out to add to the world's reservoir of understanding, as shallow as that might presently be; not yet near, but headed in that direction. He considered it a milestone that he had come to realize that some things are more important than being president of the United States. Not that being president of the United States wasn't important, it was just that there were things *more* important. Taking care of Hideko was one...being president of the world was another. *I wonder what Count would think of that?* He laughed. *I will send him a note. Count will understand.* He remembered the slogan of the School for Presidents: *Until philosophers are kings or kings philosophers states will never have rest from their evils...I wonder what Hideko can tell me about oriental philosophy? If I am to become president of the world...never mind president, I will go straight for Emperor...I'll need to know more philosophy than what I know about Socrates.* The only oriental philosophy he could think of was *'Confucius say: man who fly upside down have crack up.'* Whatever that meant.

So that was the past...he was a filling receptacle. And that was the future...he would become Emperor of the World. The present, too, was easy...he expected to wash up on the beach sometime around sunrise. He could make out the dark shape of the island against the blazing background of the familiar star-filled night sky. A pale crescent April moon added its glow. He would make his way to The Teahouse of the August Moon where Mamasan Shigetsu would direct him to find Hideko.

"She go Myako," Mamasan Shigetsu said. She looked at Booker T. suspiciously, apparently not surprised to see him. He looked carefully at the tiny lady, wondering at her equanimity. It was not possible that she had been expecting him; he had only made the decision to return as the *Agerholm* cleared the headland exiting Buckner Bay...and yet she seemed to know.

"Can you take me to her?" Booker T. asked.

"Myako far away," she said. "Need boat."

Myako was a small island about 150 miles of open water southwest of Okinawa. For centuries Myako had been famous for breeding small horses useful for riding and for light draft. The island was also noted for its beautiful marine scenery and rugged, rocky coast. And one thing more; it was the home of a lao-tzu, an old master: Zeng-tzu...Master Zeng.

"She go see Zeng-tzu. He very old. He very wise. He know future." Mamasan Shigetsu looked at Booker T., nodded her head and said, "We go Myako."

The motorized sampan slowed to enter the channel leading into the small harbor of Myako Island. The beauty of the water, sparkling in the early morning sunshine struck Booker T...brilliant shades of blue, green, and aquamarine. Schools of small colorful fish patrolled the sandy bottom. After docking, they climbed a rocky path to a small village where Booker T. was the object of much curiosity, which he returned in full measure. He saw an old man, trailed by a line of children, walking with what appeared to be a handmade paper windmill in his hand. Mamasan Shigetsu, walking ahead of Booker T. stopped, and pointed to the old man. "Kajimaya," she said, then explained. "In Okinawa, if people live sixty years it is beginning of happy old age, called kanreki. If live eighty-eight years, time to celebrate maturity of old age...called toukachi. But biggest celebration called kajimaya." She pointed to the old man with the paper windmill. "When he live ninety-seven years," she said, "he begin new life by agreement between sky god and earth god, and okay from almighty god."

Suddenly he saw her. She was running as fast as her damaged leg would allow, arms thrust out, shouting his name..."Dawg, Dawg," she cried. He ran to meet her, and scooped her up into his arms, cradling her like the lovely doll that she was, spinning around in ever widening circles. The old man with the windmill stopped, and smiled broadly. Mamasan Shigetsu found herself joyfully hopping from one foot to another. The children danced around the happy reunion, laughing and shouting. When at last he put her down, she clung to him, the top of her head reaching his chin, as though fearing that if she released him he would disappear. She began speaking rapidly to Mamasan Shigetsu.

Booker T. broke in to say, "Mamasan, please tell her that I will never again leave her. Tell her we will be like flowers linked together, never to be torn apart." When Mamasan Shigetsu told her this, Hideko's eyes, already moist with emotion, filled with tears that cascaded down her cheeks. Booker T. found tears running down his face as well. Hideko took his hand, and began walking through the village. She was taking him to Zeng-tzu.

They found the old master sitting on a large flat rock, looking out to sea. As they approached, he stood and turned to greet them. "Men-so-ree, men-so-ree," he said, smiling broadly.

"This Zeng-tzu. He say welcome," Mamasan Shigetsu translated.

Booker T. had a strange feeling that Zeng-tzu had been expecting them.

The old master came forward, and with his left hand grasped the right hand of Hideko, then with his right hand took the left hand of Booker T. Thus connected in a tight circle, Zeng-tzu looked deeply into the eyes of first Hideko, then Booker T. Tall and slim in his gray kimono, Zeng-tzu was a 75th generation descendant of a disciple of Confucius, and looking into his eyes, Booker T. felt connected to the ages. He also noted the odd feeling that, but for their almond shapes, he might well be looking into the eyes of Count.

Zeng-tzu, apparently satisfied with what he saw in the eyes of Hideko and Booker T., broke the circle, and now stood between them, Booker T. on his right, Hideko on his left. Slowly, he turned and led them forward to the large flat rock overlooking the sea. For a long time they stood silently, hands connected, in a line before the rock, looking toward the horizon. Booker T. became aware of pungent fumes coming from two incense burners placed on either side of the rock. At length, Zeng-tzu took two handfuls of star sand from a large porcelain urn in front of the rock, and sprinkled it into the incense burners resulting in a showery display of tiny points of light. He then turned and began to speak. Mamasan Shigetsu translated.

"If Heaven wishes peace and order for the world, who is there besides you to bring it about?

"In the beginning there was T'ai-chi, the great ultimate. From this came the two cosmic forces, human feelings, and human nature, the yin and the yang, which brought about the four beginnings...love, righteousness, propriety, and wisdom.

"From the interaction of the yin and the yang, all patterns, ideas, systems, and culture are evolved.

"Change is constant, simple, and easy. Whatever issues from change is good. Change goes in cycles just as the struggle between materialism and idealism, but the most important aspect of change is its progressive direction, leading to the development of society, morality, and civilization.

"Of all the social institutions, the most important, and the only one that never changes, is the family. You, Hideko, and you, Dawg, joined as the yin is joined to the yang in a never ending search for harmony, can now go from this holy place to begin a new family.

"If Heaven wishes peace and order for the world, who is there besides you to bring it about?"

>>49<<

VIRGIL'S LAST BOTTLE

"Are you sure this is what you want to do?" Count asked.

Flapper and J-four were in full agreement. They wanted to conduct another public forum; they were ready to force the issue. They had been unprepared for the Klan reaction to the first forum, On Manly Courage; this time they would be ready. They knew it was like waving a red flag at the Klan bull, but this time J-four had arranged to have national press coverage. They would exploit the Klan's penchant for murderous excess by turning the glare of national publicity on them. J-four's report to the nation on the shooting of Socrates had evoked a more than expected response from all around the country. Count had been exactly right, public outrage was aroused. Count was satisfied that the strategy was on track, and he was particularly pleased with the subject of the next forum—What Is Justice? Justice was the key to everything, could there be any doubt about that?

J-four thought about what Sadie Tanner Alexander had said to the Tuskegee graduates almost four years ago in June of 1951. She had spoken about the sacred ideals of freedom and equality. Her words were burned into his memory. He said, "The number one threat to freedom and democracy in the United States in the second half of the 20th century is unreasoned discrimination against groups because of differences in customs, religious beliefs and, God help us, in different skin color."

"Sadie Tanner Alexander," said Count.

"Holy writ," said J-four.

Flapper said, "Socrates was in favor of freedom, but he was not so sure about democracy."

"Are we sure we know what Socrates really thought?" Count questioned. "He was pretty good at confusing the issue, but I think you're right about democracy...he wasn't convinced. But then the type of democracy they had in Athens in those days was more like chaos. A jury of the whole."

J-four said, "Okay, so we're going ahead with Justice. You up to doing Socrates again, Count? I don't think anybody else could do it."

Count was raring to go as always. "Don't worry about me," he said, "I can do it, I'm feeling fine. But I wonder how many people will risk the Klan wrath again. We may be talking to the guards and ourselves. On the other hand maybe they'll decide to leave us alone this time."

J-four thought he knew the Klan well enough that they would do something in response to the announcement he planned to place in the usual places.

TUSKEGEE INSTITUTE
SCHOOL FOR PRESIDENTS
PRESENTS THE SECOND IN A SERIES OF PUBLIC FORUMS

WHAT IS JUSTICE?
A Greek Dialogue

WHERE - CARNEGIE HALL, TUSKEGEE INSTITUTE CAMPUS
WHEN - SATURDAY, FEBRUARY 15, 1955 8 P.M.

PUBLIC INVITED

J-four had met Virgil Young. After much discussion and all the friendly persuasion J-four could muster, Stanley Gordon had finally agreed to take him to Virgil. J-four found Virgil to be about what he had expected—crude but not stupid; not as smart as Stanley, but deadly devious. Also as expected, Virgil was highly suspicious of J-four, and was not easily convinced that J-four before the war had been a member of a north Alabama Klan klavern.

J-four was finally able to gain a measure of Virgil's confidence through his ability to match Virgil shot-for-shot as they polished off a full quart of Jack Daniel's sour mash whiskey. J-four's story-telling skills didn't hurt either as they swapped combat stories from their different wars. Virgil was particularly interested in the Buffalo Soldiers. He assured J-four that his quarrel was not with the Negroes, who he loved as well as anybody, but with the Jews, Catholics, and Commies who were trampling on the God-given rights of the States to run their own affairs. But as they neared the bottom of the bottle, Virgil finally admitted that he really didn't give much of a damn about that either. What really concerned him was those sissy-britches Alabama

Crimson Tide fans and their smart-assed wise cracks about the Auburn Tiger football team. Virgil and J-four sealed their bond standing on a table bellowing the Auburn fight song…"WAR EAGLE, FLY DOWN THE FIELD. EVER TO CONQUER, NEVER TO YIELD." J-four could barely carry a tune, but he never passed up a chance to give it his best shot, even with an Exalted Cyclops.

But if J-four had chiseled a small niche into the Klan facade, he was still very much an outsider. He knew they were not happy with the School for Presidents, and he expected some reaction to the announced forum on Justice, but it never occurred to him that they would kidnap Count.

They nabbed him coming out of Miz Sarah's house after a Friday evening visit, and whisked him to an isolated cabin in a pine grove near the Coosa river where he spent the night sleeping on a narrow cot in a small, locked room.

Count awoke at first light, shivering without a blanket in the cool morning air. He sat up and looked around, assessing his circumstances. The room was a square, roughly 10 by 10 feet, and bare of furniture except for the cot. The ceiling was also about 10 feet, so he was in a cube. Two small windows near the ceiling on each end of an outside wall allowed him to see pine trees shrouded in a windless morning fog. He soon confirmed that the single door was locked. There was no response when he banged on the door; he appeared to be alone. It was quiet except for the sound of insects, and the haunting, repetitive lament of a mourning dove. A damp musty odor hung in the air along with a faint smell of stale urine. He went to the corner of the room and peed.

In his long life Count had recorded about every experience it was possible for a man to have, but this was the first time he had ever been kidnapped. He apparently would have time to examine his feelings on the subject. He sensed it would be fruitless to attempt escape, but at the same time he felt an instinctive urge to try. The door was apparently bolted from the outside, and was unyielding before his frail efforts to dislodge it. The windows were too high and too small to offer any hope of exit; he was trapped. So be it; he would make the most of it. If his purpose was to provoke the Klan into stupid actions in order to bring the insanity to the attention of an otherwise occupied nation, he apparently had succeeded. He could live with martyrdom. He sat down to wait. It was a gray day. He slept and dreamed of Africa.

In the fading light of late afternoon he heard an approaching car; in it were Virgil Young and Stanley Gordon. They noisily came to the cabin; Count waited. Presently the bolt was lifted, and the door pulled open. Count stood up. Virgil walked into the room followed by Stanley. Virgil of course had seen Count before, at the first forum, but only from a distance, and he had not bothered to take a close look. Now they stood face to face and Virgil, accustomed to looking down on men of lesser stature, found himself wordless; confounded to see a man as tall or slightly taller than him who, in an odd way was familiar. They in fact were of almost identical height and build, both tall and slim, but Stanley remarked, they appeared to be photographic opposites, like a print and its corresponding negative—Count with black face and white hair, Virgil with white face and black hair. Virgil took a step back, then turned quickly and walked from the room without saying a word.

Stanley watched Virgil leave, then looked again at Count, noting his great age and commanding dignity. "How old are you, Socrates?" he asked, surprised at the unexpected question from himself, and from his deferential tone, to say nothing of the appellation.

"Why, sir," Count responded, "I am nearing one hundred ten years, but forgive me, you have me at an advantage although I seem to recall your face."

Stanley flushed slightly and said, "It was at the Unitarian service."

"Of course," said Count, remembering. "The voice from the rear."

Stanley walked to the other room where Virgil was seated at a long table pouring from a Jack Daniel's whisky bottle into a large water glass. Stanley looked back and motioned for Count to follow.

"I like to talk to very old people," said Stanley. "I think we can learn a lot from old people, like what is it like to be old? Is it hard to bear? What can you tell us?"

Virgil took a large gulp of whiskey from his water glass, and looked up at Count; it appeared that Virgil, too, was interested in the answers to Stanley's questions.

Count took a chair at the table with no objections from Virgil or Stanley and answered.

"If old people get together, the first thing they do is complain about how the younger generations don't appreciate what it means to work hard and save your money, and that young people are too busy to be interested in what the old people are interested in.

"The next thing is to lament the lost pleasures of youth…feasting, drinking, women…all of that. They are peevish that all those things have been taken from them. It is better, I think, that old people take care about looking back too much; it leads to melancholy."

Virgil, who had been staring into his glass as Count spoke, now looked up and indicated that Stanley should bring two more glasses from the cabinet. When he returned, Virgil poured Jack Daniel's into the two glasses, pushed one towards Stanley and another in the direction of Count. He lifted his glass towards Count without looking at him and took two large gulps.

Virgil had a question. "Ah wanta know somethin', Socrates…" He hesitated…Count waited. "It's about sex…can you still make love to a woman when you get as old as you are?"

Count smiled. "Hush now," he said, "I'm happy to have left all that behind…I feel freed from a wild and unreasoning master. But gentlemen, fading desires and the decreasing ability to catch up with a fast ball are not the somber problems you might imagine; the darker consequences of old age reside in the question of character. If you are wrathful and wretched in your youth and middle age, you will in all likelihood be the same in your old age."

Virgil grunted and asked. "What about money? Stanley says y'all are rich."

Count answered, "It's true, and it is also true that even a good man would find it difficult to cope with old age in poverty. But listen to this, Stanley and…" Count looked at Virgil who was occupied with pouring himself another drink.

Stanley said, "Virgil."

Count nodded. "Yes. Virgil." He paused "…Virgil, you say? Would that be Virgil Young?"

Virgil looked sharply at Count, but did not acknowledge the question. Count said, "Virgil…a name for the ages…the greatest of the Roman poets. But I stray. Listen to this, Stanley and Virgil…a bad man, no matter how rich he is, can never hope that old age will bring him happiness and contentment. You have to be careful with wealth…too many people who make money end up being bores, because money is all they ever think about or want to talk about."

Stanley was full of questions. "What is the greatest benefit money has given to you, Socrates?" he asked.

Count smiled. "You may find this answer too simple, Stanley," he said, "but the truth is that money allows a man to pay his debts, and if you don't owe anything it is easier to avoid fraud and cheating. So you can say that money strengthens virtue and gives a man honesty."

Stanley was beginning to feel the effects of the bourbon, his mind raced to keep up with the argument; he was released from inhibitions, he was excited about the debate. He said, "So are we talking about virtue and honesty and the just man? Is that what money does? Makes a man just because he can be honest and pay his debts?"

Count said, "It might seem so, Stanley, but before we fall into a deep and ill-considered conclusion about that, let me give you an example that might put a different light on it. Imagine that Virgil has a weapon that you want to borrow, let's say it is a twelve-gauge shotgun. Now let's say that when it comes time to return the weapon to Virgil you find that he has gone crazy as a coon in heat. Wouldn't you think it would be wrong to return the gun to a crazy man? It might be the honest thing to do, and it would mean paying your debt, but it surely would be an injustice to the rest of society to put a weapon into the hands of a crazy man. On the other hand, I suppose that you would consider Virgil to be your friend, and from what we have said, it is fair to say that a friend should receive only that which is good from a friend, and not something that is evil."

Stanley asked, "Do you mean to say, Socrates, that if a friend borrows money from a friend that he should not return it if he thinks that it might harm his friend?"

"Yes."

Stanley said, "This is getting interesting, Socrates. So let me ask you a question which I think follows from what we have been talking about. Would it be right to say that enemies should also get what's coming to them?"

"Yes, indeed, Stanley, you are perceptive. The debt from one enemy to another is nothing good, but something evil, and from this it follows that justice requires that everyone should receive his due."

"So Socrates, does it mean that justice is an art that benefits friends and injures enemies?"

"So it would seem, Stanley, but let me ask you this, who is best able to benefit friends and injure enemies in times of sickness?"

"A doctor."

"Good. And who on a sea voyage?"

"A captain."

"And what about a just man? When is a just man best able to help friends and harm enemies?"

"In war."

"Well said, Stanley. Now can we conclude from this that when we are well and safe on land we have no use for doctors and sea captains?"

"I believe so."

"And what about the just man? Is he useless in time of peace?"

"I don't think I would say that."

"So how would you say justice is useful in peacetime?"

"Maybe in forming partnerships in business."

"Good. Now if you were competing in a game, would you rather have a just partner or a skillful player?"

The questions and answers went on and on, while Virgil continued to drink, and listen with increasing shakes of his head.

Stanley: "Socrates, ah'm not sure anymore what ah said before because you've got me confused, but one thing seems to hold up, and that is that the just man benefits friends and harms enemies."

Count: "That brings up another question. How do you define a friend? Are they those you *think* are good and honest people or are they those who really *are* honest...and are your enemies bad or are they only those you *think* are bad?"

"Will the virtuous behavior of good men make other men bad?"

"If justice and goodness are the same, then the just man injures no one."

At long last, Virgil, who had tried to break into the argument several times, jumped to his feet and bellowed in anger. "Enough of this shit! Y'all actin' like idiots. Ah don't think either one of y'all has a idea what justice is...y'all talkin' in circles and talkin' nothin' but nonsense. Why do ah have to listen to this shit? Is this what you do, Socrates? Ask questions to confuse us and not give any answers?"

Count looked at Virgil and smiled. "Excuse me, Virgil," he said, "I should have included you in the discussion, but believe me I didn't know you had this much interest in justice. And you must also believe that I was not deliberately trying to confuse anybody, but was sincerely trying to reach an understanding of what is justice. I have to say the whole discussion would have been elevated if we had input from your superior intelligence."

Virgil stood a bit shakily, holding a half-empty glass in his hand. He spoke slowly and carefully, as if trying to ensure that his words came out clearly. "Ah know more about justice than you think, Socrates. Ah'm goin' to give you a definition of justice that is better than anything you said, and when you hear it y'all have to pay me because it's like we in a contest and I won the prize. How much you think that prize oughta be, Socrates?"

"Whatever the penalty for ignorance should be. I must learn from the wise."

"You a clever bastard, Socrates, but you ain't foolin' me, ah don't think you really know shit about shit."

"You are right about that, Virgil, but are you now ready to enlighten us with your definition of justice? The truth is that my greatest wish is to learn."

"Okay, here it is…justice is whatever the strongest man says it is." Virgil smiled sardonically. "You ready to argue about that, Socrates, you old fart?"

Count, still sitting, looked up at Virgil who was swaying slightly and looking in the vicinity of where Count was sitting. Count said, "No, I don't think I want to argue about that, but it may be important to understand what we mean by the term strongest man. Are we talking about strong in the sense that a weightlifter is strong? Or are we talking about strong as it refers to personality or character? There are of course other possibilities we might consider…are you using strong as a substitute for power as in the power of governments or organizations?"

Virgil sat down and poured yet another drink from the now almost empty bottle. He slumped in his chair, and looked long and hard at Count as if trying to bring him into focus. Finally, after a long silence, he spoke in a low voice…almost a whisper. "Ah know you, don't ah?"

Count, sitting across the table from the besotted Virgil, had received a full genealogy lesson from Miz Sarah. He knew where Virgil came from.

Virgil did not wait for an answer, but asked the question only the influence of Jack Daniel's on his soggy brain could elicit, "Are you mah grandpappy?"

Count shook his head and said, "No."

Virgil Young's lips curled into a sneer. "Yer lyin'."

"Your grandmother was my daughter; I am your great-grandpappy."

Virgil slid further down in his chair, fighting the truth he had instantly recognized and desperately denied at his first confrontation with Count. He sat now with his chin resting on his chest.

Stanley watched in a state of mild shock, a newsreel of history flashing backward through his mind.

Finally, Virgil spoke. Stanley had to lean closer to hear Virgil say, "Bring me that last bottle." They were the last words Virgil ever spoke. They were his epitaph.

Stanley straightened up, looked at Virgil, slumped in his chair, then looked at Count who returned his steady gaze and gave him the eerie feeling he was about to say, "You're next buddy."

"Git yer own damn bottle, Virgil." Stanley hissed. He stalked out the door, jumped into the car, spun it around in a fury, and roared off down the rutted road. Count watched Virgil Young struggle to his feet, stagger, then fall, sprawling on the floor. He struggled to rise, but could only manage to crawl to a pine-paneled cabinet where, moving in slow-motion, he managed to open the cabinet and bring out another bottle of whiskey. Virgil sat with his back against the cabinet, screwed off the cap, and proceeded to drain half the bottle in a series of gulps. Count looked in wonder as yet another experience was added to his lifetime list...the sensation of watching a man flood his arteries and veins with 95-proof ethyl alcohol until he lost sensibility, then consciousness, then life.

>> 50 < <

COUNT AGAIN

Count sat alone on a bench facing the Booker T. Washington statue on the Tuskegee campus. In his hand he held a scuffed white envelope. He looked at the bold, distinctive handwriting, and thought of the other Booker T., *his* Booker T., who two months earlier, Count had been informed by Booker T.'s father, was reported missing from his ship. The letter was postmarked May 17, 1955, San Francisco, California; today was May 25th. Count opened the envelope, withdrew the small sheet of paper, and read the cryptic message again: *SOME THINGS ARE MORE IMPORTANT THAN BEING PRESIDENT OF THE UNITED STATES.* Near the bottom of the page was written: *Mother McCree, Shamrock Teahouse, Sasebo, Japan.*

When Count showed the letter to Miz Sarah, she asked, "What does it mean, Count?"

Count sighed. "It means," he said, "that Booker T. is alive, that he is living somewhere in Japan, that he is hiding from the authorities, and that he has made an important discovery." Count took Miz Sarah's hand and looked into her eyes. "I think I know what it is," he said.

Miz Sarah shrugged. "I can think of a whole bunch of things more important than being president of the United States," she said.

Count nodded, but did not respond quickly. He sat holding Miz Sarah's hand and thinking. At length he looked at her and asked, "Does your list include going back to Africa?"

Flapper was incredulous. "Booker T. has deserted? I don't believe it," he said.

Count showed him the letter. Flapper read it and shook his head. "Whatever it is, he apparently thinks it's also important enough to walk away from his sworn duty. This is not what I would expect from Booker T. It must be something momentous." He looked at the envelope. "You think he is hiding in Japan? Why is the letter postmarked San Francisco. I don't understand."

"He is somewhere in the Far East," Count answered. "The letter was mailed from San Francisco by someone he knew was traveling to the U.S. He gave us an address so we could stay in touch with him...he..." Count hesitated. "...He needs help."

"What can we do?" asked Flapper.

Count had a plan, but as much as he respected Flapper, he was reluctant to share it. "This is not your problem, Flapper," he said. "...It's mine. I must find him. You can help by continuing the work here."

Flapper said, "Booker T. knows the penalty for desertion is severe...he must have been desperate." He paused, then added, "But it's not the penalty...it's the question of honor."

"The Navy does not list him as a deserter," said Count. "They think he's dead...lost at sea. One of his shipmates sent a letter to Booker T.'s parents. He came off duty the first night out of Okinawa, and was never seen again. They assume he fell overboard."

Flapper was startled. The name Okinawa evoked memories of crashing bedlam. "Okinawa?" he asked, but did not wait for an answer. "Booker T. was wounded at Okinawa," Flapper remembered. "...Ten years ago...I wonder...he..."

Flapper related the story of the girl on the beach. "...We thought he was delusional, but he insisted it was real. Could this be related to his disappearance?"

Count answered. "Almost certainly," he mused. "Nothing is stranger than fate, and Booker T. would recognize it and act upon it. You must have talked to him about destiny. He believed in destiny."

Flapper nodded. "So do I," he said, "How will you find him? Will you go to Japan?"

"I have a plan," said Count. "There is something deeper unfolding here. My crystal ball was flawed...I saw Booker T. as president of the United States. I was wrong...He will be a leader, to be sure, but it will be from out of Africa."

The next day Count posted a letter addressed to Booker T. McCan, care of Mother McCree in Sasebo, Japan.

From May through November, Booker T. and Hideko stayed on the Island of Myako. They learned each other's language, and they learned each other.

She recounted the Okinawan folktales about the seven-dragon god of the sea and one of his servants, the giant sea serpent. Booker T. told of King Neptune and Davey Jones' locker at the bottom of the sea. Hideko described the Okinawan concept of Nirai-Kansai; the belief that the abode of the gods is an idealized realm over the seas where happiness and prosperity are assured by a plentiful harvest. He told her about the Christian belief in a trinity of God, Son, and Holy Spirit. She played the sanshin for him—a 3-stringed plucked lute that occupied a position in the peace-loving Ryukyu household similar to the Japanese samurai sword as a family heirloom. He delighted her with his harmonica, performing lively renditions of "Wabash Cannonball" and "Turkey In The Straw." He was introduced to the dynamic and spirited Ryukyu dancing, which he learned was a performing art with a religious function as the songs invoked the spirit of the Buddha. He showed her how to Jitterbug, providing his own music with a babba doo-ba version of "InTheMood."

They both spent long hours with Zeng-tzu where they learned of the Shinto belief that while life had elements of evil, sorrow, and tragedy, it was nevertheless fundamentally good and beautiful. Zeng-tzu told them that the basis for understanding had been in place for more than 2,000 years with the insights of Confucius (500 B.C.), Plato (400 B.C.) and Mencius (300 B.C.). Booker T. was particularly interested in those lessons of Mencius that condemned imperialism as the result of man's unending greed and acquisitiveness, especially the insatiable ambitions and covetousness of princes, advised by selfish ministers and false counselors. Mencius affirmed that the mass of the people want to live in peace, and are disturbed and injured by imperialist wars.

In September, Booker T. received Count's letter. He read it sitting on the sand with his back to a coconut palm, a container of Awamori brandy in one hand, Hideko beside him strumming a samisen, the sun setting over the East China Sea spread out before him.

May 31, 1955
Dear Booker T.,

Greetings from Alabama, wherever you are. And of course you are exactly right, some things are *more important than being president of the United States. Flapper told us the story of the young girl on the invasion beach at Okinawa. Please give her a hug from all of us. And by all means take good care of her. And don't forget to take good care of yourself, you are still needed.*

Let me share with you some of the things that are on my mind...The world is full of change, and it seems to me that, with certain notable exceptions, weapons development comes to mind, most changes make things better than they were. It's almost as if when mankind makes some really bad mistakes...like slavery...when they finally get around to taking a good look at it, they find a way to make it better.

Maybe weapons development will be like that. But listen to this: the U.S. is beginning to show signs that it's ready to begin treating Negroes like real people, and I'll tell you how I know...It's baseball.

In 1947 Jackie Robinson became the first Negro to play major league baseball. Oh sure, in 1948 President Truman ordered desegregation of the armed forces, and oh sure, in 1954 the Supreme Court ordered desegregation of public schools, but now, in 1955, we see the surest sign of all...the New York Yankees; the 20th century symbol of white supremacy, at long last, have a Negro ball player, and a catcher at that...his name is Elston Howard. And nobody ordered them to do it.

What does all this have to do with us? Well, for one thing, it confirms my belief that in another 50 years, the U.S. will elect its first Negro president...maybe it will be Elston Howard...I'll try to get him into our school. I can't say I'm disappointed it won't be you because it's now clear to me that you have a larger destiny. Not now...the baby is only 10 years old, but certainly in the future...being Secretary-General of the United Nations will be more important than being president of the United States.

Why not Booker T. McCan of Ghana? You have participated in the first United Nations peacekeeping mission in Korea...you are off to a very good start.

Why Ghana? Maybe you never heard of Ghana. It's one of those small West African countries with the arbitrary boundaries laid out by the Europeans in the 18th century when white men descended like locusts on a defenseless landscape. The British got Ghana as part of their share, and called it Gold Coast because of the precious metal they found there in abundance. It was also known as the Slave Coast, but they weren't likely to make that its official name were they? And now, in the middle of the 20th century, things are changing, even in Africa. The British have agreed to clear out and allow Ghana to be an independent country. The new country will have many needs, and we can be a part of it. Think of it, Booker T., a new nation, conceived, as all nations should be, in liberty, and dedicated, as all nations should be, to the proposition that all men are created equal.

Why Ghana? Because it is the land of our ancestors, and it is time for us to come home. Time for us to hear the ancient folktales, to listen to the talking drums, to learn the mysteries of the forest people; to make a new beginning.

I am making plans, no, we *are making plans...my lady and me...to return to Africa, and I hope you and your lady will join us for this grand adventure. We will travel by boat, from Philadelphia, to the Far East, and from there to Ghana. Soon I will send you a schedule with exact dates when we will be in port in Japan, and Formosa; it will be some time in late November. Please meet us and we will spend a lifetime together making the world a better place.*

Friendly,
Count.

>>51<<

NYAME

The *SS Catongo* backed away from its pier six berth on the Philadelphia side of the river, slid down the wide Delaware, under the Walt Whitman bridge, past the Philadelphia Naval Shipyard, headed for the neck of Delaware Bay and the open sea beyond. The *Catongo* flew the black star flag of Ghana, and carried a mixed cargo of grain (corn, wheat, and rice), bicycles, automobiles, concrete, tobacco, and dry goods. The sturdy vessel had arrived in Philadelphia 10 days earlier carrying a supply of West African cocoa beans destined for the Pennsylvania chocolate manufacturing industry.

Captain Victoria Dzogbefia, standing behind the broad windscreen on the ship's bridge, found time to explain the barter arrangement to her passengers, Count and Miz Sarah. "It's not very complicated," she said, "they need cocoa beans, and we need food and manufactured goods. No money changes hands, just material. Sometimes the old ways work best."

Cool November breezes swept over Count and Sarah, in a state of high excitement standing next to the diminutive captain on the bridge. Plans for the African journey had developed through the summer months following receipt of the letter from Booker T. The anticipation of returning to Africa was having an unexpected effect on them; from the day plans to board the *Catongo* in Philadelphia were finalized, they began to feel younger. It was as if their bodies were responding to chemical signals that had been sequestered in their brains since the electrifying days of early adolescence. The revival would continue as they made their leisurely way, logging some 350 nautical miles a 24-hour day, over 23,000 miles of saltwater to the Gold Coast port of Takoradi. They took the long way around. Philadelphia to the Panama Canal—6 days, 2,000 miles; Panama Canal to Hawaii—13 days, 4,600 miles; Hawaii to Yokohama—12 days, 4,300 miles; Yokohama to Keelung—4 days, 1,300 miles; Keelung to Hong Kong—1 day, 350 miles; Hong Kong to Singapore—

4 days, 1,400 miles; Singapore to Ceylon—5 days, 1,600 miles; Ceylon to Mauritius—6 days, 1,600 miles; Mauritius to Cape Town—7 days, 2,300 miles; Cape Town to Congo—5 days, 1,500 miles; Congo to Gold Coast—4 days, 1,300 miles.

"Independence is in the air." Captain Dzogbefia raised a glass of palm wine in salute. She sat at a long table covered with a sparkling white cloth in the *Catongo's* dining room, along with her officers and her two passengers, Count and Miz Sarah. "To an independent Ghana," she said.

Count and Miz Sarah joined the others in a toast to a future where Africa, with Ghana leading the way, would shed the epithet "dark continent."

"Tell us about Ghana," said Count, aware of the gently rolling motion of the ship on its first night out in the open ocean.

The captain smiled and looked at her officers, Kofi Nti, the first mate, and K.K. Oduro, the chief engineer. They returned the smile. "We are a country of six million people," she said, "living in a land about twice the size of Pennsylvania. Being a land of abundant natural resources has been both a blessing and a curse to us. A blessing because the fertile soil and ample rainfall allow us to grow the plantain, yams, and cassava needed to feed the people…a curse because the land is permeated with gold and diamonds, an invitation to alien plunderers. Europeans discovered us five hundred years ago, and have been helping themselves ever since. But our time is near…the British have taught us about laws, the Americans have taught us about freedom…we are developing our own leaders."

"It will not be easy," said Kofi Nti. "There are the regional differences…the ancient animosities. The tribes."

Count raised his eyebrows expressing curiosity.

Nti continued. "The history of this part of West Africa is the history of a large group of people speaking a common language…Akan. Within this group the Fanti along the coast, and the inland Ashanti have traditionally been at odds. Also, the Ashanti do not trust the Ewe, who live in the eastern part of the country." Count and Miz Sarah looked at each other, smiling faintly at this revelation. "…The nineteen fifty constitution tried to address these differences by providing for representation in the general assembly…"

Count was listening intently, but he was having difficulty understanding the words. Nti was speaking rapidly, as though he wanted to get all his thoughts expressed before someone interrupted him, and the accent, derived from the combination of Akan and English, was strange and unfamiliar. Count held up his hands and said, "Wait, wait, Mr...." He hesitated in some confusion as he tried to remember the name of the first mate. "...Forgive me," he said, "I'm a little slow in my old age. I'm sorry, but your speech pattern is difficult for me to follow. Could I ask you to please speak a little slower? I want to hear everything you say...I heard the part about the Ashanti not trusting the Ewe, but could you repeat what you said about the constitution? That part caught me off guard...I didn't expect a British colony..." He paused, "...I guess I don't know anything about how the colonial system works."

"I think the British have had enough of Empire," said Captain Dzogbefia. "Now they talk of Commonwealth. They treat us like children who have grown up and are ready to leave home. They want us to go, but they don't quite trust us to make our own decisions. They have appointed Kwame Nkrumah Prime Minister, but they seem unsure about what to do next."

K.K. Oduro entered the conversation. "Nkrumah was educated in the U.S.," he said. "...At Lincoln University in Pennsylvania. It is not the usual thing...more often the British send us to their own universities . . ." He paused. "...or to the universities they have established in the country...the University of Ghana at Legon or the University of Science and Technology at Kumasi." He looked at Captain Dzogbefia and said, "The captain is a Tech graduate." Captain Dzogbefia smiled.

"I wonder if they have a school for Prime Ministers at Lincoln University?" Count mused.

Oduro looked curiously at Count and continued, "I don't know about that, but I have heard Nkrumah speak...he has the fire of leadership, but the hopeless dream of a foolish visionary. He sees a United States of Africa." Oduro laughed, joined by the captain and first mate.

"Imagine," said Nti mirthfully, "the Ashanti and the Fanti can't agree on anything, and Nkrumah thinks the Nigerians will join with the Ghanaians and the Ivorians? How can we take this man seriously?"

"Still, he has learned how to progress and succeed within the British system." Captain Dzogbefia said. "In nineteen fifty they jailed him for inciting insurrection...four years later they make him Prime Minister. He will be the first president of an independent Ghana, and the question to be answered is this: is it possible for a modern economic society to coexist with a centuries-old tradition of authority vested in village elders?" The captain looked around the table at the sober faces. She continued. "As much as Nkrumah might like to be the African Thomas Jefferson, he must not delude himself into thinking twentieth century Ghana is like America in seventeen seventy-six."

"Can we help?" Count asked, taking Miz Sarah's hand.

Captain Dzogbefia looked at Count in surprise. "If you can teach a mostly rural people, who only know about local authority, how a democratic government centered far from where they live can make their lives better, it would be a big help. But how can you do that? You've never been to Ghana."

Count responded with two questions. "Does it have to be a democracy? And who said I've never been to Ghana?"

"*Have* you been to Ghana?" asked the Captain.

Count and Sarah looked at each other and smiled. Count pushed back his chair, stood, and began a slow walk around the table. As he walked he began to speak in his rumbling deep voice. "Long long ago," he began, "when the earth was set down, and the sky was lifted up, all folktales were owned by the Sky God."

Captain Dzogbefia smiled. "So you know the tales of Anansi, the cunning spider," she said.

"I have worn the story hat," said Count. "I have heard the talking drums."

Kofi Nti looked skeptically at Count. "And how did Anansi earn the right to tell the Sky God's tales?" he asked.

Count smiled. "Well of course he listened to the advice of his wife Aso," he answered. Count stopped walking, and stood behind Miz Sarah, his hands on her shoulders. "In the Ashanti nation, I guess I don't have to tell you, it is always the women who are the wisest." He saluted Captain Dzogbefia. "But to answer your question," he continued, "Anansi paid for the right to the tales by bringing the Sky God a python, a fairy, and forty-seven stinging hornets."

"Who are you?" asked the Captain.

"I am Nyame," said Count.

The captain and her officers looked at Count in wide-eyed amazement. "You are Nyame?" asked Kofi Nti.

Count nodded and said, "That is my name."

"Nyame the Creator?" Captain Dzogbefia asked, her voice rising in agitation

"I would be foolish to say so," Count answered.

There was a stunned silence as the officers thought about Nyame…the Creator.

Oduro laughed nervously. Nti looked at Oduro in confusion…he wanted to laugh also, but something held him back. Captain Dzogbefia said, "Listen, Mister Whatever-your-name-is…is this some kind of joke?"

"Maybe it is," said Count. "Maybe it is. We shall see. We shall see. But for now I have some questions."

"*You* have some questions?" Captain Dzogbefia said. "My dear sir..."

Count interrupted. "Please," he said, "call me Count."

Captain Dzogbefia looked at him incredulously, then laughed loudly, almost raucously. Oduro and Nti laughed along with the captain, but clearly with less conviction, especially Nti, who continued to eye Count carefully. At length the captain contained her mirth and said, "If anything could count for anything it would be Nyame," and she laughed again. Count and Miz Sarah smiled cheerfully throughout the light-hearted demonstration.

"Captain Dzogbefia," Count said, then paused, looking at Oduro and Nti, "...this question is also for you two...have you ever heard of Osei Tutu?"

The three officers looked at each other with wrinkled brows. "I know Joseph Osei who is in charge of the University of Ghana Agricultural Station at Kade," said Oduro brightly. The others shook their heads from side to side.

Count sighed. "You are children of the twentieth century," he said. "You are the elite of your country, you know of the Anansi tales, but someone has neglected to tell you of your heritage. Osei Tutu was a seventeenth century *asantehene*...an Ashanti king. It was he who three hundred years ago established the spiritual unity of the Ashanti in the sacred symbol of the Golden Stool."

Captain Dzogbefia interrupted. "The Golden Stool is a pagan symbol; it is a relic of the past. We are now a Christian nation."

Count was not so sure. "I wonder if the village chiefs would agree with that," he said. Noting the reactions of Oduro and Nti to the captain's statement, he continued, "And what about you, Kofi Nti? How do you feel about the Golden Stool?"

Nti shifted uncomfortably in his chair. He looked at Oduro, and then at the captain before answering. "I..." he began hesitantly, "...I don't know what to believe," he said. "I'm sorry, Captain, but I have always been troubled with the concept that Jesus of Nazareth has anything to do with us."

Captain Dzogbefia jumped to her feet, and looked at Nti as if he had just planted a bomb in the middle of the table. "Nothing to do with us? What are you talking about? Jesus died for our sins...the Bible tells us so."

Kofi Nti did not want to engage the captain in a religious argument, but he could not restrain himself from saying, "Before the missionaries came we did not know about sins. We also did not find it necessary to lock our doors at night."

Before the angry captain could respond Count held up his hand and said, "Wait...wait. I did not mean to start an argument. Religious symbolism is a powerful force..."

He was interrupted again by the captain, who was still fuming. She spoke sarcastically, "And you, Count Nyame. . ." She laughed. "Have you come down from Heaven at this particular time in history to provide us with answers? To settle our disputes? To show us the way?"

"If only I could..." Count replied. "...If only I could."

The captain laughed sardonically, and continued in her biting tone. "If only you could? What kind of a god are you anyway?"

"I am no god." Count answered. "I have no power to influence events. Mankind has got to solve their own problems."

Captain Dzogbefia looked at Oduro and then at Nti. "Listen to him," she scoffed. "He gives us to believe that he is the Creator and then tells us he has no power. Why are we listening to this nonsense?"

"I bring you a tale of hope," Count said and paused. "... If you want to hear it."

No African, not even a skeptical Captain Dzogbefia could resist listening to a story, particularly a story about hope. She sat down, still frowning, but willing to listen. Oduro and Nti sat straighter, their eyes wide, like children ready for their bedtime story.

"A long time ago," Count began, "after the sky had been lifted up, and the silk cotton trees covered the land, Anansi, the cunning spider, called all the animals together." Count paused to exchange a knowing glance with Sarah. She, too, remembered the enchanting tales from long ago. Count continued. "Under the light of the newly formed moon, Anansi spoke to the animals in solemn tones. 'We are threatened by the tribe of the white-faced monkeys,' Anansi said. 'They descend upon us with sticks of fire and tongues of deception. We must choose a leader who will bring us together to resist the invasion, for if we do not they will enslave us.'

"Kwasi, the proud lion, stepped forward from the shadows into the bright light of the fire. 'I will be the leader,' he said, 'the white-faced monkeys hold no fear for me.'

"Yaw, the elephant, looked down on Kwasi the lion, and trumpeted loudly, 'I am the strongest of all the animals, it is for me to be the leader. The white-faced monkeys would not dare to challenge my strength.'

"Aku, the eagle, watching from the soaring top of a silk cotton tree, spread her wide wings, and flew in circles around the earth-bound animals gathered around the fire. 'Only I can lead you to safety and to greatness,' she said. 'The white-faced monkeys have no defense against the eyes and the speed of the eagle.'

"While the lion, the elephant, and the eagle argued about who would be the leader, Amma, queen of the ants, crawled out, and to everyone's great surprise because all knew the modest nature of the lowly ant, asked for her turn to speak.

"Amma spoke with a clear voice, but not loud enough to command complete attention from the larger creatures. Some heard her say, 'The fierceness of the lion, the strength of the elephant, and the grandeur of the eagle are well known to us all, but is it not time that someone speaks for the teeming multitudes…the termites, the mosquitoes…forgive me…the ants, who make up the vast majority of the population? We do not deny the magnificence of our societal elite, but we ask if it is possible for these brilliant few to appreciate the difficulties we, the many, must face. Forgive me for saying it, but the leader must come from the multitude.'"

Count, who had been sitting, now stood, and continued his tale while walking slowly around the table. He made occasional gestures with his hands. Captain Dzogbefia and her officers followed him with their eyes.

"Imagine the ridicule heaped upon the lowly ant when she said this. The larger animals laughed uproariously at the suggestion that a leader could come from the masses. Even the python and the cobra hissed derisively. So the debate continued, and Anansi, the cunning spider, knew with sinking heart that the time for a true leader to emerge was not at hand. And the white-faced monkeys did descend, and they did enslave, and darkness enveloped the land. And through it all, the ants continued to toil."

Count stopped walking, and for what seemed like a long time stared out a porthole at the restless sea. At length he turned back to the table and said, "This is my story, which I have related. If it be sweet or if it be not sweet, some you may take as true, and for the rest you may praise me for the telling of it."

Captain Dzogbefia looked incredulously at Count. "We are supposed to take hope because the ants continue to toil?" she asked.

Count nodded. "That appears to be the message," he said.

"Kwame Nkrumah might be a lion, and he might be a snake, but he is certainly not an ant," said Oduro.

"Jesus of Nazareth was an ant," mused Captain Dzogbefia. "You have been telling us a Bible story...Revelations: the prophecy of the Second Coming. *The grace of the Lord Jesus be with all the saints.* Amen."

She looked at Count with new interest. "Are you the new savior?" she asked.

"What is it you seek in a savior?" Count asked, donning his Socratic cloak.

"The power to deliver us from harm, sin, or death, and to redeem our souls," answered the captain without hesitation.

"Do you believe that the soul is the immortal element of the human body?" asked Count.

"Yes, I do," answered the captain.

"And do you believe that body and soul co-exist in the living?"

"It is so."

Count pressed ahead. "Would it not then follow that the souls of the living are in no need of redemption?" he asked. "And as for harm, sin, and death, is it not true that society provides for these in the form of police, ministers, and physicians?"

"It would seem so," answered the captain.

"Where then is the need for a savior?" asked Count.

"When you put it like that there is no need," said the captain. "But," she continued, "if the white-faced monkeys still rule, and we continue to live in shadows, how are we to overcome if not by way of a savior?"

Count nodded. "So," he said, "you expand the answer to my question 'what do you seek in a savior?' to include the power to deliver you from the white-faced monkeys."

"I do," said the captain.

"To say I have such power would be to engage in a sweet exaggeration," said Count. "The world is young, Captain Dzogbefia, we must be patient. We will be delivered from the white-faced monkeys only when they are delivered from themselves."

Captain Dzogbefia thought for a moment. "I don't understand," she said, "what does that mean?"

"It means," said Count , "that independence does not automatically mean deliverance. The British government may agree to independence for Ghana, but the British businessman may have other ideas. I think what you should be asking is not whether Kwame Nkrumah is another Thomas Jefferson, but whether he is another George Washington. As I read American history, it was Washington, above all others, who convinced the country to put aside regional differences for the sake of a common good. This may be the lesson for the ages…the United Nations could use a George Washington. Imagine the French and the Germans getting along; the Irish and the English; the Jews and the Arabs; the Ewe and the Ashanti. A George Washington for the world…now *there* would be a savior." He paused. "…I have a candidate," he said.

Heads came up around the room. Captain Dzogbefia laughed. "Why am I not surprised?" she said.

"You will meet him soon," said Count. "I expect to see him when the ship docks in either Yokohama, Keelung, or Hong Kong."

Captain Dzogbefia looked puzzled. Count explained. "I posted a letter giving him the dates the *Catongo* would be in those ports. He is in the Far East somewhere, I don't know for certain where, but he will find his way, and meet us at one of those ports."

"So tell us, Count Nyame, does this savior know what he's in for?" Captain Dzogbefia asked

Count nodded. "The last message I got from him was this," he said. "…Some things are more important than being president of the United States…I think he knows."

>>52<<

THE MOST PRECIOUS THING OF ALL

They stood in a row near the railing on the open deck in the bow of the *Catongo,* Count and Sarah, Booker T. and Hideko, watching the agile deckhands prepare to dock the ship at Takoradi, Ghana. They watched in fascination, as a stocky, well-muscled man, bare to the waist, his skin the color of deepest ebony, swung a monkey fist over his head like a lariat, and slung it toward the wharf with the whooping bellow, "Ahoy the quay." The three-inch hawser, secured to the heavy monkey fist, snaked toward the dock, uncoiling in slow motion, and landed at the feet of a dockhand who quickly braided it to a cleat.

Count felt the pressure of Sarah's hand, squeezing his. He turned to see tears streaming down her face. "My dear," he began, then could not continue, seized by his own emotions. Booker T. put his arm around Hideko's shoulder, and held her close. They stood near the rail, high above the dock looking out on a series of low whitewashed stone buildings laid out in rows, and beyond, spreading into the hazy distance, the sky gray-brown in the early morning light, was Africa. A hot, gritty breeze engulfed them. It was the season of the harmattan, when the hot, dry winds bring sand from the Sahara Desert, 2,000 miles to the north.

"Ghanaian snow," said Kofi Nti, coming up from behind. "In a few weeks the winds will shift and bring moisture from the ocean. The land will be transformed."

"And when at last we put our feet on the soil of Africa, *we* will be transformed," said Count as he turned and headed for the gangplank with Sarah at his side, Booker T. and Hideko right behind.

Near a neat row of majestic oil palm trees, shading a double row of cocoa trees, the Paramount Chief sat on a raised platform beneath a canvas awning, a straw mat screen at his back. He sat rigidly upright on his stool, hands on knees, looking straight ahead as if he could see Count, who was standing slightly to the side, without actually looking at him. The chief sat with a colorful Kinte cloth robe draped around him leaving one shoulder bare. His thin neck, which seemed too small for his head, was adorned with a seven-stranded necklace of blue beads; on his right wrist hung three beaded bracelets, one with blue and white striped beads, one with green and yellow striped beads, and one with yellow beads marked by a single green stripe. His head was covered with a green cloth cap that extended, like an inverted bowl, just above his ears. The chief's wooden stool had a solid foot-high base, and two sturdy upright beams positioned two feet apart supporting a wide, gently up-curving seat. The height of the stool was precisely constructed so that when the chief sat, as he did now, with his back rigidly straight, his knees bent at right angles to the ground, the soles of his two sandaled feet would exactly reach the ground. The chief was flanked on the left by his interlocutor, and on the right by the Queen Mother. His eyebrows were white, as was his wispy goatee. He was a very old man.

Count wore a patterned daishiki featuring blue and white squares separated by small orange rectangles. A wide black strip edged in white split the front of the shirt, and two large black T's edged in white were positioned on each side of the chest. Draped around his neck, and extending to the waist on both sides, was a six-inch wide ribbon of Kinte cloth featuring alternating strips colored white, magenta, orange, brown, orange, green, and white.

The interlocutor spoke to Count. "The Paramount Chief asks you to be seated," he said. A wooden stool was positioned in front, and to one side of the chief. Count took his seat. He noted a circle of spectators eyeing him curiously.

"The Paramount Chief offers you a drink of orange soda," said the interlocutor. A glass bottle of warm orange soda with a straw was given to Count.

"Mister Interlocutor," Count began, but the interlocutor stopped him with a raised hand.

"The Paramount Chief bids you welcome to the Ashanti nation," he said.

Count began again. "Mister Interlocutor," he said, "please tell the Paramount Chief that I thank him for his generosity, and for his warm hospitality. Tell him that it is always a pleasure for me to speak with very old people, from whom I can learn much from the varied paths they have traveled."

Count sipped the warm orange soda while the interlocutor leaned close enough to whisper into the ear of the Paramount Chief. The chief smiled benignly, and lifted his chin slightly when the interlocutor finished speaking to him. For a few moments the chief did not respond. Count heard insects buzzing, and felt the heat of the late morning sunshine. Then, at a signal from the chief, a small hand gesture, a man emerged from the crowd, and stood behind Count, shading him with an umbrella. At a slight movement of his head the chief signaled for the interlocutor to lean close, and gave him a message. The interlocutor looked up in surprise and said, "The Paramount Chief knows who you are. He has been waiting a long time for your return. He asks that you explain the meaning of the term 'very old people.'"

"Mister Interlocutor, please tell the Paramount Chief that the explanation for the term 'very old people' is simply those people who are ten years older than he or I."

After the interlocutor had whispered this information to the chief, Count was rewarded with a broad smile and a nod of approval.

The interlocutor listened again to a message from the chief then said, "The Paramount Chief asks that you wear the story hat."

Count accepted the wide-brimmed, high-peaked straw hat presented to him by a bashful child who backed quickly away, her head bowed. Ivory carved trinkets hung from all around the edge of the hat. Many of the carved figures were animals, but also there was a stool, an umbrella, a gold nugget, a crescent moon, a palm tree, a hut, a canoe, a machete, a drum, stick figures of a family…a man and woman on either side of a child, their hands joined.

Count stood and said, "Mister Interlocutor, I now request permission to approach the Paramount Chief for the purpose of having him make a selection from the story hat." Before the interlocutor could speak, the chief motioned for Count to approach. When Count held out the hat, the chief pointed to a globe of the earth. Count nodded, put the hat on his head, and began a slow walk around the half circle of spectators.

"A story, a story!" Shouts arose from the crowd, and children ran to tell others. A fanfare of drums sounded. "Let it come! Let it go!"

Count stopped in front of the Paramount Chief who motioned for him to take the seat of the interlocutor on the chief's left. The throng of people pressed close. Count took the seat and began to speak in his deep rumbling voice. "Long, long ago, when the Earth was set down, and before the sky was lifted up, the animals began to eat pieces of the sky so Nyame, the creator, determined to raise up the sky." Count paused as murmurs of surprise moved through the crowd and people looked at each other with nods of approval.

Count waited until they were quiet before continuing. "Lifting up the sky was for Nyame like pulling back a giant curtain for it allowed him to observe more clearly what was happening on the Earth, and with his great vision, to see to the far horizon of the history of the World. What he saw caused him to be very sad, so sad that he began to cry. Nyame's tears flowed for many days and many nights, and when at last the tears ended the Earth was seen to contain more water than land, and the oceans were formed."

The enraptured crowd now leaned forward in eager anticipation. "And Nyame saw that now he was god of the sea as well as god of the sky and god of the land. He wondered if he could ever become god of the people." Cries of "yes" arose from the crowd.

"And Nyame asked himself if he *could* become god of the people, what kind of god would he be? And the answer was: a humble god who could watch the anguish and the joy in equal measure, and allow mankind to solve its own problems, as difficult as they might be." Count heard the word humble echo around the animated crowd

"And finally Nyame asked himself a question." Count paused and heard the eager shouts "what was the question?"

Count smiled and said, "The question was just this…if there was a single message he could convey to those in peril on the sea of life, what would that message be? And the answer that came to him was startling in its simplicity. And the answer was this: all men are not created equal, some are in more peril than others. Help those in peril." Count rose from his stool, and looked out at the crowd of people gathered before him. "Help others," he said. He was rewarded with cries of approval from around the assembled throng.

Count stood, took off the story hat and said, "This is my story as I have related it. If it be sweet or if it not be sweet, some you may take as true, and for the rest you may praise me for the telling of it." He dipped his head in a gesture to the Paramount Chief.

The Paramount Chief nodded as Count handed the story hat to the interlocutor. For a long time the Paramount Chief sat looking straight ahead, lost in thought. Everyone was quiet, waiting patiently, thinking about Count's message to help others. At last the chief looked up from his meditation and nodded for the interlocutor to come closer.

The chief now pointed to Booker T., who was standing with the crowd of spectators, Hideko beside him. Booker T. came forward without hesitation when he saw the Paramount Chief gesture for him. He accepted the story hat handed to him by the interlocutor. He said, "Mister Interlocutor, please tell